INTO THE GLITTERING DARK

KELLEY YORK

Editing: Karen Meeus – karenmeeusediting.com
       Danielle Fine – daniellefine.com
Cover design: Sleepy Fox Studio – sleepyfoxstudio.net
Cover illustration: Magdalena Pagowska – artstation.com/len-yan
Cover typography: Paradise Cover Design – paradisecoverdesign.com
Interior design: Sleepy Fox Studio – sleepyfoxstudio.net
Nova drawings: Sebastian Mack – instagram.com/s.mackmypictures
Character portraits: Saira Afzal – instagram.com/friend_dumpling95

eBook ISBN: 978-1-960322-05-0
paperback ISBN: 978-1-960322-07-4
hardcover ISBN: 978-1-960322-06-7

First Edition October 1, 2023

CONTENT WARNING

Into the Glittering Dark is a dark fantasy containing morally gray characters, depictions of violence, death, and gore.

"Real magic can never be made by offering someone else's liver.
You must tear out your own, and not expect to get it back."
— Peter S. Beagle, *The Last Unicorn*

Everis   Wren

Oren   Drake

Cassia   Faulk

Ivy   Imaryllis

EVERIS

TEN YEARS AGO

They were calling it the Silent Plague. It swept into the city without warning and with no immediate symptoms. No boils, no coughing, no fever. People were fine until they weren't, and then all at once they were engulfed by fatigue and lack of appetite, wasting away before their loved ones' eyes.

Everis's mother had been one of them. She'd come home from the market, bright and cheery. Later that evening, she went early to bed, claiming to feel under the weather. Over the next few days, her health deteriorated until all she did was sleep. All Everis could do at nine years old was remain by her side and look after her.

He went out three times: once to use the last of their money to buy food, twice to visit the local doctor to beg him to come see his mother or at least give her some medicine. The doctor was of no help. Everis didn't have the funds and, according to the doctor, *medicine isn't cheap, boy*. And so Ever sat at his mother's bedside, trying to coax her to eat and drink. He kept her warm during the chilly nights and tried to cool her during the blistering heat of the day. He begged her to get better, swearing to any gods that might have been listening that he'd give anything to keep her with him, that they could take him instead. He even held her hand, eyes screwed shut, and tried to imagine he was transferring some of his own life into her body to somehow give her the strength to go on.

The city outside his window grew restless.

People were dying. Quickly. Some families packed up and left in a hurry. Others were too worried about transporting their ill; they knew they'd be turned away at the border of any other city. The doctors and healers in Balerno scurried about, tending to whom they could—but they couldn't treat something when they didn't even know what it was. A fine red fog had descended upon the town. Everis wondered if it had something to do with everyone being unwell, if some sort of dark magic had slithered its way into the city.

The city guards came then, pounding on doors, quarantining anyone sick and attempting to evacuate anyone who was not. They painted large red Xs on homes. One morning, they kicked in Everis's door, took one look at him sitting there with his mother lying on her pallet… and swiftly retreated.

They painted an X onto his door, too.

Ever didn't dare venture outside after that. The guards had broken the knob. He couldn't lock it anymore, so he pushed the kitchen table up against it, the only thing his tiny body was strong enough to move. He kept the windows closed even during the miserable heat of the day to block out the sounds and the smell of rotting corpses, and huddled inside with Mother. What would be the point of going out, anyway? No help was available. And what if the guards saw him healthy, with no signs of disease? They might take him away from Mother. No, he needed to stay right where he was and keep her safe. Surely, this plague did not kill *everyone*. Surely, some people survived. Mother could be one of them.

Then the city went deathly silent. Sometimes, the sound of someone crying carried on the wind kept him awake. Other times, the shuffle of hurried footsteps outside his door sent him scurrying into the wardrobe, afraid someone would enter to steal him away.

Someone did come for him, eventually.

He heard the footsteps outside his home, then a muffled voice. Everis scrambled for the wardrobe, tucking himself inside. Whoever it was, they would see his mother sleeping and leave. It wasn't like they had anything to steal.

The intruder opened the broken door; the kitchen table ground against the floor but didn't hinder them at all. Someone entered. No—*two* of them, at least. They spoke to each other in hushed whispers, too soft for Ever to make out. He could hear them creeping about the room, and he dared not move. But his leg was cramping, sitting as he was, and he had no choice but to shift slowly, carefully, to uncurl it and—

Creak.

He froze, heart in his throat, praying they hadn't heard the traitorous groan of the wardrobe.

Seconds later, the doors flew open and Ever gasped. He found himself staring at a boy a few years older than him, sandy-blond hair, blue eyes, freckles. He wore peculiar robes Everis did not recognize. Beside him stood a much older man with long brown hair and a beard, wearing similar clothes. Whoever they were, they weren't city guards. Healers? Had someone finally come to help?

"It's alright, lad." The older man's voice was kind. "There's no need to be afraid. Can you come out?"

Everis hesitated. Shook his head. Shrank back. "Who're you? What do you want?"

"My name is Orin Sorrel. This is my apprentice, Wren Lumina. We are magi from the capital sent by the king to offer aid to the people here." Orin frowned. "Are you ill?"

Magi! Of course, magi could fix this. Ever inched out of the wardrobe with a shake of his head.

"What's your name?" the blond boy, Wren, asked.

His eyes flicked from Orin to Wren and back again. "Everis. Everis Noctur."

"That's a good name," Orin said with a soft smile. "Everis, do you know where this red mist came from?"

Ever rubbed his skinny arms and shook his head again. His gaze darted past them to the woman prone on the floor. "Are you here to help my mum?"

Orin's expression softened. "She's gone, Everis. There is nothing magic can do to save her now. But I think you know that, don't you?"

Everis's vision blurred, his eyes filling with tears. True, his mother hadn't opened her eyes in nearly two weeks, yet she looked so peaceful, as though she were only sleeping. At any moment, she could wake up, he'd thought. He stared at her. Waited.

"Do you have family elsewhere, Everis?" the older man asked.

Large tears rolled down his flushed cheeks. "No."

Orin and Wren exchanged looks. After a long moment, Orin crouched before him, every movement slow and careful. "Would you like to come back to Midmere with us? We live in a castle. You'd have a warm bed, plenty to eat, other children your age to play with. And I might teach you magic."

Ever scrubbed at his eyes with his dirty sleeve. From his limited experience, someone had to be born with magic. They couldn't simply learn it. "I'm not a magi, though; I'm just a boy."

"I don't know about that. There's a spark in you." Orin smiled. "But even if you are 'just' a boy, I would see that you're safe and cared for. If you'd like."

He looked at Orin and then at his mother. Even now, she showed no signs of decay. By clutching her hand and willing with all his being for her to be well again, had he somehow gotten her to stay looking as she always had? Was such a thing possible? Was that the 'spark' Orin spoke of? The thought of leaving her made his chest hurt so fiercely he couldn't stand it, but he didn't want to be in this city any longer. He didn't want to get sick; he didn't want to die.

Orin offered him a hand. Everis ignored it and threw himself into the man's arms instead, clinging to him. Wordlessly, the magi gathered him up and hugged him, so protective and warm. Ever sobbed against his shoulder, letting out the wash of relief and the sorrow at once.

A new home. A *castle*. Such a thing seemed like a dream.

Whatever it was, it had to be better than this nightmare.

INTRODUCTION
THE BASICS OF MAGIC, VOLUME I

All magic is energy, and energy must come from somewhere. It was once believed that our bodies themselves fuel the spells we cast, but the Citadel came to realize that our bodies, in fact, do not generate magic but conduct it.

The energy flows through everything in our world from people to rocks and trees and animals. It is stronger in some locations than others, and a magi's ability to be in tune with the world around them greatly affects their ability to serve as a conductor. That is also believed to be why some magi excel in specific areas of magic, such as healing, potions, or written incantations. We each find our own method in which to conduct the energy from the earth into our spells.

It flows through all of us. We only need to best learn how to use it.

EVERIS

PRESENT DAY

There was nothing quite like the Friday-night banquets at the castle. Every other day of the week, Everis took his meals with Master Orin, Wren, and the other magi in the common room of their tower. The royal family dined there in the great hall. However, Fridays were a day of thanks to the gods and goddesses for another bountiful week, and commoners and nobles alike celebrated it with gatherings and plenty of food.

The table was full of honey-glazed ham, roast goose, stuffed eggs, warm bread, salad, and more that Everis hadn't yet gotten to. He'd eaten two plates already, which should've been enough, and yet he eyed a potential third helping he would certainly regret later.

As he finally gave in to the urge to reach for a few more rolls and some gravy, Wren chuckled in the seat beside him. "I really do not know where you put it all."

Everis flashed him a grin. "I'm a growing boy. Why do you think I'm already so much taller than you?"

Wren rolled his eyes and stole a roll from Everis's plate. It wasn't that Wren was particularly *short*. He was quite average, really, but when much of his time was spent around Everis—who stood a few inches above him despite being several years his junior—and Master Orin, who was taller than both of them, it made him appear smaller than he was.

On the other side of Wren were the rest of the magi in the employ of the royal family. Thirteen if one included Master Orin, Wren, and himself. Master Orin had a place in a seat reserved for a guest of honor at the right hand of the king—never mind that the king's chair had sat empty for several months.

To the left of the king's vacant chair sat Queen Danica Starling, beautiful with her crimson dress and red hair piled high atop her head. Princess Cassia sat across from him. She was sixteen with a soft, round face, dark skin, and hazel eyes, and was one of the kindest people Everis had ever met. While the queen couldn't recall that Everis even existed, Cassia knew all the magi in the royal family's employ *and* what their specialties were.

Not that Everis had a specialty yet. The first many years of a magi's apprenticeship involved learning the basics and a little bit of everything. Later, many developed a taste for a specific subject. Some magi went on to be apothecaries with a knack for healing and medicine, like Drake Reed. Others took an interest in the study of magical creatures and history, like Mace Huntly. Or they became blacksmiths, so-called scribes—the magi who could engrave their spells into physical objects such as swords or armor—like Lady Imaryllis. Everis had been Master Orin's apprentice for ten years, and he still hadn't a clue what road he might one day follow or if it would lead him away from Midmere.

He glanced askance at Wren. There were nights like tonight, with good food and wine, surrounded by these familiar faces, where he couldn't fathom his life being any other way. Even if no one else mattered, he couldn't imagine his daily life without Wren and Master Orin.

The only people he could have gladly done without were Brant and Artesia, the guards who plopped down in the seats across from his. The table was crowded, yes, but surely there were other seats they could've chosen? He purposefully averted his gaze, and yet somehow, he kept being drawn back by Brant's obnoxious, booming voice and Artesia's guffawing laughter at every stupid joke he told.

He tried his best to tune them out. At this point, he had a decade of practice under his belt, from the time he was a child and Brant a mere stableboy, and ten years of knowledge that if he got into it with Brant anywhere Master Orin could hear, he'd be lectured about it later.

Still, the low rumble of Brant's voice was so bloody *grating*. Even with the sound of chewing, cutlery against plates, and other conversations in the large hall, Everis couldn't seem to ignore it. Brant said something, and he and Artesia glanced Everis's way. They laughed. Loudly.

Anger simmered deep in his chest. He made a grab for his wine and took a long pull from it, then placed the goblet down with more force than necessary.

You're in a room full of people, he reminded himself. *Master Orin is right there. Don't cause a scene.*

Except what Everis's mind thought and what his mouth did were often two very different things, and when he made eye contact with Brant from across the table, the words tumbled from his lips unbidden.

"If you're going to have a laugh at someone's expense, you should at least let them in on the joke."

Brant rolled his eyes. "Not everything is about you. We were having a private conversation."

Heat washed into Everis's face. "You were looking at me!"

"The room's only so big," Artesia drawled, "and you *are* sitting right across from us."

They were doing this on purpose. He just knew it. Even after all these years, Brant loved needling him, making him look like a fool. When they were children, Brant had been loud and obvious with his insults. Now, he'd learned to be sneaky and backhanded, ensuring it looked as though Everis was the one acting out of line.

Before he could respond, Wren put a hand on his arm and shook his head. "Leave it alone, Ever."

Yes. Right. He would do that. Be the bigger man and enjoy his meal. No sense in letting anyone ruin one of his favorite nights of the week. *Leave it alone.*

Brant snickered and muttered under his breath, "Yeah, listen to mummy."

Or maybe not.

Everis gave a tight smile. He pushed back his chair and stood.

Then he threw his glass of wine into Brant's face.

Sputtering, Brant stood so abruptly his chair clattered to the floor. Artesia gaped for half a moment before she laughed, shrill and amused despite how red and furious Brant's face had grown.

Wren groaned and put his face in his hands. The entire length of the table—the magi, knights, guards, and royal family—were looking their way. A few spots down, Gilbert and Mace Huntly stared at him in shock, and Lady Imaryllis choked on a laugh that she swiftly covered with a hand. Magi Quinton looked on, as disapproving as ever.

"You little shit," Brant growled, snatching an offered napkin from Artesia to mop the wine from his face. Most of the other guards were laughing good-naturedly, which wasn't going to soothe Brant's bruised ego any.

Fifty-some-odd pairs of eyes were fastened on Brant and Everis. Heat flooded to Everis's cheeks, made even the tips of his ears burn, but he refused to be cowed.

At least, not until Master Orin met Everis's eyes from across the room, and Orin shook his head. Everis gulped, slowly placing the empty goblet back onto the table.

Just when Everis was certain Brant was either about to start yelling or launch himself across the table to shove Everis's face into the nearest bowl of potatoes, Wren stood. He caught Ever by the elbow, spun him around, and marched him to the door with his mouth pinched into a tight line. Everis began to protest at being dragged off like some misbehaving child, but he didn't need to make more of a scene in front of Queen Danica and Princess Cassia tonight.

Out in the hallway beyond closed doors, the almost overwhelming din of voices immediately died down to a more tolerable level. Everis's shoulders slumped as the tension eased from them.

"Now you've done it," Wren muttered, releasing him. "In front of the queen and princess, no less. What were you thinking?"

Everis tugged at the collar of his tunic and frowned but didn't get the chance to answer before the door swung open once more and Master Orin joined them in the hall. He hunkered down on himself. Being lectured by one of them was bad enough, but by them both? Time would tell if the shock and humiliation on Brant's face were worth whatever punishment he'd earned. Though, to be entirely honest, there was little worth that look of disappointment on Master Orin's face.

"Dare I ask what happened?" Master Orin asked.

Everis's face flushed all over again. "Brant started it."

"Did he, though?" Wren sighed. "You shouldn't have gotten yourself so worked up in the first place. You know if you stopped reacting, he'd—"

"He'd miraculously get over being a prick and leave me alone. Yes. So you've said for the past ten years that he's still not gotten over it."

Wren's brow furrowed. "I was watching the whole thing. He didn't say a word to you until you spoke up."

"Well, he... He wasn't talking *to* me," Everis said, defensiveness edging into his voice. "But he and Artesia were talking *about* me."

"What makes you think that?"

"They looked at me and laughed!"

"Oh goodness, they *looked* at you?" Wren folded his arms, eyebrows arched. It was times like these that Everis really felt the six years age difference between them. Wren was shorter than him, built softer where Everis was angular and lean. It was easy to forget how much time separated them. At least, until Wren started in on one of his famous lectures. "Honestly, Ever. It was a crowded room, and you were sitting across from them. It wouldn't have been the first time you were paranoid over nothing."

Everis's cheeks burned, and he dropped his gaze to study the stone floor beneath his boots. He saw no way out of this conversation. They would argue each other in circles all night if left to it.

"That's enough, boys," Orin chided. He placed a hand on Everis's shoulder. "I know things between you and Brant are... complicated."

Everis tipped his head back to look up at him. "Then you believe me?"

Orin sighed. "You can be a bit oversensitive, especially where Brant is concerned, but you aren't one to make up stories."

Was that a compliment or a jab? It felt a little like both, and yet Everis knew better. Orin was never anything but pragmatic and fair. He was never purposely unkind, but he *was* honest almost to a fault. Never did he hesitate to praise his apprentices for their successes, and he was just as quick to gently admonish them for their failures.

Everis ducked his head. He could try to defend himself until he was blue in the face, but it didn't matter. "I'm sorry, Master Orin."

Master Orin remained silent for a long moment. With a sigh, he squeezed Everis's shoulder, then released him. "Queen Danica and the other magi will expect me to discipline you for your outburst, you know. I'll have some work for you bright and early tomorrow, so I suggest you get some rest."

Orin was letting him off easy. Everis cast him a look of gratitude before giving a slight bow and turning to walk away.

He'd expected Wren to return to the great hall with their master. Instead, his friend fell into step alongside him, having to widen his stride to keep up. Thankfully, he didn't say a word. Perhaps he'd lectured himself out.

When they reached the hall that would take them to the magi tower, Wren softly asked, "Are you alright?"

Had it been anyone else, the sudden shift from nagging to concerned would have been jarring. That was how Wren was, though. He would nag at Everis about his carelessness and impulsive tendencies while at the same time gently tending to an injury sustained from trying to scale the library rooftop like a squirrel.

Everis sighed. "In retrospect, I should've just pushed him down the stairs when no one was looking."

The corners of Wren's mouth twitched in wry amusement. "Who was it that told you if you were going to exact revenge, to make sure you didn't get caught?"

A smile tugged at Everis's lips. "Lady Imaryllis." A strict swordsmaster, she never hesitated to bear down on Brant or any other soldier she caught acting out of line. She commanded too much respect from soldiers and magi alike for anyone to want to cross her.

"Terrible influence, that one," Wren mused without malice. He halted at the entrance to the magi tower, one of the tallest spires in the castle. The spiral staircase wound up a solid ten floors, with Master Orin's chambers occupying the topmost floor and Wren's and Everis's across from one another on the third. "Look, I know your dealings with Brant have never been easy for you. He's not blameless, and we all know that. But I truly think you're holding on to old grudges with a childhood rival. Brant isn't nearly as bad as he used to be. He's grown up."

Everis frowned, glancing away to stare out the nearby windows. When he didn't respond, Wren sighed, arms falling to his sides. Then his hands lifted, one to Everis's shoulder, the other to his chin, prodding him into looking up so their eyes could meet.

"Ever, you have this notion in your head that the world is your enemy, and that isn't the case. You would have so many more friends if you stopped thinking everyone you meet is out to hurt you. You're a good person. You're funny and kind and lovely—but you don't let anyone see that side of you. Let them get to know you as I do."

His shoulders sank. He'd heard this sort of thing before, and yet it never seemed to sting any less. It wasn't as though he didn't *try* to be friendly or connect with others. "Right."

Wren released him and stepped back. When he turned for the stairs and saw Everis lingering, he paused. "Going to bed?"

Everis shook his head. "I think I'll take a walk first. Clear my head."

"Well, don't stay up too late. You've got a long day ahead tomorrow." Wren cast a humorless smile his way and disappeared up the spiral stairwell.

A long day indeed. A long day of going to market for supplies, categorizing said supplies, filing, and whatever other menial busywork Orin could think of as punishment for his dinner-time outburst.

He'd meant what he'd said about taking a walk, though. He traced a familiar path to the royal gardens, which sat in the very center of the castle. A heavy oak door opened into a vibrant array of plants and flowers collected from all over the kingdom. The castle walls encased the gardens like a prison cell, towers looming like sentinels. Overhead, the moon was a thin sliver mostly obscured by thick clouds but still bright enough to cast a low, gloomy glow on every leaf and petal. Although he couldn't see the fountain from where he stood, Everis could hear the water bubbling from the stone lion's mouth.

Everis drew in a deep breath of night air. He liked this place. During the day, it was often busy, residents of the castle taking a stroll through the greenery, losing themselves on the winding stone paths, or sitting near the fountain with a game of chess or cards. At night, though, seldom did he encounter anyone there, and so it was his favorite time to meander through the foliage with his hands outstretched, allowing his fingertips to brush against every bush and tree he passed.

These gardens had been a sanctuary to him when he'd first arrived at the castle ten years ago. Everywhere else felt noisy and overwhelming, full of strangers who seemed to think he was good for nothing except being underfoot. Under a bright moon and a clear sky, the gardens had been a perfect escape where the darkness could not find him.

Wren always found him, though.

Wren, who'd seemed just as displeased by his presence there as everyone else, had bitten back his annoyance and barely contained scowls and found it in his heart to be kind to Everis. Somewhere along the way, things had shifted, that forced kindness had turned sincere, and they'd become friends. *Closer than brothers*, Master Orin said. Wren had gone from being a sullen, resentful older male figure to a constant companion, able to put him at ease with little more than a soft smile. They might bicker on a near-daily basis, but if there were anyone Everis couldn't fathom living without, it was Wren.

Everis found his way to the center of the courtyard and sat on the edge of the fountain, long legs drawn up, knees to his chest. The ripples upset the sky's reflection, distorting Everis's own face when he leaned forward enough to see himself. He could've sat there for hours listening to the running water and the whisper of trees, in a nearly meditative state as he acclimated to the magic that flowed through every living thing. He might have, too, except for the sound of a door creaking open somewhere nearby.

Everis stilled for the half a second it took to hear brisk footsteps coming his way, and then he scrambled off the fountain and around a tall topiary trimmed into the shape of a rearing horse.

Why are you hiding? he scolded himself. *There's no rule against being out here.*

Maybe he simply didn't want to encounter anyone and have to explain himself after that embarrassing display at dinner.

A black-clad figure passed through his line of vision. They stopped shy of the fountain and turned, tipping their face—which was masked from the nose down—to look around as though searching for something. Everis cast aside any thoughts of revealing himself. Who would come wandering through the gardens in the dark dressed like that? Any answer he could conjure up wasn't a good one.

The stranger seemed to orient themselves and headed off in another direction, toward a door that led into the easternmost area of the castle. Namely, the area belonging to King Faramond and his wife and Princess Cassia.

His heart hammered so loudly he could feel it in his throat. He could get a guard, but what if that allowed the person to get too far ahead and he lost them? Or what if it turned out to be nothing at all and he made a fool of himself for a second time tonight?

Everis straightened his spine and followed.

By some miracle, the door opened in relative silence, not alerting the masked person that he'd stepped inside. Being plunged back into near darkness was jarring, and he stopped, giving his eyes time to adjust to the dim glow of a few magically lit wall sconces. He strained to hear where the intruder had gone and caught sound to his left, toward the tower that housed the royal bedchambers. There would be a guard posted at the base of the stairs and, barring someone scaling the outside walls, there was no other way up. When he rounded the corner, he half expected to find Brutus or Sylvia or any number of other guards giving him an odd look for being there.

And there *was* a guard there.

A large figure lay face down on the floor, candlelight glinting off his armor. Everis rushed to the man's side, rolling him over to see his face.

Brutus... Everis lifted a shaky hand to check for a pulse and found none. Choking on a sound and clamping a palm across his mouth, he scrambled back. He could make out a razor-thin line where something thin and strong had been wrapped around the front of Brutus's throat to strangle him. He was a big man, heavyset and strong. The intruder Everis had seen was slight and shorter than Wren. How had they managed to catch him off guard like this?

There was no time for questions nor to retreat and call for help. If Queen Danica or Princess Cassia were in their rooms, they would be helpless. Even if they were still at the banquet, King Faramond, sick and frail in his bed, could not defend himself.

Everis spared one last look at Brutus and, not giving himself a chance to change his mind, skirted the body and bolted up the stairs as silently as he could. It was nowhere near as many floors as the magi tower. At every full twist of the spiraling steps, he could steal a look down the short halls to the single door on each floor. He'd only just passed the second floor when a commotion on the one above caught his ears.

Crashing. Something shattering.

Adrenaline spiking, he took the steps two at a time, nearly stumbling at the landing before propelling himself down the hall. Princess Cassia's door stood ajar. Everis had only seconds to steel his resolve before he burst into the room.

Inside, everything was dark. It took a breath for him to make sense of anything before him. On the grand four-poster bed, the intruder was bent over atop Cassia. The princess thrashed her legs beneath the blankets, violently trying to fend off her attacker.

Everis threw himself at the assassin, his steps alerting them with only enough time for them to whip their head around in his direction. In their hands was a garrote wire, which in turn was wrapped around Cassia's throat. Everis locked an arm around the attacker's neck and heaved his weight backward, dragging them off the princess.

They tumbled back in a tangle of limbs. Everis's grip wasn't tight enough—or perhaps the assassin was too nimble. They twisted and slid expertly from his hold. He made another grab for them, but he only succeeded in yanking back their cowl to expose a head of dark hair tied into a tight bun. They faced each other, and Everis got his first proper look at the assailant. It was a woman. Her eyes were a deep blue, though her nose and mouth were still covered.

The assassin came at him with a dagger in hand. He stumbled back, and the blade sliced the air where his face had been. He didn't have a chance to regain his balance before she lunged again, relentless in her assault. It was all he could do to keep scrambling away, heart racing with every narrow miss. His legs met and tangled with a chair near the balcony doors, and down he went. The woman was on him in an instant, aiming

24

the tip of the dagger straight for his neck. Everis gasped, catching her wrist, wrestling for control. She was stronger than she looked, and her full weight bore down on him.

He was unprepared against a trained killer. He didn't have his sword.

But he was a magi. He was never truly unarmed.

The air around them crackled with magic. It tingled beneath his skin, filling him with energy and strength. He focused, just like Master Orin had always taught him. The elements were there, at his beck and call. But he needed his hands to cast, and they were currently occupied with keeping this woman from slitting his throat.

Picture the essence of all magic in your mind. Open yourself to it, and it will be there for you when you need it.

Everis squeezed his eyes shut. He saw the magic like shimmering webs all around him. Brilliant, sparkling gold, something he could reach out and touch. A familiar sight any time he conjured his magic—his mind's way of making it tangible. He would normally extend his hands, draw a symbol before him, watch the threads twist and conjoin to create the spell, and when he opened his eyes, it would be to lock onto his target.

Without their hands or sight, magi were useless.

But he had to try something.

In the distance of the magical webs, a single string stood out amongst the rest, glittering a deep crimson. It looked stronger than the others. The color dimmed and brightened like the rhythm of a heartbeat. A voice whispered, somehow in his head but not.

Take it.

In his mind, Everis reached out. Tendrils of mana swirled about his fingers like floating threads.

He grasped the red one and pulled.

His eyes snapped open. The assassin froze, confusion and then fear registering on her face. Before she could react, a surging wind burst through the balcony doors, raining glass down around them. The hurricane tore the woman off him and threw her across the room while books and chess pieces and anything else in its path went flying through the open doors. In his ears echoed a howling so fierce he could hear nothing, *feel* nothing else. Magic coursed through his veins, pulsating vibrantly with the force of a storm.

Finally, the wind died down to a breeze, then faded altogether. All that remained was the sound of his own labored breathing and the faint rustling of settling papers and curtains.

What had he done? *How?*

"—Everis?" Princess Cassia called.

He pushed himself up to sit. The princess sat huddled beside her bed, her eyes wide in terror. She half-crawled over to him. Her throat was bleeding where the wire had cut into her skin and she trembled like a leaf, but she was alive. *Thank the Mother...*

She touched his arm. "Are you alright? Are you injured?"

"No, I..." He glanced at the open doors. Vaulting to his feet, he rushed onto the balcony to peer down into the gardens below. The assassin's contorted body lay on the cobblestone pathway, motionless. Cassia came to his side. She sucked in a breath when she laid eyes on the assailant's broken figure, and she swiftly turned away. After a beat, she looked up at him. Even with a tremor in her voice, she was doing her best to remain composed.

"You saved my life, Everis. Thank you."

Everis blinked once. He *had* saved her, hadn't he? Yet somehow, he felt almost embarrassed. "We should alert the guards," he mumbled, looking away.

He ushered her inside, waited while she fetched a robe to pull on over her nightgown, and escorted her down the tower steps. She startled when they came across Brutus's body at the bottom. Everis took her by the elbow and led her around, trying to shield her view as best as he could.

Foremost, he needed to find Master Orin. He would know what to do.

WREN

TEN YEARS AGO

The boy wouldn't give him a moment's peace.

Everis acted like a lost lamb, wandering about the castle at Wren's heels. Every morning when Wren came out of his room, Everis stood there waiting for him. He followed Wren to breakfast, to lessons, to market. He sat at Wren's elbow and watched as he pieced together the spells and charms Orin assigned to him. Oh, he was quiet enough and didn't chat endlessly like some of the other children his age, but his mere presence disrupted Wren's routine. What he wouldn't give for some time alone!

"He's a boy who's lost everything," Orin gently chided. "I know he's young, but the age difference between you is not that great."

No, he supposed it wasn't. Besides, the older they grew, the less that difference would be apparent. But right now, Wren was fifteen and Everis only nine. Wren didn't want to share his master with anyone, let alone some child they'd found in a plague-ridden town surrounded by dark magic.

Magic that Wren could still see in him occasionally. Always brief, always a flicker of red in his eyes and then gone, when the child got upset or frightened. Everis was just a boy. He would outgrow it with training and time. Wren ought to have told Master Orin, and yet it was so infrequent and gone so quickly that he kept talking himself out of it.

And if he couldn't bring himself to tell Orin, he certainly wouldn't tell anyone else. Someone would surely rush to the king, and Orin would be forced to send Everis to the Citadel in Aramus, where the Magi Council that ruled over all magical going-ons resided.

They might have Everis killed or locked away, his mind quietly reminded him.

Wren wanted the boy to leave. He didn't want him *hurt*. Not to mention, Master Orin might get in trouble, too. King Faramond was fond of Orin, but that didn't mean he was immune to punishment if he broke the rules. The queen would see to that. With a frustrated sigh, Wren pushed that idea far from his mind.

It was on the third week that Wren rose earlier than usual. Something had woken him, a bad dream, perhaps, and he couldn't find his way to sleep again. He washed, dressed, and opened his door, intending to head to the study and get in an extra hour or two of reading before breakfast. When he stepped into the hall, there Everis was, seated across from him and hugging his knees to his chest. His bowed head lifted sharply. He looked just as shocked to see Wren as Wren was to see him.

"Sweet Mother, you scared me. What are you doing awake?" Wren asked. "The sun isn't even up!"

Everis fidgeted, rising to his feet. "I couldn't sleep."

"So you decided to sit in the hallway? You could have sat in your room. How long have you been out here?"

The boy's eyes lowered. He tugged at the sleeve of his tunic, plucking at a loose thread.

Wren frowned. "I asked you a question, Everis."

He almost seemed to flinch, and his eyes had gone glassy. He stood unblinking, as though afraid if he did, the tears would fall. "My room is dark," he said. "I keep hearing things, and I have bad dreams… So, when my candle burns down, I come out here."

The admission came so soft, so timid and sincere, that it struck something deep in Wren's chest. All this time, he'd only thought of what a nuisance the child was, always waiting there for him, always dogging his heels. Never once had he stopped to ask himself why, or how, Everis seemed to be there waiting no matter how early or late Wren left his room every morning. Was it because he'd been spending much of his nights in the hall, too afraid to sleep in his own bed, counting down the hours and minutes until Wren would emerge and he didn't have to be alone anymore?

His shoulders slumped.

"Aren't you tired?" he asked, and when Everis shrugged nervously, Wren sighed. "There are still a few hours before breakfast. Come, to your room."

He urged the boy through his door. Sure enough, the candle at his bedside had burned down to a useless stump. Wren would ensure he had extras on hand from now on. The blankets were kicked back and strewn about as though he'd woken in the throes of a nightmare and fled the room.

Wren coaxed Everis back into bed. Instead of leaving him there and ordering him to get some rest, he slid beneath the covers with him. The mattress was as narrow as his own, but it wasn't like he took up much space and Everis certainly didn't. They managed to fit side by side with room to spare.

"Better?" he asked.

Everis curled up on his side and nodded wordlessly. Then he slid out a hand, his small fingers clutching the fabric of Wren's sleeve.

"Do you think you can rest now?" Wren glanced at him, waiting for an answer.

But Everis's eyes were closed, and he'd already drifted off.

PRESENT DAY

Wren woke shortly after dawn with the heaviest sensation that something was wrong. Instead of trying to get another hour or two of sleep, he crawled out of bed, washed, and dressed. He slipped across the hall to poke his head into Ever's room and found it empty. Perhaps he'd already headed to the magi's study to get started on his punishment work. Punishment he deserved, although it never failed that when Ever was punished, *Wren* ended up feeling bad and helping him with all that extra work.

When he emerged from the tower, the castle was abuzz with anxious energy. Guards were posted in nearly every hall. He thought of catching the attention of someone and asking what was going on, but something told him he needed to find Master Orin if he wanted any real answers.

He moved briskly through the castle, dodging servants and guards, intending to head for the study. Along the way, he spotted an unkempt ginger-haired mage close to Orin's age. Wren caught him by the arm before the older magi could disappear down another hall.

"Gilbert! What's happened?"

Gilbert halted and frowned at him. "You haven't heard? Someone attacked the princess last night. Master Orin is speaking with Her Highness about it now." He turned his head, nodding in a vague direction. *The council room.*

He released Gilbert and dashed off. Any questions he had would be best answered by Orin, not heard secondhand from anyone else.

His nerves were so frayed that he nearly burst into the council room without as much as announcing his arrival. Only barely did he stop himself at a sharp look from the two guards posted outside. He took a deep breath and lifted a hand to knock. "Master?"

The muffled voices from behind the thick wood hushed. Master Orin called, "Come in, Wren."

Queen Danica Starling sat at the far end of the round table, the first set of eyes to meet Wren's when he entered. Master Orin stood, arms crossed, to her right. The other people Wren saw were familiar. Magi Drake Reed, the head healer within the castle. General Jaquemon Groveland, head of city and castle security, and Captain Annaliese Maybury, who worked beneath him and led the royal knights. Lastly, Imaryllis Leif who, although not a person of authority amongst the soldiers and city guard, was their swordsmaster and highly respected by magi and knights alike. They were all expected presences in a meeting such as this.

The one person Wren did *not* expect to see was Everis.

Ever looked up. His mouth was drawn taut, and his brows knitted together. Shadows hung beneath his eyes, suggesting he hadn't slept. Wren gravitated toward him, bringing a hand to his shoulder. His gaze, though, went to Orin. "I've been told there was an attack on the princess last night."

"There was," Captain Annaliese said. She was a lean, steely-eyed woman with long, braided hair and bronze skin. She looked far more intimidating than General Jaquemon ever had, with a voice that instantly commanded respect. "An assassin killed the guard outside the royal tower and assaulted Princess Cassia while she slept."

Master Orin stroked a hand down his short, graying beard. "Everis intervened. He saved Princess Cassia's life."

Wren frowned, troubled. His fingers twitched tighter on Ever's shoulder, protective, and he looked down. Ever tipped his head back to meet his gaze.

"Is the princess alright?" What Wren really wanted to ask was if *Everis* was alright, but he knew what was expected of him was to show concern for the princess, first and foremost.

"Shaken," Queen Danica said gravely. "Understandably so. I had Drake give her something to help her sleep. She has some of her maids with her and extra security outside her room."

Wren sank down into the seat beside Ever. "The assassin... Did they get away?"

"She's dead," Ever muttered. "I knocked her over the balcony."

"Unfortunate that we weren't able to question her, but she did leave this behind." Orin unfolded his arms and gestured to the table where a black-bladed dagger lay. Wren picked it up for a closer look. He turned it over in his fingers, noting the intricacy of the handle—including an insignia of an owl grasping a flower in its claws—and how the blade gleamed.

Master Orin watched him. "Tell me what you gather from that, Wren."

Of course, his master would use this as a teaching moment. He hesitated, aware that all eyes in the room, including the Queen's, were now on him. "Um. Nightstone. Beautiful craftsmanship. This is no weapon for some common sellsword."

"What does that say to you?"

"It says someone with good money hired her," he ventured, looking up. "A political rival? Someone with a grudge against the king and queen who thought the best way to get to them was through their daughter?"

Master Orin nodded his approval. "We were just discussing the possibilities of that when you came in."

"We're royalty," Queen Danica said, inclining her chin. "We have no shortage of enemies and those who only pretend to be allies. But to stoop so low as to attack a child..."

Drake leaned forward, holding out his hand until Wren passed over the dagger. He studied it in his long fingers and furrowed his brow. "Your Highness, forgive me, but isn't the ichoroa blossom Duke Ryland's sigil?"

A hush fell across the room. Ryland Starling, the king's younger brother, hadn't stepped foot in Midmere for nearly a decade following an argument with his elder sibling. No one knew what they had fought over—something personal, King Faramond said—but it had created a wound between the brothers that never had healed. Where the royal family's crest was that of a brilliant sun, Ryland had taken on a new sigil, that of the elegant, blood-red ichoroa flower.

Danica started to speak, paused, and then shook her head. "A coincidence. Ryland would never... Why? To what end? He and Faramond haven't spoken in years."

"He has just as much reason as anyone else we could think of," Lady Imaryllis replied. "We don't know if Princess Cassia was the only target of this assassination attempt. She was just the one Everis stumbled across. For all we know that woman was after the princess, you, *and* His Grace."

"Duke Ryland *would* be next in line should the king pass with no surviving children," Orin reluctantly admitted. "Still, I've known Ryland since he was a boy. He can be stubborn and tactless, but I don't believe he's a murderer."

"He'd sooner wage war and meet his opponents on the battlefield than resort to such underhanded tactics," Lady Imaryllis agreed.

The queen's face had gone pale. She sank down in her seat. Wren was sure he'd never seen her look so weary before. Queen Danica was always resolute and fearless, but he supposed anyone would be rattled after nearly losing their child. "I would like to think you're right, Orin. Yet we have no other leads. I would ask you to go visit my brother-in-law, see if you can find anything out or uncover any nefarious plots."

Orin's eyebrows rose. "Under what guise, Your Grace? If he is in fact innocent, he may take offense to us marching in with accusations."

"Yes, yes, of course. I will write him a letter. Tell him about Faramond's condition and invite him to come make amends before he passes." She frowned as though mulling this idea over, then nodded once, solidifying her decision. She pushed back her chair and rose to leave the room.

General Jaquemon and Captain Annaliese followed on her heels.

Lady Imaryllis and Drake Reed remained behind. Drake regarded Orin. "I would offer my services to accompany you, my friend."

"Your talents are better served here while Faramond is ill," Master Orin said. He turned to the windows overlooking the city below, silent in the way that told Wren he was thinking very seriously. Drake bowed his head. Imaryllis gave Wren and Ever a reassuring smile and a wink, and the pair of them took their leave. The apprentices waited. If Orin had wanted them gone, he would've dismissed them, yet he lingered, fingers tugging absently at his beard. "Ever, Wren, I would ask you two to embark on this mission. We'll ask General Jaquemon to send some of his people as your escorts."

Wren started. "Are you sure? The queen said—"

"It makes more sense for me to remain here. To defend the queen and in case another assassin is sent if nothing else." Orin tipped his head. "Are you worried you can't handle it?"

His cheeks warmed at the apparent challenge. "We can handle it."

Orin smiled. "Good."

"Won't the queen be angry?" Ever asked. "It sounded like she wanted *you*, specifically, to go."

"That's for me to worry about, Ever. I will make a few arrangements. Plan to depart in the morning." He placed a hand on each of their shoulders and squeezed, smiled, and exited, leaving Ever and Wren alone.

"*We can handle it?*" Ever muttered, casting him a sidelong glance. "Are you sure about that?"

"Master Orin thinks we can, so I don't see why not." Wren rotated his chair to better face his friend. "Are you alright? What in the world happened?"

Ever sighed, looking weary to be telling this story yet again. "On my walk last night, I saw someone suspicious in the gardens, headed for the royal quarters. I followed and found the assassin attacking Cassia."

"And *you* stopped her?"

"Why do you sound so surprised by that?"

"I'm not. Well, I *am*, but not because it's you, exactly…"

Ever leveled a flat look at him. "I used magic." He paused, something on the tip of his tongue wanting to make itself heard.

Wren frowned. "What is it?"

He looked away, brows knitting together. "The magic I used, the force behind it… I've never managed anything like it before."

Wren took one of Ever's hands in his own and squeezed it, trying to understand what his friend was telling him. He cursed himself that he hadn't insisted on accompanying Ever on his walk. They could have tackled it together, and Ever wouldn't have been in danger. The thought of how poorly the entire thing could have ended up made his insides tie themselves in knots. "You were in a dangerous situation and cast a powerful spell. There's nothing wrong with that. You've always done your best casting when you feel you have something to prove." To that, Ever let out a short laugh that made some of that tension in Wren's chest loosen. He grinned. "Have you gotten any rest?"

"Not really, no. I've been too rattled to sleep."

Wren rose to his feet. "We should see about remedying that. Come.

33

Let's put you to bed. If we're traveling tomorrow, I don't need you toppling off your horse in exhaustion."

Ever didn't put up a fight as Wren saw him to his room. He bade him to get some rest and promised he'd be by with a meal later before stealing away to his own room across the hall.

He was used to trips away from the city with Master Orin and Ever. They traveled to neighboring towns for many reasons, from diplomatic missions to deliveries of medicine and charms, to investigate misuses of magic... It was, after all, on one of those missions so long ago that they'd found Everis and brought him home. Oh, how frustrated he'd been! Yet somewhere along the way, Ever's earnestness, his kindness, his eagerness to learn, and his loneliness had won Wren over. He'd stopped viewing him so much as a rival for Orin's attention and more as a... peer? Brother? Friend? Something.

Something indeed.

His cheeks warmed, and he shoved any thoughts of that *something* far from his mind.

Now they would embark on a mission all on their own without Master Orin to guide them. A diplomatic-slash-investigative mission, no less. Were they truly prepared to handle it?

He made quick work of packing his bags. They would need to visit the study for supplies, herbs and powders and potions, just in case they were needed for the road. He left the bags sitting at the foot of his bed and ventured to the other side of the castle. If Orin was leaving this investigation in his hands, he needed to know precisely what had happened from anyone who'd witnessed anything. He had Ever's story; now he needed Princess Cassia's.

As expected, there were guards posted all about the royal tower. One at each end of every hall, another two at the base of the stairs (who thankfully did not hassle him about going up) and another pair just outside her door.

A large arm shot out to block his way when he went to knock. "The princess is resting," came Brant's lazy drawl.

Wren frowned, taking a step back. "I need to speak with her about last night."

Brant and the other guard, whose name Wren didn't know, exchanged looks. The nameless guard shrugged. "Sorry, magi. We've got our orders not to let anyone in."

Before he could argue, Cassia's door opened, and a woman poked her head out. Wren knew her as one of Cassia's maids, a tall, brash girl of sixteen who could wield a sword as well as a sewing needle.

"M'lady says to let the magi in," she announced.

Brant frowned. "But—"

The girl held up a hand so abruptly that it startled him into silence. She stepped aside, nodding to Wren. He did his best not to look smug as he moved past the guards.

The princess was, in fact, awake when he entered the room. He'd never had reason to be in her bedchambers before. Cassia sat before a chessboard near the broken balcony doors, across from another of her maids. "Thank you, Sommer," she said, and the maid who'd let Wren in bowed and moved out of the way as the princess stood. "Wren, how is Everis?"

He smiled slightly. "Well enough, my lady. Resting. I'm surprised you aren't doing the same."

"Mother worries too much." She gave a wave of her hand and gestured to an empty seat to her right, which he took. He noted the bandages around her throat and grimaced inwardly. Today would've gone very differently had Everis not gotten into it with Brant at supper, gone off to mope, and happened to come to the princess's rescue. "You aren't here just to check on me. What is it?"

Wren's spine straightened. "Master Orin is sending Everis and me to investigate who might be responsible for last night's attack. I'm sorry, you must be tired of recounting the story, but I had hoped to hear your version of events."

Cassia turned to her chess table, studying it with calculating eyes and a downturned mouth. "There isn't much to say, I'm afraid. I didn't even hear her come in. One moment I was asleep, and the next... she had something around my throat, and I couldn't breathe. I must have blacked out because I barely remember Everis coming into the room. Just that weight lifting off me, and then..."

"Then?"

"Wind." She paused, picked up a piece, and moved it. "It was like... a storm blew through here, and that isn't an exaggeration. It took us all morning to clean up the mess it made. I watched it throw that woman right off Everis and over the balcony."

Wren spared it a glance. No wonder the assassin hadn't made it. No way anyone would've survived that fall. "I see. Is there anything else of note you might tell me?"

A troubled frown graced the girl's soft face, but she didn't look at him. "I don't think so."

She was holding something back. He could sense it. "Anything at all, Princess. No matter how minor. Something about the assassin?"

"No, it was…" She glanced at her maids, who were doing their best to look busy with their needlework, though they could no doubt overhear the entire conversation. "It's about Everis, actually. It's probably nothing, but…"

Wren swallowed a nervous lump in his throat. "What about him?"

Cassia leaned in, lowering her voice. "It's just… I've never seen anything quite like what he did. I've watched the lot of you do magic for years. I know the concentration it takes. This woman had Everis pinned on the floor and utterly helpless."

That didn't sound right. All magic required the use of their hands— or else some sort of written element, such as an engraved rune on a sword or a magically composed concoction in a bottle. None of which he imagined Ever had on his person last night. Cassia had to be mistaken. No magi could cast like that. Not even Master Orin.

"Are you certain?" he pressed. "So much was going on, it would've been easy to miss it."

She frowned. "I suppose you're right. It wasn't just that, though. After he did… whatever it was he did with the wind, I called to him. Repeatedly. He didn't seem to hear me at all. When he finally looked at me, I swear I barely recognized him. Something about his face was all wrong."

A chill swept down Wren's spine, along with a memory tingling at the back of his mind. He had to force his tongue to cooperate to form the words. "What about his eyes, Princess? What did they look like?"

"I remember that part clearly." Cassia shrank back in her seat, gaze dropping to the chessboard. "His eyes. They were glowing red."

EVERIS

ONE YEAR AGO

The magi's study was a looming tower near the front of the castle, overlooking the city beyond. All the magi employed by the king and queen of Midmere used it. The study was a central location for experiments, research, reading, and concocting spells—everything from charms for the local farmers to promote healthy crops to fertility potions for couples having difficulty conceiving.

Out of everything within the tower, Everis loved the books the most. They stuffed every shelf to bursting with age-old texts and scrolls. There were trinkets from Master Orin's various travels, and often Master Orin himself, seated behind his long oak desk on the topmost floor. Although there were thirteen magi within Midmere, only one was called *Master*. One the Citadel had decided was skilled enough for the title, who held rank over the rest of them, and whom all other magi in Midmere had to consult before performing certain restricted rituals or experiments. Of all the masters in the kingdom, Everis was fortunate to have Orin for his.

Master Orin wasn't the only magi he learned from, however. He took sword lessons from Lady Imaryllis, history lessons from Mace Huntly, and herbs and medicines from Drake Reed to name a few. Orin felt it important for his apprentices to learn from more than a single source.

Aside from Master Orin, Lady Imaryllis was Everis's favorite instructor, but if he'd had to choose another, it might have been Drake. He was soft-spoken and patient and kind, quick as a whip, and smiled easily. He'd witnessed Drake correcting even Master Orin on things now and again. Master Orin had once said Drake could've become a master himself, but that he refused to leave his position in Midmere to do so.

Everis's respect for his teachers meant he didn't mind doing even menial tasks for them, such as helping organize some of the upper levels of the library. So much of what lived there hadn't been touched in years. He wondered if even Master Orin had gone through all these loose papers, scrolls, and books. Magi had a habit of keeping everything written by their peers, no matter how useless it might have seemed. History was too precious to be discarded.

He balanced precariously on the edge of a chair, reaching for a leather-bound tome on the topmost shelf of the fourth floor. When his fingers finally caught the edges of the spine to drag it down, it brought with it a layer of dust that made his nose scrunch. He sneezed. Perched upon the nearby railing, Master Orin's white raven, Nova, let out a caw and beat her snowy wings.

"Oh, hush now." Still on the chair, Everis opened the book to flip through its pages. Drake had him organizing this floor by topic, a project he'd been working on for nearly a month and had not even halfway completed. Along this stretch of shelves, he'd come across old prophecies, spell books written in long-dead languages, and plenty of irrelevant history.

There were no histories or prophecies in this book. The pages were brittle beneath his fingers, the ink a deep blood red. He frowned at the first page, which was written in a thin, shaky scrawl.

True Magic for the True Mage

"There's a condescending title if ever I heard one, eh, Nova?" Everis murmured.

The bird was easy to talk at, and it felt less foolish than speaking to himself. Nova flapped her wings once, hopped to the left on her perch, and cocked her head. Everis stepped down from the chair and sat in it, turning each fragile page with care.

Hexes, curses, spells of protection and preservation... Plenty of symbolism that he vaguely recognized from his studies, although there were oddities about these that he couldn't quite place. He scoured the instructions, faded and smudged in places, but the incantations themselves written in a language he didn't know. It didn't take long to realize what all these spells had in common.

Sacrifice.

The sound of his beating pulse echoed in his ears. The use of blood magic was rarely spoken of and strictly forbidden. No exceptions. It wasn't only that such spells required living blood to be performed or that they were more powerful than most other magic, but that they took something from the caster. Life. Sanity. Everis wasn't sure, other than that sort of darkness supposedly ate away at a person. Only the basic history of the subject had been covered in his studies, and Master Orin had resisted delving any deeper into it.

He shivered and snapped the book shut. Fascinating though it was, he didn't think it would be wise to continue reading. Did Master Orin even know this was here? Did Drake or the other magi? How long had it been tucked away in their study, and who had put it there to begin with? Everis could imagine Master Orin keeping such a thing, but locked away, safe from prying eyes and bad intentions. He glanced at Nova as though the raven would have an answer to his unspoken questions. The bird ruffled her feathers and flew away.

"Has something caught your eye, Ever?" Drake called.

Everis startled and stood so abruptly he nearly dropped the book. He'd not even heard the man approach, but there he stood at the end of the aisle, smiling. His impossibly long blond hair was pulled back into a loose braid that hung just past his hips, and his green eyes twinkled in amusement that he'd caught Everis off guard.

His face grew warm. "No, I... I was just trying to figure out where some of these go, is all."

"They don't make it easy, do they?" Drake sighed, plucking a random book from the shelf and absently paging through it. "But there are some gems in here. Don't feel bad if something catches your eye. Some fascinating and long-forgotten history can be found in these pages." He chuckled and returned the tome to its place. "And I guarantee anything history-related, Mace would be happy to talk your ear off about. Do you need help figuring out where that one goes?"

Everis tried to keep his hands from trembling where they gripped the book. It almost burned beneath his fingers and he could swear that Drake, at any moment, would realize just what he was holding. He swallowed hard and forced his mouth up into something close to a smile.

"No, I've figured it out. Thank you."

Drake smiled broadly and gave him a wink. "Carry on, then. You have plenty yet to be done."

He departed as quietly as he'd arrived. Everis's shoulders slumped. His white-knuckled grip on the book relaxed. *It's fine. It's all fine. Just put the book on Master Orin's desk and say I found it; I won't get in trouble just for stumbling across it.* He knew that much to be true. It wasn't the same as someone coming across Everis invested in reading the damned thing. It would be Everis, the conscientious student, bringing attention to something important, something that likely belonged at the Citadel rather than in Midmere's personal library.

Yes. He would turn it in. Problem solved.

But… perhaps he'd wait a few days.

For now, he could just slip it there onto the shelf so he wouldn't forget where it was.

PRESENT DAY

Captain Annaliese Maybury and ten armored knights on horseback flanked Everis and Wren's carriage as they departed Midmere. It was hardly an army, but it was enough to turn this trip into an official envoy without it coming across as threatening. That morning, Master Orin had given Wren a letter with the queen's seal to be delivered to Duke Ryland, begging him to come to Midmere to make peace with his dying brother. An earnest enough request, assuming the duke truly didn't have anything to do with the hired assassin. It was a message that could've been delivered via raven, but it was the queen's hope that an official envoy would not be thought too strange.

On his belt, Everis carried the dagger the assassin had attacked him with. It would be his job to ask around the city of Patish and see if he could find the maker of such a blade. Given the rarity of the metal used to forge it, he hoped it wouldn't be difficult.

A single rider could've made the trip from one city to the next in a week and a half. In a carriage and with a few wagons of supplies, it would take their little entourage nearly twice that. Everis had insisted they could ride on horseback just as well as any knight, but Orin said it would look more official if they arrived as any ambassadors for the royal family would.

He and Wren sat across from each other as they rolled through the countryside. Wren busied himself with a stack of books he'd brought along. Everis tried to read, found the motion of the carriage gave him a headache while trying, and instead shifted around with all the restless energy of a child.

How nice it would've been to be able to sleep. Since the night of the attack, he'd gotten only a few hours. But the castle had been alive with movement and tension that Everis could feel in the air itself, and it startled him awake every time he began to drift off. Now, there on the road, his mind raced with all the ways this trip could go. They weren't alone. They had Captain Annaliese and her soldiers, and Annaliese herself had gone on countless journeys just like this over the years. She knew what to watch for. She knew how to keep them safe.

After the first few hours, Wren closed the small book he was reading and threw it at Everis. "Sweet Mother, will you stop fidgeting?"

Everis caught it and opened it somewhere in the middle. "It's not my fault this is boring. Why couldn't we at least ride on horseback until we reached Patish? We can hardly see anything in here."

"You've got a window," Wren protested, reaching for the book. Everis leaned back to keep it out of his grasp. "Give that back."

"You threw it at me. It's mine now." He paused as his eyes skimmed the page, and his eyebrows shot up. Wren made another grab for it. Everis brought up a leg, planting his boot against the front of Wren's chest to hold him at bay. "Wait, what is this?"

"It's nothing!" Wren tried to shove the offending foot aside. "Give it back, Ever!"

"*She cradled his face so softly and kissed him. Her gallant knight had rescued her again, and now they would ride off into the sunset together.*" Everis could scarcely read it with a straight face. "You and your romance novels."

Wren's cheeks turned several impressive shades of red. He pushed Everis's leg aside and lunged, snatching the book from his hands. Everis didn't try to stop him. "Oh, shut up. It's mindless enjoyment. I'm not embarrassed over it!"

"I didn't say you should be. I'm only taunting you because you're acting like I've just caught you peeping on someone dressing." He grinned, slouching back in his seat. "Read it aloud to me, would you?"

His friend scowled, mouth pulled into a tight and unimpressed line. When Everis responded by stretching out on his side of the carriage, lying back with his hands folded on his stomach, he hesitated. "You're poking fun at me."

"I am not. I get nauseated when I read with all this movement. And I... rather like the sound of your voice. So, read to me?" Everis closed his eyes, silent, waiting. It was an earnest ask. He couldn't see the way Wren was looking at him, but he suspected it was a heated glare while he debated whether he'd cave to the request.

Then he heard the rustle of paper and Wren sighing before he began to read aloud. The sound of his voice brought Everis back to every night as a child when he couldn't sleep, when he'd crawl into Wren's bed and curl up at his side after a nightmare. Even back then, listening to him had been soothing. It hadn't mattered if Wren was reading to him or simply reciting spells that he'd practiced earlier that day. Just as it did now, it allowed Everis to get some much-needed rest. One moment, he was listening to Wren go on about a lonely knight and the princess who saw past his rugged exterior to the kindhearted man beneath, and the next, his eyes were opening, and it was nearly dark out.

The next four nights saw them sleeping in bedrolls around open campfires. The weather was clear and mild, only uncomfortably chilly when they woke in the early morning hours to be on their way.

On the fifth evening, they came to the small village of Blackpool, nestled at the foot of the mountains. It would be the last sign of civilization before venturing into the mountain pass that would take them to Patish. The innkeepers brought in warm meat and mead and supplied the magi and their soldiers with rooms for the night. Everis and Wren retreated early with little interest in drinking by the hearth.

Everis collapsed into bed with a weary groan. Wren sprawled on his own bed, opposite from his. "Is it a sign we're getting old that we don't tolerate sleeping on the ground the way we used to?"

Everis muffled a laugh into his pillow. "Maybe *you're* getting old."

"Hush yourself."

"You started it." He turned his head to look across the room, one arm dangling over the edge of the bed. "Do you think Ryland sent the assassin?"

Wren had his arms folded behind his head, gazing ceilingward. "I've been thinking about that the entire trip, and I haven't formed an opinion yet. It's true that he has the most to gain by wiping out the royal family..."

"But he'd also be the first suspected of such an act, wouldn't he?"

Everis asked. Wren was better at these sorts of things than he was. His friend saw pieces of a puzzle and liked to put them together. His own tendency was to take pieces that didn't fit and try to mash them together anyway. Puzzles were dumb.

"True." Wren frowned. "There are so many possibilities. It could've been any foreign nation looking to throw the kingdom into disarray. It could've been anyone with the money to hire an assassin who held a grudge against the king and queen. I just don't know. I suspect we'll have a better idea once we speak with Duke Ryland."

Everis sighed. Waiting required patience. Not his strong point, no matter how much Orin tried to instill it in him. "I guess."

They lapsed into silence for a few moments.

Wren's bed creaked as he rolled onto his side. "Say, Ever," he paused, seeming to choose his next words with care, "the night of the attack, the magic you used..."

Tension immediately slid across his shoulders. "What about it?"

Wren watched him with a faint crease between his brows, but he seemed at a loss for what to say for a minute. "You mentioned you'd done nothing like it before. Cassia said you were not quite yourself afterward. Do you remember that?"

It was Ever's turn to frown. He'd been dazed in the aftermath, certainly. Everything had happened so fast. But it had been strange, wrong, and he couldn't recall having spoken a word when he cast whatever spell it was. "I think she's over-exaggerating. I was a bit shaken. Wouldn't anyone have been?"

"I suppose." Wren hesitated. "She also mentioned... that your eyes were red."

Everis looked at him. The meaning of those words hung in the air around them. *You tapped into something you weren't supposed to.* Neither of them entirely knew what it was, just that it was dark, and that darkness led to bad things. He remembered the crackle of magic, like a charge in the air during a storm, the strength it had filled him with when he'd grasped for it. Even now, the memory clung to his bones and whispered in the back of his mind to do it again. He shivered.

"I did what I had to do in order to save her life and my own," he finally said, rolling onto his back.

Wren pushed himself up to sitting. "I'm not blaming you, Ever. I know whatever it was, it wasn't intentional. I only thought that maybe you ought to tell Master Orin?"

Shame crept to his face as a blush. He couldn't bring himself to look at Wren. "Why? So he can lecture me on something I couldn't help?"

A pause.

Wren drew in a breath. "Because this isn't the first time." Everis flinched, looking away. "Remember the bird? He didn't judge you then. He might be able to help you prevent it from accidentally happening again. I think he'd understand a lot more than you give him credit for." When Everis only stared at the ceiling, noting the cracks and imperfections, Wren sighed. "I'm worried about you. That's all."

Everis knew that. For as much as Wren lectured, he did it because he cared. He fussed and worried over him every day. Whenever Everis struggled, Wren was the one right there, ready to give him a hand up—whether Everis wanted the assistance or not.

In this instance, he did not want it. He wanted to brush it aside and pretend he had no need of it. How many times was he likely to end up in life-and-death situations where his first reflex was to summon some kind of dark force to protect himself? Before, it had always been little, inconsequential bits of darkness that seeped out in times of high emotion; crying over a dying baby bird, an injured cat, a fight with Brant. Nothing like this.

His continued silence led to Wren sighing again and sliding out of bed. He helped himself to a washbasin atop the nearby chest of drawers, stripping down to almost nothing so he could scrub the last few days' worth of dirt and dust from his skin. Everis let his gaze wander over to him, taking in the slope of his shoulders, every soft line and angle of his body. The splash of freckles across his shoulders was fascinating. Ever swallowed hard and tore his eyes away, turning onto his side to face the wall with his back to the room. He expected Wren to pester him further on the issue, to nag incessantly as he was prone to do with most everything else.

Yet, judging by the fact that Wren washed, put out the candles, and crawled into bed without a word, he had nothing left to say.

NATURAL MAGIC
THE BASICS OF MAGIC, VOLUME I

Over the centuries, magi have strived to not only perfect their magic but to understand it. Researchers have classified various magics and the way they are used.

Natural Magic is the everyday usage of magic that is most common. The human body serves as a conductor, channeling the energy existing around them to translate it into spells. Natural magic is performed via vocal cues accompanied by hand gestures. The caster must be able to see where they want their spell targeted.

No evidence has been provided to suggest that vocal cues must be in any particular language or that any individual spell must be the same from one person to the next. Rather, the vocal cues are merely one more way for a magi to mentally focus their magic and guide it into doing what they want. For this reason, specific keywords might prove more powerful for one magi than another.

ORIN

King Faramond lay in the same position he had for many weeks past. His once vibrant eyes rarely opened anymore. When they did, they were dim and unfocused. He looked at Orin, but Orin wasn't convinced his king *saw* him.

"You need to drink, Your Grace," he murmured.

Faramond didn't respond, didn't move, although when Orin brought the vial to his lips, he parted them slightly to drink. These days, the medicine went down with difficulty. If they reached a point where they could no longer get nourishment into the king, he'd waste away to nothing. No magic would save him.

Orin set the vial aside and pulled up a chair, sinking into it with a sigh. In the early weeks of Faramond's illness, Orin had sat in this very seat, and they'd talked at length about everything under the sun. Some days, Faramond grew too weary and asked Orin to read to him or talk to him about anything. Anything at all. Just so he wasn't alone. Now, Orin had to wonder if his friend even knew he was there.

The door creaked open. Drake entered, bringing with him fresh herbs, tea, and more medicine. He frequently tried new concoctions, hoping to find some sort of miracle cure that might rid the king of his mysterious illness.

He placed the tray on the nearby table. "How is he?"

"As well as he was yesterday. And the day before that, and the day before that..."

"You sound weary, Orin." Drake smoothed his hands down the front of his tunic and poured two cups of tea. "How long have you been here?"

"Not long," Orin replied, still with his eyes on the king.

Six months. What sort of illness held on so desperately like this? Against everything they threw at it, no less. Healing spells, medicine, potions... In his darker moments, he worried their efforts to keep Faramond going were only causing him needless suffering. Were they being selfish?

"There's something we're missing, Drake. I wish I could figure out what."

Drake swept over to his side, not offering him a cup so much as placing it in Orin's hands before Orin could insist that he didn't need it. With care, he tucked some of Orin's hair behind his ear. "Some things are beyond even your ability to fix, sweet friend."

That wasn't an answer he liked nor one he was willing to accept. Yet. Despite himself, Orin sipped the tea, the flowery heat welcome as it settled in his empty stomach. "I don't just mean with His Grace. I've still been examining the attack on the princess, and I feel I'm looking at a mosaic with missing pieces."

Drake moved to the other side of the bed, leaning over Faramond. He checked his pulse, lifted his eyelids, examined his breathing. The frown on his face suggested none of these things were good. "You might've felt better going to see Duke Ryland yourself, you know. The queen was quite cross when she learned you'd sent the boys instead."

"I have complete faith in my apprentices to handle things. Besides, I'm not convinced Ryland had anything to do with this. It feels too easy."

"Sometimes easy *is* the answer." Drake straightened up with a sigh. "You often like to make puzzles more complicated than they need to be."

Orin frowned, his gaze traveling to the other magi. "I don't suppose you've finished your tests on those tablets, have you?"

"I have a few more compounds to look for, but thus far, nothing of note. Starch. Sugar. Typical filler components." Drake brought a gentle hand to his arm. "I promise, you'll be the first to hear if I find anything. If I cannot get you to eat, at least finish your tea."

He looked down into the cup. Would this be another dead end? Frustrating.

Orin ended up setting the unfinished tea aside and excused himself while Drake worked. There was nothing he could do to help, and he needed quiet to think.

Quiet could've been found in a number of places—the study tower, his room, the gardens. Yet he found himself venturing down to the dungeons. They were empty. Anyone arrested for crimes in Midmere was typically kept within the city jails. The royal dungeons had gone largely unused in recent decades... except by the magi.

It didn't matter what the weather was like aboveground; down there, it was always cold. Cold enough to store bodies. It was there that the magi performed autopsies for research and investigation. When one of the cooks had died unexpectedly the previous summer, it was in these cells that Drake and Gilbert cut the woman open to try to determine what had killed her. And it was to these cells that Orin had the corpse of Cassia's would-be assassin brought the night of her attack. The temperature, along with a few charms, would preserve her for quite a while before they'd be forced to have her interred or burned.

Orin plucked a key from inside his pocket and let himself into the locked cell. The young woman had been stripped, her clothing laid out on a table against the stone wall. He stopped there first, looking over the blood-stained garments. Worn black leather, nicely made. Tailored for easy, fluid movement. Important for an assassin. There were no identifying marks or sigils. On the belt hung pouches containing a few throwing knives, lock picks, and—previously—a handful of pills. Small, off-white tablets he'd handed over to Drake for testing, although he'd kept a few for himself, just in case. Orin had presumed they'd be condensed cypher or some other form of common poison, something an assassin might use in a pinch if they were captured and didn't want to risk being tortured for information.

She was a professional, Orin thought. *Not just anyone brought in from the streets.*

She'd known how to get in, how to take down a man twice her size, how to sneak through the castle undetected, quite possibly knew they had their Friday night banquets and much of the castle would be distracted... That was what bothered him the most. This woman *knew* what she was doing, which meant she'd likely been expensive to hire.

So why would she have been so careless as to use a weapon potentially bearing a symbol linking her to her employer? True, it could've been pure coincidence—an owl holding an ichoroa flower, Duke Ryland's sigil. Yet given that ichoroa didn't frequently grow anywhere outside of Patish, it seemed too much of a coincidence.

He turned to the body on the autopsy table, drawing back the sheet that covered her. She was slim and toned, with sun-bronzed skin and chestnut hair. The fall from the tower had snapped her neck. A quick death. Fortunate for her if the alternative had been lying there, paralyzed, while she bled out.

"What I wouldn't give to have had even five minutes to speak with you," Orin said to the corpse.

You still could.

You know how.

With a shiver, he shoved the thought aside.

Perhaps Drake was right, and he was searching for answers where they didn't exist. Perhaps this assassination attempt *was* the result of a younger brother trying to claim the throne for himself as his king lay dying. But it didn't *feel* right. Still, Drake had been his friend for decades, ever since he'd arrived in Midmere. He was talented and sharp, and his ability to see things from an angle so much different from Orin's helped to broaden his own worldview. Drake challenged him, and he needed that. Appreciated it.

But in this instance... something in Orin's gut told him he wasn't wrong. A piece was missing. He only needed to find it.

EVERIS

A storm had been raging since they packed up camp at dawn on their second day through the mountain pass. Captain Annaliese sent a scout ahead to report back any dangerous terrain or blocked passages.

Hopefully, the scout was faring better than the rest of them. Progress had been painfully slow as they maneuvered the carriage and wagons through muddy hills and narrow mountain roads. More than once, Wren peered out the window and color drained from his face when he realized it was a straight drop right outside their door.

Another crack of thunder made Everis shudder. The carriage lurched and ground to an abrupt halt, pitching Everis out of his seat and practically into Wren's lap. Wren caught him by the front of his tunic, equally startled. "That wasn't thunder."

He nudged Everis aside to lean out the window and shout through the rain to the driver. The storm drowned out whatever response he received. When he drew back inside, his sandy-blond hair had been whipped into a frenzied mess. He wiped raindrops from his brow. "One of the blasted wheels broke."

Everis bit back a groan. He shoved the door open and crawled out, minding the mud and loose gravel. He circled to the front of the carriage,

50

shoulders hunched, clutching at his hood to keep the wind from yanking it back. Captain Annaliese stood with a few knights, their carriage driver included, as they surveyed the damage where the ground had given away to reveal a ditch and the broken wheel half embedded in the mud. Everis sidled up beside Annaliese, frowning.

"There's no way we're fixing it in this weather," the captain grumbled, rubbing the back of her neck. She turned to Everis. "I propose we make camp and try to wait out this storm. We nearly lost a rider earlier because we couldn't properly see the drop-offs around the bend."

Everis grimaced, head tipping back to take in their surroundings. At least here, they were encased on either side by hills and no sharp drop-offs, but… "We're in a prime location to get buried by a rockslide."

"Right. Then let me get right on having my soldiers carry the carriage to a better location."

Everis flushed. He couldn't argue that. Besides, the knights looked exhausted and soaked through. He and Wren had the advantage of being tucked away in the safety of the carriage. Already, the rain was working its way through his clothes.

"Point taken, Captain," Wren said as he came up beside Everis, hugging himself for warmth. "We'll make camp and reevaluate in the morning. With any luck, it'll dry up in the night."

A knight let out a shout from somewhere nearby. Several others ran to him while Wren and Everis turned to watch. He looked to have stumbled into another severe pothole on the path, oddly deep for being naturally made.

Everis frowned, looking back at the carriage wheel and the hole that had nearly swallowed it. Wren was doing the same. He could see the gears ticking in his friend's head. Wren turned away, moving a few paces, scanning the mud. Everis followed, walking with care so as not to lose his footing on the slick ground. He pointed. "There's another one."

"And another," Wren said with a nod.

They counted no less than ten more holes, all similar in size and depth. What was the point of it?

"I don't like this," Wren muttered. The rain nearly drowned out the sound of his voice. He whirled on his heel and marched back toward the carriage. "Captain Annaliese! Please, I think we should try to repair the wheel and leave as soon as possible."

Annaliese regarded him as though Wren had grown a second head. "What? I've already told the soldiers to get the tents up."

"There are holes all over this road." Wren wrung his hands together in distress. "I'm fairly certain they were man-made."

Everis frowned. "Who would bother with something like that?"

Annaliese sighed. "Someone who wanted travelers to be forced to stop in this section of the pass."

Wren gave a nod. "Yes. Catch merchants with broken wagons unaware, and they become easy targets."

Everis's expression fell. "You think we're targets?"

"We could be," Wren said. "Let's keep quiet—no attempts at fires tonight—and have extra guards keep watch."

With a curt nod, Annaliese turned on her heel and began doling out orders, making it a point not to shout above the rain this time. She set a few knights to hoist the wagon out of the hole and prop it up so the wheel could be mended as soon as the storm let up enough. The others were sent to finish with the tents. Everis and Wren retreated to their own tent once it was erected, soaked through and not in the most pleasant of moods.

"Should one of us stay up?" Everis asked. "To help keep watch?"

"The knights have it handled." Wren peeled out of his cloak and tunic, rummaging bare-chested through his trunk for something dry to sleep in. Everis was tempted to sleep in his drawers, but it was too cold, and the last thing he needed was to be woken in the dead of night with bandits descending upon them and him caught in his unmentionables. Wren threw a dry set of trousers and a shirt his way, so he skimmed out of his own sopping wet outfit.

They settled in their respective bedrolls with barely a word. For a while, Wren tossed and turned, but eventually his breathing evened out and he stilled. Everis stared at the roof of the tent, listening to the rain beating against it, straining his ears to hear. Now and again, he could make out a voice or two, but little else could be heard above the storm.

He reached out to rest a hand atop his sword, which he'd laid alongside his bedroll. Just in case. Learning to properly wield a blade was just as important in their training as anything else. There would be situations, Lady Imaryllis cautioned, where they wouldn't have time to concoct charms or potions or cast spells, and the only thing between life and death would be the steel they held in their hands. Wren knew this too; his sword laid at his feet. Lady Imaryllis was skilled enough to create a blade from magic itself. He and Wren had a way to go before such a thing was possible for them.

Everis closed his eyes and focused on his breathing. In for four beats, out for four beats. Willing his heart to slow. An old trick he'd been taught by Wren when nightmares threatened to keep him up all hours of the night. He hoped it would work now.

It must have. It felt like mere seconds before his eyes snapped open, breath catching, heart lodging in his throat.

A bad dream.

Except Wren was upright in his bed, hair mussed, eyes wide and alert.

How long had they been asleep?

Long enough that the rain had let up at least somewhat.

And long enough that they were under attack.

Everis pitched himself forward, grabbed his sword, and drew it from its sheath as he rolled to his feet. Wren scrambled to follow, but Everis was already out of the tent and into the night. Mud squelched beneath his bare feet. The sound of shouting filled the pass, echoing off the hills along with the reverberations of metal against metal as swords clashed.

Their assailants were dressed in deep browns and black, damned near invisible against the dark terrain. They moved like shadows, ganging up on any soldier they could find. What they lacked in proper training, they made up for in numbers and stealth.

A knight in a neighboring tent came rushing out, nearly losing his footing in the mud. One of the bandits swooped in, sword raised. Everis lurched forward, catching the blade with his own inches before it came down on the knight's exposed neck. Swearing, the bandit drew back, refocusing his attention on Everis while the knight scrambled away.

"We aren't merchants!" Everis snapped, taking a defensive stance. "We've nothing worth stealing!"

"We'll see about that," the bandit growled, then lunged again.

Their blades met with such force that the shock sent a jolt up Everis's arm to his shoulder. He focused on his breathing. Lady Imaryllis's words repeated like a mantra in his head.

Steady. Focus. Pay attention to not only your opponent but to everything around you—even the things you cannot see.

Magic could guide a magi, even in a sword-fight. He only needed to listen to it. Which was difficult when he had this ox of a man bearing down on him with one heavy swing after another, driving him back and away from the camp, away from anyone who might have come to help. It was all Everis could do to block and dodge.

Focus.

Imaryllis had put them through combat drills for years. Taught them how to fight, how to create offensive spells and hexes, how to fashion poisons to be smeared on blades and arrowheads and flammable oils that would create a blazing sword or a blade of ice. But they'd never needed to use those skills outside of a training yard.

Everis lost his footing, plummeting to the ground. His back struck the mud with a wet sound while a rock jabbed sharply into his left shoulder blade. He winced, caught a glimmer of steel overhead, and rolled to one side before it came down on him. Gracelessly, he got to his feet. Practicing in the training yard on a clear, bright day with someone who knew the rules of honor was one thing. This was another.

He breathed deeply and tried again to concentrate. The man was larger than him. Stronger. Quicker than he looked, but still not as quick as Everis. He seemed to be favoring his right leg. An old injury, perhaps. His strokes were vicious but clumsy. His opponent relied on that sheer strength and stamina—so Everis just needed to beat him before he grew too tired to lift his own sword. Even if the bandit was used to this terrain, he wasn't immune to its hazards.

Everis ducked beneath another wide swing. This time, when the mud shifted beneath his feet, he went with it. He let himself go with the momentum down to one knee, skidding forward a foot. Far enough that he could bring his blade across the back of the man's right calf. Leather and skin parted like butter, and his blade struck bone. The bandit howled in pain, leg buckling beneath him. With one last surge of adrenaline, Everis pushed to his feet, grasped his sword with both hands, and drove it into the man's back.

He felt every bit of it. Visualized it. The blade glancing off the spinal column, gliding through muscle and lungs and ribs before the tip exited the other side. The bandit slumped forward, gurgling on his own blood.

For a few seconds, Everis didn't move, his chest heaving and heart racing. It wasn't like he'd never killed someone before. Just the other night he'd thrown a woman to her death from Cassia's window. This was different. *Felt* different. He sensed the split second the man died. The sensation raced through his veins, and the rush brought everything into crystal-clear focus.

They'd gone forty or fifty feet from camp. He could make out silhouettes fighting in the darkness. Metal against metal. Screaming. Cries of anguish and fury. He sensed...

Wren.

Everis planted a foot against the dead man's back and yanked his sword free before dashing off for the camp as fast as his legs would take him. Everything around him seemed sharper. His adrenaline spiked, the earlier fatigue and achiness little more than a memory now. He vaulted over a fallen soldier, bringing his sword up across the back of a bandit who was engaged with Captain Annaliese. Annaliese didn't even appear winded, though there was blood on her chain-mail. Everis couldn't tell if it was hers.

"I had it covered," she said.

"Where's Wren?" Everis demanded.

Annaliese frowned, whipping around. "He was just over there, last I saw. Stars, Everis, I can't keep track of everyone right now!"

Everis scarcely heard her. He was already off like a shot, making his way through the fray. The knights were holding their own, years of practice and superior skill allowing them to drive the thieves back.

At the far edge of the camp, where the pass narrowed and the hills rose sharply on either side, another knight stood back-to-back with Wren, surrounded by a handful of bandits. He didn't need to get closer to tell they were both barely hanging on through their exhaustion. This was their last stand.

I won't reach them in time.

A blade sliced the air a fraction of an inch from Wren's face, interrupting a spell he was trying to cast, and another took the knight in the shoulder while he tried to deflect yet another coming in from his left. The bandits attacked in pairs, making it difficult to block or dodge.

In seconds, the soldier hit his knees, doubled over, and clutched his stomach. He must've been one of the ones sleeping because he wore no armor, only the leathers he'd gone to bed in. Blood pooled from between his fingers and he gasped, unable to do a thing as one of the bandits lifted his blade with the clear intention of taking the soldier's head right off. Wren knocked away the sword before him and whirled, narrowly catching that blade against his own to protect his companion.

Everything crept along slowly. The large bandit knocked Wren back. He stumbled, tried to turn in time to meet one of his original attackers. Block, block, parry—

Until a sword took him through the stomach, and his expression went slack.

Everis screamed.

BLOOD MAGIC

THE BASICS OF MAGIC, VOLUME I

Also known as the dark arts or sacrificial magic, blood magic is a long-outlawed practice within the magi community and punishable by the Citadel for any magi found dabbling within it. Whereas natural magic uses the existing energy within the world around us, blood magic seeks to generate new energy with the sacrifice of life and blood. Nothing carries stronger essence than ichor, after all, and spilling it provides a blood magi with frighteningly powerful abilities.

However, with great power comes a catch. The inherent darkness surrounding blood magic corrupts those who use it. Blood magi are known to become addicted to the sensation of the magic flowing through them, and it becomes an insatiable beast difficult to ignore. There is not a blood magi in recorded history who has not succumbed to this madness, and few are able to make it out again without intervention. Those few who have survived have had only one thing to say: "The magic, it is always hungry."

EVERIS

Lightning split the sky wide open. Everis could feel it in his bones, just as he'd felt the dying soldier, just as he'd felt the man he'd run through moments ago. It crackled across his skin like a second pulse, cold and thrumming, fueling his rage.

The bandits were waiting when he descended on them, five in total. He slashed one across the chest and took the next one's arm off at the elbow, leaving him to howl in pain.

The lightning wasn't only in the sky anymore. He could feel it—see it—sparking across his fingertips and up the hilt of his sword, flickering across the blade. When the next bandit swung for him and their weapons met, it was in a shower of sparks and electricity. His opponent's blade crackled, splintered, and snapped in half. Everis's sword came down on his shoulder, catching halfway down the man's chest, lodging in muscle and organs and bone.

With a hiss, he relinquished his hold and spun to the next man. The bandit's sword caught his face, tip raking across his cheek and the bridge of his nose. Heat flooded from the open wounds, and he tasted blood on his lips.

Everis gripped the bandit's wrist, squeezing so tightly that the rogue's

57

hand spasmed and lost its hold on his sword. Lightning crackled from Ever's fingertips, surged bright and hot through his skin and into the bandit's, racing up his arm and shoulder and beyond. The bandit seized, his head snapping back. Everis shoved him into the final foe, and the pair stumbled, hitting the ground. Everis retrieved the bandit's fallen sword and ran them both through.

He turned, chest heaving, and with a brutal yank, dislodged his own blade from the nearby corpse. The man who'd lost his arm lay writhing on the ground, and he scrambled back as Everis stalked toward him.

"Mercy!" he begged. "Mercy, please—"

"Like the mercy you were about to show to my friend?" His lips drew up into a snarl, grip tightening on the hilt of his sword.

"*Ever...*"

He stopped.

Just like that, the second pulse dropped away. The electricity died from his fingers. Everis sucked in a deep breath, disoriented. Who had called him? What had he done?

Wren called for him again.

All but forgetting the bandit, Everis dashed back to Wren's side, dropping to his knees and gathering him up. The front of Wren's tunic was stained red, and he clutched at it as though trying to apply pressure but not having the strength.

"I'm here," Everis said, ignoring the tremor in his own voice. "I'm here, Wren. Hang in there."

"I don't think..." Wren started to reply, voice trailing off. His face was so pale.

That could be the darkness, that's all.

He'd lost so much blood.

He's going to be fine. He'll be fine.

Everis gathered him into his arms, staggered to his feet, and mustered enough energy to hurry back in the direction of the camp. Wren didn't make a sound. His head dropped against Everis's shoulder. He was dying.

HE'LL BE FINE.

What good were all his years of training if he couldn't do something about this now? What sort of magi was he? What sort of friend?

"Stay with me," Everis said, again and again, until he was too breathless from moving with dead weight in his arms. Annaliese and her soldiers had fought back the remaining bandits, many of whom now lay strewn across the camp. She fixed her gaze on Everis as he approached, realizing who the injured man was.

"Help the magi!" she barked.

Two knights hurried to meet Everis, hefting Wren from his arms.

"To my tent," Everis panted, already moving around them to head there himself. "Captain, I need the trunk from the carriage. All our medical supplies are in there. Bring any of the other injured to me."

He didn't wait for an answer. He marched for the tent, flinging aside the flap, and ducked inside. The pair of guards arrived just as he got the lanterns lit. They laid Wren down on Everis's bedroll instead of his own, and he didn't try to stop them. He dismissed them with a wave of his hand and dropped to his knees at his friend's side, yanking up the blood-stained tunic to have a better look at what he was working with.

His hopes plummeted. The sword had taken Wren almost straight through the belly. It was a miracle he was still alive... But that miracle would not hold out for long. Everis grabbed his own tunic and yanked it over his head, balling it up to press it against the wound as firmly as he could, unable to do much else until his things were brought to him.

Two soldiers hauled the chest in, placing it within reach, while another two carried in an injured knight, who they laid on Wren's bedroll. Everis only gave him a passing glance.

"Hold this," he instructed one of the lingering soldiers. She crouched and took over pressing the fabric to Wren's stomach while Everis opened the chest and rummaged through it. He needed herbs and bandages, antiseptic, quillcorn, bramble weed, snakeberry... Wren had been smart enough to make up some salves prior to their trip, but some things had to be mixed right before use because they were only effective for a short time.

With shaking hands, he ground the leaves and seeds with a mortar and pestle, and formed a poultice. He shooed the knight back, scooting forward to take her place. The bleeding had slowed but not stopped. Wren's breathing had grown unsteady. Sweat dotted his brow. Everis untied a brown roll of leather, sliding out a needle and thread. In silence, he hunched forward, keen eyes focused on the task at hand.

"You there," he said to the knight still kneeling nearby. "The blue bottle by the mortar—yes, that one. Pour it into his mouth. See that he drinks it all."

She moved to obey while Everis focused on closing Wren's pierced skin. He'd stitched plenty of wounds during his apprenticeship, but none quite like this. None that *mattered* like this. Yet his hands remained steady, his breathing even. When he finished, he had the knight help him roll Wren onto his side. The blade hadn't gone all the way through. Good.

He grabbed for the mortar, scooping the cold mush onto his fingers and smearing it over the wound. It would harden in a matter of minutes, better than any cloth bandage. In about twenty-four hours, it would start to chip away, and he would apply a new one.

That done, he rocked back onto his heels and stared helplessly at Wren. He could patch him up, could have him drink every medicine they'd prepared, and it *still* might not be enough. He squeezed his eyes shut. The gash on his own face throbbed. He'd honestly forgotten about it.

"Magi Everis," the knight spoke quietly. "My friend… He still needs tending to."

Ah. That was why she'd stayed.

As loath as he was to leave Wren's side, he couldn't sit there idle, either. He had a job to do. This was what he was trained for.

The knight—Sanda was her name—helped him tend to the injured soldier. He couldn't have been more than twenty, certainly no older than Wren. He'd not been armored during the attack, and that had been his downfall. An angry red gash ran from his right shoulder clear across his chest, exposing muscle and bleeding profusely. Another blade had taken him in his left side. He was awake, more or less. Everis had Sanda hold him down while he cleaned, stitched, applied a poultice to the wounds, and forced him to drink the bitter-tasting liquid that would not only aid in healing the internal damage but also help him sleep.

Sanda sat back on her haunches, biting her lip. "Will Maliel be all right?"

Everis sat cross-legged in the middle of the room, stealing an anxious look at Wren before turning his attention to cleaning his suturing needles. "Hard to say just yet. I'll have a better idea come morning."

She hesitated as though more questions were on the tip of her tongue.

Everis sighed. "Go see if your fellow soldiers need anything. I'm sure they could use help clearing the bodies and taking stock of anything that was damaged."

And whoever we lost, he thought grimly.

Wren had been right. This had been a trap. They should've been more careful or, at the very least, tried harder to fix the carriage—weather be damned. They should never have gone to sleep.

Sanda left him alone with nothing but Wren and Maliel's unsteady breathing for company. Now that the immediate need for him to stay vigilant and focused had passed, his adrenaline had crashed, leaving him nauseated, dizzy, and trembling. Again and again, that image of the blade sliding through Wren's belly with little resistance played in his head. He could not shake it. If he had moved faster, if he had not gotten distracted running through the camp, if he had been even *five seconds sooner*...

The thoughts played in an endless loop. Everis squeezed his eyes shut and gave himself a few moments just to breathe, to allow his body to settle—as much as it was willing to, anyway. When he felt he could move again without throwing up, he scooted to the trunk once more and rummaged through it as though he might come across something he hadn't already thought to use. Herbs for sore throats, rashes, earaches. Salves for burns. Berries that, when mixed with quillcorn, would help an upset stomach. Nothing useful. Of course.

What would Master Orin do?

His gaze darted to the other trunk—the one containing his clothes and personal belongings, at the foot of his bedroll. He wet his lips and could swear he still tasted lightning there.

"Ev...?"

He whipped around to see Wren's face tipped toward him. He lifted a hand, seemed to decide he didn't know what to do with it, and let it drop again. In a heartbeat, Everis was at his side, taking up that hand in his own and holding it against his chest.

"Easy," he murmured. "You got yourself roughed up pretty good."

"Hurts," Wren sighed, face screwing up.

"I gave you something for the pain. It ought to kick in any moment." He lifted a hand, stroking back the hair from Wren's flushed face and sweat-covered brow. His skin was too warm for Everis's liking.

"You look worried." Wren curled his fingers against Everis's, trying to focus on him, although his gaze wandered now and again.

Everis tried to smile. "You scared me.. What made you run off from the camp on your own?"

Wren shifted, winced through gritted teeth, and lay still again. "Looking for you..."

Guilt struck him hard in the chest. He swallowed it back, blinking away the tears that blurred his vision. "You shouldn't have done that."

The corners of Wren's mouth slowly turned up in a delirious smile. "Have I told you... that you have the loveliest eyes?"

Heat crept into his face. He almost laughed. Almost. Any other day, Everis would have fallen all over himself for Wren to give him such a compliment. "Ah. That must be the medicine hitting. Get some rest, Wren. I'll be right here."

"Hmm. S'true, though..." Wren's voice slurred and trailed off as his eyelids drooped shut. Everis didn't know if he was asleep or passed out, but there was little he could do either way.

Except sit and wait and look after both his charges.

Again, he glanced toward the chest at the foot of his bedroll, wetting his lips anxiously.

Give it time, he told himself. *Patience.*

Everis waited and watched until dawn. A few more soldiers filtered in as the night progressed, mostly with injuries that needed tending to but weren't life-threatening. Sometime in the early morning, Captain Annaliese swept aside the tent flap to step in to greet him.

"The carriage is repaired," she announced. Her gaze roamed across Wren and Maliel, a frown tugging at her face. "Can they travel?"

Everis didn't want to risk moving either of them. Maliel had woken once or twice, and each time Everis had checked his wounds again and given him more medicine to help him rest. Wren had scarcely moved. His fever had worsened; his breathing was weak and shallow.

I need more time.

He brought a hand to rest on Wren's bicep. "If we were to stay here another night, do you think those bandits would return?"

She folded her arms. "Hard to say. Suppose it depends on what their numbers are like. A fair number left here injured. I would like to think if they had reinforcements, they'd have come back already, striking while we were still recovering."

"But…?"

"But these are hill people, not trained soldiers and strategists. They abide by their own logic and rules."

Everis spared a look at her. "So, you think we should depart now and not risk another night."

"If you're asking for my opinion, then… yes." Her expression shifted, the normally harsh lines to her gaze softening. "You and Wren are technically the leaders of this trip, Everis. If you order us to stay, we will stay."

If the bandits return, we aren't likely to be so lucky this time.

He looked down at Wren, worry eating away at his insides. What was the right answer? Exhaustion had overtaken him hours ago, but he couldn't bring himself to sleep. What would Master Orin do? What would *Wren* do? He wouldn't want to endanger anyone else for the sake of a few. He would do his best to keep the injured safe and stable, and he would press onward.

He rose tiredly to his feet. "Ready the knights. Have two of the wagons unloaded into the carriage to free them up. One for the dead, the other for Wren and Maliel. I'll ride with them."

Captain Annaliese bowed deeply and retreated from the tent, leaving Everis alone with his decision and wondering if it was the right one.

ORIN

"It's greywitch." Drake laid a piece of paper before him. "I missed it the first time around because it's lacking creeping cress."

Orin sat back in his chair, sliding the reading glasses from his face to look over Drake's breakdown of the tablets that had been on the assassin's person. "It had gloriosa as a binding agent?" He lifted his chin. "Gloriosa doesn't grow here. Too much rain." And the greywitch itself was considered too dangerous. Magi outside of the Citadel weren't permitted to cultivate it at all, not that it was a rule easily enforced.

"Correct. We've tried a few times to grow gloriosa in the castle gardens, and it never took root." Drake folded his arms across his chest. "But do you know where it grows in abundance?"

Orin wasn't sure he wanted the answer to that. "I'll wager a guess. Patish?"

"Patish," Drake agreed. "I worry your apprentices may be on a mission that will prove more than they can handle, Orin. Are you sure we shouldn't go after them?"

That was a question to make Orin hesitate.

He'd woken from a dead sleep the night before, shaken and broken out into a cold sweat. Sometimes, he could feel his apprentices on a

64

metaphysical level. There existed a sort of shared link between their hearts, the strings of magic that wove them together. They were more than master and apprentices. They were family, and that bond was one Orin felt to his very core. If the boys were in danger, he would know.

And I do, he grimly thought. *Something's happened, and I can do nothing about it.*

He ran a hand down his face. He had every bit of faith in Wren and Everis. When the pair of them were together, their strengths complemented one another. Wren was cautious and possessed common sense. Everis had a good feel for people and had mastered the mechanics of every spell and sword lesson his teachers could throw at him. Still, his chest ached with a heaviness he could not so easily dismiss.

"They'll be fine. You used up all of the tablets, I presume?"

Drake's eyebrows lifted. "Planning on poisoning someone, Master?"

He smiled pleasantly. "No. Not today, at least."

"I'm afraid I did. There were only a few."

He sighed. "I appreciate your hard work, Drake."

Drake left him, descending the stairs. Perched on the back of his chair, Nova flapped her wings and croaked, hopping down to the desk and eyeing the paper with a tilt of her head. Orin extended a hand, smoothing a fingertip up her beak.

"One question answered and a million more to go, hm?" His eyes roamed over the notes, hoping for something that would jump out at him that he'd missed. All signs pointed to Duke Ryland. It might've been wisest for him to take that lead and follow it, and yet…

He glanced at the white raven, meeting her red eyes. "What do you think, Nova?"

Not that he expected an answer, but often he worked through conundrums by speaking aloud to her. She was a good listener. Now, she walked to the ledge of his desk and pecked at a wooden box where Orin kept treats tucked away. With a chuckle, he lifted the lid and allowed her to duck her head inside. She emerged with several seeds and took flight, heading into the rafters above.

It was not only a treat box, however. Orin reached in, removed a small pouch, and slid his thumb across it. He could feel small tablets inside—the few he'd not handed over to Drake for processing.

How many times had he told his own apprentices never to use up all their samples during initial testing? One never knew if another test would need to be run. While such tests weren't Orin's specialty, he still knew how to do them and how to utilize the vast library to make sense of the results. Perhaps he would find something Drake had missed.

He circled down the spiral staircase to the ground floor where their supplies and lab equipment lay. Drake had his own private lab in his rooms where he could concentrate on his work uninterrupted. Orin removed two of the three tablets from the pouch, fetching beakers and tubes, snatching dyes and chemical compounds. He used only as much of the tablets as he had to for accurate results and to run as many tests as he could think to run, the pills cut into multiple small pieces. Many of the samples would need to sit for a day or two before he could determine much of anything. He tucked them away in a back room, out of sight of anyone who wasn't specifically searching for them.

Thankfully, the first of the results was one of the most important. By the time he checked them the following day, he was able to rule out the most common poisons, something Drake had already done. But one of the results gave him pause.

No traces of greywitch or gloriosa.

He set up a second test, just to be certain. Either his results were wrong, or Drake's had been. It seemed more likely that the error was his. Drake had been doing this for far too long to make a careless mistake that would yield inaccurate results.

When he checked back the following day, the results were the same. Not a trace of greywitch.

But there *was* cypher.

A common poison, it was used often in combat on arrowheads or to coat blades—though it made them rust if not cleaned after a battle. It wasn't nearly as deadly as greywitch on its own and had to be prepared and cooked in a very specific way to make it effective. Where greywitch could make a man drop dead within five minutes of ingesting even a small amount, cypher caused seizures, heart palpitations, and death, but only in high or extended doses. It was far more effective as a means of rendering a person unconscious if they inhaled or ingested too much of it at once.

Orin braced his hands against the table, the possibilities of what this meant running through his head. He'd ruled out nineteen other poisons. Only traces of cypher had come back positive. How had Drake's tests been so very wrong? Had the results been tampered with? Not for the first time, he felt like he was going in circles with answers that only opened more questions.

Nova sat nearby, watching him through those unsettling eyes. Orin met her gaze. She seemed to be telling him, *You still have an option left.*

If he couldn't find answers any other way except from the dead assassin…

Then it was the assassin he needed to speak to.

EVERIS

The only blessing that day was that the worst of the rain had let up. Any time the drizzle got to be too much, Everis dragged a woolen blanket over his head and draped it over the sides of the wagon to keep the water off Wren and Maliel as best as he could.

It was slow-going getting through the narrow pass. What had once been ten knights was now six—if one counted Maliel and the scout that had not yet returned. The dead were kept in a cart at the end of the procession, just behind the wagon Everis himself rode in. It was impossible not to stare at it, directly in his line of vision as it was; four linen-bound bodies, jostling every time the wheels hit a bump in the road. There was little place for proper graves here in the pass, and it seemed fitting that the soldiers be returned to their homes and families. Everis had, thankfully, just enough supplies to place a preservation charm on each of the dead knights. It would hold until they reached Patish.

Now, he just needed to keep the injured two alive.

Maliel opened his eyes now and again to stare blearily around, and he smiled when Sanda rode up to the side of the wagon to check on him, but otherwise he slept soundly. The more time passed, the more Everis was convinced he'd pull through.

Wren, on the other hand…

He'd been right that the journey wouldn't be good for his friend. By the time they stopped an hour short of sunset, Wren was racked with shivers and scalding to the touch. Everis made sure that theirs was the first tent pitched so he could get Wren lying down properly and have a look at his injury.

The poultice was black and dried, and it peeled away beneath Everis's fingers like a flaky second skin. Beneath, the stitched wound was raised and angry and, worst of all, oozing. Wren's abdomen was swollen, hard to the touch.

Tears stung his eyes, and he swallowed, blinking them back. "Wren… I need you to tell me what to do," he whispered. "I can't figure this out on my own."

Silence, of course. Save for the sounds of soldiers making camp. Sanda came in at some point to offer him supper and check on Maliel, but Everis politely asked her to leave so he might try to get some rest.

Not that rest was what he intended to do.

Once most of the camp was asleep, he approached the trunk containing his personal belongings. Hammering away in his chest, his heart threatened to burst free.

How long are you going to put it off?

You might not have any time left.

He unlocked the trunk and dug to the bottom for a satchel buried beneath the clothes and spare blankets. From the satchel, he removed the old, worn tome he'd filched from the magi's study before they'd left. He wasn't sure why he'd taken it, only that it had seemed to call to him. Something in the back of his head wouldn't relent, whispering that he might need it. That it might be a matter of life and death.

That voice might not have been wrong, he thought, returning to Wren's side as he thumbed through the pages.

After all this time, he practically knew the book by heart. Every now and again, as he swept the aisles or dusted shelves in the library, he'd slide the book from its spot, sit, and peruse its spells and charms. He knew there was something in there that could help him. No—something that could help *Wren.*

Healing
The reversal of grievous wounds for those on the cusp of death.

All the supplies required by the spell were present in his other trunk. There was no reason he couldn't do this. Except for the one very obvious reason that'd had him putting it off this long to begin with.

Everis looked at Maliel, sleeping soundly. The injured knight had managed to eat a few bites of dinner. Just soup, but it was something. Sanda had been so happy. She thought he was out of the woods, that within a few days, he'd be up and talking and laughing with her again, ready to get back on a horse for the remainder of the journey.

"It's still touch and go," Everis whispered. "It could get infected. He isn't safe yet."

Wren would tell him he was making excuses, trying to justify what he was thinking of doing. No, not just thinking about anymore. What he *planned* on doing.

He poked his head out of the tent long enough to ensure that most of the camp was settled for the night and he wasn't likely to be disturbed. Then, he gathered the needed supplies, sat with his pestle, mortar, and a knife, and began to prepare.

From the ingredients, he formed a thick paste, blood red in color, the sweet scent of weeping nightshade nearly overwhelming. He scooped a generous amount into his hands, smearing it with care across Wren's skin, coating the wound itself and spreading it across his distended abdomen.

He moved to Maliel next, staring down into the knight's resting face. He'd taken his medicine with supper. It would keep him asleep—Everis hoped.

He gathered the remaining paste onto his fingers, coaxed Maliel's mouth open, and pushed it past his lips, onto his tongue. Swallowing it wasn't necessary, although he could see the man's throat moving reflexively as his face scrunched at the taste. Everis rested a hand on his chest and sat with him for a long moment.

"I'm sorry," he whispered. "I wish it wasn't you. I wish I'd grabbed one of the bandits instead. But we can't afford to lose him. *I* can't. I..." His voice caught, words tripping on their way past his lips. It didn't matter. Nothing he said was going to make this fair or right. It only mattered that it *worked*.

Everis returned to the book, kneeling before it and reading over the spell a final time. There was a short incantation to speak, but the rest wasn't something that could be placed into words on a page. All magi saw their magic differently. His were threads to be grasped and pulled. He could speak the words even in a language he didn't know and hopefully pronounce them all correctly, but ultimately, it was up to him to guide the magic into doing what he wanted.

Everis squeezed his eyes shut and slowed his breathing, deep and even, as the words fell from his lips. He tried to open himself to the magic around him. It had been so effortless that night in Cassia's room, but he'd been spurred on by the life-and-death situation he'd found himself in. This time, he wasn't afraid for his own well-being. He was afraid for Wren's. The only true friend he'd ever had and the person who knew him better than anyone. They'd grown from boys into men together, always at each other's sides. He couldn't call Wren simply *friend* or even *family*. It was more than that. A deep, undeniable urge to love and protect him, no matter the cost, because Everis couldn't live in a world where Wren did not exist. Any time he'd slipped up, stumbled too close into that which was forbidden, Wren had been there to gently guide him back and see him through it.

Wren was his light when the darkness felt so tempting.

It happened sooner than he'd expected. One by one, those magic threads formed all around him in his mind's eye. Varying shades of shimmering silver and gold, except deeper, beyond those in the glittering darkness on the furthest outreaches… A crimson thread.

He tried not to think about Maliel and how his death would devastate those who cared for him. He was doing this for Wren, for Master Orin, for all the people Wren could and would help in his life. He *deserved* to live. Everis couldn't allow himself to think any other way. He could not allow his resolve to waver, not on something this important.

Hot tears streamed down his face. He swallowed the lump of remorse in his throat.

I'm sorry.

Everis reached. Curled his fingers around the red thread.

I'm sorry I'm sorry I'm…

He pulled.

ORIN

Something woke Orin from a dead sleep. Not a nightmare, not a noise, but something cold and dark creeping into the recesses of his mind and jarring him into sitting upright, sweating despite the cold, staring into the darkness of an empty room for the second time in a week.

He was alone. A pang of melancholy and remorse hung heavy in his stomach.

The energy in the castle was skewed. Tense. Orin closed his eyes, reaching out. His links with the other magi may not have been anywhere as strong as they were with his students, but they were physically close enough that he could pick up the inkling of *something*.

Most of them were quiet, calm. No doubt asleep at this hour.

Magi Rue Brevil, however… *Panic. Fear.*

From the nearby windowsill, Nova shrieked and jostled him from his thoughts. He sucked in a breath, cast his blankets aside, and lurched out of bed. He threw on a robe and hurried into the halls, Nova's pale wings flapping after him. She flew ahead, careening gracefully down the corridor, leading the way to where Orin needed to go. As though he didn't already know.

Rue was a young magi, fresh out of her apprenticeship from a neighboring city. She was bright-eyed and kind but not as confident as Orin would've liked her to be. She second-guessed her decisions on everything, deferring to others instead of trusting her own judgment. Like Drake, she was a healer, a medicine magi.

She was also the one who often kept vigil over the king at night.

Dread weighed heavily on his heart as Orin swept through the castle at a brisk walk that eventually turned into a run. As he rushed to the king's tower, he nearly collided with one of the castle guards. Artesia stumbled back. Her eyes were wide and intense, but it took her only a second to overcome her surprise.

"Master—I was being sent for you! It's the king—"

"I know." Orin was already stepping past her. "Go wake Drake Reed immediately."

Artesia wasted no time in obeying. She whirled with a flick of her long braid and ran off down the hall. Orin wished he'd had the forethought to wake Drake on his way there, but panic had clouded his thinking.

He rushed up the stairs and could hear the others before he even reached the king's floor. Queen Danica and Princess Cassia stood outside Faramond's door, the princess with her face pale and drawn, Queen Danica pacing while she fought back sobs into her hands. Two guards whose names Orin didn't recall stood with them, at a loss for what to do.

Cassia spotted him, her small shoulders squaring. "Master Orin! Father—he's…"

Orin did not stop to wait for details. He brusquely moved past them into the king's chambers where another guard stood with Rue Brevil and the king himself.

Faramond's blankets had been kicked off, his nightgown soaked in sweat and vomit. He was seizing, spine arched off the bed, eyes rolled back so all that could be seen were the whites of them. The guard was attempting to roll the king onto his side at Rue's instruction, to ensure he didn't choke on his sick or his own tongue. Rue herself was trying to maintain control of the situation, trying to remember her training. Yet the relief in her eyes was unmistakable when she turned and saw Orin enter. She stepped back as he rushed over.

"Your Grace, can you hear me?" The answer to that was surely no, but Orin spoke to his king regardless, voice level and calm despite the fear coursing through his veins. He grabbed for a nearby washrag, using it to shove his fingers into the king's gaping mouth, ensuring nothing was lodged in the back of his throat and blocking his airway. Faramond convulsed, jaw snapping shut around Orin's fingers hard enough to draw blood. The magi winced but didn't jerk back, waiting until Faramond's mouth went slack again. Orin shoved the corner of the rag into the king's mouth, letting him bite down around it to preserve his own tongue.

There was little else Orin could do. He helped the guard keep Faramond on his side through the seizure, spoke softly to him, pressed a hand to his sweat-dampened forehead, and channeled what calm energy he could. Finally, Faramond's body went rigid, every limb coiled and tight, his hands tucked to his chest, and long, thin fingers curled like gnarled branches. Then he went boneless, limp against the mattress. He sucked in a slow, quaking breath—*finally*—and for a moment, the man's brown eyes looked into Orin's. Dazed, distant, but it was the first time in months Orin thought the king actually *saw* him.

And he looked terrified.

Orin held his gaze, unwavering, unflinching. He took one of Faramond's hands in his and squeezed it. What had been a blinding panic surging in his own chest had given way to resignation. Whatever had led them here, his king was suffering.

"It's all right, my king," Orin whispered.

Slowly, the fear drained from Faramond's face. He breathed in weakly a few more times, twitched his fingers around Orin's, and went still.

Orin sank back into a nearby chair. The same chair he'd spent so many hours in over the last six months, watching over his king. Speaking with him and, eventually, *to* him when Faramond could no longer respond.

Faramond was only a prince when Orin had first been employed at the castle by the previous king, long before he'd received the title of Master. They were close in age, Orin only a few years older. They'd gotten along immediately. The young prince had a zest for life and a caring heart. He liked to come visit the magi in their tower to watch them work, lamenting his lack of any sort of affinity for magic himself, much like his daughter now did.

You don't need magic, Orin had told him once. *You will work your own magic and be a good king to your people.*

And he had. Faramond was loved and respected. He'd been a good husband, a good father, a good friend. Strict but not unfair. Just but not cruel.

It dawned on Orin as he sat there, staring into the king's dead eyes, that while he'd thought he'd lost all hope of him getting better, some small part of him had still thought: *Maybe. Maybe he'll pull through.* The grief struck him soundly in the chest and he had to look away.

The rest of the world slowly came back into focus. The guard who'd been holding the king had moved back, at a loss for what to do with himself. Rue stood at Orin's side, shaking like a leaf, her face tear-streaked. Blaming herself, perhaps, that this had happened on her watch. He ought to comfort her but found he couldn't muster the words.

Cassia stepped into view. Steady despite her tears, she sank onto the edge of the bed and took one of her father's hands in her own. She touched his face, pushed back his sweat-matted hair, and bowed down to place a kiss upon his brow. Danica remained in the hall, sobbing.

He'd lost a dear friend tonight, yes. But a wife had lost her husband, a daughter had lost her father, and a kingdom had lost its king.

Orin wasn't aware of Drake in the room until he felt the magi's hand on his shoulder. Drake put his other arm around Rue, holding the girl to his side reassuringly. That hand squeezed gently, and Drake said, "Orin, perhaps we ought to let the queen and princess have a moment?"

Yes, Orin meant to say, but he still couldn't find the words. He nodded and got to his feet. Drake ushered everyone from the room save for Cassia. When they stepped into the hall, Danica rushed inside. The door closed behind her. Orin didn't protest against them being left alone; they deserved some time to process their grief without guards and magi hanging over their shoulders.

Drake drew Rue aside, speaking softly to her. "It's not your fault, dear one. You've helped with his care for months and have done very well. We knew this was coming."

Rue couldn't meet his eyes. Her short dark hair was mussed, her cheeks splotchy and red from crying. Drake's words didn't seem to reach her even though she nodded to show she was listening.

"Rue," Orin said, finally finding his voice. "Let me walk you back to your rooms."

Again, she nodded and fell into step beside him as he led her to the stairs. No one tried to follow.

It was like stepping into another world as they crossed the castle. Gone was the urgency and alarm. Here, everyone was still sound asleep in their beds, unaware of the tragedy that had just taken place. Orin could feel Rue's weariness like a weighted blanket on his shoulders. He got the sense she wanted to speak but didn't know what to say.

When they reached her chamber doors, she turned to him, head still bowed. "Thank you, Master Orin."

He brought a hand to her shoulder, the other gently prodding the girl's face into looking up at him. "Drake was right. This was not your fault. You do understand that, yes?"

Her dark eyes filled with fresh tears. "I fell asleep, Master. I'd been reading and must've dozed off. I didn't mean to, but when I woke, the king was already seizing, and I just…"

Orin grimaced inwardly. The point of having someone watch over King Faramond in the night was to have eyes on him in case of something like this. Any other night, he'd have lectured her on not being vigilant. It seemed out of character for her, and yet…

"Do you think if you'd woken any sooner, it would have saved him?" Orin asked.

Rue hesitated. "I… I don't know. I don't think so."

"I don't think so, either. So, there's no point in berating yourself for what we all feared was inevitable."

"Do you think he's at peace now?" Rue bowed her head once more.

Orin squeezed her shoulder and stepped back. "I hope so, child. I hope so."

He left her there, bidding her to try to get some rest.

For the second time that night, he crossed the castle, this time at a more leisurely pace. By the time he returned to the king's tower, Princess Cassia had gone to her rooms escorted by some of her maids, who would no doubt ensure she was looked after. Drake and a few woken servants were cleaning the mess that was the king's room, clearing away the soiled linens and mopping the floor. Queen Danica stood near the window, hugging herself as she stared out into the night.

Orin went to her side, hands folded before him. "My lady…"

"I had fooled myself into thinking he would get better," Danica said. No longer was she crying, but the traces of her earlier tears stained her cheeks. "What do we do, Orin? I nearly lost my daughter and now I've lost my husband."

"Princess Cassia is safe and will continue to be, Your Grace. As for the rest of it… We mourn. We celebrate the life he lived and the legacy he leaves behind." He took a deep breath. "Cassia is old enough to take the throne."

Danica's head swiveled to stare at him. "What? She's so young!"

"Young, yes, and inexperienced. But your daughter is smart and kind, and not much younger than Faramond himself was when he donned the mantle of king. He did it alone. The princess will have you to turn to for guidance."

In truth, Orin thought it would be wiser for the queen to serve as regent over the realm for a year or two, but that wasn't the way of things. The kingdom didn't care if a man or a woman sat on the throne as long as they were of royal blood. Cassia was. Danica was only royalty by marriage. The people would struggle to accept her as their leader.

Danica returned her attention out the window, nodding gravely. "She has no shortage of people to support and guide her, I agree. Cassia is well-loved. I know it's asking much, but could I impose the task of funeral arrangements on you, Orin? You were Faramond's friend as well as his servant."

It wasn't a task he wanted to be saddled with, but he would never say as much. He dipped his chin, lashes lowered. "You honor me with such a duty. Of course, my queen."

Orin remained at her side until Drake finally persuaded her to retire to her chambers in the early hours of dawn and escorted her off. Orin stayed behind to dole out whatever instructions remained. He had the servants strip the king of his soiled clothes to be wiped down while Orin watched with a heavy heart. It was more apparent than ever how much weight the king had lost over the last few months. He'd once been broad and sturdy but was now little more than paper-thin skin stretched tight over a skeletal frame

When they finished, the servants wrapped his body in a linen sheet with the utmost care, and the guards entered to transport him. He would be kept in a locked and guarded room where the magi would later gather to wash and prepare him for his funeral once arrangements were made.

Finally, Orin was alone in the king's room. He collected some of his own books from the bedside, along with a mostly empty teacup. The room still stank of death and sickness. To be honest, it had for weeks. It would be cleaned. Incense would be burned. Rituals would be performed to cleanse the space spiritually. Tradition decreed that this room would now be Cassia's, but only after she was crowned. Even then, Orin couldn't see her being in any hurry to relocate into the room where her father had suffered and died. Tomorrow, he would want to check on her, but for now, he was swamped with the desperate urge to retreat to his own rooms.

His body felt so heavy with grief that halfway there, he had to stop in one of the halls, set his things aside, and brace his hands against the window archway overlooking the gardens. In the silence, with nothing to occupy him, no orders to give, no one to take care of, it all swept over him. His head bowed; his shoulders slumped. With only Nova as a witness, he allowed his tears to fall.

EVERIS

The endless patter of rain hitting the tent lulled Everis into a near-sleep, even sitting up. A gentle, soothing ambiance, far more welcome than the previous thunderous storm. All he wanted to do was lay down and sleep. Any time he tried, he startled immediately back upright, suffocating in a blanket of darkness and magic.

Even now, he could feel it all around. The silence in the pass was unsettling. No birdsong filled the morning. No rustling in the trees. It was all too quiet, too still. The air had a tangy, metallic taste to it—although Everis couldn't be sure if that was the weather or simply the remnants of last night's magic.

Now, as the sun was barely rising, he thought perhaps he might be able to nap—even if sitting upright at Wren's side. His eyes drooped closed and his shoulders relaxed. Perhaps he even had dozed off, but it was soon interrupted by the tent flap sweeping open and Sanda ducking inside. He bit back a wince, keeping his eyes closed.

"Is he still sleeping? What a lazy brat." Sandra crossed the tent, although her steps slowed as she neared her friend.

Everis forced himself to his feet, dragging in a slow breath. Everything ached. He was drained, exhausted, and it was painful to stand. "Sanda…"

She knelt beside Maliel and took his hand. Everis caught the way she nearly flinched back. Whatever she might have suspected upon seeing Maliel would be confirmed by the cold of his skin. Everis's shoulders slumped and he lowered his gaze to the ground.

"He began seizing late last night. There may have been internal bleeding or some other damage I wasn't aware of. I'm so sorry."

Sanda didn't budge. She stared at Maliel; the faintest sheen of tears was visible in her eyes.

Everis stepped up behind her. "It was unexpected, Sanda. There was nothing any of us could do."

Sanda gave a slow nod and swallowed hard. "May I sit with him for a few moments before having him brought to the wagon?"

"Of course." Everis retreated, returning to Wren's side.

Wren stirred, mumbling for water, which Everis hurried to fetch.

He glanced askance at the two knights. Sanda squeezed Maliel's hand. When he didn't squeeze back, she let out a quiet sob. The sound struck Everis straight in the heart.

This was *his* doing. He had caused this. He could try to say as much as he wanted that Maliel could have taken a turn for the worst, yet he couldn't lie to himself well enough that he believed it. Maliel could have—likely *would* have—made a full recovery.

But Everis had made his choice.

And that choice had involved murdering an innocent man.

CASSIA

Cassia Starling fell straight to sleep. She did not dream, and she woke in the morning as she had any other day, with sunlight on her face and a cool breeze whispering in from the balcony window. It could've been any other morning in her life.

Still, her world felt darker.

Her maids fussed over her more than usual despite her insistence that she was fine. They helped her wash and dressed her in a black mourning gown she'd never had cause to wear before. They pinned up her long dark hair with beads and pins and clips and draped a black, fur-lined shawl about her shoulders. They brought breakfast to her room, and Cassia did her best to eat but found herself only picking at it. Her maids' worried glances didn't go unnoticed. Honestly, she would have liked some time to be alone, but they *really* would've fretted over her then.

Father's first few weeks of illness had felt stranger than this, without his jovial voice to fill the halls and his smile to greet her at meals. Now she had grown used to his absence, except for after lunch when she finally secured a bit of time alone and found a hollow in her chest as she stood in the doorway to his chambers. She used to spend an hour or two here with him almost every afternoon. Now only an empty room greeted her.

All day, she felt as though she were walking in a dreamworld that mimicked reality with subtle differences. She stared at the bed her father had lain in for six months and tried to recall what his last words to her had been. Perhaps they were *I love you*. She wasn't sure. They could've just as well been telling her that he was tired and wanted to sleep.

"Princess?"

Cassia jumped, gaze jerking from the bed to where Master Orin stood by the window. He'd been so still and quiet she hadn't even noticed him. "Oh—goodness, I'm so sorry."

He held up a hand, then gestured, beckoning her in. "I apologize for startling you. Would you like to be left alone?"

Yes, she thought. Hadn't she been seeking that all day? Yet resting her eyes on Orin, on his kind face that looked as though he'd not slept a wink last night, she couldn't bear to dismiss him. She moved to his side by the window instead, tugging her shawl around herself for warmth.

"No, please. Your company is always welcome. What brings you here?"

"The same thing I suspect brought you." Orin folded his hands before himself and looked out the window. The breeze brushed back his long, graying hair. "Habit, perhaps. I spent so much of my time here that I felt at a loss for where else to go."

"I suspect there are many other matters that demand your attention."

"Indeed, but even I need some time to process all of this."

Cassia paused, blushing. "I'm sorry. I didn't mean to imply... You and Father were close, I know. This must be hard for you, too."

Orin stole a look at her, understanding in his deep blue eyes. "Do you know what your father said when he found out your mother was expecting you?"

"I can't say that I do."

"He was *ecstatic*. Someone said they would pray for him to have a strong and healthy son. Faramond scoffed and slammed his hand on the table and said, '*No, give me a strong and healthy daughter who will nurture this kingdom into prosperity.*' Even when the queen insisted that she'd give birth to a boy, Faramond somehow knew his child would be a little girl." A small smile played across his mouth at the memory. "Even before he met you, he loved you so much."

Tears sprang to Cassia's eyes. She blinked them back. It wasn't a story she'd heard before, and it warmed her beneath the cold veil of her sadness. "Was he proud of me, Master Orin? I know Mother feels I'm too soft sometimes..."

Orin shook his head. "Faramond liked that about you. He admired your compassion and your empathy. He knew you would make a good queen when the time came."

How much of that was true and how much was Orin merely projecting what he thought she wanted to hear? No. He was too honest for that. Orin was a kind man, but never had she known him to mince words to make someone feel better.

Cassia looked down at her hands, small and slender and fine-boned. After Father's funeral, she would be crowned queen. What a terrifying thought. At sixteen, she was old enough to rule by their traditions, but just barely.

Her thoughts were interrupted by the sound of the castle bells ringing. Ten booming peals that would echo across the city, alerting everyone to the king's death. They would gather at the gates, and Cassia would be expected to address them. She knew what was expected of her, even if the idea made her feel queasy.

Master Orin laid a hand on her shoulder. A gesture many would've seen as disrespectful to a princess, but Cassia found it comforting. It helped steel her resolve. No matter what happened now, she wasn't alone. She had the magi at her side. They would guide her, counsel her, teach her. She would find the strength within herself to be the sort of queen Father would've wanted her to be.

Mother didn't seem confident that she was ready.

She would have to be.

WREN

EIGHT YEARS AGO

"He's been up there nearly an hour in tears," Gilbert huffed as they hurried across the training yard.

Wren had to move his shorter legs at twice the speed to keep up with the taller man. "So why am I the one being brought to fetch him? Why not Master Orin? Or even Lady Imaryllis. She's just in the armory."

"He didn't ask for them. He asked for *you*."

Wren bit back a sigh. He could try to guess what was wrong with Everis, but there was never any telling. The boy still struggled to find his footing in the castle even after two years. Oh, he was sharp as a blade with his studies, and he picked up new spells with an ease that made Wren a little jealous… but when it came to making friends, in adjusting to life at court, he floundered like a fish out of water.

Gilbert brought him to the base of the single towering willow tree at the far end of the training yard. It stuck out like a sore thumb there but had been planted so long ago that no one had been able to bring themselves to cut it down. Its drooping branches brushed the ground in places, and Wren had to part them like a curtain to slip inside its cover and peer up in search of his friend.

"Everis?"

From above came a sniffle and a rustling of leaves, and he saw Everis's round little face peering down at him. There was a glint of red that Wren couldn't quite make out from this distance, but something about it made a lump form in his throat.

"Ever, come down from there."

"No! You have to come up!"

"I'm not climbing trees because you're—What *are* you doing?"

"Please, Wren, just…"

Wren sighed. He pushed up his sleeves, grabbed the lowest branch he could reach that looked like it would support his weight, and began to climb with all the grace of a dog walking on its hind legs. He'd never been the sort of child who climbed and swam and played stickball in the streets. Still, he managed to weave his way up to Everis, who sat perched amongst the limbs like he was part squirrel. Up close, Wren could see it now—the dim, crimson glow in his eyes. It was faint, visible only when it caught the light like the reflection of a cat's eyes in the dark. Before he could ask what Everis had done, the boy held out his hands. Nestled in his palms sat a baby bird.

Wren only needed one look to know something was not right with it. At first glance, he would've guessed it had been injured, likely having fallen from its nest, but that wasn't quite right. It sat deathly still, and when Wren dared to venture closer until he could straddle that branch himself, he saw the array of open wounds on Everis's fingers where the bird had assaulted him with its beak.

"It fell," Everis whispered.

"What did you do, Ever…?"

"Nothing! I found it. It was hurt. I didn't want it to die, so I…"

"You healed it?" Wren extended a hand, hesitating as the bird twisted around, small beak snapping at his fingertips.

Silence.

"Everis."

"Yes. No. I… I think I brought it back."

"You brought it…" He stopped, the words catching in his throat.

"It was an accident," Everis insisted with such earnestness that Wren couldn't help but believe him. "I just kept thinking I wanted to save it, and it started to move around. I was going to return it to its nest."

A sinking sensation filled Wren. Whatever this creature was now, it was no longer what they would have called a bird. Its disturbing red eyes stared up at them, intense and fierce, and now and again it twitched and convulsed as though possessed.

Everis had brought a dead creature back to life all right, but how? And at what cost?

Slowly, Wren brought his hands to cover Everis's, folding his fingers closed around the baby bird. "I think we should take it to Master Orin," he softly said.

Everis's eyes filled with tears anew. "He'll be angry."

"I don't know about that. Do you want me to take it on my own?"

He bit his lower lip, gaze flicking down, the dim red glow glinting deep within his gray eyes that reminded Wren of the day they had found him in a plague-ridden city. "No. It was my fault. I should take it to him."

Could he convince Everis to tell someone else? Imaryllis, Gilbert, Drake... Except there were very few people Wren would trust with the knowledge that Everis was capable of tapping into questionable magic, especially so easily. As far as Wren knew, only he and Master Orin were privy to that information, and it was better that way.

Wren climbed down first, receiving scraped palms and a bruised knee for his efforts. Everis followed him with ease, managing to handle both himself and the bird. He dropped the last few feet to land in the dead grass beside Wren and peered at the little white creature in his palm. It twitched, head twisting to peer at them.

It didn't make a sound.

PRESENT DAY

Wren's throat and eyes felt coated in sand. He blinked at the ceiling, willing his vision to clear as he took stock of where he was and what had happened. His back and shoulders ached from lying on his bedroll for so long, and his abdomen throbbed something fierce. Gingerly, he touched a hand to his belly, finding some sort of poultice there. It flaked beneath his fingers. He thought he smelled mint, or maybe choir berry. Whatever it was, it wasn't a scent Wren was familiar with in a healing aid.

We were fighting, he dimly recalled. *I got stabbed.*

He remembered Everis screaming for him. Remembered being carried. And then... nothing.

The world swam around him for a while. He heard other voices in the tent, movement, thought he saw a few armored knights carting something heavy outside, but it was difficult to concentrate on any of it. The room fell silent, and Wren's eyelids began to drift shut, sleep threatening to claim him once more.

Then Everis returned with water, kneeling at Wren's side as he uncapped the flask. With effort and dizziness, Wren pushed himself up onto one elbow while Everis held the flask to his lips for him to drink. And drink he did, until he'd damned near gone through the entire thing, but at least it quenched his thirst and soothed his parched throat.

Sated, he sank back again, dragging his tongue across his lips. "Where are we...?"

"Still in the pass," Everis said. "Only about a day's ride from where we were attacked."

That felt... wrong. The severity of the injury he'd received would've downed anyone much longer than a day or two. He pressed a hand to his abdomen. While it ached, it certainly didn't feel like a fresh wound. Everis was good with his healing spells, but he wasn't *that* good. He didn't know anyone who was.

Wren's eyes locked onto his friend's face. Everis glanced away.

Oh, Mother...

He pushed himself up to sit properly with a wince, bracing against one hand while the other picked at the poultice, flaking it off his flesh. Everis started to reach for him, but Wren swatted him away, refusing to stop until he could see his skin beneath the dried salve. Where he ought to have seen a raw, angry wound, he found a mostly mended suture line that looked *weeks*, not *days*, old.

"Ever," he whispered, "what did you do?"

Everis bit the inside of his lower lip. His shoulders squared and he inclined his chin, meeting Wren's eyes. "I saved you. You're welcome."

"Yes, but *how?*"

A pause. "You were getting worse, and I knew..." Everis ducked his head, staring down at his hands folded in his lap. "You were going to die. I couldn't let that happen."

"Everyone dies." He sat up fully. His insides throbbed, but the urgency ate into him, had the words spilling from his lips in a frantic whisper. "That's why we've been trained to *fight*—because things like this happen. Our lives are not always safe. You can't just grasp for dark magic every time you're *afraid*."

Everis plucked at the hems of his sleeves. His brows knitted together, mouth turned down, chastised but defiant. "I'm not apologizing."

Wren scrubbed his hands over his face. He wanted a bath. And food. And maybe a drink at this rate. He turned until he was sitting cross-legged, facing Everis, and brought his hands to rest atop the other man's. "Look…"

Everis yanked his hands back, eyes turning stormy. "Do you have any idea what it's like to watch someone you love slip away from you? Have you ever lost someone like that?"

"I…" Wren paused. "No."

"I pray you never do. You watch the light fade from them until they're out of your reach. You watch their body shut down, give up. It's the single most devastating, helpless sensation imaginable. I couldn't do it, not again." His voice rose in pitch, a frantic edge to his words. "I couldn't lose you. I couldn't wake up every day for the rest of my life to face a world that didn't have you in it. I can't…" He was spiraling, wildness creeping into his eyes.

Wren caught Everis's face in his palms and forced Ever to look at him, *really* look at him. He pressed their foreheads together, voice soft. "Shh, shh… Alright. I hear you."

Everis dragged in a shaky sigh, eyes brimming with tears. It took him a moment and several deep breaths to calm himself. "I'm sorry, Wren. I'm sorry. If I could've thought of any other way…"

He smoothed the pads of his thumbs across Everis's cheeks, catching a stray tear that had snuck its way free. "What's done is done. We will, however, be speaking more about this when we reach Patish. *And* telling Master Orin when we get home. Alright?"

"He's going to be angry."

"When have you ever known Orin to be angry when we've come to him with the truth? Annoyed, frustrated, but never angry. You remember the incident with the bird, don't you?"

Everis looked away. It was impossible to forget, even so many years later. Orin had taken the resurrected bird from Everis's hands, and before his students could say a word about what had happened, Orin knew. He had sat with the creature, expression etched with sadness and regret. Regarding what, Wren hadn't been sure. Still wasn't, even now. He wished he'd asked at the time.

Yet Orin hadn't been angry, not in the slightest. He'd turned his intense gaze to them as he spoke, *You have such great capacity for love, Everis. In that love, there is so much fear in you at the idea of losing something. But sometimes the best thing you can do for something you care for is let it go.*

Those words still rang clear in Wren's head. It was difficult to say he regretted whatever Everis had done because he had no interest in dying, and were their situations reversed—well, wouldn't he do anything in his power to help Everis? Or Orin? The conflict within himself was great. He could only imagine how Everis had felt, struggling with loss the way he did. The one thing he knew for certain: Master Orin needed to know. He would know how to address this where Wren did not. Although maybe it was something to think about later, after they'd completed their current mission.

"We've lost time with me being injured, I imagine."

"A bit," Everis agreed, tension easing out of his shoulders at the change in subject. "We traveled, but it was slow-going."

"Then we ought to pick up the pace today and try to make up lost time." Wren pitched himself forward to get up. He made it as far as getting to his feet before the ground spun out around him and nearly brought him back to his knees. Everis was there, catching him by the elbows. Wren leaned into him, cheek pressed to Ever's chest where, for a few long moments, all he could think about was the world careening wildly in his periphery, the warmth of Everis's skin, and the steady beat of his heart.

"All right?" Everis murmured.

He gulped and straightened himself. Everything eased back into focus. "Yes, just a little light-headed."

"I healed the worst of it, but you'll need to take it easy for a bit." Everis kept hold of his arm as they crossed the tent. He helped Wren wash and dress, and it brought back a memory from a few years back of when Wren had come down with a wretched cold. He'd refused to stay in bed. Everis had been there, helping him do the simplest of tasks while lecturing him that he ought to be taking it easy. Of course, Master Orin had taken one look at him and ordered him back to his room for medicine and bed rest.

Now, though, that wasn't an option. He needed to be fit enough to travel, and he'd not have anyone fussing over him. For as happy as Annaliese and the other knights were to see him up and moving, there was a heavy blanket of melancholy across the party as tents were packed and wagons loaded. It only took one glance at the wagon of dead for Wren to understand why.

By the time they were on the road again, Wren had exhausted himself by moving around. He slumped into the carriage with a sigh, head resting against the side, and dozed off and on throughout the day. Even remaining stationary within the carriage was exhausting. They traveled for as long as they safely could, and when they set up camp that night, Wren scarcely made it to his bedroll before falling asleep.

The following day, he felt better. Stronger. Better still the day after that. As they neared the end of the mountain pass, Wren was getting through most of the day without needing to nap. He expected the energy of the group to lift at least marginally the closer they grew to their destination, yet the more alert and back to his old self he became, the more he noticed just how off everything felt. It wasn't just a dip in morale from losing friends in the attack; it was... something else.

It was Everis.

Or rather, it was the knights' attitude toward Everis.

They quieted when Everis walked by the campfires. Only spoke with him if he addressed them directly, otherwise they brought their comments and questions to Wren. One of the soldiers—Sanda, he thought her name was—often stared at Everis with such a burning intensity it was a wonder Everis couldn't sense it. Maybe he could and simply chose not to react. He'd been quiet and lethargic himself the last few days.

Only Captain Annaliese seemed to be acting as though nothing was amiss. Wren approached her on the fifth morning to ask if she'd noticed anything odd, and she paused, in the middle of saddling her horse, and seemed to debate that question. She resumed her task and didn't look at him.

"Has someone been acting disrespectfully? If so, I'll have a word with them."

"No, that's not it at all. I just..." He scratched a hand over his jaw with a sigh. He needed a shave. "Since the attack, I've noticed a strange air about the group. I can't put my finger on what it is. An unrest, almost."

Annaliese's brows drew together. She straightened and turned to him, mouth pulled taut. "We've lost several brothers and sisters on this trip. Surely their unrest is understandable."

"You're being purposely obtuse, Captain," Wren pointed out with an edge of heat to his voice. "I think you know what I'm talking about isn't just grief."

They stared one another down for several ticks before Annaliese turned away, resting a palm against her horse's neck, scratching her fingers through the mare's dark mane. "Look, everyone is immensely pleased that you pulled through. I saw the extent of your injuries, and it's a miracle you're standing here right now, but..."

Wren frowned. "But?"

"The night of the attack, I don't pretend to have seen everything that happened. But several of us caught glimpses of Everis during the fight. There was something unsettling about it, although I could mark that down as us being unaccustomed to battling alongside magi." She sighed. "And I don't put any stock in idle gossip and speculation, but… Maliel was on the mend. He'd been up and talking and eating the night before. It seemed so strange for him to have gone downhill the way he did."

Cold swept over Wren, chilling the blood in his veins. He remembered waking that morning, seeing that still body across from him and the woman who'd been crying over him. "I'm asking you to speak frankly, Captain."

"He was doing better, and you were at death's door." Annaliese paused for a breath. Her dark gaze slid over to him. "Yet come morning, he was dead, and *you* were the one walking out of that tent."

ORIN

FIFTEEN YEARS AGO

"What happens to us when we die, Master?"

Wren had asked Orin that question when he was a small boy, after one of the elder magi in the castle had passed away in his sleep. Orin had sat with Wren in the gardens after the funeral, knowing what a precarious subject death could be, how frightening it was to face the unknown.

"They say our souls go to be with the Mother," Orin replied.

Yet even at his young age, Wren had clearly begun to learn the purposefully evasive way Orin often answered things because he asked, "But what do *you* think?"

"I think… only a fool would answer that question with any certainty." He nodded once, satisfied with that answer. "Because how can we truly know? Without having died ourselves or speaking to someone who has died, all we can do is speculate."

A crease formed between Wren's brows. He looked straight ahead out over the gardens, his small hands folded in his lap.

Orin watched him from the corner of his eye. "What do you think, Wren?"

"I don't know. I think it would be nice to think we go on after, that there's some world after this waiting to greet us. But…"

"Speak freely. It's alright."

"But like you said, how can we know?" He tipped his head back to look up at Orin, blue eyes distressed, the wind tousling his hair. "It's scary, not knowing. Isn't there magic that can bring people back?"

A chill slithered down Orin's spine, but he met the boy's imploring gaze without flinching. "There is," he softly confirmed. "But magic like that is forbidden."

"Why?"

"Because life and death coexist in a delicate balance. If something dies, it permits something else to be born. So, if you try to bring something back, you must be willing to sacrifice life to overcome death. Equivalent exchange."

Understanding blossomed across Wren's face. "You would have to kill someone to bring someone else back?"

"That's an oversimplification, but yes. And that sort of dark magic eats at a person. It gets inside you like an infection, and it spreads." He shook his head, dismissing old memories and refusing to allow them to take root. "I've known magi who fell into blood magic before."

Wren's blue eyes went wide. "What happened to them, Master?"

Orin could have gone into detail. What it was like to watch the people he cared for deteriorate in body and mind and spirit. How different they became until he looked into their faces and saw not a trace of the men and women he once knew. He could have said that there was a time when he looked in the mirror and found it difficult to recognize his own reflection.

Instead, he brought a hand to rest atop Wren's head and said simply, quietly, "Very few of them found their way out again."

PRESENT DAY

Even in the cold recesses of the dungeons and with the charms placed upon her, the young woman had finally begun to decay. Now that Orin had made the decision to do what he needed to do, he cursed himself for waiting so long. He worked in the dead of night, wanting to ensure no one interrupted him. Nova kept vigil nearby; she would make noise if anyone descended the stairwell.

It had been some time since he'd read up on spells for resurrecting the dead, but the knowledge was still burned into the back of his mind like a nightmare he couldn't shake. Recalling the details was like trying to ease open floodgates and hoping only what water you wanted would trickle through rather than the entire dam bursting open. He'd worked too hard to distance himself from that. If he had any other course of action to take, he would've gladly taken it. But the king was dead, and Orin was no closer to finding an answer than when he'd started. Perhaps it was paranoia, but he was afraid the princess and queen were still in danger.

More important to him than that: he had no idea if Wren and Everis were in danger.

He readied the various plants and ground them together into a viscous paste, some of which he spooned into the woman's mouth and used the rest to paint a rune in the shape of a four-fingered hand on her chest, above her heart. Then he picked up a dagger from his supplies, pressed the tip to his forearm, and dragged it down, parting skin and spilling blood. He needed to move swiftly. The blood would have to continue to flow if he wanted this to work.

Orin pressed his eyes closed and focused, reaching out for the swell of magic. Normally, it came to him so easily, a flock of shimmering ravens whose feathers would float into his outstretched hand.

What he needed now, though, was deeper than that. Darker.

After all those years, it was still far easier than he would've liked. He extended a hand, and a lone crimson feather emerged from the blackness and settled in his palm. The jolt of power sent a shudder straight up his arm, made his lungs suck in a breath and his eyes snap open. Suddenly everything in the room seemed so clear, every color and texture glittering with astonishing clarity.

This was what it was like—the dark arts. The power it imbued him with was intoxicating.

He twisted himself free of its grasp to concentrate on the task at hand. He had a purpose. That was all. And when he placed his blood-drenched hand over the mark on the assassin's chest, he focused that power and lifeforce from himself into her.

With a jolt, the woman's spine arched off the table, her limbs contorting, toes curling. Her mouth gaped open wide, and she choked in a long, low, rasping rattle. Orin kept his hand firmly in place, his blood spilling down his arm, trailing in rivulets across the assassin's bare skin. As soon as her eyes opened, milky and unfocused, he began to speak.

"What is your name?"

She twisted beneath his touch in agony. The voice that escaped her lips was cracked and brittle. Her spirit was there, but just barely.

"What's happened to me?"

"You died," Orin said simply. Already he felt a bit light-headed. "You tried to assassinate Princess Cassia, and you failed. Tell me your name and who hired you."

"Dead," the woman moaned. *"Dead, dead, dead… I've died, and it's so… so dark. Where is my mother?"*

A deep pang of guilt coursed through him. *Where are you? What's dark?* he wanted to ask. There was no time. "Tell me your name and who hired you."

With another convulsion, the assassin's eyes locked onto him. *"Mateen Sha'ren. One… job. One last job. I would've had enough to live the rest of my days in… in peace."*

"One last job from whom, Mateen?" Orin pressed. "Who had that kind of money to offer you?"

With a wretched scream, Mateen jerked upright, sending bottles and the dagger and various other supplies clattering to the floor. Still Orin kept his hand in place, even when her face was now inches from his. Her hands flew to him, bony fingers wrapping about his forearm as though the blood pouring from it called to her.

"Queen Danica… will be next," she rasped.

Orin wrenched his hand away. Partly in shock, partly because he could hold her there no longer without endangering himself. With a moan, Mateen collapsed lifelessly onto the table, glassy eyes staring at the ceiling and her lips parted in mid-scream. Orin stumbled back, falling into a nearby chair and gasping for breath. He blindly reached for the rags nearby and, with shaking hands, cleaned his injured arm and wrapped it tightly.

Everything reeled about him. He pressed his eyes shut, and the magic was still there, pulsating beneath his skin, beating in time with his heart. Fiercely, he shoved it back into the darkness, envisioned himself shutting a door and locking it until the sensation faded. It left him with a dull, empty ache in his chest as though he were mourning the loss of an old friend—as well as a pounding headache behind his eyes. His arm throbbed. His blood was all over the girl, the table, the floor. He would have to clean it up before morning.

Queen Danica will be next. Had Cassia not been the only target after all? If Duke Ryland was behind the attack, it would make sense. Take out the princess and the queen, and no one stood in his way.

What he wouldn't have given for someone to talk to about all of this. With his apprentices gone, Orin felt unbearably alone. There was too much at stake here, too many factors, too many missing puzzle pieces. What was more, he found himself eyeing everyone in the castle with suspicion, even people he regarded as good friends.

Once the lightheadedness ceased, he set himself to cleaning the cell and the body, erasing the evidence of the ritual he'd performed as best as he could. It was two hours until dawn by the time he emerged from the dungeons, heading for the magi tower rather than his own rooms with Nova perched on his shoulder. He'd left a test running and wanted to check on it before falling into bed for a few hours.

It wouldn't have been unheard of for other magi to be there, even at that time of night. Sometimes their work required them to keep odd hours. Sometimes someone wandered in because they couldn't sleep. There were many such nights for Orin where he stayed long into the early morning hours, hunched over his desk and working by candlelight until his eyes hurt and his back ached. Everything appeared silent tonight, though. All the better.

He passed through the ground floor and into the small back room where he'd stashed the other test results from the assassin's pills. On the table were the remnants of those tests, and beside them, a teacup. Next to it lay a small glass strip containing a few droplets of the tea the cup once held.

There had been enough liquid for only one test. Orin needed to make it count. Now the results were staring back up at him, and all the fears he'd hoped would be unfounded bore down on him. The sample had turned silver, indicating a foreign substance mixed within Rue Brevil's tea the night of Faramond's death.

Rue hadn't fallen asleep watching over the king.

She'd been drugged.

EVERIS

Everis spent his days doing little more than sleeping. The fatigue was worse than with any illness he'd experienced before. Immediately following the ritual to save Wren's life, he'd been flooded with a burst of adrenaline. The world rang crisp and clear, and nothing seemed impossible. By the time Wren had woken, though, that sensation had faded. Now every movement was like slogging through knee-deep mud.

Wren let him rest. A few times, Wren touched his cheek or forehead as though checking for a fever or to administer some salve to the wound on his face, but other than the exhaustion, Everis felt fine. Whatever he'd done, it had simply taken more out of him than he'd expected.

Not as much as it took out of Maliel, he reminded himself.

The guilt sat heavy and immovable in his stomach. Exhausted or not, he noticed the looks the knights were giving him. More than once, he felt Sanda's gaze boring into him until he turned to meet it, unflinching, and she was forced to look away. They couldn't possibly know what he'd done, but they could speculate at the strangeness of it. They could wonder. Everis had made his choice between a knight he hardly knew and the person who meant more to him than anything else in the world. He could feel remorse and guilt for his choice, but he refused to regret.

Anyone else would've done the same in his place.

He was dozing late into the evening several days later when a horn sounded in the distance. He recognized the tune as one of their own and opened his heavy eyelids to meet Wren's gaze. "Is that our scout?"

"Sounds like it." Wren leaned out the window to peer ahead. The roads had widened as they were nearly out of the mountains and onto flat land again.

"I'm surprised he made it." Everis stifled a yawn against the back of his hand and sat up, trying to work the crick from his shoulders and neck from sleeping at such an odd angle. "I figured the bandits would've caught him."

The horn was met with a blast from their own party, affirming they'd heard and were on their way. Captain Annaliese brought her horse to the side of the carriage to address them. "Our scout has returned. Duke Ryland has sent some people for us. They have a camp not too far ahead."

Wren and Everis exchanged looks. Queen Danica had ensured a letter was sent informing the duke of their arrival, though not their reasoning, because it would've been in poor taste for them to show up unannounced.

Within the hour, their small envoy had traversed the last stretch of mountain path and emerged through the trees into wide, flat lands as far as the eye could see. Two days northeast lay Patish. There at the base of the mountains sat a small camp, its fires glowing warmly in the chilly evening. The scent of cooking meat met Everis's nose as he breathed in. When had he eaten last? It had been a few days. Sleep had been more important, and some of their better food and rations had been ruined in the bandit attack.

They drew up to the camp and the two magi stepped out of the carriage. Everis, light-headed and half-asleep on his feet, and Wren, still moving stiffly from his healing injuries. A group of armored knights with a red flower crest upon their cloaks were waiting for them. Leading them was a woman, perhaps in her late thirties, tall and thin, her raven hair cut short. Her robes, cowl, trousers, and even her boots were black with deep-red accents; all that darkness only amplified her umber skin and piercing green eyes. She wasn't dressed as a knight or even a noble. She was most assuredly a magi.

"Magi Wren, Magi Everis," she called when they approached.

Wren took the lead, extending his hand. "I'm Wren Lumina. And you are…?"

She gripped his hand and gave it only the briefest of shakes. "Magi

Ivy Amaranth, at your service. Duke Ryland requested that we escort you the rest of the way to Patish."

"A kind gesture but an unneeded one." Wren offered a smile. "We could've found the way on our own."

Magi Ivy did not smile. If anything, she frowned as though bothered. "I would speak with you two in my tent, if you don't mind." Without waiting for a response, she turned and strode across the camp.

"That doesn't bode well," Everis murmured. "Do you think they know why we're here? Is Ryland planning something?"

"Be still, Ever. Don't jump to conclusions." He brushed a hand against Everis's arm, and together they followed Ivy. Her tent smelled of incense, something that reminded Everis of the sea and instantly made him want to lie down and sleep.

Ivy gestured for them to have a seat. Neither of them did so. She didn't appear to take offense and merely sank down atop a trunk, watching them. "We received a raven from the capital two days ago."

A headache was making itself known behind Everis's eyes. He pinched the bridge of his nose. "Yes, the queen said she was sending a raven to inform the duke of our arrival. What of it?" He felt Wren's disapproving gaze on him and couldn't bring himself to care.

Ivy's lips pulled into a thin line. "It would seem you're impatient, so I'll not drag it out. We received a *second* letter from Midmere. Your king is dead."

The words landed like a physical blow to Everis's chest. He stared at the woman, stunned into silence. Wren grabbed at his arm, fingers twisting in the fabric of his sleeve. "He... *What?*"

"Two nights ago. The letter said he's been ill for quite some time, so I suspect this does not come as a surprise?"

Everis tried to absorb this information. Yes, the king had been ill for months, and yet the news still rocked him to his core. Oh, poor Princess Cassia and Master Orin. He could only imagine how they were grieving.

"That's why we were being sent to Patish," Everis said. "We were to deliver a letter to Duke Ryland from the queen, begging him to come make peace with his brother."

"Bit late for that, it seems." Ivy lifted her chin. "All the same, I'm sorry for your loss. You are, of course, welcome at the castle to restock your supplies and rest before you head back. I'm sure Duke Ryland would still like to see that letter."

This could be tricky. They still needed time to investigate—time they would've had if they were trying to convince Ryland to return to

Midmere with them, regardless of whether or not he actually agreed. Now they had to hurry home for a funeral.

Undeterred by their silence, Ivy continued, "We'll depart first thing in the morning. Help yourselves to a warm meal and a good night's rest. You look like you could use it."

They said their thanks and stepped out of the tent. Annaliese lingered nearby, waiting for them, her brows knitted together in concern. The knights needed to be informed of Faramond's death, and none of them would be happy. Everis's head was spinning, spinning, spinning…

"Ever," Wren murmured. A soft hand came to rest against his cheek. "You look dead on your feet. Go lie down."

He closed his eyes to stop the world from swimming. As much as he didn't want to leave all the dirty work to Wren, he wasn't sure how much use he'd be in his current state. Without protest, he headed back to where the knights were busy erecting the tents. His and Wren's wasn't yet assembled, and he had no interest in waiting for it, instead crawling into the carriage and curling up on the bench seat there. Not even the sound of people working outside was enough to keep him from plummeting immediately to sleep.

When Everis woke, it was dark, and Wren was at his side with a platter of food. His head was still a muddled mess, but sleep must have helped somewhat because his stomach actually growled at the prospect of a meal. Slowly, he sat up, scrubbing a hand across his eyes. "I'm sorry. I didn't mean to sleep so long."

Wren sank down beside him, nudging the platter over so it sat half on Everis's lap and half on his own. "I'm guessing whatever it was you did the other night took a lot out of you. Are you sure you're alright?"

Everis breathed deeply, considering that question. "Yes. I'm just so bloody tired."

"Eat, then. Get your strength back. Look, there's roast boar. Your favorite."

They ate in silence. It was no Friday evening banquet back home, but it was better than what they'd had during much of the trip there and the first thing Everis had put in his stomach for days. They picked at their food listlessly. Hungry or not, Everis's mind was elsewhere. He found himself asking, "Do you think Master Orin is all right?"

Clearly, that had been a concern of Wren's, too. A frown creased his brow, and he lowered the bite he'd been about to take. "I hope so. As well as one can be after losing a friend. I wouldn't be surprised if much of the funeral planning has fallen on his shoulders."

Everis stared down at their platter. Bacon grease had pooled in the corner, leaving some of the dinner rolls soggy. He knew he needed to eat more, but every bone in his body felt so damned heavy. "What are we going to do now?"

Wren leaned back. "We still have a job to complete. Master Orin is counting on us to investigate, and that's what we're going to do. We may just have to make quicker work of it than originally planned."

"Oh, that should be easy."

"Did you have a better idea? Ought we turn right back around and head home? I'm sure the soldiers will be thrilled their friends lost their lives for nothing."

Everis's cheeks warmed. "I didn't say that."

Wren paused, sighed, and rested a hand atop one of Ever's. "I'm sorry, that was uncalled for. I'm a little on edge."

Everis studied that hand on his, struck with the image in his mind of a few nights ago, looking down at Wren's long fingers and thinking how pale he was, lying at death's door. He swallowed hard. His hand turned over, fingers curling about Wren's, holding on to him. "I think we all are."

They sat in silence long after their food had gone cold. Wren dropped his head to Everis's shoulder. He never did pull his hand away.

ORIN

EIGHT YEARS AGO

Orin gazed down at the baby bird in his hands. He'd dismissed Wren and Everis—the latter had been in tears as the older boy escorted him out—because there was nothing either of them could do. He could hardly fault Everis's kind heart for wanting to save the life of another living thing. But his magic, no matter how strong, was clumsy and unrefined. He knew what he wanted to achieve but not how to achieve it. Unfortunately, resurrecting the dead wasn't a skill Orin intended to ever teach his apprentice. Forbidden magic aside, the sacrifice required for it was too great. What had Everis given up, even for such a small life?

Nova croaked. Orin lifted his chin to look at her. She fluffed her feathers as though sensing his distress, her red eyes a mirror image of the baby bird in his palms.

"Sorry, my girl. I believe this one is past my ability to help."

The white raven walked closer, head tipping, studying the chick, which twisted and twitched. Even she seemed to decide it was a lost cause because she spread her wings and took flight.

All Orin could do for the warped creature now was to put it out of its misery. It would live like this otherwise, suspended in this very state, and who knew for how long? He might know more about such things than any of the other magi in the city, but he was hardly an expert.

After all, Nova was the only creature he'd ever brought back from the dead.

PRESENT DAY

Rue hadn't left her room since the king's death. Orin had instructed someone to check on her daily, ensuring she received meals and wasn't allowing her guilt and grief to impact her own well-being.

The day after he'd resurrected Cassia's would-be assassin, he saw fit to visit her himself. He knocked once, waited for her to give him leave to enter, and stepped inside. If he'd been expecting to find Rue huddled in the darkness and withering away, he was mistaken. The curtains were open wide, and a cool breeze swept in. Rue herself sat before her fireplace. She wasn't languishing around in her nightclothes, though the outfit she wore did appear a bit rumpled and her hair was mussed. Her cheeks were faintly pink from the cold. Other than looking as though she'd only just woken, she did not seem any worse for wear. When she glanced back, though, her eyes grew large and she lurched from her seat, fussing with her clothes and hair.

"Master Orin, I'm so sorry. I had no idea you'd be coming by. I know I haven't been to the tower in days—"

Orin held up a hand, stepping forward. "I only came to ask how you were, not to lecture you on missed work. Some time off is warranted, I'd say."

Rue settled, shoulders slumping. "Of course." She wrung her hands together and nodded at the second chair before the hearth. "Um, please. Make yourself comfortable."

Orin crossed the room to take the offered seat. Sitting on a table between the chairs was a tray of untouched food and tea. No, not entirely untouched; the bread had been nibbled at, perhaps. The tea was mostly gone.

"How have you been?" he asked once she'd sat down. "Eating, resting?"

"Yes, Master. I've been doing little other than sleeping, honestly." She bowed her head, examining her hands. "Not that it's any sort of reprieve."

He frowned. "Nightmares?"

She nodded, embarrassed. "Only, even when I'm awake, I keep replaying that night in my head. How things could've gone differently. I know what you said before, about how it would've happened whether I'd been awake or not, but... but *what if?* What if I'd known how to save him? What if I'd been able to get to you or Drake before the worst of it?"

"I won't say those aren't valid questions, but there is little to be gained by asking them now." He paused. "I have a question for you, however, regarding that night."

Rue swiped the back of her hand across her eyes briefly with a sniff. "Yes?"

"You had a tray and a cup of tea set aside."

She blinked. "I often took a small meal with me, yes."

"Took it with you, or someone delivered it to you?"

She frowned. "I'm not sure I understand where you're going with this, Master."

Orin leaned forward, elbows coming to rest on his knees. "I'm asking if someone delivered your meal to you that night."

Rue shook her head. "No. I brought it with me." Then she paused. "But my tea... That came later."

His gaze sharpened. He could sense her uncertainty, as though she knew that his line of questioning meant something was amiss and she was afraid to find out why. His voice remained calm. "Rue, please. I need you to tell me who brought you your tea."

A heartbeat of silence passed before Rue managed to look him in the eye.

"Drake Reed."

Orin had known. He'd known from the moment his tests hadn't matched up with Drake's. Still, he'd pushed the truth aside, refusing to acknowledge it. If he pretended it didn't exist, if he found someone else at fault...

Drake had been his friend for decades. They'd arrived at the castle around the same time—Drake only two or three years before him—and although Orin had earned the title of Master, Drake had all the makings of one, too. But there was only one Master to a kingdom; that was a rule of the Citadel and not a rule they'd ever permitted to be broken. There would be one person responsible for the magi within a given city, one who granted permission and guidance in precarious research.

Not that it had mattered. Drake might not have been a Master by name, but the title was merely a word, a ceremony, a formality. As far as sheer ability went, Drake matched Orin in most subjects. They were friendly rivals, research companions, and now—

He drugged Rue. How far does this go? Did he poison Faramond, as well? Did he take out the contract on Cassia's life?

One question had been answered. One door closed. A hundred more opened wide.

Why, why, why…

Orin's jaw clenched, and his expression blanked, masking the turmoil beneath it. "Thank you." He rose to his feet, intending to take his leave.

Rue stood abruptly. "Is there something I should be aware of?"

Yes. No. What did he tell her? How much did he let her in on? His mind was spinning with questions and anger and guilt. Every inch of him wanted to find Drake and beat him bloody for his apparent betrayal. He knew better. He needed to tread carefully.

"I don't believe falling asleep was your fault, Rue. I think the king's death wasn't as natural as we initially thought," he said, gauging her reaction.

Rue wrung her hands together and took a step forward. "Please, Master Orin, if there's something I can do to help…"

He studied Rue's earnest face and desperate eyes. He could feel the guilt and remorse radiating off her. Even now, she blamed herself and was searching for a way to make amends. Orin's heart went out to her. Yes, he needed to be cautious, but he shouldn't proceed alone, either.

"Actually," Orin said, "there is."

WREN

EIGHT YEARS AGO

"Is it true that magi can see their magic in shapes and stuff?" Cassia asked.

She was eight, and as such, Wren tried his best to be patient with her. Hunched over a worktable, studying old texts and writing down notes, he didn't want to admit that he secretly didn't mind the occasional break from work even if it was to answer a child's incessant questions. Perhaps he also enjoyed her wide-eyed stares and amazement over little things a magi considered second nature.

He heaved a sigh and set down his quill, straightening his spine. "Yes. Well, not out here, but in here." He tapped his forehead. "When we cast, we envision it in our minds. Over time, most magi conjure up specific imagery that helps tie them to their magic."

Sure enough, Cassia's big hazel eyes grew even bigger. "What does yours look like?"

Wren's brow furrowed. "You know, truthfully, for a long time, it didn't look like much of anything. And then for a while it sort of... changed every time, like it couldn't decide what it wanted to be. But a year or two ago, it seemed to settle. So now, it looks like fireflies."

"Oooh, fireflies?"

"Yes. I envision myself in a big field beneath a starry sky, and the magic of the area around me twinkles like fireflies. I hold out my hand, and I call upon the one I want."

"That sounds so pretty!"

He smiled softly. "It is, yes. And comforting. I suppose that's why we all have our own individual conjuring that we envision. It's very personal to each of us."

Cassia wriggled in her seat with excitement. "What about Everis and Master Orin?"

"Ever says his is like a web of fine threads. Master describes his as ravens."

Cassia grinned. "Like Nova!"

"Yes, like Nova."

The princess grabbed a spare piece of parchment and a hunk of charcoal that had been laid out especially for her. She leaned over the paper, beginning to draw. "I think... I think my magic, if I had any, would have to look like puppies—no, wolves! Puppy wolves. Because they're strong and pretty and they would always protect me. How does that sound?"

Her words softened his gaze. "I think that sounds wonderful, Princess. Absolutely wonderful."

PRESENT DAY

Duke Ryland's home was more manor than castle. Wood and stone loomed high and ominous over their heads, framed against a gray sky and the sea stretching out beyond it. Patish sat nestled against the mountains and the coast. They had minimal luck growing many crops and instead relied heavily on the export of fish, ore mined from the mountains, and wool. Despite Ryland and Faramond's fifteen-year feud, the two cities had retained their trade agreements. It was simply left in the hands of others, so the brothers didn't have to deal with each other directly.

Wren admired the architecture as they exited the carriage. Oh, he was looking forward to a warm bed and a clean change of clothes! Seeing new sights had always been something he loved. It was *traveling* to and from those destinations that he couldn't stand. Patish was a beautiful destination to finally arrive in.

News of Faramond's passing must've traveled fast through the city. Even moving through the streets, people gathered to watch them, many bearing the traditional black and purple mourning colors. When Ryland himself emerged from the double doors of the manor he, too, was dressed from head to toe in black with a purple cloak about his shoulders, lined in dark fur.

Ryland was six years younger than Faramond—a striking man with sharp features and long, dark hair pulled back. Wren had met him only once, years ago, when he was just a boy. He recalled the duke being rigid and aloof, very different from his jovial brother.

Everis came to stand at his side, spine straight and shoulders back. Wren knew he hated political meetings, but it was entertaining to watch him fumble his way through them.

He wants to make a good first impression, Wren thought with a smile.

"Welcome to Patish, magi," Ryland greeted as he descended the stairs. He didn't smile, though he did offer a hand, which Wren took in a firm grip.

"Thank you for your hospitality, Duke Ryland," Wren said with a polite bow of his head. "And for sending your people to see us safely the rest of the way. We encountered some trouble through the mountains, and the assistance was appreciated." He didn't need to look at Everis to know his companion was trying not to roll his eyes. The *assistance* hadn't really assisted them at all, but manners were rarely about being truthful and more about saying what was considered socially appropriate.

Ryland sighed. "Yes, we've been having some issues with the bandits in the hills. It's something we're attempting to deal with. Please, come in." He turned and marched back up the steps.

Wren and Everis followed, with Ivy on their heels.

The interior of the manor was not nearly so lavishly decorated as the castle back home, yet it seemed reflective of Ryland's personality. Simple. Effective. To the point. It was tidy and warm, surprisingly cozy, and even inside, Wren could breathe in deep and catch the scent of the ocean.

They were brought to a large den, with walls lined with artwork and tapestries and shelves of books. A fire had been lit in the hearth. Ryland beckoned them to have a seat in the plush chairs across from his own. They sat, and Everis hunched forward, warming his hands by the fire. Ivy remained standing beside the duke's chair, her hands clasped behind her back. Ryland signaled a nearby servant for refreshments to be brought. Only once the servant returned with a rolling tray of tea, sandwiches, and fruits, did Ryland decide it was time to speak.

"My brother is dead, I hear."

Wren flinched. "I'm afraid you would know that better than us, my lord. He still drew breath when we departed Midmere."

Ryland's gloved fingers drummed atop the arms of the chair. "How long has he been ill?"

"About six months. I've a letter for you from Queen Danica—it's in my trunk."

A scowl crossed the duke's face, intense and distasteful, but it smoothed out quickly enough. "I'm sure you can summarize what it says for me."

Wren paused, startled by his brusqueness. "She... um. She bade you come to Midmere to make peace with your brother. We feared he wasn't long for this world."

"And she waited six months before making this request?"

It was a perfectly valid question. Oh, Wren wished Master Orin were there. He was far better at these sorts of conversations. No doubt the duke was staring at the pair of them, insulted the queen had sent two *children* to speak with him.

Everis spoke up without lifting his gaze from the fire. "We had high hopes for a while that he would recover. He went downhill quickly over the last few weeks."

A lie, but a necessary one, Wren supposed.

"Yes, well, be that as it may, a bit late for it now." Ryland sighed, looking askance, following Everis's gaze into the fire.

Was that a thread of regret in his voice? Wren hoped so. "It's a tragedy, to be certain, my lord. But not all is lost. If you would be willing to accompany us back to Midmere for the funeral, I have no doubt the queen and princess would be thrilled to forge a closer relationship in the wake of the king's death."

Ryland scoffed. "No, I don't believe that's going to happen."

Wren frowned. "May I ask why?"

Ryland rose to his feet, restless. As he began to move about the study, he stroked a hand over his short dark beard. "Everyone knows that my brother and I were not on speaking terms."

Everis inclined his head. He and Wren exchanged a look. "King Faramond preferred not to speak of your quarrel," Wren said.

"Of course he did. He would rather pretend nothing happened.

But I can say with assurance that I would not be a welcome presence in the capital, magi. I'll not dishonor my brother's death by pretending otherwise."

"With all due respect," Everis said, "Queen Danica and Princess Cassia are alive and well. Shouldn't their wants matter more than those of a dead man?"

Wren inwardly winced at the brashness of such a comment.

Duke Ryland stopped beneath a portrait on the wall, staring up at it. Now that he was paying attention, it occurred to Wren that the portrait was of the Starling brothers. Much younger, in their teens or thereabouts, but still very recognizable with Faramond's bright grin and Ryland's steely stare.

Silence reigned over the room for several moments before Ryland spoke again. "How is Cassia?"

A chill settled in Wren's bones. It could've been a simple question, an uncle asking after the well-being of his niece or...

Everis didn't skip a beat. "The princess has grown up well. Mature, intelligent, kind. She'll be a good queen."

"Good. She's young yet, but she'll grow into the position."

"She will," Everis agreed. "Even better if she had the guidance of an uncle in her life."

Ryland turned to pin him with a stare. "I will not be returning with you to the capital. I won't repeat myself again."

Wren put a hand on Everis's arm in hopes of silencing him before he could say anything more. They didn't need to bring Ryland's wrath down on them when they were guests in his home—especially when they had investigating to do.

If Everis noticed that warning touch, he ignored it. "I was not implying that you ought to come with us, just that perhaps you could reach out. A letter, maybe. An invitation for Cassia to visit you here."

One corner of Ryland's mouth twitched. His face was otherwise an impassive wall, unreadable to Wren. "I will see to it that your supplies are restocked, and your soldiers and horses are tended to. Help yourselves to refreshments. When you are ready to retire, Ivy will show you to your rooms." He strode out without another word, leaving the three magi alone.

Wren's shoulders slumped and he sighed.

Everis reached for a sandwich and a cup of tea. "That went well."

"If you could watch your mouth," Wren muttered. "Honestly. What's gotten into you?"

"He wasn't being very forthcoming." Everis shrugged and looked at Ivy. "How has he been since he received the news?"

Ivy folded her arms across her chest, eyebrows arching. "As anyone would when they find they've lost a sibling. His heart was broken."

"He didn't look terribly broken up to me."

"Ah, yes. Because he has reason to spill his feelings in front of strangers. He doesn't owe you or anyone else a display of his grief."

Everis opened his mouth, and Wren grabbed his wrist to silence him. "I'm sorry, Ivy. It's been a long couple of weeks, and we're still reeling with the news ourselves. Tensions are high."

Ivy's eyes remained on Everis, her mouth downturned. "Of course."

They lingered long enough for Everis and Wren to fill their bellies with sandwiches and tea. After which, Ivy took them on a tour of the manor. It was maybe a quarter the size of Midmere's castle but no less impressive. She showed them their own magi study—a converted great hall rather than a tower—and the gardens, stables, training yard, and kitchens should they need anything to eat later. Lastly, she brought them to their rooms. They were one of the only places they'd seen thus far with any sort of effort put into decorating. No doubt even Duke Ryland understood the importance of ensuring his guests were comfortable and felt worthy of frivolous things.

Just like back home, Everis's room sat directly across from his own. They parted ways long enough to wash up and change. The sunset from Wren's balcony window was nothing short of incredible. Ocean as far as the eye could see. It gave him chills. If he looked to the right, he could make out the docks in the distance, small fishing boats gliding in from a hard day's work.

The bedroom door creaked open. Wren didn't bother to look back. Everis never knocked anymore. "I could get used to a view like this," he called back.

Everis stepped up beside him. Gone were his dirtied linens from the trip. He wore a black tunic, purple breeches, and black boots. It was an outfit perhaps a little too nice for lounging around in, but no doubt the only thing in mourning colors he had with him.

"Why didn't we just take a ship here if they're right on the coast?" Everis asked.

"We would've needed to travel west to Nolis and tried to hire a ship that was headed straight here. Depending on the weather, sailing around the peninsula would've taken longer."

Everis frowned. "Longer maybe, but probably safer."

Wren could've pointed out the dangers of sailing, of pirates and Mother knew what else out there, but he bit it back. Everis was still rattled by the bandit attack. Wren had been trying not to dwell on it. Not only over the lives of the soldiers they'd lost, but his own brush with death.

And whatever it was Everis had done to save him.

He swallowed hard, guilt and uncertainty snaking around his heart. "How are you feeling?"

Everis blinked, and it cleared the haze of melancholy from his face. "Fine, I guess. Why do you ask?"

"You've spent the last few days either sleeping or looking ready to fall over."

"Oh." He rolled his shoulders back into a stiff shrug. "I'm better now, I think. What about you? How is your injury?"

"It aches at times, but it's bearable." A pause as Wren debated what he wanted to say and how he wanted to say it. "You know… Master Orin gave me a brief rundown of the history of blood magic years ago. He said that the sheer power of it is achieved by the rule of exchange. You sacrifice something in order to gain something in return."

Everis had gone still. Staring straight ahead, arms folded across his chest, the ocean breeze caressing the hair from his face, he looked beautiful and dangerous and like a complete mystery to Wren. He didn't like it.

"Ever," he murmured. "Please. Don't I deserve to know what was sacrificed that allowed me to be standing here now?"

Everis's tongue swiped out across his lips, which parted with the intention of answering. Still, he hesitated. "It's not your burden to bear. I made the choice."

"You did, and I'm not convinced it was the wisest choice. I'm also not foolish enough to think I would've acted any differently were our situations reversed." He stepped in front of Everis, grasping his elbows, wishing Ever would look at him instead of the horizon. "Please. Don't go to someplace I can't follow. If you have a burden to bear, I will bear it with you."

Finally, Everis's attention dropped to Wren's face. For half a moment, he looked like that little boy Wren and Orin had found hiding in a wardrobe, lost and uncertain. Wren held his gaze, unrelenting, until his friend sighed and tore his eyes away.

"Maliel," he said softly. "I sacrificed Maliel's life to save you."

Captain Annaliese was right.

111

Wren's heart sank. Of course he'd had every reason to suspect. Hearing it from Ever's lips, though, struck a deep pain in his chest that he didn't know what to do with. He mourned for the loss of an innocent man and for the heartache the other soldiers now carried because of it. His own life wasn't worth that. Nothing made him more valuable a human being than that young knight.

Still, he didn't falter. He squeezed Everis's elbows, then cupped his cheeks. "All right. What's done is done."

Everis slowly met his eyes once more. He'd never been good at masking his emotions, and now was no exception. The shame was plain as day on his face. "You aren't angry with me?"

"Angry isn't the right word, no."

"Then what is the right word?"

Wren paused. Sighed. How did he describe it? He was horrified, and the guilt weighed heavy on his chest that an innocent man had been killed so that he could live. Wren's life didn't matter more than any one of the soldiers who accompanied them. "I don't know. I won't lie and say I'm unfazed by this, but... You made a choice, Ever. It cannot be taken back. So now, we live with the aftermath of that choice. We move forward. We try to make amends for what was done, as much as we can. We will inform Maliel's family ourselves when we return to Midmere and ensure he's given whatever burial they wish for him."

The influx of emotions that passed over Everis's face made him utterly unreadable. Unnervingly so. His eyes glassed over, and his arms lifted, coming up around Wren, drawing him into his arms and against his chest. Wren's breath hitched. He felt the press of their bodies, Everis's fingers clutching at his back as though afraid Wren would slip away into oblivion if he didn't hold tight. Ever's breath fell against the curve of his neck and shoulder when he spoke, so achingly sad and lost.

"I was so scared. I couldn't lose you."

Oh, his heart could've broken with the weight of the anguish in those simple words. Wren clung to Everis just as tightly, too overwhelmed to manage an immediate response. He spoke with his hands instead, deft fingers sliding into Everis's perpetually messy hair, breathing in deeply to soothe the ache in his own chest. Eventually, though, he became aware of the time, that the sun had dipped below the horizon and they were standing there in the dark. Reluctantly, he drew away.

"We should get some sleep. We've got a busy day tomorrow."

Hesitation flashed in Everis's eyes. That was a look Wren hadn't seen for some years, and yet he still knew exactly what it meant.

"Do you want to sleep in here tonight?"

A faint blush crept into the younger man's cheeks. "We're not children anymore."

Wren smiled. "Please? I would sleep better."

That did the trick. Ever's shoulders sagged. "Well, if you need me…"

"I do." He did not. He slept fine on his own, and he vividly recalled how, as a boy, Everis hogged most of the blankets and insisted on shoving his cold feet and hands against Wren's body. At least back then he'd been small enough that Wren could shove him to make some space.

Everis left long enough for them both to get changed. Now when they climbed into bed, Wren was distinctly aware of how different this was from when they were children. Oh, they'd shared close quarters while traveling in recent years, bedrolls laid out next to one another. Now they lay on a single mattress that shifted every time Everis moved. They had a single blanket, so he was aware of the shared body heat that would warm them both throughout the night.

Suddenly, Everis's breathing, moving, his entire existence seemed more real, more intimate.

They lay on their sides facing each other. Ever's eyes were already closed, but Wren stared at him. The cut across his face was finally starting to look a little less angry but still no doubt painful. He found himself reaching out, fingertips touching the spot just beneath the wound.

Everis made an inquisitive noise. "What is it?"

"Does it hurt?"

"Not so much." He shifted, subtly turning his head into that touch. "Just a scratch."

"It will scar."

"Probably. So will yours."

He smiled. "Mine isn't on my pretty face."

Everis opened his eyes, and Wren almost wished he hadn't because now it wasn't him watching Everis, but him and Everis watching each other, close enough they were sharing breath. Wren swallowed hard, trying not to let his smile falter.

"You think my face is pretty, do you?" Ever asked.

"You do all right."

"*I do all right,*" he repeated with a soft chuckle. Then he brought up a hand, brushed a bit of hair from Wren's face, and cupped a palm to his cheek. Just for a moment. Long enough for the warmth of his skin to make Wren flush, long enough for him to smooth a thumb across his cheekbone before he drew back, closed his eyes, and lay still. As though this were the most natural thing in the world.

Peculiar, then, that Wren was positive it would be awhile before he could sleep himself.

ORIN

TWENTY-SEVEN YEARS AGO

The castle was new and terrifying. Granted, *everything* had felt new and terrifying these last few weeks. The city, the castle, the other magi. He'd dragged himself from the clutches of darkness, had clawed his way back into good standing with the Citadel, and this was where they'd chosen to place him. A kingdom two hundred miles from his home.

It was for the best, really. Home still carried too many reminders Orin didn't need. Even if his circle of friends was gone now, he'd still see their ghosts everywhere he looked and glimpse the shadows of what used to be.

The call of their magic still crackled beneath his skin even after all these months. Would it ever let go?

He hoped so.

No, you don't.

He hunched over his breakfast plate, his eyes pressed shut. Sometimes, the noise and bustle of the dining hall were too much. Too many people. Too much brightness. Too much, too much, too—

"I like your bird," a voice announced.

115

Orin's head snapped up. He recognized the face of the magi presently taking a seat across from him at the otherwise unoccupied table. Most of the magi would be dining in the tower, not there in the hall. So why Drake Reed was there was a mystery to him.

"Oh. Um. Thank you."

On the table beside him, Nova cocked her head, patiently awaiting whatever morsels of food Orin might send her way. She turned, studying Drake Reed thoughtfully, before strutting across the table to investigate.

Drake smiled, lifting a hand. "Will he peck me?"

"She," Orin corrected. "And I don't know. She might." There was never any telling. Nova was never aggressive with him, but with others…

Drake took the chance and brought a finger down to stroke the soft white feathers of her head. His smile widened in delight. "So far, so good. Does she have a name?"

"Nova." Orin dropped his gaze to his plate. He really needed to eat. It had been a day or two, but his stomach never seemed to settle enough for it.

"And you're Orin Sorrel, the new magi sent by the Citadel."

Orin stilled, waiting to see if there was more to that statement. *The magi sent by the Citadel after being locked away for nine years for using blood magic.* No. No one here would be aware of that. Not the king, not the other magi. The king knew Orin had been reprimanded and sentenced for *something*, but not the severity of the crime. Only that he'd served his time, made amends, and been cleared by the Citadel to take on an official position.

Drake continued to pet Nova. Orin studied the other young man thoughtfully. Around his age—mid-to-late twenties. His long, pale hair was pulled back and braided, his eyes a deep emerald. Handsome, even. He had a pleasant and disarming smile.

"You're Drake Reed," Orin said. "Why are you eating in here and not the tower?"

Nova abandoned Drake in favor of returning to him, taking the opportunity to steal a fig from his plate.

Drake chuckled. "I could ask you that same question, couldn't I? You don't seem to be enjoying the noise much, so why are you here?"

One corner of Orin's mouth twitched in displeasure. "Because I wanted to be alone," he answered crisply, wondering if his meaning would come across loud and clear.

"Not really alone in here, are you?" Drake glanced around. No one might have been seated at Orin's table, but there were plenty of guards, soldiers, and other castle inhabitants eating nearby.

Orin stared at him. This man was going to be his peer in this new place. He couldn't allow himself to be short-tempered and abrasive so soon after his arrival. Still, he couldn't think of a polite way to ask, "What can I help you with, Reed?"

"Oh, posh. Just Drake is fine." The magi waved his hand. "You don't need to help me with anything. I only thought... well, I thought you could use a friend, on account of..." He trailed off. For the first time, his smile faltered.

"On account of...?" Orin asked.

Drake looked down at his own plate, wrapping his fingers around his fork. "Ah. I meant to say—I figured you might be feeling out of place, is all."

What little appetite Orin had was lost. He set his spoon aside. "And why is that?"

The other man hesitated. "I'm only being friendly, Orin."

"Friendly or curious?" he snapped. "Go on, then. Tell me. What are the others saying that had you feeling sorry for me?"

Drake's mouth downturned, and his eyes dropped to his breakfast. "They... they say there are rumors you were locked up for a time at the Citadel."

"Hm. Did those rumors say why?"

There was another pregnant pause, accented by Drake shifting uneasily. "No one seems to know for sure, but there are some guesses being tossed about."

"Such as?"

"Ah, well, everything from stealing sacred texts to defrauding citizens with fake charms to blood magic."

Yes. There it was. "What would your guess be?"

Drake took a deep breath, finally meeting Orin's steely stare. "I think it probably doesn't matter much what happened before. You're here now, and everyone could use a friend. Our pasts do not define us. If you committed some sort of wrongful act, then you've served your time and it's no longer relevant."

The answer caught Orin off guard. He'd met most of the magi in the castle by now, had greeted them with uncertain smiles and handshakes. Every one of them had looked at him as though he had the plague. Rumors or not, he was an outsider with a tall shadow looming over him. The fact that he still felt that shadow hanging so prevalently over his shoulder didn't help matters any. Would he slip up? Would the call become too great to withstand?

Drake didn't give him time to dwell on his insecurities, however. He smiled again and picked up his fork as though their topic of conversation had been nothing more important than the weather.

"Well, Orin. You should eat before your breakfast gets cold."

PRESENT DAY

Nova fluttered nervously. She might've been gleaning emotions from Orin, really, because *he* was nervous. Some small part of his brain still wondered if he'd assembled this puzzle all wrong. Drake had been a loyal member of the Citadel of Magi for as long as Orin had. No—longer, technically, seeing as Orin himself had been disgraced and locked away for years.

That was why he'd sent for Drake. Just to talk. To try to get some answers. He wanted to hope beyond all hope that Drake was innocent and there was a rational explanation for all of this.

You know there's not.

You know you could force him to tell the truth…

Crimson burned at the back of his mind. He shuddered. Resurrecting that assassin had done a number on him. For years, he'd turned his back on the dark pull of that voice, and it had grown easier with time. Now that he'd dipped his toes back into it, he was ever aware of its presence again, like the steady drip of a water pump he couldn't quite shut off.

The door to the magi tower swung open, letting in a shot of light that was briefly obscured as Drake stepped inside. He had two cups of tea balanced on a tray, along with a smile for Orin that made his chest tight.

He had always loved that smile. Could it really have been a lie, too?

"Good morning." Drake crossed the room to place the tray atop one of the research tables. "I hope you didn't call me here to deliver bad news from Patish."

"No," Orin said, unable to shake the tension from his shoulders. His voice may've remained amiable and calm, but inside, his emotions were coiled tight in apprehension and grief. His instincts told him something was wrong. "It's not about Patish."

Drake bowed over the tray as he spooned sugar into his cup. "What is it, then?"

Orin circled around the back of him, keeping a careful distance. "The night Faramond died... Rue was looking over him."

"As she does most nights, yes. Poor thing. She's still so rattled. Hasn't left her room and isn't taking visitors."

Orin came to a halt a few feet away. "Did you deliver her tea that night, Drake?"

Drake's gaze slid over to Orin. "Hm, I believe so. That's something I would do from time to time—checking in on her and delivering snacks and drink while giving the king his last dosage of medicine for the day."

"You prepared this tea yourself?" Orin pressed.

This time, Drake straightened his spine and turned to him with an inquisitive tip of his head. "Is there a reason you're giving me such leading questions, my sweet friend? If you have something to say, please say it."

The tension in the room was palpable. Orin inclined his chin. "Rue didn't fall asleep that night. She was put to sleep. I'm asking if you drugged her tea."

"Oh." Drake considered this as though Orin had merely asked him what he wanted for lunch. "Why, yes. I suppose I did."

Orin's breath hitched at the casual admission. "Why?"

Drake flipped his braid back over his shoulder with a dismissive shrug. "I thought I was doing her a kindness, truly. I'd intended for her to sleep through the king's death. The seizures were... unexpected."

Dread coursed through Orin's veins. He braced himself against the table, too stunned to speak.

Drake took one look at him and chuckled. "Oh, come now. Don't look at me like that. You shouldn't ask questions you don't want the answers to. Unless you were hoping I would lie?"

Orin forced his mouth to cooperate, anger scorching the edges of his words. "You killed Faramond. *Why?*"

"I don't owe you my reasons," Drake scoffed. "But I *had* hoped to keep you in the dark about it, at least for a bit longer. You get so worked up about matters regarding the king."

Orin bit back his fury. He tried to focus, to calm himself. The answers to his questions could come later. For now, it was his duty to bring a traitor into custody and deliver him before the queen.

"Drake Reed," he said, "I hereby condemn you to imprisonment and judgment."

Drake smiled, almost sweetly. "All by your lonesome, dear heart?"

His jaw clenched. "Never. Guards!"

Above them, several castle guards stepped into view at the railings, swords drawn and their expressions a mixture of anger and confusion and horror at what they'd just overheard.

Drake's smile didn't falter, though, as the guards descended the stairs to the ground floor and surrounded him. On the contrary, he picked up his tea and took a sip as he scanned the group. Five guards, ones Orin had felt confident he could trust, and Orin himself. Six to one were good odds in their favor.

Or so Orin thought.

Drake slammed his cup onto the table, sending tea and shards of porcelain every which way. He wrapped his fingers around one of the shards, whirled, and plunged it into the throat of the nearest soldier.

The burst of darkness that washed over Orin was instantaneous. He saw the flash of Drake Reed's eyes, a brilliant burning red. The guard staggered back, clutching his neck, choking on his own blood. As he died, he unwittingly fed into the powers Drake was harnessing. An unwitting sacrifice for Drake's blood magic.

The other guards surged forward, no longer concerned with simply capturing Drake. They would kill him if they had to, and Orin wouldn't stop them. Drake raised his bloodied hands, fingers painting symbols in the air as he chanted in a language dark and deep that Orin still remembered even after all this time. The room quaked around them, sending one man sprawling on his face. The other three were swept off their feet by a spinning whirlwind that gathered them up like ragdolls. All about the tower, books and herbs, parchments and beakers, paintings and supplies were ripped from their shelves, hurtling in every direction.

A fireplace poker narrowly missed Orin as it zipped past his head. The guards were suspended in mid-air, hanging there by invisible nooses, clawing at their throats for air. But it meant Drake was concentrating on them, and it gave him just enough of an opening.

He ducked past the debris, making a dive for a knife about to be plucked off the table by the fierce wind. In one fluid motion, Orin murmured a spell beneath his breath, whirled, and flung the dagger at Drake's exposed back.

It might've hit him square between the shoulder blades were it not for the wind. It pitched too far to the left and a few inches too high. The blade skimmed the side of Drake's face, drawing a thin line of blood in its wake. But it did the trick. His concentration faltered, and there was a stutter in the wind before the guards came crashing to the floor in varying stages of consciousness.

Drake faced him with a sneer. With his attention refocused, he thrust his hands forward, chanting. A fine red mist had begun to creep into the room, and with that movement, the mist roiled together, forming the smoky shape of a large, bony hand.

Orin wasn't fast enough. The incorporeal fingers closed around his throat as he tried to dive to one side, hoisting him several feet off the ground. The darkness swept over him, made him see stars when he squeezed his eyes shut.

And red. Red feathers just within his reach, if he only wanted to grab for them, to harness their power...

A gust of wind burst past his face, accompanied by a beating of wings and an ear-piercing screech. He opened his eyes as the hold on his throat loosened, just in time to see Nova flying at Drake's face. She attacked with such ferocity and speed that she had one of his eyes bloodied before anyone could register what was happening. Orin concentrated on the magic holding him, prying the fingers from around his throat until he could drop to the ground. He gasped in a lungful of air, turned, and raced for the stairs. Nova could only distract him for so long.

"Bloody bird!" Drake howled.

Orin tore up the first flight, reaching the topmost step before he heard Drake ascending the steps after him. Ducking between the first row of bookshelves, he weaved in and out through the maze-like structure. There was only so high he could go in the tower. Drake would catch up with him, eventually. That was fine; he only needed some extra time... Time to draw Drake away from the unconscious guards and think of a plan.

When he reached the second flight of stairs across the floor, he took the steps two at a time. Behind him, books and papers went flying. The old redwood shelves creaked perilously beneath the onslaught of magical wind.

On the third floor, Orin had enough of a lead that he ducked between a few shelves to catch his breath. He could hear the storm-like flurry quickly catching up. From a nearby table, he snatched up a quill, fumbling hastily with its bottle of ink. He needed just a minute or two. Thirty seconds. Enough time to ink a spell onto the back of his hands.

For half a moment, he stopped, eyeing the bandages on his arm. It would take little prodding to open the cut he'd made the other night and use his own blood to fuel the magic that sat at the edges of his mind.

The blood spilled on the first floor could have helped him as much as it helped Drake. The thought of it made that flicker of darkness surge into a bright and tempting flame.

You could end this quickly.

Orin shuddered, thrusting it away. He would not. He *could* not. This was a fight he needed to win on his own without allowing himself to fall.

He turned his attention to the ink drying on his hands, willing it to hurry, to not smudge. Behind him, the roar of the wind had grown stronger. The shelf at his back groaned ominously, then pitched forward. It connected with the shelf before him, trapping Orin in the triangle of space between the two shelves and the floor. He remained still, breath held, listening.

"Orin, Orin, my dear Orin… I've been trying to spare you all this, you know," Drake called. Nearby, but not near enough. "You should've gone to Patish with your boys. Even then, I tried to take care of things without you knowing. It would've been fine if you'd only kept your nose out of it."

Orin closed his eyes. He couldn't stomach listening. So many thoughts danced on the tip of his tongue. *How could you do this? Faramond was your king. You were sworn to protect him and his family.* He bit it back, concentrating instead on those approaching footsteps.

"It isn't too late. You know how this magic works as well as I do. Think of all we could teach each other! Me, you, and your apprentices, too. The four of us would be *unstoppable.*"

A chill ran down his spine. Drake said *apprentices*, but Orin knew what he meant. *Everis.* Of everyone in the castle, the only person aside from Wren and himself who knew about what they'd discovered in Balerno was Drake. He'd been the only one Orin had trusted with that information, as one of his dearest friends.

Damn it all.

He couldn't help the anger that washed over him. Drake's steps were close enough now—he hoped. He straightened as much as his cramped spacing allowed him, pressed his hands against the worn wood of the bookshelf, hissed out the incantation, and the magic did the rest.

A wall of force took the shelf, table, books, and everything else in its way and sent it skidding ten, twenty feet across the floor. Drake gave a shout, followed by a thud as he was caught up in the chaos. In the seconds that followed, his storm immediately died down.

Orin scanned the disaster before him. Years and years of organization and research and hard work now lay scattered in haphazard piles across the floor. Papers floated aimlessly down the center of the tower to the ground floor. His gaze swept around until he spotted Drake, one arm jutting out from beneath a pile of shelves and books.

Cautious, Orin crossed the rubble to him. He nudged the magi's arm with his foot. It twitched. Drake groaned, twisting, trying to drag himself free from the debris. Orin loomed over him, ready to grab him and restrain him by any means necessary.

Not that he had to. A voice called from below, "Master Orin?"

He exhaled. "Third floor!"

The sound of chainmail and pounding footsteps greeted his ears as three of the guards rushed up to find him. Orin gave a flippant gesture to Drake and stepped back.

"Restrain him. Hands behind his back and cover his eyes," Orin ordered. That would ensure Drake didn't have any more tricks up his sleeve. Even his blood magic wouldn't do him any good that way.

Artesia lifted her head to look at him. "What do we do with him then?"

Orin turned away, shoulders slumping in relief as he saw Nova perched on the railing nearby. Red stained her snowy feathers, but she appeared unharmed as she tipped her head and studied him like she was thinking the same about him.

"Take him to the dungeons," he said in a voice as heavy as it was tired. "I want two guards watching him at all times. Do not take your eyes off him. You've seen what he can do."

WREN

Wren laid the dagger on the counter. "If you'd just take a quick look... It's a unique blade, and I'm certain you'll remember it if it has crossed your path."

Sighing, the burly blacksmith set aside his hammer and scooped up the dagger. He studied the dark, gleaming blade and the intricately carved handle, and although Wren thought he saw a bit of awe in his eyes, there was no recognition.

"Gorgeous piece of equipment," he admitted. "You're right 'bout one thing: I'd remember it if I'd seen it. But sorry to tell ya, it's new to me."

Wren sighed. His entire day had comprised going from blacksmith to blacksmith and anyone else in-between who might make or peddle knives such as these. Where else should he try? Had someone he'd questioned lied to him? He took back the dagger, unable to hide the weariness in his voice. "Thank you for your time, and I'm sorry for taking you from your work."

He got as far as the door before the blacksmith snapped his fingers and said, "Oh, Asher Belmont. That's the fellow you ought to see."

Wren turned back around, frowning. "Who's that?"

"A bloke with a shop down in the southernmost district. Jewelry, antiques, oddities. I hear he occasionally deals in unique armor and weaponry." He shrugged. "Might be worth a go if you're out of leads, anyway."

He wasn't feeling particularly hopeful, but Wren smiled and thanked the blacksmith all the same.

It took him nearly an hour to cross back down to the southern district. Even in the cool coastal weather, he felt overdressed and overheated. An hour to get there and another hour of asking around about Asher Belmont finally led Wren to an elegant storefront. Behind the window sat a display of all sorts of things: exotic jewelry, taxidermied animals, blades, whips, and potions.

A tinkling bell atop the door announced his presence. The inside was no less peculiar than the window display. Upon closer inspection, Wren realized the posed animals along the shelves weren't simply taxidermied creatures but entirely new species the maker had fabricated themselves. Upon the head of a stuffed owl sat intricate deer antlers. A cat's head had been neatly sewn to a raccoon's body. Butterfly wings had been attached to the backs of mice and rats. It was difficult to pay attention to anything else in the shop with so many glass eyes staring at him, and he was simultaneously fascinated and unnerved.

"This is not a museum," a clear voice announced.

Wren turned to see a clean-shaven gentleman standing behind the counter. He was tall and lean, neatly dressed in beautiful golds. His wheat-colored hair was done up into braids, decorated with beads and baubles, and his gray eyes stood out against his ebony skin. The man arched a brow and gave a glittering smile. "Although if you want to treat it as such, I suppose I would be agreeable for the cost of admission."

A faint flush rose to Wren's face, and he stepped over to the counter. "My apologies. I was fascinated by the work here. Did you make all these?"

The man Wren presumed to be Asher Belmont shrugged. "It is a hobby that can occasionally prove profitable. If nothing else, it ensures no one forgets about my shop when they leave. How may I help you today, young sir?"

Wren removed the dagger from his belt and held it out. "I've been investigating leads regarding this dagger. I was told you might be the person to ask about where it might have come from."

Asher started to reach for the blade, paused midway, then took it. The hesitation was so slight, so brief, Wren wasn't certain if he'd imagined it. Asher's expression had deadpanned into a carefully constructed mask. *That* much, Wren knew he wasn't imagining.

"You know it," Wren said, not making it a question.

The merchant's eyes lifted to him. "Where did you get this?"

Wren's heart skipped a nervous beat. "I don't believe it matters, unless it's familiar to you."

Any fleeting trace of friendliness upon the man's face was long gone. His eyes were sharp, and his posture straight and tense even as his gaze flicked about the shop. "I believe it's time for you to go, my friend."

"Please," Wren begged, just shy of wringing his hands together. He was so close to finding out something; he *knew* it.

"Go," Asher repeated, voice cold. He turned away to retreat into the back of his shop.

Panic rose in Wren's chest. What would Master Orin do?

No… What would *Everis* do?

In a flash, he lurched over the countertop and grabbed the merchant's bicep, wrenching him around so they were nose to nose.

"Listen," he hissed. "I've been all over this blasted city today, trying to find answers for Master Orin Sorrell, and I'm not leaving until I have them. The life of the royal family is at stake, and I will throw myself upon my sword if it means keeping them safe."

Dramatic, but dramatics were the Everis way, weren't they? Sometimes, they worked.

Asher tensed and looked down at him, but his brows drew together. "The royal family?"

"An assassin snuck into Midmere's castle and attempted to kill Her Highness, Princess Cassia. This was the dagger on the assassin's person."

"I see. What happened to this assassin?"

"Dead, hence why I'm not in Midmere questioning *them.*"

Asher's expression flickered with resigned weariness. He sighed. "Flip the sign in the window." He drew his arm away and ducked past the curtain partition leading into the back. Frowning, Wren switched the window sign from *open* to *closed*, snatched the dagger from the counter, and followed.

The back was darker than the shop itself. There were no windows or candles as Wren followed Asher down a long, narrow hallway, stealing looks into the few rooms they passed as his eyes adjusted to the dark. Workshops, it looked like. Storage areas. Asher brought him to the only closed door at the end of the hall, removed a key from his pocket, and let them in. With a wave of his hand, he brought light flooding into the room. Not from candles, but from crystals. Small, sharp-edged rocks etched with light runes that were placed strategically about the room. Wren marveled at them. Even at the castle, they had only a handful of these. They were difficult to craft so that non-magi could use them, and expensive. Asher possessed nearly a dozen.

With the light came at least twenty creatures staring at him from shelves—taxidermied mythical animals in progress. Wren shivered at the way the crystal light danced across their vacant eyes and made it appear they were watching him.

Asher stopped before a floor-to-ceiling bookshelf. Something felt off. Wren clutched the dagger as though he might soon need it. Maybe it would've been wiser to bring Everis after all. The merchant grabbed two of the books and tipped them forward. The bookcases opened like massive, creaking double doors to reveal an alcove. With a step back, he gave a dramatic gesture of his hand as though this revealed compartment contained the answers to all life's questions.

It was a weapons cache. They covered every wall of the alcove from top to bottom with daggers, blades, maces, arrows, and more, hanging neatly from silver pegs or in ornate wooden cases. Wren stepped closer, inspecting the dark metal used to forge them. More importantly...

"The emblem," he whispered, lifting the dagger to compare it with others much like it. Without a doubt, the intricate owl and flower engraving on the hilt matched perfectly. Not just on a few of the weapons, but every single one of them. "I don't understand. What is this?"

Asher crossed his arms, shifting from one foot to the other. "The Dusk Court."

Wren frowned. "I don't know what that is."

"No, you wouldn't. Few do. Not by name, at least." Asher plucked the dagger from Wren's unsuspecting hand, holding it up alongside another that could've been its twin. "The Court is an assassin's guild. Difficult to find, difficult to hire, unless you know the right people or run in the right circles."

An assassin's guild. Wren's chest cinched tighter. Oh, there were rumors about organized groups of assassins, but like Asher said, never by name.

They were careful. Deadly careful. It would make sense that someone who wanted the royal family dead would hire only the best. "Why are *you* in possession of their things?"

"Because I furnish them with their weapons, of course. Nightstone is notoriously difficult to come by. I get it, I have someone who forges it, and I sell it to the guild."

His brain scrambled to catch up with this. He spun around to face the merchant with wide eyes. "Then *you* gave this to the assassin who went after the princess?"

Asher's mouth curved into a grim smile. "It would seem that way, yes. Though not with the intention that it be used against someone of royal blood."

"Do you have a way of finding out who she was? Or who hired her?"

Asher held up his hands. "I'm merely a merchant, my friend. They only trust me with the information I need to supply them and take their payment. Nothing more, nothing less. I prefer it that way. I'd rather they have no reason to ever doubt my loyalty."

A cold prickle of dread worked its way down Wren's spine. This was a lot of information. Information he suspected Asher wouldn't give to just anyone. "And yet you're betraying their trust to help me. Why?"

Asher smiled and tipped his head. That sensation of dread coiled tight around Wren's insides.

He needed to leave.

Without further questions, he whirled on his heel and dashed for the door. Asher made no move to stop him.

Wren stepped out of the room. He caught sight of a shadow at the end of the hallway just in time to dodge left, narrowly avoiding a throwing knife that zipped centimeters from his face and embedded into the wall behind him. As a large man in black moved toward him, frighteningly fast and silent, Wren thrust a hand forward, fingers painting symbols within the air before him as he shouted out a frantic incantation.

A ring of fire ignited, flickered, and shot down the hall. The assassin skidded to a halt, but his reflexes were such that he dropped to the floor and rolled beneath the flames. Wren kept his hand outstretched, eyes intense and focused. Surely even an assassin wouldn't want to go toe to toe with a magi, especially in a small space that Wren could easily light up.

"That was a warning," Wren said. "Lower your blade, and let's discuss this like adults."

The man rolled to his feet and drew his sword in one fluid movement, taking a guarded stance. For half a second, Wren was positive he would attack again.

The door to Wren's right opened once more, and Asher stepped out, dagger in hand, tapping the flat of the blade thoughtfully against his chin. "He's a magi from Midmere sent by Orin Sorrell," he announced to the assassin. "One of your people went after the king's daughter."

That seemed to catch the man's attention. He stilled, sword dipping. With his face half obscured by his mask, Wren could make out very few details beyond tanned skin, deep scars, and a set of brilliant golden eyes, which narrowed in his direction. Wren didn't lower his own hand.

"It's up to you, of course," Asher continued with a casual shrug. "But seems to me a rule was broken, and tradition states you owe a debt for that."

The frown turned to an all-out scowl, but the assassin slid his sword back into its sheath and crossed his arms. Not a word was spoken, and yet Asher smiled, seeming to understand the silence. He turned to Wren.

"The Court has regulations in place to keep things running smoothly. They don't take just any job that falls into their hands but choose appropriately to better maintain balance within society. For instance, a hit on a simple farmer over a petty squabble would be overlooked, but a contract on a wealthy lord known for bleeding his people dry with taxes would be a prime target."

"Murderers with a moral compass," said Wren dryly. "How quaint. What does that have to do with the princess?"

Asher exchanged looks with the stranger, who nodded in reluctant approval. "Royalty is off-limits. The slaying of a ruler throws everything into chaos. The last king to be dethroned was over a hundred years ago, and it was done only after the entirety of the guild met and voted on the matter."

Finally, Wren felt safe enough to lower his arm, flexing his fingers that still tingled with traces of magic. "Then this woman broke the rules... Why?"

"That's a matter for the Court to look into, not you." Asher gave him a pat on the back. "I can assure you, however, had she survived the ordeal, she wouldn't have been around long to enjoy the victory."

"What about who hired her?" Wren pressed. "That's what I really need to know. There's got to be a way to find out, hasn't there?"

Again, Asher and the assassin looked at one another, conversing without saying a word. The assassin sighed, gave a flippant wave of his hand, and turned away. As he departed, he seemed to melt into the shadows. Wren couldn't even tell whether he'd left through the main shop or vanished into one of the other rooms.

Asher smiled. "It would seem he intends to look into it. No promises that he'll find anything, of course."

Wren pinned him with an unimpressed scowl. "How did he even know I was here?"

"They keep watch over me, naturally."

"I thought you said they trusted you."

"Oh, they do." His eyes positively twinkled. "They watch me because I'm an irreplaceable asset."

"But how—" Wren paused. "The sign…"

"Merely a handy way of alerting whoever's watching that something might be amiss. I knew someone would show up in short order to… discuss things with you."

"Or he'd have slit my throat."

Asher laughed. "Either way, the situation would've been dealt with, no?"

EVERIS

"I *should be going with you. It's not smart to split up.*"

That was the argument Everis had made repeatedly the night before. If Wren wanted to question blacksmiths in town about the dagger, that was all fine and well, but he might need backup. Just in case. What if he crossed the wrong person or got in over his head?

"Someone needs to stay here and keep an eye on things. See if you can't get some more information out of Ivy," Wren had said before departing.

Right. Because Ivy was such a chatty, forthcoming woman. She hadn't spoken a word throughout breakfast, had scarcely even looked their way. Not until Wren had amiably asked if she had plans for the day and could spare some time to get a few lessons in for Everis. *"Master Orin is big on encouraging us to learn from as many teachers as we can."* Everis had flushed, annoyed that *he* was the one who supposedly needed training, but managed a tight smile all the same.

So, it came to be that he headed to the hall-slash-magi study shortly after lunch. It was empty upon arrival. Everis perused the various experiments and notes laid out on the tables, partly out of curiosity, partly to see if anything suspicious caught his eye. Even though Ivy was the only magi who worked for Duke Ryland, others lived in the city of

Patish. They would conduct much of their more extensive work there in the study, leaving their personal workshops for minor charms and potions. As such, there were notes on a variety of topics.

As he looked over a ledger of magical qualities of different types of field mice, the door opened and Ivy swept in, chin up, shoulders straight, cool as ever. Everis set down the ledger and put on his most awkwardly polite smile.

"Thank you for meeting with me, my lady—"

"Ivy is fine," she cut him off, swinging the cloak from her shoulders to drape it on a hook near the door. "Come. We'll be training in the yard."

He paused, realized she wasn't waiting for him, and fell in line to follow her. "Outside?"

She led him through the back door into a small training yard complete with wooden, padded dummies, a rack of weapons, and a few articles of old, dinged chest plates and bracers. A bit pitiful compared to what they had back home, but something told Everis this wasn't the main training yard used by Ryland's knights and city guards. It was more likely for the children to beat their wooden swords together and pretend they were soldiers.

Ivy gestured to the weapons rack as she walked to the center of the yard. "Choose one. I know they aren't much, but a blade is a blade."

Everis picked up one of the battered wooden swords, testing its weight as he twirled it in his hand. It was awkward and poorly balanced, nothing like his own sword back in his room, but it would do for—ah, well… "Um, what are we doing, exactly?"

Ivy came to a stop and faced him, her hands clasped behind her back. "You're going to attack me."

He started. "Sorry?"

"Are you having trouble with your hearing, apprentice?"

Heat crept into his cheeks. "I heard you fine. It just didn't make any sense."

"You wanted to train, and we are going to train in combat."

"You don't even have a sword. What brought this about?"

She sighed. "Listen, I may not be some well-to-do royal magi, but I'm not a fool, either. You two are up to something. I know Wren is off poking around about whatever it is, and he probably wanted you here, hoping to get information out of me."

Everis almost laughed. So much for their plan. Wren would be quite vexed to learn about this later. Spinning the sword once, he meandered across the yard toward her. "Very well, you've figured us out. What does

132

that mean for me now?"

"It means," Ivy said with the patience of someone speaking to a toddler, "if you can best me in a fight, I'll answer any questions you have."

He squinted. "Honest answers only?"

"I swear it. I have nothing to hide." She smiled. "Do we have a deal?"

Everis pursed his lips. He didn't have a clue what kind of warrior Ivy was. He didn't know her strengths or weaknesses, didn't know what weapons or spells she favored. It occurred to Everis that he'd spent so many years training with the same people—Wren, Lady Imaryllis, the knights and guards—that facing a new opponent felt a little daunting. With the bandits, he hadn't been given a choice. Yet, what was his weakness was also hers; she didn't know anything about how he fought and judging by the overly saccharine smile on her face, she would likely underestimate him.

"Suit yourself," he said.

Then he attacked.

The first few swings, Ivy sidestepped with speed and grace, and Everis kept his strokes easy and simple, void of any intricate moves. Let her feel settled and secure that she had the upper hand while he figured out some of her techniques because if she wasn't going to attack with a sword, then he anticipated magic.

Ivy ducked and rolled out from beneath another of his swings and, sure enough, murmured a swift incantation he couldn't quite make out. With a flick of her hand, the dirt beneath Everis shifted and rolled, nearly knocking him off his feet. He yelped, struggling to maintain his footing, and this time, the swing he took at Ivy missed only because he couldn't reclaim his balance.

His knees hit the rippling ground. From beneath the dirt, tree roots snaked to the surface, slithering toward him. As he tried to lurch back to his feet, one wrapped around his ankle, threatening to topple him again. With a snarl, Everis reflexively hacked at the thick coil, but a wooden blade wasn't much use against anything.

He gritted his teeth, pivoted as much as his restrained position allowed, and launched the sword like a javelin in Ivy's direction. She ducked, but it did the trick of catching her off guard enough that her concentration flagged, and Everis kicked the root loose and yanked his foot free.

"Hardly fair," he snapped. "I have to use a fake sword, but you get to use real magic?"

"I never said you couldn't use magic too," she pointed out, kicking the training sword aside. "Unless you aren't experienced enough to wield spells in battle yet, of course."

Flushing, Everis flicked a hand in her direction, uttering a few simple words that brought a flare of heat to his fingertips. This time when the tree roots came for him, he grabbed them, his burning hands scorching the wood and rendering it useless. One by one, the roots recoiled and dropped like snakes at his feet.

There were more where that came from, though. Ivy was relentless, tossing spell after spell, hands moving to direct more of the plants that crept from all reaches of the training yard toward him, faster than Everis could fend them off. He was forced to retreat, two feet, three, ten, until he felt the manor wall at his back. He was cornered.

Thin tendrils of some sort of plant stretched from the wall, sliding around his throat. He choked on a sound, grabbed the plants by the handful and burned them, but there were too many. They coiled about his wrists and ankles and neck, squeezed until he couldn't utter another spell to try to break free, until the rows of tiny, razor-sharp thorns pierced his skin.

Trapped. His panicked mind raced. *This isn't training. She's really going to kill me.*

Ivy stood amongst the foliage, bright eyes glinting expectantly. Everis choked in one last breath before the vines tightened and cut off his air supply. The image of Ivy before him began to fade as his vision went dark.

But with the darkness came a crimson light within his reach.

She can't win against you.

No one can.

Everis's drooping eyelids snapped open. He grasped the vines, envisioning himself drawing the very life from them, and they loosened their grip on his limbs and fell limply around him. He could breathe again. Ivy took an abrupt step back as he straightened himself and kicked away the withered remnants of roots at his feet.

"You'll pay for that," he sneered, fury and power flooding through his veins. Everything felt sharper. Nothing was impossible.

Ivy braced herself, jaw set, unmoving, hands clasped behind her back.

Everis lunged.

At least, he tried. Two steps forward, his legs gave out, and he hit the ground.

This time, everything did go completely dark.

BRANT

Brant offered to take the first watch alongside Artesia. Together, they sat across from Drake Reed's cell, a small table between them with a modest lunch to fill their bellies after their… adventurous morning. Brant was sporting a few cuts and scratches. They both had bruising around their throats where Reed's dark magic had attempted to strangle the life out of them.

Brant stared at the magi. He sat beneath the window of his cell with his head tipped back, still bound, and with a scarf tied securely about his eyes. Over the years, he'd witnessed plenty of magic performed by the magi who resided in the castle. He'd seen their charms and potions work small miracles. Had witnessed firsthand their enchantments that transformed the guards' own swords into magical weapons capable of shattering stone and steel.

But he'd never seen anything like what Reed had displayed in that tower. Nothing so violent or loud or big. It wasn't even the display of it as much as the *feel* of it. Even now, he could swear she felt the remnants of his power crawling on her skin.

"I would be very appreciative," the magi finally spoke, "if you were to release me."

Artesia and Brant exchanged looks. Master Orin had warned them not to engage with Reed, that a blood magi wasn't a thing to be trifled with, but Brant couldn't let it lie.

"And *why* would we want to do that?"

"Because it would be beneficial to you in the long run," Reed said, shifting his shoulders as though trying to get comfortable. His arms had to be aching by now.

Brant sneered. "You killed some of our friends and injured the rest of us. If you think I trust a word out of your mouth, you're stupider than I thought."

A soft, almost kind smile crossed Reed's face. "Fair enough. Although I feel I should point out I only attacked because I was surrounded. Wouldn't anyone have done the same in my place?"

"Not if they were innocent," Artesia chimed in. "You could've gone before the queen and pleaded your case, and it would've been a lot stronger than trying to escape first."

"So you say. Tell me, have we received any word about the funeral arrangements for the king? I know Orin was working on them."

Gods, this man was giving him a headache. Was he really so oblivious to his predicament that he thought small talk was appropriate? Or was he plotting something?

Brant snorted. "Doesn't matter. You won't be attending anyway. What in Mother's name made you think poisoning the king was a smart idea? And if you wanted him dead, why not just poison him once and get it over with? No sense in dragging it out for months."

Artesia placed a hand on his arm, shooting him a look. And yet to his surprise, Reed answered.

"Sometimes the long game is the one that needs to be played. Faramond was healthy as a horse. If he'd dropped dead so quickly, everyone would've suspected foul play. An illness, however... That gave me more time to set some other things in motion."

Artesia paused. "Do you mean the attempt on Princess Cassia's life?"

A serene smile passed over Drake's face. "A misstep on my part. I grew impatient. I certainly hadn't anticipated Everis intervening and saving her."

A wash of anger surged through Brant. Princess Cassia was a good girl. Sweet and kind and never the sort to wish harm to anyone. Brant remembered the night of Faramond's death, how grief-stricken the princess had been, and yet still, she'd placed a hand on Artesia's arm and asked, *Are you alright?* Drowning in her own sorrow, she'd been concerned about those around her. The idea that this man was behind the assassination attempt had him seeing red.

Brant lurched from her seat and approached the bars, voice low. "You're lucky Master Orin wants you unharmed for your judgment. I'd be happy to open your throat right here and now for that admission."

Reed inclined his chin, and he could almost swear he could somehow see Brant even through his blindfold. "By all means, feel free. But you've seen what I can do with the blood of others. Imagine what I could do with my own."

It was a thinly veiled threat, but a threat all the same. Brant shivered. He could feel Artesia at his back, a steady and assuring presence to remind him that they were safe. Not even a magi could hurt them in his current state. "Were you always this disgusting, or is it the blood magic that makes you that way?"

"Oh, dear." Reed pressed his back to the wall, using his legs to push himself up the stone until he was standing. He took a few precarious steps across the cell until he stood a mere inch from the bars. Too close for comfort. "If *my* blood magic offends you so, you'll be quite disturbed to hear I'm not the only one in the castle who does it. Ask Orin about his own foray into the dark arts. Or—oh! Ask Everis. He's a friend of yours, isn't he?"

He spoke the word *friend* in a way that dripped venom. Artesia tensed behind her. She caught his elbow and drew him back a step. *Were* there more blood magi within the castle walls?

"Time for you to shut up before I shut you up," Brant said icily. He flopped back into his chair and grabbed his mug of cider. Artesia sank into her seat slowly, though her eyes never left Reed. He'd set out to get them wound up, to make them question things. Just like Master Orin had warned them. They wouldn't allow themselves to fall for it.

But was he telling the truth?

WREN

Upon his return, a guard informed Wren that Everis was waiting in his room and wanted to speak with him. An odd request, given that Wren would've sought him out anyway. A knot of dread formed in his stomach as he ascended the stairs. He tried to reach for Everis, for the warmth of the connection they shared through their magic, but the flame was barely a flicker.

Something is wrong.

He took the steps two at a time, out of breath as he reached Everis's door and threw it open.

"Ev—"

A moment's glance revealed Everis in bed, seemingly asleep. Wren willed his racing heart to slow as he approached, kneeling on the edge of the mattress and reaching out for him. He didn't so much as stir.

"I hope your day was as eventful as ours," Ivy said from her seat in the corner of the room.

He twisted toward her, eyes narrowed. "What's happened to him?"

She lounged back in her chair, all long limbs, in possession of the lazy grace of a cat. Still, he thought she looked on edge. Defensive. "Your friend likes to tap into the dark arts."

He tensed. "I don't know what you're talking about."

She raised a brow. "Your troops were shaken when they arrived, and I overheard whispers that something happened in the mountains. From what I was able to make out, it seems *you* made a miraculous recovery while one of your men took an unsuspecting turn for the worse."

He slid off the bed to face her properly, shoulders rigid. What did he do? What *could* he do? What was he *willing* to do to keep Everis—and his secret—safe? The words to fix this situation wouldn't come to him.

"Relax," Ivy drawled. "If I'd wanted him dead or in chains, he would be. Instead, you see him as he is, sleeping peacefully. Drugged, but peaceful. I suspect he'll be cross with me when he wakes."

Wren's jaw clenched. "What do you want?"

"I wanted to ensure he wasn't a threat." Ivy stood, sweeping over to the window and opening the shutters. "But Everis appears to be... a bit of a unique breed."

The initial surge of fear that rose at her admission was briefly quelled. "Unique... how?"

"Blood magi are traditionally bound by the same rules we all are. Magic requires a spoken or written element. We need our eyes, our voice, our hands. Everis, it seems, does not."

Cassia's words echoed in his mind. She'd told him Everis had used his magic without uttering a word, and he hadn't believed it. Why would he? Never had he met a magi who could cast without vocalizing or signing. But then again, he'd never spoken to a magi other than Master Orin who had any firsthand knowledge of blood magic... and Ivy seemed to as well.

"I don't understand."

She leaned a shoulder into the wall, eyes fixed out the window. "Before I came to work for Ryland, I was employed by the Citadel. In specific, I was part of a team that investigated reports of rogue magi and inappropriate uses of magic—including blood magic. I had to hunt down, fight, imprison, and try to rehabilitate dozens of them. I know the signs to look for, so when your soldiers' whispers reached my ears, I knew what I was hearing. I engaged Everis in a sparring match and backed him into a corner. Even the trickiest of blood magi, when threatened with death, will slip and reach for the darkness. It's as much a reflex for them as breathing."

Wren narrowed his eyes. "So, you made him afraid for his life... to test him?"

She blinked at him as though the answer to that were obvious. "Oh, should I have just *asked* him?"

"What if you'd been wrong? Would you have just killed him?"

"I bound him with gloriosa vines. Their thorns inject just enough toxin to knock a person out. He'd have fallen unconscious and woken up in short order, no doubt angry with me, and I would've owed him a great apology."

"You..." He stopped, took a steady breath, and counted to five. "If you don't plan on handing him over to the Citadel, what do you want?"

"Oh, I *had* planned on turning him over, make no mistake. But, like I said, he's..." A frown tugged at her brow. "What do you know about the workings of blood magic?"

"What every student learns, I suppose. Sacrificing life in exchange for greater power, but it corrupts. It changes a person." Wren glanced at Everis. He couldn't imagine his sweet Ever being different. The boy who cried over dead baby birds, turning hard and cruel and obsessed with power... It was why he'd turned a blind eye to those peculiar slipups over the years. Until Maliel, Everis had never harmed anyone when utilizing any form of forbidden magic.

"All true but your description is limited in scope. Blood magi do not *have* to kill for their power. The simple shedding of blood from a living creature is the easiest method to draw power from, yes, but I've seen magi who didn't need to. They could leech the life directly from a person to tap into their dark magic, all without spilling a drop."

He swallowed thickly. "And you're telling me Ever can do that?"

"He can do more than that." Ivy beckoned him to follow her. Together, they left Everis sleeping, descended the stairs, and took a few hallways, first to the magi's study and then to a small yard beyond.

The ground looked freshly disturbed, every blade of grass brown and dead, wilted vines drooping lifelessly down the walls. The trees were little more than hollowed-out, ashy husks. Wren stepped forward, trying to place the odd sensation creeping up his spine. Old and familiar and dark...

Suddenly, he was back in Balerno ten years ago, in a plague-ridden village, coaxing a frightened boy from a wardrobe while surrounded by the remnants of his dark magic.

"I don't understand," he repeated softly, even if some part of him secretly did.

Ivy stood at his back. For the first time, she sounded almost sympathetic. "Everis can draw the life out of not only people, but other living things. His connection to his magic is *that* strong... and it makes him that much more lethal."

Tears pricked his eyes.

Ever... What do I do?

"Your friend is dangerous, Wren, but that doesn't mean he's beyond help. For all that I saw today that worried me, I saw hope too."

He blinked to try to clear his vision, but he felt the tears on his cheeks regardless. "What hope?"

Ivy gave a curt nod. "Tell me, is this tree dead?"

Wren pressed his palm flat against the trunk. He could feel the inkling of life still within. It was wounded, but it would survive. "No."

"And am *I* dead?"

"Clearly not. What are you getting at?"

"What I'm getting at is that Everis had the ability to draw the life straight from me. He could've drained me and every plant in this yard to save himself, yet even when presented with impending death, he didn't." She took his shoulders and turned him to face her. "He tapped into his *own* lifeforce before he would touch mine. What a person does to save their own skin is very telling, and what that told me is he still values the life around him. He doesn't see it—even subconsciously—as a tool or a means to an end."

I could've told you that, he thought. "Ever is... He's temperamental, a bit moody sometimes, but he's *good.* Ivy, I swear to you. He's always been so sensitive to the loss of life. No magic can change that. I won't let it."

"Then he's got a better chance at reform than most." She released him and stepped back. "That's why I didn't arrest him or tell anyone. I think it's early enough that we can help him. And..."

"And?"

"I don't know what you're looking for here in Patish, but as repayment for my extreme generosity, I think it's time you told me."

ORIN

Orin sent word to Queen Danica regarding Drake's betrayal and saw to the removal of the fallen guards from the magi tower, then to his own cuts and scratches. Nova appeared unharmed. She stood patiently while he checked her over, and he gave her a generous portion of nuts and fruit for her assistance.

Afterward, he picked his way through the chaos of the tower. Where did he even start in putting it all back together? A few of the other magi had come in, balked at the scene before them, and were now studiously gathering books and papers to at least stack them and ensure they wouldn't become damaged more than they already were.

Lady Imaryllis looked at Orin, concerned, questioning. Orin only shook his head. He wouldn't discuss details with anyone, not yet, not even her. Imaryllis was a steadfast, loyal woman and a good friend, and as far as Orin knew, he could trust her. But a few days ago, he would've said the same thing of Drake in a heartbeat. Until he was *certain* no one else was involved in Drake's plans, Orin would remain quiet.

Eventually, he knew he would need to stop dragging things out. A guard came to tell him the queen was waiting, and the sooner this was dealt with, the better.

A heavy lump of dread formed in his chest as he made his way down to the rarely used dungeons. Brant and Artesia were still there, keeping watch, hunched over their table with a game of cards. Orin noted the bruises and scratches on them both with a frown. Still, they seemed to be in one piece, and Drake hadn't moved from his cell.

Brant and Artesia stood abruptly when they saw him. Everis might've been cross with him for asking the pair to accompany him to confront Drake, but whatever rivalry existed between them and his apprentice, Brant was steadfast and loyal to the late king—even if he was a bit hotheaded—and Artesia was alert, quick, good with a blade, and one of the guards Princess Cassia frequently relied on. He trusted them with this, as much as he could trust anyone.

Orin gave the pair a curt nod and stopped in front of Drake's cell, hands clasped behind his back.

Although he didn't say a word, Drake lifted his head and smiled. "Is that you, Orin?"

"It is," he replied, voice steady and unreadable. "The queen has requested you be brought before her. She will hear your case and pass her judgment."

"So she shall." Drake pushed himself up with some difficulty and approached the cell door. He was just as bruised and scratched up as the guards. Orin supposed getting buried under a pile of bookshelves would do that to a person. A significant black-and-purple welt had formed across one of his cheekbones, and his right eye was likely a lost cause thanks to Nova. Blood had soaked through the blindfold.

At Orin's beckoning, Artesia stepped forward to unlock the cell. She and Brant grabbed Drake by the elbows, leading him out. They ascended the stairs in silence, making their way to the great hall where the king and queen commonly held their meetings with the public.

This might be the last time Orin would have the chance to speak to Drake Reed. He stopped just outside the double doors and turned to his friend, wishing he could remove the blindfold so he could look at him and try to get a sense of what he was thinking and feeling.

"Will you tell me why?" Orin asked softly. "What made you step this far into the darkness?"

Drake inclined his chin. "You ask me that, but you know why, don't you? You did the same thing."

"When I was young and foolish," he admitted, feeling Brant's and Artesia's eyes on him. "I made amends for my mistakes. I learned from them. It isn't too late for you, either; beg the queen's forgiveness, ask her to send you to the Citadel. Serve your time, and you could still walk away from all of this."

Any and all trace of good humor vanished from Drake's face. His mouth formed a thin, tight line. "I will not go back to sub-par magic and parlor tricks, Orin. Tell me honestly, have you ever once felt as alive as you did when you wielded that kind of power? Have you ever been able to reclaim that feeling?"

The words burrowed under his skin and made it prickle.

No. No, he had not.

"That is how it gets you, my friend," he murmured. "And that's how it ruins you. The magic is always hungry."

He turned away, pushed open the doors, and had Drake escorted inside.

Queen Danica stood on the dais awaiting them. A dozen of her personal guards were on hand, which was typically only a formality during meetings like this. Still, the more people present, the better, in case Drake tried anything foolish.

Brant and Artesia pushed Drake to his knees, stepping back a short distance while Orin took up a spot alongside Drake with his hands behind his back. "Your Grace."

Danica frowned, but otherwise her expression remained nearly unreadable. "You say Drake Reed is responsible for my husband's death?"

"He is, by his own admission in front of myself and several of the castle guards." Orin felt Drake shift next to him, displeased. "He poisoned King Faramond's drinks and medication for months leading to his death, and he even put a sleeping draught in Magi Rue Brevil's tea so she would fall asleep the night he died. In addition, he hired the assassin who attacked Princess Cassia."

Danica laced her fingers together, mouth pinched tight. "Where is my daughter? I sent for her."

A guard stepped forward. "She was not in her rooms, Your Grace. No one has seen her today."

Orin cleared his throat. "If you'll forgive me, I took the liberty of having the princess escorted somewhere safe for the time being. Protective custody if you will."

Danica's gaze snapped back to him, bright like fire. "You took my daughter out of the castle without my permission?"

"I had *her* permission," Orin pointed out carefully. "I felt it prudent to ensure her safety, as the next ruler of Midmere."

"You've certainly been busy," Danica said. "Remove Drake's

blindfold."

"Your Grace, I'm not sure that's a wise idea given his—"

"I did not stutter, Master Orin."

Hesitating, Orin reluctantly pulled the scarf from around Drake's eyes. Or eye, rather.

Danica pressed a hand over her heart and gasped. She rushed forward, dropping to her knees in front of Drake and taking his injured face in her hands. "Oh... Drake, what did they do to you?"

"Nothing I won't gladly return tenfold as soon as I'm unbound," Drake said with a smile.

Orin went still.

"Untie him," Danica ordered, rising back to her feet. Two of her guards moved to do so even as Danica's eyes found Orin's again. "And arrest Orin Sorrel immediately."

Orin stared, too stunned to fully process what was happening even as guards were closing in around him, cautiously, as though expecting him to fight back. "Arrest me—*why?*"

Danica inclined her chin with a cool reply. "For conspiracy against the throne, abduction of the princess, and murder of the king."

EVERIS

Everis dreamed of his mother for the first time in years. Her face often felt faded in his memory, and yet in that dream, he saw her with startling clarity. She smiled, got off the floor where she'd lain sick for weeks, and opened her arms to him. He should've been a boy still, yet he towered over her now, head bowed as she brought her warm hands to his face.

"Everything will be all right, sweet boy."

He woke with tears on his cheeks, staring blearily up at the stone ceiling above his bed.

Oh, mercy, everything in his body felt heavy and weak. It took him three tries to roll onto his side and sit up, longer still to swing his legs off the edge of the bed. He didn't hurt, no. He felt… drained.

Ivy tried to kill me.

At least, he thought she had. If that were true, though, why was he here now, in his bed, alive and apparently free of injuries? His head swam too much to think on it. It was all he could do to pitch himself forward, legs shaky and buckling beneath his weight as he struggled to stand.

He needed…

He wanted…

Focus. Focus, Everis.

By the time his bedroom door swung open, he'd clumsily made it halfway across the room in search of his sword, as though he were in any sort of condition to wield it. His fingers wrapped about the hilt, and he tried to slide it from its sheath in the same breath that he whirled around to face whoever had entered.

For a dizzying moment, his vision went blurry and then black. All the air rushed out of him as he crumpled to the floor. Only vaguely did he make out a familiar voice that sounded so very far away.

"Ever!"

Arms came around him and helped him to his feet. He tried to move his legs to assist. Wren managed to get him into the chair his sword had previously occupied. As soon as Everis was still, his sight began to return. The first thing that came into focus were Wren's soft, worried blue eyes. Everis smiled, lifting a hand and tracing unsteady fingertips along Wren's jaw.

"Oh, you're back."

Wren covered Everis's hand with one of his own. "What were you trying to do?"

Everis blinked once, twice. What *had* he been trying to do again? "That woman," he muttered, leaning forward. "She attacked me."

Wren's mouth downturned. "She told me. Look, you're still a bit drugged right now, so you're not going to be getting up and running around just yet. Will you let me help you back to bed?"

"Tried to kill me *and* drugged me?" Everis groaned. "What'd I ever do to her?" He didn't protest as Wren helped him to bed. Truthfully, lying down felt wonderful and eased the spinning sensation.

"We'll talk about it when you're able to think a bit clearer. Why don't you get some more rest?"

"I don't *want* to rest," he protested, reaching for Wren's arm, momentarily panicked that if he dared to close his eyes, he'd open them and Wren would be gone again. "Don't go."

A small smile tugged at Wren's mouth. "I'm not going anywhere, I promise."

Everis made a sound somewhere between disbelief and exhaustion. It wasn't even that he needed to sleep, just that his head was too muddled to think straight, and he kept recalling his mother in his dreams.

As promised, Wren stayed with him. Whether it was for a minute or an hour, he wasn't certain, just that eventually the fog in his head began to clear, and rational thought edged its way in.

Yes. Ivy had attacked him, but he wasn't sure why. He'd blacked out, and she could've killed him, unless—

Was he forgetting something?

"Wren, did I do something?" he whispered, not opening his eyes. "Did I hurt anyone…?"

"No," Wren assured, stroking the hair back from his face until Everis dared to look up at him. "You didn't hurt anyone. Ivy brought you up here."

"And drugged me."

"Well, the vines in the yard did that. She wasn't certain how you'd react when you woke." He cut a thin smile. "Which is fair. You're an absolute bear when you wake up in the mornings."

Despite himself, Everis gave a short laugh. He tried to sit up. Although his head felt clearer, his body still didn't want to cooperate. Only with Wren's help was he able to sit, propped against the headboard. "Why do I still feel so bloody awful?"

Wren retrieved a glass of water from the bedside, lifting it to Everis's lips and helping him drink. "I couldn't say for sure, but I'd wager it has something to do with that gloriosa toxin and tapping into dark magic."

There was nothing accusatory in his tone, but Everis flinched all the same. He swallowed a few gulps of water, found it made him feel a bit better, and slouched back again, eyes focused on his hands in his lap.

"We should talk about it," Wren said.

"Should we? I could tell you it was an accident, but you must be tiring of that excuse by now."

Wren sighed. "I don't feel you were entirely at fault for this, Ever. Ivy overheard some guards talking about what happened with Maliel on the trip here. She used to work for the Citadel, capturing and rehabilitating blood magi. She was testing you—and that meant purposely pushing you into doing what you did."

"I shouldn't be able to be *pushed*," Everis growled. "I should be stronger than that. If I slip up so easily… why am I still here? Why am I not in a cell or on my way to the Citadel?"

Wren touched his face, gentle fingers caressing his cheek, coaxing Everis into looking at him. "She thinks she can help you. Help *us*. I trust her."

"I don't know that I do."

"Will you trust me, then?"

Everis faltered. "I trust you. Doesn't mean I always trust your judgment."

He pinched Everis's side. "You're impossible. Do you want to hear what I've learned?"

"As always, I suspect you'll tell me whether or not I want to hear it," he teased, even if the attempt felt half-hearted.

Wren recounted his return to the castle and his conversation with Ivy. Everything from how he'd sucked the very life from nearly everything in the training yard but hadn't actually killed anything, to how he'd likely used his own lifeforce and that contributed to why he was so exhausted now.

He looked out the window. Hearing it put into words, Everis knew every bit of it to be true. That pulsing anger, that desperate grasp for power... He'd envisioned it flowing into him from everything. Even himself.

"Talk to me," Wren softly pleaded. "I can't help if I don't understand what it's like for you."

"I don't know what it's like," he admitted. "It's complicated."

"At least try. Please?"

Everis bit at the inside of his cheek. "Any time I've tapped into that side of myself, it's felt... necessary. Like protecting Princess Cassia. Protecting myself from Ivy."

"And the bird when we were younger?"

He paused, cheeks reddening. "Like I said, it *felt* necessary. Not something I meant to do, but something that just happened, without me having to say a thing."

"Something you wanted badly enough to trigger it," Wren softly finished, "like when I was dying."

Ever's jaw clenched. "I told you. I couldn't bear to lose you. When I think about it, I can't—" The words caught in his throat, and his vision blurred. He couldn't get the image out of his head of Wren lying there, dying, small and frail and vulnerable. It had been too close. "Saving your life was the one time I purposely called upon it, and I would've sacrificed the entire camp if I'd had to. Nothing in this world matters as much to me as you, Wren. I would burn entire kingdoms to the ground to keep you safe," Everis met Wren's eyes, and the heat in his voice only validated his conviction, "and I would not regret it."

Wren faltered, speechless. He seemed to grasp for words and failed, and Everis tried to swallow the fear of what he might say when he found his voice.

Instead, Wren bridged the gap between them and pressed their mouths together.

Everis had never allowed himself to think of what it would feel like to kiss Wren. Yet the warmth of his lips so insistently against his felt righter than anything ever had. It took no thought at all to kiss him back, to wrap his arms around Wren and drag him closer. He still felt as weak as a kitten. Wren understood, though, all but crawling into his lap, leaning over him as he slumped against the pillows, holding Everis's face between his hands as if he were something delicate.

When Wren drew back, he cradled Everis's cheeks and pressed their foreheads together, voice so achingly soft. "I'm with you, Ever. You aren't alone."

Strange how those few words could make his chest constrict so tightly. Those simple words brought his guilt over Maliel surging to the surface. Wren was so good, so *just*, and Everis knew that the knowledge someone had died to save him had to be eating at him. Never had he wished so much that he were a better man, someone more deserving of Wren. "I'm sorry. I've made things difficult."

Wren gave a soft laugh. "From the day we met. I wouldn't have it any other way."

Everis's eyes fell shut. Despite the exhaustion that weighed so heavily on him, despite the lingering guilt that kept its vice-grip on his heart, he also couldn't recall the last time he had been filled with this level of warmth. Wren shifted, drawing Everis's head to his shoulder, and stroked his long fingers through Ever's messy hair. They remained like that, enjoying the nearness, simply *being*, until Wren gently prodded Everis from bed so he could help him get changed and they could retire properly for the night.

They ended up in Wren's room, bundled beneath layers of thick blankets. Wren held him, and neither of them said much. It wasn't necessary. They were there. They were safe. They were together.

That was all Everis needed to fall into a peaceful sleep.

ORIN

Drake *must be having quite a laugh right about now.*

He'd been bound and placed in the same cell Drake himself had occupied, with a blindfold pulled tight over his eyes. He knelt in the damp straw strewn about, shoulders aching from his arms being restrained. With little else to do, he had plenty of time to think and wonder, to try to figure out how in the world they'd gotten to this point.

Queen Danica and Drake Reed. Working together.

Something told Orin there was more to their relationship than anyone could possibly have known. When had it started? How long had it been going on? Had Drake turned to blood magic because of the queen, or had he used it to sway her? Why would the queen sanction the murder of her own daughter? It was true that the throne was meant to stay with the bloodline while it existed, and that meant Cassia would take her father's place as ruler. Danica would become the queen's right hand, an adviser to help her as she grew into the shoes left for her.

Was that not enough for Danica? Did she want so badly to retain her title as queen that she would kill her own husband and child for it? Even then, with Cassia dead, the throne would pass on to any other living Starling. In other words, Ryland.

Orin heaved a sigh. *Which is why she wanted Ryland framed. With Faramond dead, she could spin it that Ryland wanted the throne and sent an assassin after the princess.* Everis had tossed a wrench into those plans, and since that night, Cassia had been watched over carefully. Another assassination attempt would've been difficult, if not impossible.

Whatever Drake and the queen's initial plan had been, they'd certainly been forced to alter it. He couldn't begin to guess what they would do now. Would Orin be sent to the Citadel? It seemed unlikely. If he were able to spread word about what he'd witnessed here, they'd send a task force to capture or kill Drake for his crimes.

No, it was far more likely Orin would be executed.

The thought left a cold, heavy knot in his stomach. Brant, Artesia, and the other guards had been forced to swear their loyalty to the queen and denounce Orin's actions. It would be said they'd only been following orders and hadn't known any better, that Orin had tricked them. No doubt Danica was now trying to get them to tell her where Princess Cassia had been taken—not that any of them knew.

But he feared for Everis and Wren. When they returned, if they found him locked up—or worse—how would they react? How long before they were bound and thrown in here alongside him? If only he could get a raven to Patish to warn Ryland. He wasn't sure what action, if any, Ryland would take, but he had to try *something*. At the very least, he needed to get a message to Rue and Princess Cassia. The pair were holed up at an inn near the city gates, with instructions to leave at the first sign of trouble. Danica would have men searching the town for her now, and he could only hope the two women could flee before they were found.

Orin made out footsteps coming down the stairs and into the dungeons. He strained to hear as words were exchanged between his guard at the door and whoever had entered.

"No, I don't think so," the guard said, voice rising.

Orin stilled as a struggle ensued, listening to the sounds of boots scuffing against stone, the grunts of a person being attacked, and the thud of a body as it hit the floor. Orin held his breath. Two sets of steps came his way, and a familiar voice greeted him.

"Are you alright, Master Orin?"

He exhaled through his mouth. "I've been better, Gilbert, but I've also been worse."

Someone unlocked the cell door. Not a moment later, the blindfold was pulled from Orin's eyes, and he blinked rapidly in the dim lighting. He saw Gilbert's freckled face twisted in concern as Artesia helped Orin to his feet and removed the shackles from his wrists.

"We don't have much time," Gilbert said. "We need to hurry before they realize what we've done."

Orin stepped out of the cell after them, rubbing his wrists. "And what is it you've done, exactly?"

"Some of your magi friends drugged tonight's meat and mead," Artesia said in amusement. She grinned and gave Gilbert's shoulder a playful punch that was just hard enough to make the lanky man wince. "Not everyone is out, but enough people for us to come get you. So, let's get moving."

They were committing treason, by all rights. If they were caught, Artesia and Gilbert and whoever else was involved would face the same fate as Orin himself. His jaw clenched. Telling them as much would be useless. What was done was done, and they had made their choice.

Orin hurried after the pair, stepping over the guard's unconscious body. Brant awaited them at the top of the dungeon stairs, poised as though he were merely standing guard. When he heard them approach, he looked both ways. "It's clear."

Together, the four of them moved through the darkening halls. The candles should've been lit by now—in fact, that was normally one of Gilbert's jobs. He had a spell to ignite each hallway with a single word. Darkness was better for their escape. They had thought this through in the few hours they'd had.

They crossed through the courtyard, which was just as dark as the castle with the moon hidden behind thick clouds. A figure moved near the gates, and Orin almost faltered until he saw Imaryllis, her smile lighting up her face. She beckoned to them with her free hand, her sword in the other.

"Horses are saddled and waiting for you," she said when they neared. She caught Orin by the elbow, her brows knit in concern. "Are you alright?"

"I'm fine." He clasped her arm and squeezed. Without a shadow of a doubt, he knew that Imaryllis was the one who'd orchestrated this entire plan. "Although now I'm immensely concerned. You know what this means if any of you get caught."

"We do." She gave him a thin smile and nodded at Artesia, Brant, and Gilbert. "Which is why they're going with you. You'll need another magi, and those two will be the prime suspects when the queen wakes up and finds you're gone."

"They're going with me, but you aren't?"

"I can shake off any suspicion." Imaryllis released him and stepped back. "I'll keep an eye on things to the best of my ability and try to slow them down."

Something struck Orin in that moment, a sense of uncertainty and loss, as though he were looking at Imaryllis for the last time. But she was right; she had the greatest potential to help them there at the castle and get word to Patish.

"Please, be safe," Orin murmured. "No unnecessary risks."

The swordsmaster grinned and gave him a salute. "Hurry now. Quit dawdling."

She ushered them through the gates and heaved the doors shut behind them. Orin stared over his shoulder until a nudge from Gilbert prompted him forward.

As promised, four horses were saddled and tethered to posts, waiting for them inside the stables. Orin went straight to his horse—a mare he'd considered his own for the last several years—and hauled himself into the saddle. They made haste from the castle grounds and into the city beyond, knowing they had only so much time before Gilbert's sleeping draught wore off and the castle went on high alert looking for them.

And as soon as they realize I'm no longer in the castle, Orin thought dismally, *they'll start tearing the city apart.*

WREN

He'd never been a particularly heavy sleeper, and in a room so far from home and concerned about his bed companion, Wren woke often. The first few times a noise roused him, he dismissed it as a trick of the wind, the sounds of the old manor settling around them.

This time, when his eyes snapped open, it was different.

Everis was a heavy weight lying half atop him, head upon his shoulder, an arm and one leg slung across Wren's smaller form. Whatever it was he'd heard, it hadn't done a thing to disturb the younger magi.

Wren scanned the room. Nothing. Nothing except the wind, anyway. It had grown chilly, and he'd apparently left the balcony doors open. Untangling himself from Everis—who didn't so much as stir—Wren slid from bed, shivering as his bare feet touched the floorboards. He parted the curtains to let the moonlight spill in and drew the double doors shut.

He caught the reflection of a man in the glass panes and had no time to scream before a gloved hand clamped over his mouth and one of his arms was grabbed and twisted behind his back.

"Quiet, magi," a voice hissed against his ear, muffled by the mask that covered his mouth. "Don't wake your friend. I've brought you the information you wanted."

Wren stilled. He smelled cloves and worn leather. Incense. *Asher's shop*. His shoulders slumped. Only then did the assassin release him and step back.

"Did you really have to sneak into the manor in the dead of night to see me?" Wren asked in a whisper, twisting around.

Now facing the assassin, he recognized those sharp gold eyes and warm, scarred skin.

"Yes," the man said bluntly, keeping his voice low. "I did this as a favor, which means you can work on my schedule."

Wren resisted the urge to roll his eyes. "Of course. What news do you have for me?" When the assassin's gaze flicked warily toward the bed, Wren shook his head. "He's fine, and I'm fairly certain nothing shy of a parade would wake him right now." Which would've been unfortunate had the intruder meant him harm.

The man crossed his leather-clad arms over his chest. "So you say. Anyway, the Court started receiving tentative offers for the lives of the royal family about six months ago. Always through intermediaries, always from people careful not to reveal the client. The fee offered was... well, *very* fair."

Wren frowned. "Then why not take it?"

"Like Asher said, we don't just take any job that falls into our laps," he replied. "We have rules. Lines that are not to be crossed. Every request that makes it past the recipient goes to a vote. The more influential a target, the wider that vote stretches across the Court. Think of the ramifications of murdering an entire royal family, not just for the line of succession, but for everyone. Jobs lost, everyone in the extended royal family a suspect, the upset of an entire kingdom. It could mean *war*. Faramond may've had his share of enemies, but as a whole, his people cared for him and have approved of the job he's done."

"So, a ruler is only removed if—"

"If the chaos caused by overthrowing them is still a better option than allowing them to rule."

Wren sank heavily into a chair by the doors. "So, the Dusk Court turned down the job. Alright. Then what?"

The man shrugged. "The Owl who took it upon herself to accept the job did so without our knowledge. As far as I can determine, she took the contract out of Midmere, not Patish; she hasn't been here in over a year. She would've kept the entire fee herself and never had to work another day in her life. It's admittedly a tempting offer to many, isn't it?"

The Owl. Was that how they referred to themselves? He supposed it had a better ring to it than assassin or killer. "I suppose that depends on whether someone's a member of the Court for the right reasons or not... if there's such a thing as a right reason for murdering a person in their bed."

The assassin gave him a sidelong look, lashes lowered. "Trust me. There is."

There was a trace of something so haunted in his voice that it made Wren falter and stumble over the hundred questions he now had. "At any rate, what do we do from here?"

"We? *We* do nothing, magi. The assassin has been killed. We can't punish her for breaking the rules any more than that."

Wren scoffed. "For a group that claims to care so much about morals, you don't seem concerned about the repercussions of one of your people's actions. Whether she acted on your orders or not, she never would've been privy to the information in the first place if the Court had been better at concealing it."

Anger flashed through the man's eyes, his posture tensing. "Watch your mouth. I was not obligated to help you."

"No? Asher implied that you were."

They locked eyes, unblinking, neither willing to back down. Wren willed his shoulders to remain relaxed, expression easy, confident, but not foolishly so. It was the way he'd witnessed Master Orin handle difficult people countless times over the years. Never overbearing, but stalwart and steady.

Finally, the assassin turned away, taking a moment to calm himself. "Right. What would you have us do if you had your way?"

"Find me the name of who hired that woman," Wren replied. He couldn't keep the tinge of pleading from his voice. "A name. A date. *Anything* for me to go off. Help me prevent this from happening again."

"I will speak to the others. This isn't a decision I can make on my own."

It wasn't what he wanted to hear, but it wasn't a *no* either. Wren took a slow breath. "Of course." As the stranger began to walk for the balcony doors, Wren stood. "Ah—how do I keep in touch with you? Through Asher?"

He opened the doors. "No, not Asher. If you have need of me and it cannot wait, there's an old woman begging for coin in the fisherman's district. Seek her out, give her a single silver, and tell her it feels like a storm's coming, and she should get inside. She'll take it from there."

Wren rolled his gaze to the ceiling. Such dramatics. Everis would've found it hilarious if he were awake. "And then what? How do I ask for *you* specifically?"

The man paused, seeming to debate his options for a long minute. "Faulk," he finally said. "Ask for Faulk."

ORIN

Brant had spent his early years in service of the crown as a city guard. He'd been a night guard, patrolling the streets in the dark hours. He recounted this to Orin as the young man led them through the darkest of streets and alleys, avoiding the main roads that would be lit by oil and magical lamps. The fewer people who spotted them, the better.

Their destination, Orin told them, was an inn near the eastern city gates. They left their horses in the care of a sleepy-eyed stable boy they had to rouse from his bed. This time of night, only a faint flicker of light greeted them from a front window, but Orin tried the door and found it unlocked. It swung open without a sound.

No innkeeper sat behind the counter, not that he'd expected one. Orin had chosen this place, and he was acquainted with the husband and wife who ran it. He'd made charms and potions for them over the years to battle the husband's chronic ailments. As loath as he'd been to call in a favor that would endanger an innocent couple, he'd needed somewhere safe for Princess Cassia. Someplace close to the city limits, so she was within easy distance of escape if necessary. He feared that the need to flee would arise sooner rather than later.

Orin headed straight for the stairs then brought them to a door at the far end of the hall, lifted a hand, and rapped lightly three times in a quick, rhythmic pattern. After a moment of silence, the door cracked open, and Rue peered out. Her eyes went wide at the sight of Orin, somewhere between surprised and relieved as she yanked the door back further to allow them in.

The room was neither large nor lavish. There was scarcely space for a bed, a small dresser, a wash table, and maybe enough floor leftover that they could all sleep without lying on top of each other. Princess Cassia rose from the bed, pulling her robe tightly around herself.

"Master Orin! We hadn't expected you back so soon. With friends, I hope?"

"With friends," Orin agreed.

Artesia stepped around him, bowing her head to the princess. "We're here to help look after you, my lady."

The sight of a familiar face made Cassia smile, albeit briefly. "And yet I have a feeling this visit doesn't bode well. What's happened?"

Orin realized then just what it was he had to tell Cassia. She was already mourning her father's death, but now she'd have to carry the knowledge that her mother and a magi she'd trusted were behind it... and that they wanted *her* dead, too. He was still trying to reconcile that with his own head. If it made so little sense to him, surely it would make even less sense to Cassia.

He took the princess's hands between his own. He remembered her as a baby, the first time Faramond had proudly brought her to see him in the magi tower. Orin had taken her hands then too and marveled at how tiny they were in his, how even at only a few days old, the infant was the striking image of her father.

"Your Grace... What I must tell you will not be easy to hear."

Cassia met his eyes without flinching, jaw tight. "I'm a grown woman. I can handle it."

He knew she could, but that didn't mean he wanted her to have to. With a sigh, Orin bowed his head. "Drake Reed was behind your father's death," he said after a long moment. "But... I'm afraid he wasn't acting purely of his own volition."

Something akin to uncertainty crept into Princess Cassia's eyes, along with a resigned sort of sadness. She pulled her hands back, hugging herself as she turned to the window overlooking the city streets below. "My mother."

"You knew?"

"No," she admitted quickly. "But I... I wondered. I don't know why, exactly. Something just seemed *off* about the whole thing. Mother urged me to not take the throne yet. To let her serve as queen for the time being until I was 'older and more mature.' She began to question me on it the very night Father died, and I'd thought then how odd it was. His body wasn't even cold, and she was concerned over who would rule? As though a few more days would make a difference."

"She likely wanted to use your grief to coerce you into making her a promise that wouldn't remove her from power," Gilbert said. "Though what I cannot say I grasp is *why*. She may not be the queen regent, but she'd still have been the queen mother and held a respectable place in the people's eyes."

The raspy, guttural words of the dead assassin rang in Orin's head. *Queen Danica will be next.*

She hadn't meant that Danica would be next to die, but that she'd be next for the throne. Not that he felt comfortable relaying that information just yet. The last thing they needed to hear was that he'd resurrected a dead woman for vague answers that had led him nowhere.

Orin stepped forward, standing at Cassia's shoulder. "I don't know that her reasoning is of importance now. I suggest we leave, and leave soon, Your Grace. We'll hurry to Patish and ask for Duke Ryland's assistance with whatever needs to happen next."

Cassia looked at Orin's reflection in the window, her own face drawn and sad. "Are you so certain my uncle will help us?"

As much as Orin wanted to reassure her, he wouldn't lie. "Do I think he'll rally his armies and lay siege to the city? Maybe not. But I don't believe he would leave you in harm's way, either. He may be our only hope."

"Couldn't we petition the people?" Artesia asked. "If they see the princess hasn't been kidnapped, if she speaks up, surely the citizens will stand behind her, and the other knights will turn on Danica and Reed."

"A possibility, but I suspect they've thought of that and planned accordingly." Orin shook his head. "I urge all of you not to underestimate Drake. He's been a few steps ahead of me this entire time. Had he not grown impatient and slipped up by drugging Rue's tea, I would no doubt still be in the dark."

"Do we leave now?" Cassia asked. "While it's dark?"

All of them looked at Orin. He took a breath and closed his eyes, thinking. There were benefits to it, yes. Leaving under the cloak of nightfall, getting a head start. But it wouldn't be *much* of a start. All it would take was one wrong turn, one fast rider to catch up with them...

What will Drake expect us to do?

His old friend knew him too well. He knew Orin's top priority would be getting Cassia to safety. He would know they'd leave as soon as possible. Which meant...

He opened his eyes. "I think we should wait."

Gilbert frowned. "Master? I thought you said..."

He stroked a hand down his beard in thought. "I did, but I'm reluctant now. They'll expect us to make a run for it and may focus most of their attention on catching up with us. But if we wait a few days, try to keep our eyes and ears open... We can lie low until their attention is so focused elsewhere that we can slip by unnoticed." He paused then, observing the trusting faces of his companions. "But I'm not the leader here, I hope you realize. It's only a suggestion. I'm a magi, not a strategist." Oh, he wished Imaryllis had joined them. She would've known what to do.

There and then, Cassia was in charge. They could advise her all they wanted, but the decisions would be hers to make. Orin met her gaze, knowing that such a burden wouldn't be easy. She was still a young woman, working through so much grief and betrayal, and now to be told she needed to set all that aside to lead them if they wanted to survive...

Cassia stared back at him, her mouth pinched tight as resolve settled into her soft features. "I think Master Orin makes a good point. We'll wait here for a few days if our hosts are amiable to that. Is there any way we might get a letter to Patish?"

"Imaryllis said she was going to try," Gilbert said. "But I suspect the queen will be watching any incoming and outgoing messages carefully."

"If anyone can think of a way around it, it would be Imaryllis," Orin said. "For now, let's see about getting us some plain clothes, something to eat, and some rest. I fear we're going to need it."

WREN

Ivy had breakfast delivered to Wren's room the next morning. Everis was still fast asleep, scarcely budging even when the serving boy knocked and rolled the cart into the room, so Wren dined alone and left plenty for Ever for when he finally woke.

Sleep hadn't come easily after Faulk left. Oh, he'd crawled back into bed and curled up with Everis again, warm and safe, but too many worries plagued his thoughts. If only he had a way to speak to Master Orin. A raven was out of the question, given the nature of the information he wanted to share. Too many hands that might intercept it. Unfortunate, because his teacher would know how to put him at ease. He would handle all of this with much more grace and care than Wren knew how to. Orin often said he foresaw Wren graduating from his apprenticeship within the next few years, but Wren didn't share that confidence. He felt so very far from where he wanted to be.

After eating, Wren sat near the open balcony door with a cup of tea, watching the sun glitter off the ocean in the distance and trying to sort through things on his own. If everything worked out, Faulk would have a name for him. Any sort of lead was better than nothing. If he could question whoever had hired the assassin, he could trace it back to the source.

Assuming they know the source. Whoever it was, they were clearly being very careful.

That was a scenario he didn't want to think about. It would mean another dead end, and he wasn't certain where he would go from there.

He could also speak to Ivy again, to see if she was harboring any information she'd not previously let them in on. Now that she was privy to their secrets and had proven (to some degree, anyway) that they could trust her, he hoped he might learn *something* new. Now that they were more confident that Ryland wasn't behind the assassination attempt, they could ask Ryland about it directly. Hopefully, he wouldn't be too offended that they'd ever suspected him in the first place.

Everis finally stirred. He shifted and sighed, long limbs stretching out, his mess of dark hair appearing from beneath the blankets drawn over his head. Even as he sat up, he looked no less tired than he had the previous night, but he had a smile for Wren despite that. "Morning."

"More like late morning, early afternoon." Wren smiled against the rim of his cup. "Still some breakfast, though it's a bit cold now, I'm afraid."

"I don't care. I'm starving." Everis dragged himself from the bed. At least he was moving easier, a little more like his usual self. "Why'd you let me sleep so late?"

"You needed it. You were dead to the world. We even had a visitor last night, and you slept right through it. Quite rude, actually."

Everis pulled up a chair across from him, pulling the food cart closer. "Ivy?"

"No, his name is Faulk, the man from the—" He paused at the odd look the other magi gave him. "Ah, I haven't had much of a chance to catch you up, have I?"

"Might be a good time to start while I'm stuffing my face," Everis said, already wolfing down a piece of honied toast.

Wren filled him in on his previous day's outing, about the blacksmith and Asher and the assassin—which had Everis giving him a sidelong look that spoke worlds of displeasure that Wren had gone out alone to begin with.

"An assassin's guild," Everis repeated. "And this assassin attacked you."

"Well, yes, but—"

"I told you we shouldn't have split up. We ought to be working together, not flouncing off on our own merry ways."

Wren sighed. So, Everis was still sour over being left behind. It had been necessary. Wren felt that now more than ever. The fight between Faulk and Everis would've turned ugly very quickly; Ever wouldn't have tried to resolve matters diplomatically. It would have been fire and brimstone, ask questions later.

"At any rate, that assassin—Faulk—he's the one who dropped by last night."

Everis scowled. "How did he even get in here?"

"Well, I mean, he's an assassin. That likely includes being sneaky. I suspect he's just good at his job?"

Sighing, Everis sat back, palming a few grapes from the tray to pop them into his mouth. "So, what now? We just... wait on this Faulk? For how long?"

"I don't know. I figured I'd give it two or three days, and if he hasn't come to see me, I'll seek him out again."

Everis chewed while staring out the balcony doors. "I have a bad feeling about all of this."

"To be fair, you have a bad feeling about most things. You're a highly skeptical man." Wren smiled.

Everis's grim expression didn't waver. "It's not just that. Don't you sense it? Something is just... *off*. I can't place it. I feel as though there's something right in front of our faces and we're completely missing it."

Admittedly, Wren felt the same. Had felt it ever since they left Midmere. Some sort of niggling sensation in the back of his mind that they shouldn't have left at all, that they were chasing ghosts in this city. He'd shrugged it off after finally finding some leads about Princess Cassia's assassin, but it hadn't soothed the uncertainty in his gut. "Would it put your mind at ease if we sent a raven to Master Orin, just to ask how things are? It will take a few days, but it might make us feel better."

For a moment, Everis seemed to slip away from him, his eyes distant and even his breathing going still. There was no red glow, no rush of darkness, yet somehow the distance between the two of them felt so vast. Wren reached across the cart to touch his arm. Everis inhaled sharply. In an instant, he was back again. "I don't know. Something tells me he wouldn't get it."

"That sounds ominous," Wren began to say. He paused when he caught the sound of footsteps outside the room.

Then came a knock, followed by Ivy's voice. "I'm coming in." She didn't wait for a response before opening the door to let herself in. If it surprised her to see the pair of them still in their nightclothes together, it didn't register in her expression.

Everis's face wrinkled up, but he managed a curt, "Morning."

Ivy stopped a few feet away, hands clasped behind her back. "Good to see you up and moving. Are you up to putting proper clothes on? Your boyfriend may not mind your manner of dress, but the rest of the castle may."

Everis's cheeks went apple red. "What for? Are we going somewhere?"

"We have work to do, apprentice." The arch of her eyebrows accented her patronizing tone. "Or has Wren not discussed the concern of your magic with you yet?"

"I have. I just thought he could use some rest first."

"Quite the opposite, actually. Better that we push him while he's exhausted. There's less room for him to blow things up." She smiled, amused by that idea.

Everis got out of bed. Ivy likely wouldn't have noticed, but Wren caught how he wobbled ever so slightly on his feet and the careful manner in which he walked across the room to fetch clothes. "And what, exactly, are we doing to train?"

"First, I have some texts for you to read. Second, focus. Meditation. Exercises to keep your mind calm so you don't lose yourself in the heat of anger."

"Well, temperamental as he is, Ever isn't usually angry when he… slips up."

Ivy pointed in Wren's direction. "Stop that. Tiptoeing around this helps no one. Call it what it is. Everis has been tapping into dark magic, and he doesn't know how to control it."

Everis had begun to pull his nightshirt off over his head, and he startled, the garment balled up in his hands as he looked at Ivy. "Does that mean I *can* learn to control it?"

She shrugged. "That remains to be seen. So, hurry up, both of you. We have a long day ahead of us."

EVERIS

Ivy set him out in the withered training yard with several old scrolls so brittle he feared cracking the parchment and a tome as thick as his forearm. They were from her own collection, she told them. Things she'd kept from her time working at the Citadel. In return, he reluctantly handed over the book on blood magic he'd brought from home, and she disappeared into the study to go through it.

Wren sat beside him beneath the shade of a tree and an overcast sky, accompanied by the smell of rain. At least the company was agreeable, and Wren would likely gain more from reading all this than he would. Still, the documents contained many things Everis's teachers had never taught him. Not rituals and spells like his book had contained, but genuine history and records by and about the users of blood magic from hundreds of years ago.

"It didn't use to be forbidden," Wren murmured. They looked up, eyes meeting. "This says blood magi even used to sit on the council at the Citadel."

Everis frowned. "What changed?"

"I don't know." Wren flipped through the pages again. "It's like there's this gap in history. Maybe Ivy can fill it in for us."

167

"What about Master Orin? Do you think this is something he knows?"

With a shake of his head, Wren closed the book. "I can't imagine he'd have kept something like that from us. Do you?"

Everis didn't want to think so. Learning this history would have brought him such comfort growing up, to be assured he wasn't broken or defective for this innate connection he couldn't cut himself off from. Delicately, he rolled up the parchment and set it aside. "Perhaps. Unless he worried that I'd get the wrong idea and think it was permission for me to delve further into it."

"If Master Orin thought you that inept, he'd have not kept you as his apprentice."

Everis wanted to believe that.

They spent the afternoon poring over the texts, reading and rereading, hoping to learn something new. Astra was the first name to truly catch Everis's eye. She was a magi who didn't need to speak to cast her spells. Astra didn't have to tap into the magic that was present in an environment; she could draw it from the life all around her. No bloodshed, no death, unless she willed it. There was an entire page dedicated to the good Astra had done with her magic: the people she'd healed, the wars she'd ended, the tyrants she'd helped to overthrow.

And then, abruptly, all mentions of Astra ceased.

Everis flipped back through the pages in case he'd missed something about her death or retirement from the Citadel. Nothing. *Strange.*

Ivy returned shortly before supper and took a seat before them. "Well, that book was informative... I suppose. If you're into that sort of thing."

Everis scowled. "What's that supposed to mean? The spells in it are legitimate. I used one to save Wren."

"I'm not so sure about that." Ivy lounged back, her hands braced behind her. "I want to try an experiment."

"That bodes well," Wren mumbled.

She ignored him, pulling a piece of parchment from her pocket and offering it. "Read this. Cast it."

Everis took the page. There was nothing written except a short, three-word incantation. The words weren't familiar to Everis, written in a language likely long dead, but any spell so short ought to be ridiculously simple.

"This looks like a novice spell," he said.

Ivy inclined her chin, gazing skyward. "Then you should have no problem casting it, hm?"

Everis sighed and set the paper before him. He closed his eyes, felt the magic still present even in this now-barren training yard, and spoke the three ancient words loud and clear.

Nothing.

Not so much as a pull of magic, not a single thread for him to grab. Everis opened his eyes, frowning at the paper. Wren and Ivy's eyes locked on him, and his cheeks warmed with embarrassment that such a simple spell could be so beyond him.

"Are you sure you wrote it correctly?" Wren asked.

Ivy studied Everis in something akin to fascination. "I did. Now, I'm going to ask you to perform something without an incantation. Visualize what needs to happen and go from there."

Everis glanced at Wren, who shrugged. It seemed a tall order. He'd proven he didn't need to use verbal incantations or hand signs, but that had always been with his dark magic, put out there in the heat of the moment and coated in fury or fear.

Ivy pointed to one of the tree root husks snaking lifelessly across the ground between them. "I want you to grow something from that. A sprout, a flower, doesn't matter."

He blinked. "But..."

"It's an experiment, apprentice. Just do it."

Sighing, Everis brought his hands over a portion of the root. When he closed his eyes and *focused*, he could sense that it wasn't dead, that he hadn't truly killed it the day before. However, the life he felt shivering within it was a flicker where it should've been a fire. He swallowed the nagging guilt and visualized the life still within the tree, trickling down from the trunk into every branch and leaf, every withered root. Not just before him, but buried deep beneath the ground. He took it a step further; he envisioned those roots entangled with the other roots to other trees, with the grass and ivy and flowers. That system could've stretched across the entire yard. Not any one entity, but a cohesive system that flowed and worked together.

Grow.

In his mind's eye, he grasped hold of a silvery thread before him, drawing it to his chest, navigating the mana through himself and into the surrounding environment. He opened his eyes, centering on the root. They felt heavy and tired again, yet for a few moments, his body thrummed with the remnants of energy. It was not so great and powerful as dark magic, but he found it comforting and warm.

Beside him, Wren gasped.

There was not one sprout, but many poking from the tree root. Across the entire yard, the grass had sprouted anew, and the beginnings of leaves had formed on every tree. It was a subtle change, to be certain, but no longer did the yard look as though they had razed it to the ground. It looked like a forest coming out of a winter thaw, renewed.

A slow smile spread across Ivy's face. "Well, you didn't need to show off."

He flexed his hands, still tingling with magic, though it had begun to fade. "Growth spells aren't exactly difficult."

"I couldn't do what you just did," Wren pointed out. "Not without a lot more focus and an incantation."

Ivy retrieved the parchment and held it up. "This was a growth spell, designed to do what you just did on your own. Well, not quite so glamorous, but you get the idea. Do you want to give it another try?"

Everis frowned. He didn't see a point in humiliating himself yet again, but they were watching him expectantly, as though he were some lab experiment. He squirmed, sighed, and held his hands over the root again and repeated the spell aloud.

This time, the sprouts beneath his hands grew, forming small buds that eventually blossomed into tiny flowers. Everis drew back, frown deepening. Wren scratched a hand down his jaw, thoughtful, like he was on the precipice of understanding what had just happened. "Fascinating."

"What?" Everis looked from him to Ivy and back again. "What's fascinating? Why did it work that time?"

"The spell didn't work the first time, because you couldn't envision what it did," Ivy explained. "You could do the spell once I told you what it was, and then even with no incantation at all. You only need to *imagine* what you want your magic to do, Everis."

Everis gazed down at the scattered blossoms. What Ivy said rang true; he could remember struggling with recreating spells and potions in books when he did not know what the outcome would be. He couldn't experiment just to see what something would do. Wren had that talent; he did not.

"The same goes for my dark magic?" he asked quietly, recalling the night in Princess Cassia's room. What he'd experienced then had been a brief but thrilling explosion of power, created without words, without writing, without gestures, and with a freshly dead guard's spilled blood a few floors down. He'd pictured the assassin being thrown off him. His magic had made that happen.

"Likely." Wren laid a hand on his arm. "This is new for all of us, Ever.

No one's been allowed to experiment with this kind of magic before. At least, not in any research I've ever come across."

Ivy interjected, "There was one."

Everis glanced at the book beside him. "Magi Astra."

"That would be her." Ivy drew up her legs, elbows coming to rest upon her knees. "It might be possible there are others too, but that they've been silenced by the Citadel or else hiding their unique abilities out of fear of retaliation."

"Do you know what happened to Astra?" Everis asked. "These texts talk about her, but then it's like she vanishes from them completely."

"Most records of Astra have been long since sealed away in the Citadel archives."

"But you worked for the Citadel, so..."

Ivy's smile slipped. For the first time he'd met her, she looked at odds with herself. Uncertain. "I will tell you what I've read, but know that I tell you this in confidence. Restricted information from the archives is not meant to be shared abroad."

Everis gave a thin smile. "It's a shame you don't know some big, dark secret of mine."

"That's the only reason I'm willing to share." With a sigh, she continued. "Magi Astra sat on the Council for years. She was well-known and well-loved for the work she did. Her magical abilities could be... questionable, at times. Astra could sacrifice animals to boost the power of a spell, and on the battlefield, the spilled blood made her a force to be reckoned with. She didn't need incantations. She was *powerful*. Certainly more powerful than any other singular member on the Council.

"The official transcripts from the archives say that the Council caught Astra making human sacrifices, and perhaps it's true. But I also came across a journal of a past councilwoman. In it, she mentioned Astra only briefly, but the implications of her words were that the Council feared how strong Astra had become and executed her. They felt her mere existence upset the balance of the Citadel."

Wren balked. "They punished her because her magic was more powerful than theirs? If there's a trick to casting without needing spells, wouldn't the Citadel *want* to learn more about it?"

She shrugged. "They probably tried. Maybe it's something they couldn't learn. Maybe they felt it was too risky to bother. Maybe they were simply jealous. There's no telling. What I can say of the Citadel now is that there are many magi who are brilliant, talented, powerful, and kind. Maybe even most of them, but..."

But not all of them, Everis finished in his head.

Corruption ran through every government, monarchy, and large organization he'd ever learned about in Everis's history lessons. Why would the Citadel be any different? Being a magi hardly made someone a good person by default.

His head hurt. This was so much to wrap his mind around. It had been a while since he'd craved Master Orin's advice so deeply or even a hand upon his shoulder, giving it a reassuring squeeze. Orin would've had answers. Or if he didn't, he would've found them.

As though sensing his need for comfort, Wren placed a hand over his and laced their fingers together. "What are you thinking?"

Everis swallowed the lump of uncertainty in his throat. A lot of thoughts raced through his mind, far too many to point to any one or two. Nothing except, "I'm really missing home right about now."

THE SCRIBES

THE BASICS OF MAGIC, VOLUME I

Some magi have formed the ability to cast spells as they carve it into a material such as metal or wood, imbuing the object with a magical property that can be called upon later with little to no preparation time and no verbal casting. Some magi are skilled enough at this trade that they can create lasting charms powerful enough to sustain themselves even when not in the magi's possession. Such magi are often referred to as scribes, and their abilities are highly sought after in industries such as blacksmithing.

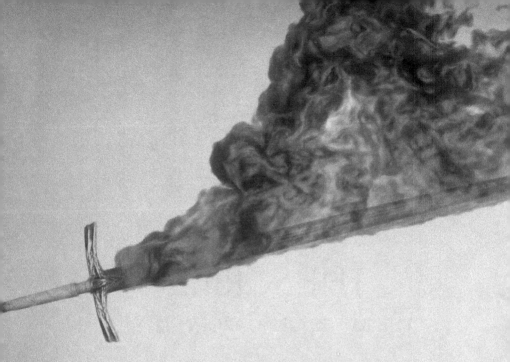

IMARYLLIS

The castle was in chaos. Tension rang through every hallway, the queen's foul temper seeping into every stone. Gilbert's sleeping draught had been a brilliant idea, executed with speed and precision he ought to be proud of. Imaryllis had seen that they placed the draught in nearly every dish and pitcher of mead and ale served at dinner that night, including those meals brought to the guards stationed on duty. Imaryllis herself had sat at the table, observing, watching as the first few nodded off and others realized something was amiss. The swordsmaster pretended to be under the effects herself, not wanting any suspicion thrown on her after the fact.

The queen had locked herself up in her quarters that evening and refused food and drink, but that was fine. She wasn't the true target. Imaryllis had only needed Drake to fall asleep. That was all. He could've been apprehended along with the queen. Cassia would've been free to return to the castle.

But Drake, toward the head of the table in the seat of honor, had not laid down his head. He'd sworn and risen to his feet, unsteady, bracing himself against the table. He'd stumbled from the hall. Imaryllis had held her breath, waiting several minutes before she got up to follow.

Drake was gone.

Wherever he'd slinked off to, he'd undoubtedly realized he needed to get himself somewhere safe before the draught could take full effect. She hadn't been in a place to hunt for him just then, either; her priority had been freeing Orin and getting him out of the castle. Afterward, she hurried to the raven's tower, made quick work of getting a letter attached to one of the birds, and sent it off to Patish.

She'd returned to the table to make sure she was there when everyone began to rouse and to witness the queen's ire after the fact. Danica looked at everyone with disdain and mistrust—particularly the magi. She was no fool. She had to know that if given the choice, many of the magi in the castle would side with Orin. Fear kept them in place.

To no one's surprise, Drake summoned them all to the magi's tower before the sun had barely risen. Drake was alert, while others were still trying to shake off the effects of the sleeping potion. Imaryllis feigned the same fatigue. Seeing Drake stand before them in the spot Master Orin usually occupied during their meetings made her insides twist in fury and betrayal.

If only I'd had time to hunt him down last night. All this could be over.

"As I'm sure we're all aware by now," Drake drawled, hands clasped behind his back, watching them with his one good eye, "last night, a plot was hatched to free the traitor Orin Sorrell from the dungeons. Magi Gilbert Galliel appears to be missing, and as we know one of his specialties is potions, I think it's safe to say he helped orchestrate the whole thing.

"Two of the guards have also failed to report for duty, two who attacked me in this very tower. Six to one is hardly a fair fight, but I digress."

He smiled at his fellow magi almost fondly. Almost. It felt too wolfish for Imaryllis's liking.

"Which is why I've asked you all here. I am to take over the role of Master for the city, at the queen's behest. I thought I would give all of you the opportunity to ask any questions you have so that I may lay your worries to rest."

The group shifted uncomfortably, looks exchanged between friends and colleagues. It was Mace Huntly who stepped forward first. He was broad-shouldered and tall, not the sort who looked like a scholar and record-keeper. His voice was a low rumble, and yet it held the resonance of authority that made everyone stop to listen when he spoke.

"Rumor has it you've delved into the blood arts," Mace announced. It was what everyone was thinking, but were too afraid to say. "I don't know about the rest of this lot, but I wouldn't let a blood magi lead me to the dinner table, let alone in affairs of the kingdom."

Drake tipped his head. "You've studied our history, Mace. Surely you know the power this magic can unlock."

Mace's gaze did not waver. "I do. And I know the cost of that power is far too great."

"A sacrifice some of us are strong enough to make," Drake said, a dangerous lilt honing the edge of his words.

"Except the sacrifice isn't yours to make, is it? I doubt those whose lives were stolen for your powers were so willing."

Slowly, the smile dropped from Drake's face, replaced by something dark. A red, sinister glint flickered across his eyes, sending a shiver straight down Imaryllis's spine. They'd all learned about blood magic and those who used it. The Citadel drove that into their brains from an early age. But never had she met a blood magi face to face—nor had she witnessed the power they could wield.

Surely, if they all stood up against Drake as a group, he wouldn't stand a chance. He could be injured just like any of them. A sword through his heart would kill him the same as any other man. It was trying to catch him off guard to get close enough to strike that would present an issue.

Imaryllis rested her hand atop the hilt of the sword at her hip. Her blade had never failed her before. She'd embedded it with charms and spells, etched into the very metal itself, and she had confidence she stood a change of driving home a killing blow before Drake knew what hit him.

"I'm afraid," Drake said coldly, "that you are more alone in your way of thinking than you realize." He lifted a hand and gestured. From the small group, several of the remaining magi stepped forward. Beatty, Quinton, and Arabella all dropped to their knees before Drake, heads bowed in something akin to reverence.

Imaryllis's blood cooled. The only ones left standing were Mace, Pava, Carlisle, and herself. The scales were suddenly not so much in their favor.

"As you can see, I've already acquired a few students of my own. Their knowledge is still limited, but I assure you, they know enough." With a smile, Drake reached out, patting Beatty atop his blond head as though he were a loyal hound. "I'm offering you the same opportunity. Learn from me. Help me track down the princess and the traitors."

Mace's face grew red in fury. "The Citadel will never allow this," he spat. "*I* will not allow it. Orin is no traitor, Reed. *You are.*"

Drake moved like lightning. He closed the distance between him and

Mace in the blink of an eye. He split open the old man's throat before any of them could react.

Mace's eyes went wide, mouth agape but silent. Carlisle cried out in agony, catching Mace's body as he sank to his knees. Blood spilled down the front of his soft brown robes. "Mace, Mace—please, no…"

Drake wiped the dagger off on his sleeve. A sudden darkness blanketed the room, and with the spilled blood, Drake's eyes burned deep and fierce. Death and blood empowered him. Every person he struck down would only strengthen him, give him more magic to pull from.

Drake regarded Carlisle, licking his lips. "Now, you see, if you had knowledge of my powers, you would know that I have the ability to save him."

Carlisle's head snapped up, voice wavering. "You've lost your mind. If you can save him, then save him!"

Drake smiled. "No."

Mace lifted a shaky hand, covering one of Carlisle's. It fell away, and he went still, dark eyes staring off into nothing. Carlisle let out a howl of fury and lurched to his feet, lunging for Drake. Imaryllis wasn't close enough to grab for him, to beg him not to let his temper get the best of him. This wasn't a fight they could win right now.

Drake stopped the young magi with a palm to his chest, and a phrase uttered beneath his breath. Something in a language older than anything Imaryllis was familiar with, something that rang dark and dangerous. Carlisle's eyes went wide and his jaw slack. The sound of cracking bones filled the room, a shattering sort of sound that made her skin positively crawl. Carlisle staggered back, choking on his own blood where he hit the ground beside Mace. The entirety of his chest cavity looked wrong. Caved in. Blood leaked from the corners of his eyes and from his nose.

Imaryllis's fingers wrapped tightly around the hilt of her sword. Of every magi present, she held the best chance facing Drake in combat, and yet she'd only stood there, struggling to weigh the options of what to do, paralyzed by uncertainty.

Useless, she scolded herself, staring at the bodies of Mace and Carlisle.

Mace had been here longer than most of them, strict but wise and kindhearted despite his grumpy demeanor. Carlisle was his apprentice, one of the youngest magi at the castle; impetuous, stubborn, but eager to learn. They'd been her peers, her friends. Her eyes burned with the threat of tears, and she fought them back, breathing slow and even. There would be time for justice and revenge later and grief later.

Drake licked his lips and turned to Imaryllis and Pava. Pava drifted closer to Imaryllis's side as though seeking refuge there. Any chance for action was long past. Blood had been spilled, fueling Drake's magic, and he had others on his side. Imaryllis would stand no chance against them, and Pava was not known for her offensive magic.

"Pava? Lady Imaryllis? Did you have any further questions?"

Every muscle in her body screamed for her to attack, no matter that it would be a battle swiftly lost. Her jaw clenched. "With all due respect, Reed, you are no Master in the eyes of the Citadel, and in the absence of a Master, all magi are to report directly to their kingdom's leader. That is what I intend to do until I'm told otherwise."

Pava tensed beside her, a look of horror passing over her features at Imaryllis's defiance. Yet Drake's smile didn't waver. "Fair enough. Go on then. I'm certain the queen is expecting you."

He dismissed them with a wave, turning to his apprentices and instructing them to *remove the trash* from the tower. Imaryllis spun on her heel and marched out, fury simmering beneath her skin, knowing if she did not leave now, her temper would get the best of her.

Pava kept pace with her as they crossed the training yard. She was older than Imaryllis, well into her fifties, though she could've passed for ten years younger. Her hair was a mousy brown, her skin fair and freckled, only the hints of age lines at the corners of her eyes. The pair of them had never been close, though it wasn't because of animosity, rather they simply had nothing in common. Now, though, it seemed they would have no choice but to stick together. They were the only magi left in the castle who saw through Drake Reed.

"He could've killed you," Pava whispered.

"No. He would've killed me if I'd pledged my allegiance to him," Imaryllis corrected. "He would've seen it for the lie it was."

The older woman caught her by the sleeve, drawing her to a halt. "And yet what point was there to it? Clearly, he's working under the queen's orders. Danica will simply command us to fall in line."

"I am a woman of my word." The swordsmaster smiled, thin and humorless. "I said I would defer to our ruler."

Pava paused for a beat, gleaning her meaning. "But Danica—"

"Danica is not our rightful queen," Imaryllis said. "Cassia is."

ORIN

When he'd first left Rue and Cassia at the inn, Orin had instructed Rue to place wards discreetly around the building. They would alert her if someone with malicious intent entered and grant the magi some time to get the princess to safety. Now, Orin intended to take it a step further. Simple wards by a novice magi weren't enough.

In the early morning hours, Orin took Gilbert outside. They parted ways, armed with bits of charcoal, and penned intricate diagrams along each wall of the building and beneath every window. Orin had worried they would be too noticeable for anyone passing by. For that reason, he also made his way down the quiet streets, repeating the symbols elsewhere. If it was enough to throw Drake off their trail when he came sniffing around, that was all that mattered.

He lingered over the last of the spells.

You could make it stronger.

You could make it so, so much stronger.

Orin thrust the voice aside and straightened up. He refused to be swayed by the darkness again. If he caved to the desire now, it would make him no better than Drake himself.

After his task was complete, he met up with the others back in Cassia's room. The princess had curled up alongside Rue and gone to sleep. Artesia and Brant sat side by side on the floor, holding a quiet vigil over them. Orin moved with care so as not to disturb the sleeping women, sinking onto the floor for lack of anywhere else to sit.

Gilbert took up residence near the door and sighed. "Do you really think all that will do any good?"

Orin drew his knees up, elbows resting atop them. He closed his eyes. "Perhaps. Perhaps not. It certainly won't hurt, however. Between those wards and Nova, we ought to have fair enough warning if anyone we'd rather avoid comes this way."

"Nova?" Artesia asked.

"His bird," Gilbert said. "The white one with the strange eyes."

Everyone in the castle had seen Nova at some point. If she wasn't in the tower or flying around the training yard, then she was perched on or near Orin. A white raven was a difficult thing to miss.

"Always thought something was strange with that one," muttered Brant. "Hasn't she been around forever? How long do birds live, anyway?"

Gilbert shrugged. "Can't say that I know."

Orin took a deep breath. "Ten, fifteen years at the most, if they're healthy."

Gilbert considered that with a frown. "But she's been with you longer than I've been here, and that's been…"

"Longer than fifteen years," Orin agreed, voice soft. The three of them had their eyes on him, waiting for an explanation. He sighed. "I found Nova when I was about Everis's age. During a time where I had fallen away from the Citadel's teachings and found myself alongside a group of blood magi."

Gilbert's eyes went wide. "Blood magic? *You?*"

"Yes. I initially sought it to heal people, to bring them back from the dead." Orin looked down at his hands. Sometimes, he could still see the red that had once stained them. The lives he'd sacrificed to save others… It weighed heavily on him, even after so many years. "I thought I had tapped into this power and was using it responsibly, but anyone I tried to bring back—they weren't the same. If I was lucky, their memories were intact, but something was never right in their heads."

Artesia asked, "And the bird?"

"Nova was the one creature I resurrected successfully." Orin frowned. "Instead of sacrificing the blood of another, I used my own. And it worked. She's been with me ever since. I don't know if her life is somehow tied to mine or what it would take for her to die naturally. I couldn't bring myself to destroy her."

As though summoned, there came a fluttering of wings at the open window and a glint of moonlight reflecting off Nova's snowy feathers. She cocked her head as everyone's attention turned to her, yet her eyes met Orin's. As he always did, Orin felt the connection of magic between them. Nova wasn't a pet. She was a friend. She was a piece of his heart and soul—in a very literal sense. Sometimes he felt what she felt, and he suspected the same was true for her. No matter where he went, Nova could find him.

He continued to speak unbidden. "I served my time with the Citadel and went through their rehabilitation. When they released me, I stepped out into the gardens, and there Nova was. She'd waited for me all those years, and she's been with me ever since."

Silence fell over the room. Nova ruffled her feathers, croaked, and took flight again.

Brant said slowly, "So... you have an undead bird."

Despite himself, Orin smiled. "She's very much alive. Heartbeat and all."

"Then, could you bring a person back the same way you brought her back? Could you have saved the king?"

That smile faded quickly. After Nova, he'd never tried to resurrect anyone again—except for Cassia's assassin, and he'd *intended* that to be temporary. The processes were very different. Could he have saved Faramond at the expense of his own blood? Should he have tried? Would it have made a difference to buy him a little time before Drake and Danica found another way to have him murdered?

"I don't know," he admitted. "Resurrecting Nova took so much out of me. I can't imagine how much it would take to revive a human being... or if he would've been the same after."

"Faramond wouldn't have wanted that," Gilbert said. "You know how he felt about the dark arts. He'd have been horrified to find out you gave into them because of him."

Orin found comfort in those words, even if he still wondered if it would've been worth it. Had it been Everis or Wren, would he have tried it? There was no one else in this world as precious to him. More than once, he'd vowed to do anything to keep them safe.

How far did that vow extend?

Beyond the grave? Into the darkness?

A shiver of uncertainty and dread slithered down his spine. "We should get some sleep while we can," he instructed, tone suggesting the conversation was over. "We have a lot of waiting around to do."

WREN

For the first time since they'd arrived, Ryland's cool demeanor appeared fractured, worry and unease clear at the edges of his expression. Wren spotted a rolled parchment—small, a raven's message—upon the table.

"News from home?" Everis asked.

Ivy nodded toward the scroll. "Read it."

Wren couldn't bring himself to move. Dread rooted him to the spot. Everis picked up the tiny scroll, squinting to make it out. Slowly but surely, the color drained from his face. "This says that Cassia's been kidnapped." He looked up. "By Master Orin."

Wren paused for the span of a breath, and then... he laughed.

Everyone looked at him. He pressed a hand to his mouth. "I'm sorry, I just... *What*? Master Orin? That doesn't sound completely ludicrous to anyone else?"

"It does," Ryland agreed. "However, *why* someone would make such an outrageous accusation concerns me."

He still wanted to laugh, but it was a nervous laugh, brought forth by fear and anxiety. The last few days, he'd felt something was off and now he knew what it was. Orin was in trouble. Orin needed them, and they were miles away. Wren closed his eyes against a sudden wave of dizziness.

183

His insides buzzed with anxiety.

Everis's hand came to rest against the small of his back. "We'll have Captain Annaliese ready our men immediately."

"I would advise against it," Ivy said. "You do not know what you're walking into. If this is some conspiracy, what good do you think you're going to do other than put yourselves in danger?"

"What if he's being set up?" Everis snapped. "Orin is our master. Our *family*. We're not going to abandon him when he needs us. Not to mention the princess and all the other magi."

Ryland ran a hand over his jaw, sighing heavily. "We aren't asking you to. This has Danica's handwriting all over it. My brother's illness and death, the assassination attempt on Cassia, and now this."

Wren's brow furrowed. "The queen? But why? Why would she want her husband and daughter dead?"

Ryland seemed to debate with himself before he admitted, "Because Cassia isn't her daughter."

The information struck them like a bell, drenching the room in silence with the words still reverberating in Wren's head. *Cassia, not Danica's daughter?* It made sense and yet no sense at all. Even Ivy looked startled.

"Does Cassia know?" Everis asked. Even spoken softly, it sounded loud in the stunned quiet of the room.

"At the time I learned the truth, no. It's been nearly as many years as Cassia is old, but I'd be surprised if my brother ever told her."

"But I remember..." Wren deflated into a nearby chair, suddenly weary from trying to process this. It altered so much of what he thought he knew about his life living amongst the royal family.

Ryland arched an eyebrow. "You remember... what? Danica with child? Danica giving birth in Midmere?"

Ever and Ivy frowned at him, waiting, as though *he* somehow had special insight into this. It had been a few years before he and Orin had found Ever and brought him home, and although it might've been mentioned in passing over the years, Wren couldn't recall a specific instance where they'd had reason to discuss the queen's pregnancy.

Or lack thereof.

"When they announced Danica was with child, she left with a select few maids and a cook to a countryside estate," Wren relented. "She was gone the entire time. When she returned, it was with a newborn."

Ivy scowled. "But why fake it? Was she unable to conceive on her own?"

A sharp laugh escaped Ryland's mouth. "That wasn't it at all. More like my brother saw fit to share someone else's bed shortly before he and Danica were married. One last *hurrah*, so to speak, since he intended on being faithful to his wife once they were wed. *That* woman ended up pregnant. Faramond insisted on taking the child in and raising her. To spare Danica the public humiliation, he concocted the plan to simply pass Cassia off as their daughter. Danica wasn't pleased with this."

"If she'd had a child of her own with Faramond, that child would've had a more legitimate claim to the throne, technically. If the truth were to ever have come out," Ivy said.

"Yes, but the relationship between husband and wife had soured from the beginning. Danica had no love for him, nor he for her, and he had an heir." Ryland shook his head. "He would never have brought himself to share her bed if she didn't want him in it."

Wren looked out the nearby windows at the view of the city stretching beyond the manor. They had so many answers and yet so many more questions. Danica and Cassia had always had a strained relationship. Wren had marked it up to Cassia being so favored by Faramond, by the fact that the people were more partial to Cassia than to her mother. They were both good people in their own right, but Cassia had a gentle charm and kindness to her, where Danica was calculating and critical. He'd witnessed Danica lecture her daughter over the most minute things many times. He'd shrugged it off as it simply being Danica's nature. There was nothing wrong with it; it was simply... who she was. Her aloofness was her strength and her weakness. She was a force to be reckoned with.

The only thing Wren could do was speculate. Did Cassia know? Would she have cared? She'd grown up with Danica as her mother, no matter how contentious a relationship it might have been; Wren knew from experience that blood didn't matter when you *felt* someone was family.

"Whatever happened to the other woman?" Wren asked. "Cassia's birth mother?"

Ryland scowled, years of defensiveness creeping into his features. These were secrets he'd harbored for so long, and now he was spilling them to a pair of boys he'd only just met. He took a steady breath. "Her name was Elly. Faramond sent her to me, of course."

Wren grimaced without meaning to. As much as he wanted to know more, prodding into the duke's personal relationship with his brother so soon after his death seemed unkind.

Everis possessed no such filter. "That's why you two weren't speaking?"

"My brother and I... We've argued about a great many things over the course of our lives. We are very different people. He is—was—a good man at the heart of it all, but a good man prone to rash decisions. He initially wanted to keep Elly in Midmere, but Danica wouldn't hear of it. Rather than ask me, he simply sent Elly here to Patish with a letter, a request to ensure she would be taken care of. Not much of a request, if you ask me. The poor woman had been through enough. She was convinced Faramond loved her and would send for her, that she would get to see her daughter, eventually.

"I saw to her, of course. Gave her a lovely home near the ocean. She never needed for anything. Not once did she ask for anything, except for word of her daughter and the man she loved."

"So, where is she now?" Everis asked.

"She's dead, I imagine," Wren said softly. "Given that Duke Ryland's been speaking of her in the past tense."

Regret flickered across Ryland's face. He turned away. "When Cassia was about five, yes. She fell ill. I had all the best healers I could find treat her, but I fully believe she died of a broken heart."

Wren couldn't envision a woman he'd never seen, so he instead pictured an older Cassia, removed from her only child, heartbroken and alone in a city far from home. His chest ached for her and for the loss of a relationship that Cassia would never get to explore. A part of him hurt for Ryland too, witnessing the grief on his face even after all these years.

He shook his head. Despite all these answers, the biggest question he could not figure out was, "Why now?"

He hadn't meant to ask the question aloud, but there it was. Three sets of eyes turned to him, each of them thoughtful.

Wren continued, "Danica. Why risk so much trying to kill the king and his heir so close together? After all these years. Surely it would've been easier to denounce Cassia as a baby or even have her... removed from the picture. Babies die all the time. No one would've questioned it."

"Maybe she'd hoped she would come to love Cassia as her own." Everis shrugged. "But even so, you're right. It was reckless. It reeks of desperation. Could she have felt she was running out of time?"

"Out of time for what?" Ivy asked.

"I don't know. It was just a thought. Maybe something happened. Maybe someone found out."

Wren sighed. No amount of dwelling would give them answers. All of this felt too large, too much.

Did Master Orin know about this? Has he been harboring this secret?

He closed his eyes and tried to breathe to still his reeling mind.

Everis quietly inquired, "Wren, what should we do?"

Wren opened his eyes and looked at him, somber yet determined. "You and I have someone to speak to."

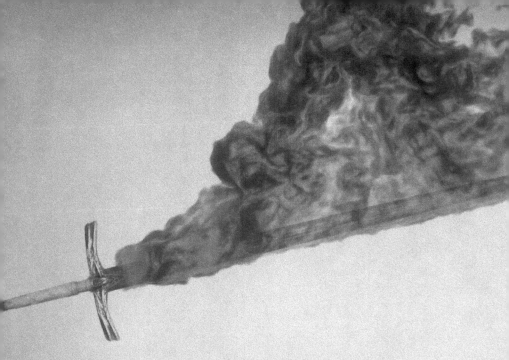

IMARYLLIS

Imaryllis caught sight of Nova on her windowsill early that morning. The bird was a common enough sight fluttering about the training grounds, which Imaryllis's own window overlooked, but it was a rare thing for Nova to pay her a visit directly. She sat up in bed, noting the parchment tied to the white raven's leg.

She slid to her feet and soundlessly made her way to the window. Nova waited with the utmost patience as she untied the tiny scroll and unrolled it.

All is well. C is safe at the rivers. We await your word.

She would've recognized Orin's handwriting anywhere. But... the rivers? There was a single river that wound through the city, cutting it in half.

The Twin Rivers, she realized. It was an inn near the eastern gates, if she recalled correctly. Smart of Orin to stay put and not immediately head for Patish. Queen Danica had already deployed a hundred soldiers in every direction in search of her missing daughter and the 'traitors.' Others were armed and searching the city, yes, but they had extended most of the effort outside the city walls.

Imaryllis took a seat at her desk, flipping Orin's note over to scribble on the back in small letters so it would fit.

Soldiers on the roads. Avoid. Will send all clear when safe. Drake has others.

With deft fingers, she tied the note back to Nova's leg and stroked a finger over the top of her head. "Look after them for me, would you?" she murmured.

Nova let out a squawk as though in response, turned, and flew away.

Imaryllis watched until she was gone from sight. No matter where Orin and the princess were, it was dangerous. Orin was the most skilled magi she'd ever met, but she doubted even he could hold his own against a blood magi with a handful of apprentices and an army of guards at his back.

She washed, dressed, and went about her day as though nothing was amiss. There were knights-in-training to be taught in the yard, spells to be crafted for battle. It seemed foolish to overdo it on those, lest they ended up being used against her allies in the coming weeks, so she purposely botched most of every spell she did. A charm to prevent breaking on one sword was altered by a single glyph to make it *more* prone to shattering. The bow strings were frayed instead of reinforced. Some fletches on the arrows were snipped so they wouldn't fly true. It wasn't much, but it was all she could do.

That afternoon, she took her lunch to the training yard rather than eat in the magi tower. Not unusual in and of itself; she often ate alone beneath the old willow tree. When Orin's apprentices were younger, she enjoyed watching the pair of them scurry about the yard with their wooden swords or seeing Everis scaling the willow itself.

She wondered how they were faring in Patish, if they were safe, if her letter had reached them. Even barring weather and the potential for getting lost, a raven could've been taken out by a larger predator. It wasn't uncommon to send three or four birds with the same letter just to ensure that one of them made it through, but she hadn't wanted to risk anyone noticing so many birds missing.

"Lady Imaryllis?" came a quiet voice.

Lady. That had always made her respond with an uncertain smile. She'd been born a lady, yes, but she'd left that life—and a family who'd not been fond of magic, nor those who wielded it—behind a very long time ago. *Little Lady Imaryllis.* What had started as a taunt at the Citadel from a young age had, in recent years, become a title the other magi spoke with respect and fondness. She lifted her head, squinting against the sunlight to where Pava stood over her, a bowl in hand.

"May I join you?" the older woman asked slowly, as though she expected to be turned away.

Imaryllis gestured to the stone ground and scooted over a bit. "I don't believe I have a claim on this spot, so by all means."

Pava took a seat beside her so they were hip to hip. For several long minutes, they ate in silence, dunking chunks of bread into their soup. Finally, Pava asked, "You spoke with the queen yesterday?"

Imaryllis swallowed a warm mouthful of broth and vegetables, gaze fixed straight ahead at the magi tower. Drake was in there, but not alone. She kept waiting for him to be on his own so that she might catch him off guard and unprotected. If she could simply dispatch him... "I did. She insists that Master Orin confessed to the murder of the king and that all magi orders are to be taken from Drake henceforth."

That statement seemed to have killed Pava's appetite. She stared down into her bowl.

Imaryllis took a slow breath. "The princess is safe within the city. As soon as he can, Orin will get her out and take her to Patish. Assuming we can't secure the castle first, that is."

Pava's freckled face gaped at her in surprise. "Secure the castle? What are we supposed to do?"

She could still hear Carlisle's agonized scream echoing in her ears. She could see the look in Mace's eyes as he died. There was no honor in what Imaryllis had planned. Yet, if being branded a dishonorable coward helped to save the lives of those she cared for... she would wear that badge with pride.

"We wait until Drake makes a mistake. Whatever he's become, he'll be as dead as any other with a sword in his back."

EVERIS

The north-easternmost part of Patish sat close to the docks, littered with warehouses, ships, and all manner of sailors passing through. The scent of fish had wedged itself into everything, including Everis's clothes. He kept close to Wren's side as they scanned the dim streets. Wren had said they were looking for an old woman, but that hardly narrowed it down. They'd passed half a dozen of them so far, but Wren seemed to know what he was looking for even if he couldn't describe it.

"You're looking so sour, Ever," Wren commented as they rounded a corner.

"I'm not *sour*. I just don't understand what we're doing. You really think a band of assassins is going to drop everything to help us with our problems?"

"They're a… bit of a unique bunch. I wouldn't rule it out. Besides, for the right price, I suspect their help could be bought."

Everis sighed but dropped the subject. It wasn't as though they had many other options.

They roamed the streets for the better part of two hours. Even Wren began to look frustrated, muttering something about how they ought to give up and return to the merchant that had previously assisted him, but his grumbling fell short as they came across a woman on the nearby corner. Her hair was ratty and thin, her spine bent, and her eyes stared off at nothing as she shook a tin cup at any passerby who came near.

Wren pressed a hand to Everis's chest. "Wait here," he instructed before crossing the street to approach her. He flicked a silver coin into the cup and murmured something too quiet for Everis to hear. The crone shook the cup. The single coin rattled within. Then she turned and hobbled into a nearby alley.

Wren looked back at Everis, who raised an inquisitive eyebrow. They exchanged shrugs and followed.

If the streets were dirty, the dark, dank alleyway was outright filthy, and the fishy aroma was overpowering, tainted with the scent of rotting food. Still, Ever could hear the clink of the old woman's cup as she disappeared around the far end of the building. When they reached that same spot, she was nowhere to be seen, but a door to a nearby building stood ajar.

"Why does this feel like a trap?" Everis whispered.

Wren bit his lip. "You worry too much."

They slipped inside. Before them loomed a steep staircase to the second floor. The bottom step creaked ominously as Wren placed a boot upon it. An uneasy feeling gnawed at Everis's insides. Judging by the way Wren hesitated, he assumed the feeling was mutual. Then Wren took a deep breath, squared his shoulders, and pressed onward. The wood groaned with every step, killing any element of surprise if they'd need one. The top of the stairs brought them to the end of a hall where the old woman tarried in front of another door. She limped inside, out of view, not giving them as much as a cursory glance.

"Wait!" Everis dashed after her. He skidded to a halt beyond the door, looking around in bewilderment at an empty room. He didn't see the old woman.

"Ever—"

Wren's warning came a second too late. Everis whirled as the woman dropped from the rafters overhead and landed directly before him. With one well-positioned blow to his jaw and a foot hooked behind his leg, she sent him slamming face-first to the ground. One arm lay trapped beneath him. She twisted the other behind his back at a sharp angle, threatening to dislocate it with a single shove.

With a hiss, Everis tried to squirm and throw her off. He halted at the press of a blade to the back of his neck and the feel of a bony knee digging between his shoulder blades.

"Who are you?" the woman sneered.

He turned his head as much as his compromised position would allow, just enough to meet Wren's eyes. The door had fallen shut during the scuffle, and Wren slumped back against it, one hand raised and ready. There was no way he could fire off a spell without risking hitting Everis, too. Panic bubbled up inside Everis's chest. The darkness simmered beneath his skin, ready to be summoned. Wren pinned him with a stare, imploring him to remain calm.

"My name is Wren Lumina. We're looking for Faulk. He told me this is where I would find him."

The woman didn't appear fazed. "What's your business with Faulk?"

"None of your fucking business," Everis growled. The offending knee bore down painfully against his spine, almost enough to make him cry out.

"He came to speak to me at Duke Ryland's," Wren said quickly. "He said if I needed to reach him, to give a silver to the old woman on that corner where I found you and say those words, and I'd be able to speak with him. It's urgent. *Please.*"

The crone scoffed, "I'll show him *old,*" but the weight lifted from Everis so he could roll over and sit up. She scowled at the pair of them. Even standing straight, her back had a curve, and she was most certainly up there in age, but she now moved with a nimbleness and grace he'd never have expected from her. She sheathed her blade, though not before he saw it was another of the dark daggers Princess Cassia's assassin had carried.

"Have a seat," she said gruffly. "I'll fetch him."

She left through the door, shutting it behind her. Everis and Wren stood in the near darkness; no windows, no light save for a candle on a nearby table. The door latched behind her, and Everis's shoulders tensed. Had she really locked them in like wild animals?

For the first few minutes Everis remained still, occasionally shifting his weight from one foot to the other. Then he began to pace. Even now, the pull of magic had his heart racing and his senses sharp. Perhaps he'd been calling on it too often lately; it shouldn't have been so readily available.

Wren leaned against the wall beside the table, arms folded, and he looked perfectly calm. The faint firelight cast shadows across his face. "You're making me nervous, Ever. Relax."

"I *am* relaxed," he snapped.

No sooner had he said those words than he wanted to swallow them whole. Stricken by his vicious tone, Wren looked away.

Everis grimaced and pushed his hands through his hair. "I'm sorry."

"It's fine." The way Wren said it suggested it was *not* fine.

"I'm wound a little tight, is all. With so much going on…"

"Oh, yes. I wouldn't know what that's like."

Everis turned to face him, brow furrowing. Before he could comment further—or make things worse—the door swung open again. In place of the elderly woman, a man dressed from head to toe in black and brown leathers stepped inside.

He was shorter than Everis but broader shouldered, lean, and solid. He wore a cowl and a mask that obscured his nose and mouth, leaving it visible enough that one could see the glare he set upon them and the ragged scarring that climbed half his face.

Wren smiled as though greeting an old friend. "Thank you for coming, Faulk."

Faulk crossed his arms, unimpressed. "The invitation was for you alone, magi. Cara would've been within her rights to kill you both."

"She could've tried," Everis growled.

Faulk met his eyes, unflinching. Rather than acknowledge that Everis had said anything at all, he merely turned his head away and ignored him.

"We've received word from the Owls in Midmere that things have gone awry. I assume that's why you've sent for me."

"I'm sorry. It was urgent that we speak with you."

"I'm listening."

Wren hesitated, wringing his hands together. "We believe Queen Danica is responsible for hiring your assassin and for murdering the king. Princess Cassia isn't really her daughter."

Faulk paused, still managing to scowl somehow even as he looked thoughtful. "Suppose that makes sense."

"It does?" Everis asked.

"Doesn't it? Only a member of the Starling bloodline can sit on the throne as long as one remains living. With Faramond dead, Cassia becomes queen. Danica, not being her real mother, could be tossed to the streets."

It was Everis's turn to glare. "Princess Cassia would never do such a thing."

"How certain are you of that?" Faulk asked.

"Positive," Wren said, even though he glanced at Everis as though reluctant to agree with him at that exact moment. "There must be more to this. I've known the princess all her life. Besides, I don't think anyone other than Faramond and Ryland knew about Cassia's parentage, including Cassia herself. No one can spill a secret they know nothing about."

Faulk turned from them, leaning a shoulder into the door. "Is Danica aware that Ryland knows?"

The question gave Wren pause. "I... I'm not sure."

"Common sense says no. Otherwise, she'd have had Ryland dealt with first, probably ages ago, so that he couldn't spill her secret when all of this happened. Instead, she's framing him for the king's death and the princess's assassination attempt, isn't she?"

Wren's spine straightened, and his eyes widened in understanding. "If Ryland were to be tried and executed for treason and Cassia was dead, Danica could take the throne even though she isn't a Starling."

Everis shook his head. "This all seems like a terribly convoluted plan when she could've simply enjoyed her time as the queen's mother and adviser."

"Then," Faulk said, "something pushed her to do it. Or someone. A fear of being found out, perhaps."

Wren took a step toward the assassin, buzzing with this new information. "She's trying to hold the pieces together of whatever secret she's carrying and secure her position!"

Everis watched them. The pair seemed so much on the same page that he couldn't help but feel left out. He swallowed the spike of jealousy. Foolish. Still, his voice came out more tense than he'd meant it to. "That doesn't answer the question about what we're supposed to do now, and if you'll help us."

"We aren't helping you, magi." Faulk sighed. "But we will help the queen."

"Danica—?"

"Did we not just clarify that Danica has no claim to the throne? Cassia is queen. Our allegiance is to her. The Owls of the Dusk Court in Midmere are attempting to locate her now, whether she's in the city or has left it. They want to find her first, and they can keep her safe if they do."

Everis couldn't help a faint flicker of hope. If Cassia could be protected, perhaps Master Orin could be, too.

Faulk peered back at Wren. "There's something else I received word of that you haven't mentioned."

"What?"

"Word of something strange from the royal magi. Saying the city's

Master is responsible for kidnapping Cassia, and the magi are reporting to someone new now."

Wren's face flushed. "Orin would *never.*"

"And do the other magi know him well enough to know that, too?"

"Well, they—they should!"

Faulk shrugged. "If they know him to be innocent, then they're willingly betraying him. That's something to keep in mind. Danica, and whatever soldiers she has at her disposal, is not your only enemy."

Wren looked at Ever, and their eyes met, heavy hearts reaching for one another. Everis bit his lower lip. "This is going to be an all-out war, isn't it?"

"It's beginning to look that way," Wren quietly agreed.

Faulk cleared his throat. "Suppose you boys ought to ensure you've got the winning side, then." A pause. "A vote has already been passed. We will send a few of our members with you to help expedite your passage through the mountains. By the time you arrive in Midmere, our Owls there ought to have more information."

"Ryland said he'd send troops," Everis began.

"He can, and he should, but do you know how long it will take an army to get through the pass? They'll likely go by ship. It's faster for a large group, easier to transport supplies and keep the soldiers rested."

"You've thought of everything, haven't you?" A smile crossed Wren's face. He looked almost in awe of Faulk, of how sharp he was.

Everis's face warmed. He crossed his arms, slumping sullenly back against the wall.

This time, even Faulk seemed to smile behind his mask. It made his eyes crinkle slightly. "That's what we do, magi. Prepare to depart by tomorrow morning. Horses and a guide will be waiting for you. I hope I don't have to caution you against speaking about the Court. A simple 'we've hired a few blades' will suffice."

"Understood."

Faulk beckoned for them to leave first. They departed the way they'd come, slipping into the foggy city streets. The woman named Cara had returned to the street corner, but when they passed her, her eyes moved right over them as though they didn't exist. Wren said nothing as they walked. It was more than obvious that Everis snapping at him had struck a nerve. As loath as he was to bring up the situation again, he hated having Wren angry with him even more.

"About earlier…"

Wren cut him off in a clipped tone. "Focus on the matters at hand.

196

Do we tell Captain Annaliese, or do we have her travel with Ryland's men? Never mind. Strategy isn't your strong point."

It was a purposeful barb, one that struck home and burrowed deep. Everis looked away. "We can't all be Faulk or Master Orin, I guess."

Wren didn't respond.

With the tension lingering, they returned to the manor in silence.

A servant greeted them when they entered through the main double doors, sending them to a waiting Ryland and Ivy. It went without saying that Everis wasn't to mention anything about the Court, so he kept his mouth shut and let Wren do the talking.

"We've hired a few sellswords to help expedite us through the mountain pass," Wren explained. "It's our hope that we can locate Master Orin and Princess Cassia before Danica's soldiers do."

Ryland frowned. "But the troops…"

Wren shook his head. "Whatever men you can spare should travel with Captain Annaliese by boat and approach from the north. It will give her ample time to go over strategies with your captains and figure out how best to handle this. A few magi and sellswords can reach the capital faster and slip in undetected."

Duke Ryland heaved a sigh. "As you wish. When do you depart?"

"First thing in the morning," Everis said. "We've wasted so much time already."

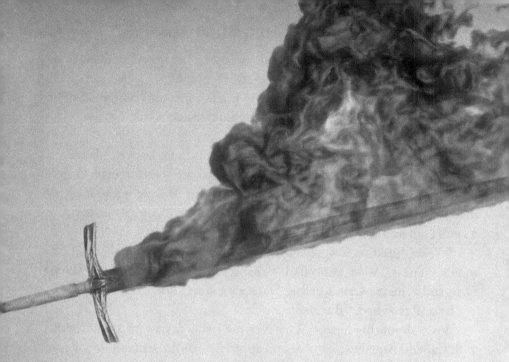

IMARYLLIS

Danica had kept a food tester at her side every meal since Orin's escape. She didn't seem bothered that her meal would grow cold while she waited, nor did she require that everyone else wait. Drake always waited, though. So did the magi working for him. They were the only ones who had something to worry about.

These were people Imaryllis had once thought of as her brothers and sisters. They looked like strangers to her now. Foreboding filled the castle halls, void of Cassia's cheerful voice or the king's boisterous laughter, of Everis and Wren's bickering and joking and sparring in the yard. Now it was just her and Pava and people she thought she knew. They attended suppers in the hall out of obligation, but neither spoke much, and Pava could scarcely make eye contact with any of her fellow magi.

Imaryllis met any sideways looks with a cool and collected stare. Perhaps she ought to have pretended to go along with the state of things, to feign some interest in Drake Reed and his teachings. The idea made her sick to her stomach. Would Drake believe the act if she tried? No, he knew she could not be swayed. There was only one reason he hadn't simply had her locked up or executed.

Drake was playing with her.

He knew damned well she would slip up, that she'd take any opportunity to attack him, and he was waiting for it.

She wrapped her fingers tight around her fork, drawing in a steadying breath at the sound of Drake's laughing at something someone said. All around them, people pretended nothing was amiss. As though this were any other dinner, as though the king's funeral wasn't a day away.

A fact that Danica brought up toward the end of supper. She rose from her seat, lightly tapping a fork upon her wine glass so the room would silence and grant her full attention.

"As you all know," she announced, "my husband's funeral is tomorrow. I will speak to the city after the service, as is customary. During that time, I shall announce a reward for the head of Orin Sorrell or any information that will assist with the safe return of my daughter."

Imaryllis's stomach plummeted. Why was she telling them this now? Knowing well that some of the people present weren't truly on the queen's side, had only bent their knee and sworn their loyalty out of fear of Drake…

It's a trap.

They had no doubt kept a close watch on the goings-on within the castle. They knew who their possible problems were. Imaryllis would be on that list. They were hoping someone would try to warn Orin and subsequently lead Danica right to them.

But did Imaryllis have a choice? If they put a bounty out to the entire city of Midmere, the common folk would be out for blood. They would turn everything upside down. Not even for Danica, but for the safe return of their princess. Imaryllis studied the cooling plate of food she'd scarcely touched. Did she take the bait and try to reach out to Orin? Did she do nothing and hope he and Princess Cassia would escape unscathed?

She pushed back her chair and stood, ignoring the curious look from Pava as she went. Drake stopped her as she headed for the door, grabbing her loosely by the wrist and drawing her to a halt.

"Oh, dear. Were you not hungry, Lady Imaryllis?" he asked in that too sweet tone.

Imaryllis stiffened, willing herself not to jerk away lest she draw attention or else be seen as disrespectful. Yet the words that fell from her mouth held such barely concealed contempt. "Tasted a bit off tonight," she drawled. "I believe it's soured my appetite."

Drake smiled widely, eyes positively sparkling with amusement. He released her. "Do get some rest, my lady."

Her stomach did turn then. She retreated to her chambers, barely able to refrain from breaking into a run. Every hallway she turned down, every doorway and window she passed, she was certain something—someone—lurked in the shadows, watching her. Nowhere felt safe. Not until she closed and locked her bedroom door behind her. Only then did her chest uncinch, and she regained her ability to breathe. How much longer could she keep wading in a nest of vipers, not knowing which ones were poisonous and when they would strike?

Habit had her looking to the window, hopeful Nova might've returned with a word from Orin. She stepped to the sill and looked out, scanning the dimming sky and trees. No flash of white wings caught her eye. She swore inwardly. It was too much to hope that the raven would've returned, so she might relay a letter to Orin without having to put his location at risk. Still, she gave it a few hours. Long enough for the rest of the castle to go to sleep, for even the servants to have cleared the halls, leaving only the night guards making their patrols. Still no sign of Nova.

"All right," Imaryllis muttered. "Then let's do this the hard way."

Night patrol or not, Imaryllis knew the ins and outs of the castle like the back of her hand. It took little effort to sneak past the guards, her steps light, a hand at the ready should she need to summon a weapon. Not that she planned to. Coming to blows with anyone now would ruin any chance she had of making it out of the castle alive. Not even she could fend off the entire castle guard and the traitor magi.

She didn't dare risk waking the stableboys by taking a horse. She left the castle on foot and, in case she was being trailed, took a roundabout way through the city, heading in the opposite direction of the inn Orin had taken refuge in.

The streets stayed mostly empty around her, save for the occasional passersby in the dark. In the business districts, torches would be lit, and taverns, brothels, and gambling houses would still be bustling with patrons. There in the outer reaches of the city, however, it remained quiet and unnervingly still. And yet, Imaryllis couldn't shake the feeling she was being followed. It took effort not to steal a look over her shoulder. No sense in tipping off whoever it was—if there was anyone at all beyond her own paranoia.

She ducked into a vacant storefront with boarded windows and shut the door behind herself. It took a moment, but the sound of footsteps on the road outside met her ears as someone passed. The steps paused not far from the door, lingered a moment, then continued on and vanished down the street. Imaryllis breathed a sigh of relief. It felt too easy, but perhaps she was giving Drake and the soldiers too much credit.

After another ten minutes of silence went by, she emerged from the shop, squinting both ways down the road. She appeared to be alone. Good. Imaryllis headed back the way she'd come, intending to cut through another few alleyways, then head to the Rivers to find Orin.

No sooner had she passed the opening to an alley than a hand shot out from the darkness, grabbed her, and dragged her into the shadows.

It took a split second for Imaryllis to light a glimmering blade of pure magic and pin her attacker to the wall—but the black-clad person had a dagger at her neck as well. She stared into a pair of dark eyes set within a mask-covered face. In fact, the entire ensemble of the person was eerily similar to the assassin who'd tried to claim Princess Cassia's life.

Imaryllis gritted her teeth. "Think you can slit my throat before I slit yours?"

"I'd rather not find out," the assassin admitted in a voice lighter than Imaryllis had expected. "I'm here to help you."

"You have an odd way of showing it," she growled, not releasing her hold just yet.

The assassin lowered her dagger, tucking it into her belt and holding her hands up. "Better?"

Imaryllis narrowed her eyes. Slowly, she drew back, putting some distance between them. She allowed the blade in her hand to dissipate, returning the empty hilt to her belt. "Who are you?"

"A friend," the woman said. "But you're being followed, and I don't have much time to explain."

"I'm aware I'm being followed. That was the whole point."

"You were hoping to lead your pursuers to the wrong place, aye?" Even in the darkness and with her mask covering her mouth, Imaryllis could tell the woman was smiling. "I'm afraid they may know where the princess and the runaway magi are. Did you tell anyone their location?"

Her blood cooled in her veins. How? *Who?* No one knew where Orin was hiding.

Except Pava.

Imaryllis sank against the opposite wall, eyes closed, pained. How foolish she'd been to assume that, just because Pava hadn't immediately fallen in line with Drake, she couldn't be swayed.

No. It isn't that she was swayed. She was afraid.

Pava had likely bargained for her safety or to get into Danica's good graces by supplying her with the information. Imaryllis hadn't told her everything but enough to put Cassia and the others in harm's way.

Oh, she wanted to throw herself onto her damned sword.

Several hurried sets of footsteps echoed from the street. Her companion touched her arm. "We should be going."

Reluctantly, Imaryllis allowed herself to be led away.

They sped through the alley to the street on the other side, crossed to a set of stone steps leading up, and followed a walkway along the canal that overlooked the city's river. The Waste Water, they called it, because there was no drinking from this river. It was where most of the citizens tossed their waste, and even with the steady current, the odor was a slap in the face.

"That way!" a voice shouted, too close for comfort.

The smell and the chilly night air were enough to make her lungs hurt. Imaryllis yanked her hood up high, jogging after the assassin. If they could reach the bridge leading to the other side of the canal, it would be easier to lose their pursuers and hide.

The guards were a few steps ahead of their plans. A group of them raced up another set of steps ahead, crowding onto the canal walkway. Behind them, Imaryllis could hear others at their heels. The pair of them came to an abrupt stop.

Imaryllis pulled the hilts from her belt, sliding a thumb along the incantations engraved into the metal. Fire. Ice. Stone. Each with its own purpose. She touched the lightning runes. Her magic flared to life, rippling through her arms and wrists and palms, forming the very blades themselves. They were an extension of her, strong and hot and unyielding, and the sight of the glowing blades gave a few of the soldiers pause. She'd no doubt trained with some of these people. They knew what she was capable of.

"Lady Imaryllis," one of them called, her voice splitting in fear. "Please, unarm yourself and come with us peacefully."

Imaryllis made no move to do so. "You're all being used. Princess Cassia needs our help, and the queen has you fooled. You're on the wrong side of this fight. If you'll just—"

"Kill the other one," a guardsman barked over her. "Take Imaryllis alive—if you can."

She opened her mouth to plead further, but the guards descended, and the assassin wasted no time clashing with them head-on. Even with only a dagger at her disposal, she met their swords and dodged their blows with ease. Imaryllis turned to the three guards at their backs and did the same.

With her magic-formed weapons in hand, she could've slain every one of them with little effort. But these were soldiers merely doing their jobs, terrified, not only for their lives but likely the lives of their families. She didn't want their blood on her hands if she could help it. "Don't kill them!"

The assassin stopped just short of driving her dagger into one man's throat. She spun at the last second and slammed her elbow into his jaw instead. There came a *crunch* of breaking teeth and a howl of pain, but at least he was alive.

"Must you make this difficult?" the assassin grumbled, scarcely winded by the battle.

Imaryllis pressed forward, meeting blade after blade. The walkway was too narrow for them to surround her. She crowded them as close to the edge as she could, where a wooden railing prevented them from toppling over. She canted backward, dropped to one knee, and drove one of her magic-formed blades into the stonework of the canal wall.

"*Shatter!*"

Sparks tore from the blade, splitting the stone as it went. The wall beneath the guards' feet crumbled. The railing wasn't enough to hold the weight of the three of them as they flailed and scrabbled for purchase. Down they went into the Waste Water. Her companion knocked the remaining guards in after them, each with a shout and another plunk or splash. They leaned forward, watching the dark, stench-filled water whisk the soldiers downstream.

Imaryllis winced. "That smell will never come out."

They were both winded by the time the assassin led Imaryllis into another building. No sooner had they heaved the door shut than a large man with the muscled arms of a blacksmith lumbered out from a back room, lantern in hand, to stare at them. It took only a nod from the assassin for him to relax his broad shoulders. He bowed his head in return and retreated without a word.

With the immediate danger gone, Imaryllis allowed herself to catch her breath and steal a look around. Nothing about the building suggested it was anything more than a blacksmith's shop. What business did an assassin have here? And why was she carting around a dagger like the assassin who'd come after Cassia? Oh, certainly, there were whispers of organizations of thieves and bounty hunters, mostly used to frighten children into behaving.

Maybe you ought to have paid more attention to the stories, she scolded herself. Every rumor had some seedling of truth.

The woman in black stole another peek out the window, then moved away to meander about the shop, familiar enough that it was clear she'd been there before. She vanished through another door, searching for something, while Imaryllis slumped against the wall and folded her arms across her chest with a frown. "So?"

"So?" the woman called back.

"You obviously know who I am. Are you going to grace me with a name?"

There was no immediate response. She appeared again with a bottle of ale in hand, which she uncorked and drank from after yanking down her mask. In the near darkness, Imaryllis couldn't get the best look at her face before she yanked the mask up again.

"Gwyn," she said.

Was that her real name? Not that it mattered at the moment. It was something to call her by, at least. "Fine, Gwyn. Thank you for your assistance. However, your timely presence brings up a number of questions." Imaryllis's eyes raked over the woman. "Such as what sort of organization you're a part of."

"I don't believe there's a reason to answer that. At least, not yet." Gwyn approached, extending the flagon of ale.

Imaryllis didn't take it. "There is when you're donning the same clothing and sigil as the woman who tried to murder Princess Cassia."

Gwyn sighed, troubled. "That assassin is no longer affiliated with my organization. She chose to abandon her post when she took on that job, and if she hadn't died a failure, we would've killed her ourselves."

Imaryllis scowled but finally uncrossed her arms and took the offered drink. She would no doubt need it if they were going to be doing any more running about tonight. "What are you after, then? What is your group after?"

"I belong to an organization that stretches across the continent. We've known something was off with the king's illness for a while but couldn't pinpoint what it was or who was responsible. I recently received word from my siblings in Patish that something had gone awry here and that the queen was responsible. We've been on high alert ever since, trying to evaluate the situation."

"Evaluate the situation? To determine what?"

"If we ought to interfere. We don't meddle in affairs of the crown unless it's necessary." She paused. "Although by the look of things, it's quickly becoming necessary."

Imaryllis pinched the bridge of her nose. She took another long pull from the ale and sat in a creaking chair near the fireplace. "Princess Cassia's being hidden within the city, along with a few loyalists who are looking after her."

"We know."

"But I believe it was one of my fellow magi from the castle who gave away that hiding spot."

Gwyn tipped her head. "I see."

"It's my fault. I should never have trusted her with the information."

"Probably not."

They stared at one another. Had Imaryllis expected some sort of comforting words from a stranger? Rather than be annoyed, she found a tired smile twitching across her mouth. A laugh escaped her lips. Even Gwyn appeared to grin behind her mask.

They finished the bottle together as they rested. Outside, the street remained quiet. Perhaps they'd lost their pursuers for good. Not that it mattered. If they knew where Cassia was...

Imaryllis stood. "I need to go. I have to warn Orin."

"He's being looked after," Gwyn promised. "There's no way to get him out of the city without a confrontation right now. My people are watching and waiting. We'll help get him and the princess to safety."

Imaryllis gave her a sidelong look. "Well, you're on top of it all, aren't you?"

She shrugged. "We do our best."

"If your intentions are to protect Cassia, can't you simply get into the castle and sever the head of the snake? Kill Drake Reed and take Danica prisoner? The rest will fall in line."

"I wish it were that easy. As I said, we only do as much as is deemed necessary. My organization hasn't stepped into the light with any major conflicts in over a hundred years. Already we've had to make ourselves known to too many people and give too much information. Those higher in the family than me are still deciding, and the vote is split."

"Yet you're helping me."

"We've been given leave to prevent the princess's death, but nothing more until a final decision is made."

"Democracy at its finest," Imaryllis muttered.

Gwyn started for the door, ensuring her mask was securely fastened and her hood pulled up. "That democracy might be what saves your princess and friends."

Together, they slipped back into the night.

ORIN

The unrest in the city was palpable. Orin knew from their hosts that security at the city gates had been increased within the last twenty-four hours, despite the troops dispatched to the main road not having returned. It didn't bode well. If, somehow, Drake and Danica knew Cassia was still within the city…

We're running out of time.

He stared out the window of their small room, stroking his fingers over his beard, lost in thought. He and Gilbert had noticed more city guards patrolling the area, too, which made going out to get the lay of the area more and more difficult. Orin didn't enjoy having to rely upon their hosts so heavily to fetch supplies or serve as a lookout. Although they swore they were happy to do so for the true queen's sake, Cassia had expressed her displeasure at how much they were putting on the line for her.

She has a good heart, but she still has much to learn.

Cassia was young yet to be a ruler. She could do it. She had the desire to do right by her people, the compassion and understanding that every life was precious and that her life didn't mean more than anyone else's. And yet…

A flutter of wings drew him from his thoughts. He'd left the window open enough for Nova to come and go, not wanting the patrols to notice her pecking at the glass. She hopped to the small table before him, clawing at the feather of his quill pen as though inquiring about what he was working on. Smart though she was, Orin couldn't say just how much she properly understood when he spoke to her. It sometimes helped, though, to jar his thoughts from spiraling in endless circles.

"I feel we'll be trying to make our escape soon," he whispered to her. "I wish I had more confidence that it will go as planned."

He placed the quill aside and brushed a finger up her beak. "If something were to happen to me, I can't promise what will happen to you as a result. Your life may fade if my magic does. But if it doesn't, you'll look after Wren and Ever for me, won't you?"

Nova cocked her head. She strutted across the parchment, leaving a smudge in the ink and a footprint or two. Orin lowered his lashes. He'd spent the better part of an hour on this letter and still wasn't certain he was done. It felt incomplete. Perhaps it always would, no matter what he wrote, no matter how long it carried on.

A disruption in the atmosphere sent a shiver through him, accompanied by a sudden spike of anxiety that flooded the magic he'd placed all about the inn. Orin lurched to his feet, almost dizzy with the sensation. He reached for the magic, and although there was a sense of urgency, there was no danger. No immediate danger, anyway.

Downstairs, he sought the others in the cellar, which the innkeepers had offered to them. It was some place they could sneak to when the inn was quiet, and they were desperate to get out of their cramped quarters. It was cold and dim, kegs and boxes of supplies and foodstuffs organized in an orderly fashion against the walls. In the center sat a table they'd had many a meal at over the last several days. He'd often looked around at his companions—two fellow magi, the rightful queen, and two soldiers—and wondered how any of this could ever have come to pass. It felt surreal.

Now, though, there were two fresh faces in the group. The first he didn't recognize save for her clothing, similar to those of Cassia's would-be assassin. Reflexively, he tensed until his gaze traversed to Imaryllis standing beside her.

Imaryllis had her hands on Cassia's shoulders. They were smiling at one another, speaking in hushed but excited tones at seeing each other safe. She took swift notice of Orin entering the room and turned, relief flooding her features. "*Orin.* Thank the Mother you're all right."

"I could say the same of you." Orin gave her a gentle smile as she came to him. "Although if you're here... Has something gone wrong?"

Just like that, her smile withered away. Dread twisted at his insides. It could've been many things, and yet Orin's first thought jumped to his apprentices. "Wren and Ever..."

Imaryllis shook her head. "I have no reason to believe the boys are in any danger, though I haven't heard from them. I suppose you know about Danica's speech today."

He took a slow breath to settle his nerves. Their hosts had listened to the speech and relayed its contents to Cassia, of course. Missing her father's funeral had been difficult for her. "We've been informed, yes."

"I have good reason to believe she knows where you are. Not the exact location, thank the gods." Imaryllis turned to Cassia. "Your Grace, it's time to get you out of Midmere."

Cassia wrung her delicate hands together, though her gaze flicked to Orin, searching for guidance.

He crossed his arms. "How certain are you?"

"Certain enough," the stranger spoke up. "It's likely that someone within the castle tipped off Drake Reed."

"Who the fuck are you again?" Artesia snapped.

Imaryllis held up a hand. "This is Gwyn. She helped me escape the guards when they followed me from the castle and tried to have me arrested."

An impending headache made itself known behind Orin's eyes. "Clearly, we have some things to catch up on."

"I don't know that we have that kind of time, Master."

"Gilbert and I have runes all over this area of the city. If danger approaches, we'll have warning." Orin gestured. "Please, start from the beginning."

They gathered round the small table with enough chairs for all but two of them. Orin remained standing, as did the assassin, who lingered close to the edges of the room. As Imaryllis recalled the last few days, Orin studied the stranger named Gwyn, taking in what he could about her. She was small, thin but solid, and brown skinned. She stood straight and poised and carried about her the air of someone who'd grown up in a noble household. Her hazel eyes gave away absolutely nothing. It was unnerving.

When Imaryllis reached the end of her story, Orin most definitely had a headache. Danica knew what she was doing. Either they stayed where they were and risked discovery by the guards tearing apart the city, or they attempted an escape like foxes being smoked from a den and running right into the mouths of waiting hounds. They'd already lost so many at Drake's hand... Magi Drake had lived with, worked with, trained with for decades. Had that not mattered to him at all?

Orin pinched the bridge of his nose, then turned back to the assassin. "Gwyn, is it?"

She dipped her head, surprisingly demure. "Yes, Master Orin."

This woman was a stranger to him, and he didn't trust her yet with Cassia's safety. "May I ask what sparked you to assist Imaryllis?"

"I've been charged with watching the comings and goings of those in the castle. When I saw the magi sneaking out, I followed. She needed aid, and so I provided it."

Orin studied her face, what little he could see with the mask that covered the lower half. "What you did could be considered treason by Queen Danica."

Gwyn shrugged. "Danica isn't the queen."

Good answer. Not that it meant anything other than she might be a good liar.

His head hurt. His heart hurt, too. He could only imagine how Cassia felt, no matter the strong front she put on. Orin closed his eyes for a moment.

"I need to collect my thoughts," he finally allowed. "We will formulate a plan for what to do next. Imaryllis, with me." He turned and headed back upstairs with the swordsmaster at his heels.

They slipped into the small room. Imaryllis looked around, eyebrows raised. "Cozy."

"Isn't it, though?" Orin sat at the table with a sigh, staring at the letter he'd left there. "Our options are looking rather bleak at the moment, aren't they?"

"Try to escape with every city gate heavily guarded or wait to be sniffed out? I would say so." Imaryllis leaned her hip against the table, arms crossed. She kept her eyes on the floor. "I'm sorry, Orin."

He frowned. "What for?"

"It's my fault," she mumbled. "I let it slip to Pava that you were still in the city. I should never have trusted her."

Orin shook his head. "You were alone and surrounded by enemies, my friend. Please do not let someone else's failings become your burden. We're all doing our best in unprecedented situations."

Her shoulders sagged with the weight of her guilt. No matter what he said, she would blame herself. Still, he could see the way she granted herself only a moment of self-pity before she straightened her spine and forced a smile. She paused, touching questioning fingers to the letter. Orin sighed a bit.

"For Wren and Ever," he said. "In the event we're unable to reach them."

Imaryllis's expression softened. "We're the ones in the viper's nest, and yet your thoughts still go to them."

"They do, foolish as it might be."

"I wouldn't say it's foolish. Those boys are family. You love them, and they love you. No doubt they're worrying over your well-being just as you're worrying over theirs."

Orin studied the paper until the words blurred and stopped making sense. He'd never been a man with many *close* friends. Those near to him looked up to him as someone in a position of power, as an authority figure. Aside from Nova, whom could he confide in about personal matters? Only Drake knew of his previous ties with blood magic, and even then, what he knew was minimal. He and Imaryllis had spoken of many things over the years, some more personal than others, but when it came to his apprentices...

His eyes closed. "Do you think Wren is ready? Have I taught him well enough?"

"I think Wren is a smart, capable young man and a talented magi," Imaryllis said without hesitation. "He couldn't have had a better teacher. But I hope you realize such questions don't matter."

Truly, he'd expected no other answer from her, and yet it was what he'd hoped to hear. What he *needed* to hear even, whether or not it was true. "I digress. We came up here to discuss leaving the city."

Imaryllis's expression hardened in determination. "Would you like my professional opinion?"

"You have far more combat and strategic experience than I do. Your input is valuable."

She considered. "Then my vote is to attempt an escape. Through the closest gate, if necessary. Or Gwyn insists she knows a hidden entrance that could lead us through the flood caverns. But no matter the route we choose, unless we're incredibly lucky, I don't foresee us getting out of the city without some sort of a fight."

That's what I'm afraid of.

He took a slow breath. Between Gilbert, Brant, Rue, Artesia, Imaryllis, and himself—plus whatever help this assassin and her companions could offer—they could certainly handle groups of soldiers. But an army? *Several* blood magi? All while trying to protect Cassia? He didn't like those odds.

Orin could feel Imaryllis's eyes on him, an unspoken question on her lips. He lifted his gaze. "What is it?"

Imaryllis chewed at her lower lip, appearing to choose her words carefully. "If you had to fight Drake one-on-one... could you win?"

Oh, what a question. One he'd been mulling over a lot in recent days. "Honestly? I don't know. I've not had reason to stretch my skills so far in a very long time, whereas it would seem Drake has been keeping his finely tuned. A well-trained blood magi is worth ten ordinary magi."

"*Ordinary* magi, yes. But you are no ordinary magi." Imaryllis straightened, turning to look at him head-on. "You are a *master*. You've fought wars and gone against entire troops all by yourself! I've witnessed you on the battlefield. You're incredible."

Orin took the praise with a small but sad smile. Imaryllis didn't yet know about his past, riddled with darkness. Would she look at him the same if she did? He wanted to tell her, and he would, once they got Cassia safely out of the city, when he had enough time to answer all her questions. "Quite a compliment, coming from you."

"We all have our strengths, as you often told me when you trained me." Imaryllis smirked. "With your skill and my specialty in close combat, I'm confident we can get Cassia safely out of the city."

Orin opened his mouth to respond, but a burst of magic zipped through him, making his fingertips tingle and his spine stiffen like a small electric jolt. Imaryllis must've noticed the shift in his demeanor because she, too, tensed. He exhaled and pushed back his chair.

One of the wards had been tripped.

"I hope you're positive about that," he said to her, "because I fear we're out of time."

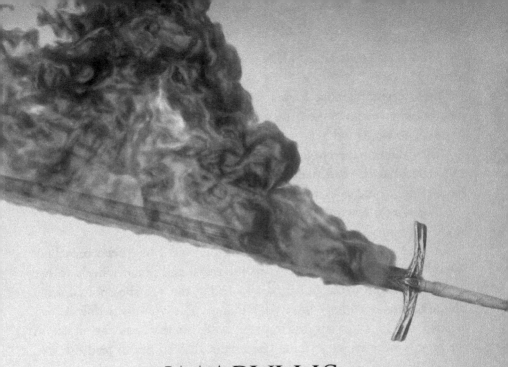

IMARYLLIS

They gathered only the belongings they needed most and fled into the night.

"The city gates are closed and guarded. Where are we supposed to go?" Brant asked.

"There are more ways to exit the city than through the gates," Gwyn said, her tone still mild. She made no move for any of the horses, only helped them prepare theirs. "However, you will need horses when you escape. We will get to the nearest gate, and I will ensure it remains open long enough for you to get through." She didn't elaborate. She helped Cassia onto her horse, bowed deeply to her, and disappeared out of the stables and into the darkness.

Brant scowled after her, letting out a huff. "Are we sure we can trust her?"

No, Imaryllis thought. But what choice did they have? If she had help to offer, they needed to take her up on it. Gwyn was gone only a moment before stepping back into the stables. After taking a long look at the lot of them, she approached Brant and took the reins of his horse. "I'm going to need this."

He pulled back, staring. "Wha—hey! She's mine!"

"And I need to be able to lead you where we have to go," she replied patiently.

Brant cast a plaintive look at Imaryllis and Orin, and when he saw they would give him no help, he groused quietly and pulled himself onto Artesia's horse behind her.

They didn't have enough horses. Cassia and Rue doubled up, and although Imaryllis had planned to do the same, Master Orin instead saddled up behind Gilbert, leaving her with a mount all her own.

Because we're expecting a fight, she thought grimly. *And he knows I will need no one in my way.*

A *crack* pierced the air outside. Another ward had been breached. Imaryllis gritted her teeth, took up the reins, and put her heels to her horse to exit the stable. When she looked at the sky, she spotted a red plume of smoke curling above the buildings. Easy to miss if one weren't looking for it. That was the broken ward, so that was the direction the guards were coming from. The others allowed her to lead the way, galloping down the dark cobblestone roads. Another crack. Another plume of smoke, closer this time.

Then another, from a separate direction.

And another.

Behind her, she heard Gilbert swear and Orin's fretful voice. "They're trying to surround us."

"*Trying?* Seems like they're succeeding," Imaryllis muttered.

Yet another cracked to their left, a few blocks away. Gwyn plunged ahead of Imaryllis, taking a sharp turn down the next alley. Imaryllis didn't hesitate to follow.

Gwyn led them through back streets and closes so narrow their horses barely fit through. Now and again, she looked to the rooftops and lifted a hand, signaling to something or someone that Imaryllis couldn't see.

What she *could* see as they fled were glimpses of guards on the street, their armor glinting in the moonlight. Some were on horseback, others on foot, all of them armed. Their shouts echoed off every wall until she could no longer tell which direction they were coming from. Left, right, back, and ahead. Wards continued to go off.

Danica and Drake were holding nothing back. Likely, every guard in the city was hunting them now.

They rounded one last corner. Gwyn had brought them down so many strange routes that Imaryllis was utterly turned around, but when they exited onto the main street once more, she spotted the eastern gate looming before them. *So close.* They only needed to get through the square.

They pushed their horses as hard as they could. It wasn't enough. By the time they crossed into the square, soldiers were filing in from every direction—including in front of them. They formed a tight row across the opening of the gates, spears forward.

The group pulled their steeds to a halt. Without needing direction, they circled Cassia and Rue's horse, guarding from every angle. Brant and Artesia drew their swords. Imaryllis looked at Orin, whose face remained calm and indifferent. She would do her best to reflect the same sense of confidence.

Soldiers had them surrounded, corralled like livestock, armed with bows or blades or spears. For several long minutes, no one moved. Then the crowd parted, and through the valley rode Drake Reed with his new apprentices at his side. One by one, they dismounted. Drake greeted them with a snake-like smile. His voice rang clear and pleasant across the square.

"Orin, Orin… Hiding is so *very* unlike you, sweet friend."

Orin's voice betrayed nothing. "It's become quite apparent we do not know each other as well as either of us thought."

Drake scoffed and gave a dramatic wave of his hand. "I would like the princess back if you please. Her mother is sick with worry."

Before Orin could respond, Princess Cassia spoke out. "I'll not be returning to the castle. You will allow me and my companions to leave the city unharmed. That is an order!"

He *tsked* and spread his hands out as though in apology. "I'm afraid I cannot allow that, my dear. The queen's orders outrank yours, you see."

Imaryllis's temper flared. She brought her horse around to address the assembled soldiers, so many of whom had trained under her. Many avoided her gaze. "Danica is not our queen. You all know this to be true. With our king gone, *Cassia* is our true heir. Only a Starling may hold the throne!"

A soft murmur rippled through the crowd. Soldiers shifted uncomfortably, exchanging glances. A few lowered their weapons. Some stepped back and stood down.

"Normally," Drake called, not skipping a beat, "what you say would be true. However, if the princess is currently indisposed and under the influence of a magi's charms, she cannot very well give consent or orders, can she?"

Cassia's eyes widened. "I'm under no charms!"

"You wouldn't know if you were," Drake replied sweetly.

Imaryllis scanned the troops. There was enough uncertainty trickling through them that they might make it through this. Just might. Most of these men and women did not know what was going on or what to do about it. They were following orders as they'd been trained to do, but the unrest and confusion were there.

Beside her, Gwyn spoke softly enough that she could barely make it out. "Buy us a minute longer, magi."

Oh, she hoped that meant Gwyn had a plan. Imaryllis would fight their way out of the city if she had to, but it wouldn't be pretty. Before she could open her mouth, Cassia's horse stepped forward, bringing her steed between Orin's and Imaryllis's.

"If I go with you, will you allow the others to leave the city unharmed?"

Imaryllis's gaze snapped to the girl. Artesia swore, and Gilbert's face paled. Orin kept his expression carefully neutral. Whether Cassia meant it as an actual bargaining tactic or as a means to buy time—it didn't matter.

Drake folded his arms, considering the offer. "Tempting. But I'm afraid not, little one. Orin here is wanted for the murder of the king. I cannot very well let him go. And I believe Lady Imaryllis and your other companions are under suspicion of conspiring against the throne and drugging the queen's supper."

Imaryllis glanced at Orin, but his eyes were locked with Drake's, whose face sparked with fierce amusement. For Danica, it might've been about maintaining the throne. For Drake Reed, this was only about Orin. This was personal.

"I propose a different solution," Orin said. "A duel. I know much of your quarrel is with me alone, and in that case, we shouldn't involve so many others."

Drake raised his eyebrows, threw his head back, and laughed. "Tricky of you, Master, but no. Only the losing side begs for one-on-one combat. I can take all of you without breaking a sweat."

Was that true? None of them had seen the extent of his powers yet. Perhaps he was bluffing.

Oh, please, let him be bluffing.

Drake gave a flick of his wrist. The guards at his side advanced.

They got no further than a foot before an arrow took one of them in the throat.

The guard choked, staggering forward as he grasped for the shaft jutting from the front of his neck. Before any of them could fully process what had happened, a volley of arrows came raining down from the city walls and rooftops like a storm.

Many of them hefted their shields up and over their heads to block the onslaught. Drake, however, sneered. The blood spilled at his feet would do nothing but empower him. This was a battle that needed to be ended quickly. Knowing she'd never be able to fight properly on horseback, Imaryllis slid from her saddle. Orin joined her, tipping his head to look at Gwyn.

"Can one of your people get the gates open?"

She inclined her chin. "Already working on it."

He nodded once, then turned to Imaryllis and grasped her elbow. "Whatever happens, you are to get Cassia to safety. Do you understand?"

Imaryllis startled, looking up at him. "Master Orin—"

"Do you understand?" he repeated.

She opened her mouth, closed it, then clenched her jaw. "Understood."

It was a promise she would keep, but only if she had to. Before it came to that, she would fight. She drew her swords. The magic pooled from her hands, the shimmer of white and gold fire that formed the blades in her grasp.

When the torrent of arrows ceased, those soldiers left standing—and there were many—charged. Imaryllis lurched forward, cleaving through the first man to cross her path. The next lifted a mace high above her, and she feinted left. Let him bring the club down as she dodged right and put a sword into the exposed joint of his pauldron and chest plate.

One by one, she cut through the soldiers. Familiar faces blurred together and smeared with red, and she couldn't stop long enough to see what the others were doing beyond the glimpses she caught in her periphery. Cassia's horse reared. She and Rue clutched at each other. Artesia pulled up beside them, and Brant grabbed the reins to keep the beast from throwing its riders to the ground. Although she couldn't see them, Imaryllis could feel the ebb and flow of magic from Orin and Gilbert, trying to stem the stream of guards with whatever spells they could.

Still, the onslaught was relentless. Beyond it all stood Drake in the distance, smiling, enjoying every blood-drenched minute of it. In her distracted fury, a guard found his way to her side unawares. She pivoted, but Gwyn drove a dagger into his jugular before she could respond. Breathless and blood-soaked, the assassin hissed, "To the gates!"

As though on cue, the portcullis began to rise with a groan. Imaryllis cast her gaze to the walls. She could see movement, but no details. All she could do was pray that Gwyn's people had indeed overtaken the soldiers there... and that they could hold it a bit longer.

She ran back to her horse and hauled herself into the saddle, cutting foes down as she went. She swept up alongside Cassia and Rue, giving their horse a smack on the rump to get it running. With a lurch that nearly sent Rue tumbling, the mare took off. Imaryllis, Artesia, and Brant hurried after.

The portcullis had opened enough that they could clear it, and from there, it would be a matter of outrunning Drake's magi and soldiers. Freedom was so close.

Almost, almost…

Mere feet from the gates, the ground crackled and split, and from it surged a wall of flame, blocking their path once more. Heat washed over her skin. Imaryllis swore, drawing the horse back around. Beyond the chaos, Drake, face twisted into a snarl, had one hand raised above his head. Imaryllis took in the massive square. From the shadows, Gwyn's allies had emerged, moving in and out of groups of soldiers like shadows and dropping them like flies. Yet their numbers were too few. She could no longer see Gilbert, and Master Orin was surrounded. He wavered on his feet. Even at this distance, she could see the slump of his shoulders, the fatigue that had set in from trying to buy them time. The more bloodshed there was, the stronger Drake would become.

Was this unwinnable from the beginning? she wondered, dull horror setting in.

As though he could pluck the very thoughts from her head, Master Orin looked over his shoulder. The world slowed. In that moment, Orin's eyes locked onto hers. He smiled and mouthed words she couldn't make out.

Orin whirled away, grabbed an advancing guard, disarmed him, and dragged the blade across the soldier's throat. He cast the body aside, his hands bloodied, and dropped to one knee with his palms to the ground.

Orin's magic rippled throughout the square, but it differed from anything Imaryllis had felt from him before. Powerful, raw, *dark*—and it stilled her with a chill to her core. A shockwave burst from where Orin's hands connected to the ground, sending violent cracks splintering outward across the cobblestones. The earth shook, toppling the soldiers close to him. Drake kept his footing, but the rumbling fractured his concentration for just a second.

That was all they needed.

The flames surged brighter, then abruptly died. Imaryllis wouldn't forfeit their chance. She shouted to the others and put her heels to her horse.

"We can't leave him!" Cassia cried, but her protests fell to the wayside.

They had no time. Master Orin had issued an order, and Imaryllis would follow it.

Before anyone could stop them again, they raced out the city gates and into the night.

CASSIA

Cassia clutched at the reins for dear life, but it didn't stop her from twisting in her saddle as she begged for everyone to stop. They couldn't leave their people behind. Not Gilbert, not Gwyn's companions who'd come out of the woodwork to aid them… and not Master Orin.

She thought of Orin tending to her as a small girl when she was sick. Of how gentle and kind he'd always been. She thought of the evenings when she would intrude on her father's chess games with him and how she would crawl into one of their laps while they explained the game to her. When she got older, they even allowed her to play now and again. Orin always let her win. She sat in on some of the lessons he gave his apprentices. He took in the small animals she found injured or abandoned. He'd been warm and attentive and ever present for her when Father had been busy or away.

Now Orin looked back at them with a red glint in his eyes that sparked familiarity only because Cassia had seen it before, from Everis. Orin tore through the guards that came after him with horrifying ease until Drake Reed's apprentices advanced on him. One man against a group of blood magi… Was he strong enough to win this? Something in the set of Lady Imaryllis's jaw and her hardened eyes gave her an answer she didn't want.

She carried with her a letter Master Orin had given her before they left the inn. The parchment in her pocket felt heavy. She clutched at it to ensure it was still there.

"When you see them, please give this to Wren and Everis."

Had he known it would come to this?

The frantic pleas to turn back fell from her lips unbidden. No one listened. What could they have done for him even if they'd stayed?

Even so, Cassia begged and begged until the portcullis slammed shut behind them.

She turned and pressed her face into Rue's tunic and sobbed.

ORIN

Relinquishing himself to blood magic was like sinking into a warm bath after a long journey. Comfortable. Familiar. Invigorating. The city gates were closing again. It no longer mattered. The princess was on the other side. Now it was up to him to keep Drake and his soldiers from going after them. He needed to buy time.

A blade grazed Orin's ribs, wrenching him to one side with a hiss. He held fiercely onto his concentration. If he could win this, everyone—the city, Cassia, Everis, Wren—would be safe. The surge of power washed over him, and he whipped around, chanting beneath his breath. The ground trembled, bits of stone and wood breaking free from the surrounding buildings. A beam came crashing down onto a few soldiers. Their screams rang through the night.

A soldier narrowly avoided the collapse, ending on his knees in the dirt. Orin was on him before he could get up, splitting his throat open wide with one quick stroke of his blade. The man clutched at the wound, staring at the crimson pouring down his front with wide eyes. The sensation sent a shiver down Orin's spine, slaking a thirst he'd ignored for far too long.

Finally.

It was time to deal with the head of the serpent.

Drake.

Orin slid his palm along the flat of his blood-covered sword and drew another rune on his arm.

Keep going.

Exhaustion made his vision blur.

Everyone is depending on you.

Drake made his way through the soldiers, eyes flashing in fury and lips curled into a snarl.

Orin dropped his sword, extending his hands to either side and closing his eyes. Around him, the raindrops froze in mid-air, the pitter-patter turning into a deafening silence. The words fell from his lips like a prayer, and the water gathered against his palms, swelling and swirling into tumultuous watery spheres. Drake closed in on him. Orin's arms lifted. The storm circulated through every nerve of his body.

Another incantation. The gathered water split again, hardening into glass-like shards, thousands of little knives suspended in the mist. His eyes snapped open. The ice ripped through the air with magnificent force, unpredictable in its trajectory. They tore through the leather of soldiers' armor, penetrated the joints where metal plates met, shredded through exposed skin. All around him, Orin could hear, see, *feel* the guards dying. Could feel the air clouding with a fine red mist of rain, magic, and blood.

The fallen were people he'd known for decades. He saw them now as a snuffed-out flame, an insignificant sear against his skin.

It serves them right.

The effects of the spell slithered out of him. He gasped, doubling forward to catch his breath. His heart raced with the possibilities. Why had he ever given this up? He differed from Drake or anyone else. He could harness it, control it, use it to *protect* those he cared for. And he would start by ripping Drake Reed to pieces and avenging everyone whose life had been lost because of him.

The mist cleared enough that he could see Drake kneeling several feet away, gripping his bleeding side where he'd not been fast enough to avoid the barrage of ice. Orin scooped up a fallen soldier's sword.

Nearby, a small voice wailed.

Orin stands in a rundown home in a plague-infested city, staring at a boy with wide, frightened eyes. He knows that look. He knows the crawling sensation of dark magic. He knew it intimately for so many years.

Everis. His name is Everis.

Later, he holds the young boy's hand as they enter the castle, and Everis is filled with fear and uncertainty that Orin can feel to his bones. He squeezes that tiny hand, smiles down at him, reassuring.

"I know it looks intimidating, but this will be your home. We will be your family, and I will keep you safe."

Orin stumbled, whirling toward the sound. He spotted a boy near a building desecrated by the ongoing battle, spotted the crumbling bits of that same building that were precariously close to falling. Only in his periphery did he see Drake extending a hand toward the building to coax the debris along. The smirk on his face spoke volumes.

What will it be? Which will you choose? Your power and your revenge?

Orin bit back a cry.

Wren is seven, a force to be reckoned with, a boy easily overwhelmed by his emotions. He will be a good magi someday, but he has much to learn.

Orin finds him on the second floor of the tower, in tears, hunched over a collection of books and potion bottles—several of which are broken. Concerned, Orin steps up behind him, though it only takes a moment to see that Wren's attempts at replicating potions have not worked and he's shattered the bottles in his frustration. Orin only watches, silent.

Wren sniffs, swiping a sleeve across his eyes. "I can't do it. I can't. It's too hard. I'm not going to be a magi."

"Aren't you? That's disappointing to hear." Orin takes a seat on the bench beside him. Wren looks at him, eyes filling with tears anew before he lets out a sob.

Orin planted a foot into the cobblestone and twisted to change direction, making a dash for the boy. He snatched the child into his arms as the rubble came crashing down, and they struck the ground rolling, hard enough that Orin's shoulder wrenched out of place upon impact. The child clung to him, dirty-faced, big green eyes and blond hair, howling in fear.

He says nothing as he gathers Wren into his arms and holds him, allowing his apprentice to cry into his robes. It's not just the spells, is it? Wren is only a child, trying to adapt to castle life and to the expectations placed upon him. Worse yet—the expectations Orin knows he places upon himself. Wren's own family didn't want him, so how must it feel now, in a new place with new people, afraid of failing? Afraid of further rejection?

Orin gently strokes Wren's hair back from his face. He allows Wren to cry because sometimes tears are necessary for healing, and he will not make his apprentice think there was anything wrong with his grief. They were family. He was Wren's and Wren was his. His actions would speak louder than any words ever could.

Orin stared at the child, pain radiating through his shoulder. With his still-functional hand, he pried the boy from him and whispered urgently, "*Go.*" The boy didn't need to be told twice. Orin rolled to his side, trying to reorient himself amongst the settling dust and rain and the ringing in his ears. He reached for the magic again, rallying his strength so he could stand and fight.

He got as far as his knees before pain shot through every nerve in his body.

He didn't need to look down to know he was bleeding. Shards of broken armor, spearheads, splinters of steel and iron, magically propelled, pierced him from every direction. Orin could feel each and every one where they bit into his lungs and stomach and ribs.

He breathed in to try to speak. Coughed. Choked on the taste of blood.

Footsteps. The overflow of Drake's magic rushing over him. Drake stood behind him, bending down. But no longer did his voice hold its melodious taunting lilt. Rage radiated from him like fire.

"Why, Orin? Why did you make me do this?" Drake dropped to his knees before him. The beautiful, clear eyes Orin had once admired were barely recognizable. His friend, his companion, was little more than a stranger to him now. That stranger grabbed Orin's face. "*Why did you make me do this?!* I always meant for this to be both of us. We would have taken the world by storm. Why were you willing to use blood magic to fight *against* me rather than *with* me?"

It took Orin a few tries to speak.

"I am disappointed in you."

There, in that moment, Orin saw a flicker of the Drake Reed he knew and loved in those eyes.

Drake flinched back as though scalded. He lurched to his feet. Tore away from Orin and *screamed*, fury and resentment and grief ripping through the night like the same shards that had ripped through Orin.

Orin felt his ability to breathe leave him as he slumped forward to the ground, clutching uselessly at his chest. It wasn't quick. It wasn't painless. Drake wasn't kind enough for that. He raged on, snarling orders to his apprentices and guards. It sounded so very far away. Drake left him there in the dirt to either bleed out or suffocate on his own blood, whichever came first.

It gave him time to think. Time to regret, to grieve. For the lives that were lost. For Cassia, being stripped of both her parents so young. For the friend he had lost. For all the moments in Wren's and Ever's lives he wouldn't be there to see.

Oh, but he was so *proud* of them. Of everything they were, everything they would ever be. Brilliant and kind and wonderful. They would have each other. He found comfort in that, even if in nothing else.

As Cassia mounts her horse, Orin takes her hand and presses the freshly penned letter into her palm. She pauses, looks down at him, frowning. "What is this?"

"It's for Wren and Ever. In the event you see them before I do. Would you see that they receive it?"

She meets his eyes, the worry and concern clear in her soft face. Yet the urgency of their present situation isn't lost on her. They have no time for questions. She takes the folded parchment and tucks it away with a curt nod. "Of course."

Orin steps back. Bows. "Thank you, Your Grace."

"However, it's my intention that we will all see them together."

Orin offers her a small smile. "Yes. That is my hope as well."

He spotted Nova, perched amongst the rubble of the homes he and Drake had destroyed.

How many people did I hurt?

She fluttered over to him. The soft brush of her wings against his face brought him comfort. She didn't make a sound but bowed forward, pressing her head into his hand as her eyes met his. He couldn't speak, but when had they ever needed words? Perhaps she would continue to live on with whatever magic he'd once imbued her with. Perhaps he could give her whatever little he had left.

Look after Ever and Wren for me, my friend.

She remained with him until the end, as she always had.

WREN

Wren woke to the fluttering of wings against his face and the scent of rain and the taste of ash on the back of his tongue. The sound of clashing metal and a slowing heartbeat echoed in his ears long after his eyes snapped open. He bolted upright, breathless and soaked in cold sweat. He reached for the spot next to him in bed and found it empty. Everis stood by the windows, bathed in cold moonlight. By the shadows beneath his eyes, he didn't appear to have slept yet, or at least not slept well.

Wren tried to make his mouth work. No sound came out. His chest heaved with dread and terror. Something was so very *wrong* in a way he'd never experienced before. His vision blurred, tears overflowing.

When he tried again to speak, his voice caught in a sob. He brought a hand to his face, touching the tears on his cheeks. Where had they come from?

Everis didn't ask if he was all right, but came to him immediately. It was all Wren could do to grab Everis the moment he was close enough, pulling Ever's tall frame into his arms to embrace him. Everis enveloped him in a tight hug. They clung to one another in silence while Wren tried to reel in his whirling emotions.

"Something's wrong," he finally managed, barely a whisper against Everis's throat.

"I know." His fingers slid through Wren's hair, reassuring, although his anxiety was palpable. Whatever Wren was feeling, Everis felt it too. He only wished he could pinpoint what *it* was.

Wren pulled back to look at him. "We should be home. We should've left days ago."

"You know that wasn't an option. We couldn't have known what was going on," Everis said gently. How odd of *him* to be the practical one, but he was right. "But…"

"But?"

"We could leave. Right now."

Wren scrubbed a hand across his eyes, frustrated with himself and his confusing emotional outburst. "It's the middle of the night. We can't possibly wake everyone to leave."

Everis paused. "I didn't say everyone else. I said *we*."

That earned him an incredulous look. "Are you mad? You think we can go through the mountain pass, just the two of us, and make it out alive?"

"I can protect us." Defiance glinted in Everis's eyes as he spoke, his spine stiffening.

"You've only just begun training to keep your power in check. Don't go thinking you're a master in your own right just yet."

Ever flushed in embarrassment, yet the barb seemed to do the trick of shaking some sense back into him. "I only meant, if we don't have time to spare, if you feel we need to be home…"

Wren closed his eyes. He wanted to grab his things and dart out that door immediately, just like Ever said. But it would be suicide. What would they even do if they made it to Midmere in one piece? Stage a two-person rescue mission for Master Orin? Go up against Drake and whoever had sided with him?

Faulk said they had friends there that could help us, he remembered.

Yet Orin's voice lectured in his head. *Don't be reckless. Patience.* It was so crystal clear it made his eyes fill with fresh tears all over again.

What's wrong with me?

He swallowed the lump in his throat, forcing himself to take a few deep breaths. Perhaps he was homesick. It wasn't as though he was used to being away from Midmere without Orin.

"Thank you, Ever, but no. We'll leave in the morning, as planned."

With great effort, he lay back down, pulling Everis with him. Everis kissed him, full and desperate and just as afraid as Wren felt. They curled there together beneath the down blankets, their limbs intertwined. Wren was hyperaware of every breath against his neck and bare chest. Everis's eyes were closed, but Wren knew he was wide awake.

The world felt empty and wrong. His heart hurt.

Neither of them slept much the rest of the night. When morning arrived, Wren's eyes were heavy and tight, his limbs weighted. Still, he moved with purpose, hurrying Everis along. They bade their farewells to Ryland, Ivy, and Captain Annaliese. Wren wondered if the soldiers were secretly happy to see Everis leave.

Faulk had said they would wait at the city limits. Wren didn't spot the growingly familiar Court outfits, but there was a group of six people dressed in riding leathers lingering with their horses. They might've looked like any other band of riders, but something about them made Wren glance twice. One of them had his eyes on them. Ever flanked his left as they rode closer. The watchful man tugged the reins, drawing his horse toward Wren's. His long silver hair had been pulled back out of his face, which was marred by angry scars across one cheek, but it was his striking gold eyes that caught Wren's attention.

He drew to a halt, stunned. It was the first time he'd seen the man without his mask and hood. "Faulk?"

"Magi," Faulk replied easily, turning to coax his steed into a brisk walk so they could begin their journey away from the city.

Wren rode up alongside him, a smile playing across his mouth. "Here I was beginning to wonder if you had a face under there after all."

Faulk snorted. "Trust me. I'd have preferred us wearing our uniforms, but we're meant to be common sellswords and these clothes attract less attention."

A cursory look over the others didn't reveal anyone Wren knew— although Everis was eyeing one of the young men in surprise.

"I saw him at Ryland's manor," Ever said. "He came in to stoke the fire and bring our supper, remember?"

Wren squinted. The young man did have a slight air of familiarity about him. He was unremarkable looking. Short dark eyes and hair, olive complexion.

Faulk cracked a smile. "I needed a way to keep an eye on you, didn't

I?"

They really are everywhere.

"Have you heard anything from Midmere? Any word about our master?"

"There wouldn't have been time to receive anything if they did send it. But they know to expect us, and they should hopefully be at work looking for the princess in the meantime."

If they find Cassia, they'll find Orin.

That was what Wren wanted to believe, at least.

They rode until the sun went down. Although the weather was clear and Wren wanted to beg Faulk to let them continue, doing so would be at their own peril. The horses were tired, and his body ached from being in the saddle for so many hours. With no rain in sight, they didn't bother with tents and instead laid their bedrolls around the fire. Their companions took turns keeping watch and had them up and moving again before dawn.

The further into the pass they ventured, the less Wren recognized it. This must've been the stretch of the trip he'd been unconscious. They would enter bandit territory again soon. He only hoped they weren't holding a grudge over their failed attack last time.

Every evening when they made camp, Everis spent a few hours working on his magic and the exercises Ivy had given him before they left—specifically on his focus and control. Wren kept nearby, always with a watchful eye. He remembered watching Ever and Ivy the day before they left, and the one time he'd thought to praise Ever's progress, Ivy had scoffed.

"*This?* This *is practice with wooden swords in an empty training yard. The real test will come when something disrupts his calm, when he feels threatened or afraid.*"

Not comforting, given the situation Wren suspected they were about to step into.

When the weather took a windy and rainy turn, it required the small convoy to erect their tents and turn in earlier than any of them cared to. None of the assassins were talkative round the campfires at night, at least not with him or Ever. They kept to themselves, speaking in hushed tones and with bowed heads. Faulk pointed out that they were a group used to working to maintain their secrets. Part of that, no doubt, meant distancing themselves from others to avoid anything slipping.

For the first time, Wren felt a flicker of a connection to them. Regardless of whether he agreed with their way of life, he realized just how committed they were to it. So much so that they forsook any family outside of the Dusk Court. They were each other's family, and it made them all that much more determined to protect what they had. To some extent, it was like that with him and Ever, wasn't it? He would guard the secret of Ever's origins as carefully as he could. Would protect him with his own life if it came to that.

The following day, as they neared the site of the initial attack, Wren could sense Ever's unrest. The sunlight had burned away most of the morning fog, but not all of it. They took their time through the pass, minding the holes to avoid anyone's horse breaking a leg.

Faulk pushed to the head of the group, inclining his chin toward the cliffs. When he came to an abrupt halt and gave a sharp snap of his fingers, everyone stopped. In eerie synchronization, the assassins drew their masks over their noses and mouths. Beside Wren, Ever shifted, spine rigid.

From the hillside, a group emerged from the lingering fog and descended on them. Others remained atop the ridge, crossbows raised. Heart pounding, Wren reached for his sword. He grasped the hilt, but didn't draw it yet. Faulk had made no defensive move, and Wren wanted to follow his lead. If they could get out of this without a fight, all the better.

One man, his face a mess of scars, stepped away from the armed group, favoring his left leg when he walked. Faulk removed his left glove, revealing an owl tattoo that adorned his wrist. "We're just passing through. I believe your treaty with the Five Guilds is still in effect?"

The man sniffed, broad shoulders lifting in a shrug. "'Course, m'lord. Your people are welcome to go." He raised a hand to point at Everis. "That one, though, he comes with us."

Wren's heart about climbed into his throat. "What—"

Faulk silenced him with a stern look before turning back to the bandit. "Not a request I will grant. We're escorting these two, which means they're under our protection."

"Wasn't a request. That fuckin' demon slaughtered a buncha my people," the man sneered. "He ain't human, nor is he worth protectin'."

"If it's a rematch you want, I would be happy to oblige," Ever growled, drawing his sword.

Wren placed a hand on his arm, a silent plea to wait.

"To my understanding, you attacked their camp while they slept,"

Faulk drawled, unperturbed. "They acted in self-defense."

"Don't matter. No one with that sort of power ought to be walking about." The man's eyes burned into Ever, brimming with contempt. "Take the other bloke if you want, but if you'd seen what we saw, you wouldn't be so quick to defend this one."

"We've defended worse." Faulk swung down from his saddle. He strode over to the bandit, who towered over him by a good foot and outweighed him by an easy ten stone. And yet, Faulk still managed to look down his nose at him. "Your opinion of my charges is irrelevant. You've made an agreement with the Guilds. Am I to understand you wish to break that contract?"

The end of his sentence was punctuated by each assassin drawing their blades in unison, so in sync that the sound of steel against sheathes made a single unsettling sound. Wren looked around. Every assassin had their eyes locked onto somewhere different: the bandits before them, the ones on the hillside... They were silent, still, poised. Dangerous. He'd never been more grateful that the Dusk Court was on his side.

The bandit leader's fierceness faltered. He glanced between Faulk and Ever and back again, weighing his options. The bandits outnumbered them by a lot. Was Faulk talking big, or could this small group take on the two dozen bandits surrounding them?

Finally, the man licked his chapped lips and stepped slowly to one side. "'Course not. Wouldn't dream of breaking a treaty with the Guilds."

Faulk gave the curtest of nods. There was no smugness in his actions, no air of superiority as he strode back to his horse and swung into the saddle. Wren tried to remember how to breathe as the bandits cleared their path. Beside him, the tension eased from Ever's shoulders. They rode past without another word.

When he was convinced the bandits were well out of earshot, Wren drew his horse up alongside Faulk's. "Who are the Five Guilds?"

"Hm?"

"The Dusk Court is one, obviously. Who are the others?"

Faulk gave him a sidelong look, somewhere between amused and exasperated. "Aren't you privy to enough information that you shouldn't be, magi?"

"Perhaps, but if you were to find out there was some secret guild you'd never heard of, wouldn't you want to know more about it?"

"Yes, but I wouldn't expect them to spill their secrets just because I asked nicely."

Wren grinned. "Have you ever asked nicely for anything?"

"An assassin asking *nicely* is probably accompanied by a knife to someone's throat or prying off their fingernails or something," Everis muttered from his other side.

Wren shot him a look and opened his mouth to chastise him, but Faulk gave a short laugh.

"He's not wrong," he said before flicking his reins and trotting on ahead.

EVERIS

On the other side of the mountains, they stopped at the same inn in Blackpool they'd stayed in on the way to Patish, though their numbers were significantly fewer this time. Rather than retreat upstairs, Everis and Wren stuck with their companions for supper, soaking in the warmth of a fire and a good mead and a hot meal.

Everis still found it tricky to get a read on the assassins in their company. Something about Faulk ruffled his feathers, though he'd grudgingly admit he didn't mind the man as much as he minded that Faulk seemed so familiar with Wren.

There was Stryder, a lean, steely-eyed woman nearly as tall as he was, who looked as though she could've flattened any of the men in her company with little effort. Yet she spoke warmly and had offered him some sweets she'd brought along on the trip, so he couldn't help but like her.

Sitting off on their own were a pair of red-haired twins named Sevin and Vesir. Everis couldn't tell them apart, not that he really needed to. Neither of the women had spoken a word to him or Wren the entire journey.

Elias was wiry and small, with olive skin and dark eyes. He was loud with a habit of singing by the campfire—something he thankfully didn't do there in the tavern, lest he draw attention to them.

Jade was the last to make up their group. He was polite, smiled easily, was strikingly handsome with his long, dark braided hair and gray eyes, and yet he had an unsettling aura about him that made Everis feel about three inches tall whenever the man addressed him.

It was Elias, Jade, and Stryder who sat across from him and Wren at the table over supper, with Faulk seated on Wren's other side. Conversation stayed light and focused on topics that were of little importance. A precaution, Everis imagined, just in case anyone happened to be eavesdropping.

He was halfway through his meal when Wren froze beside him, and the fear spreading from him immediately made Everis drop his spoon. Before he could look up, Wren had grabbed his thigh beneath the table and dug his fingers in, bruisingly tight. Everis winced, stole a glance askance, and mimicked what Wren was doing… keeping his head down and trying to focus on his meal as though nothing were amiss. But when he turned his gaze toward the window on his left, he spotted several armored men on horses bearing the sigil of House Starling.

Royal soldiers… all the way up here?

"Keep eating," Faulk's low voice rumbled. "Don't acknowledge them."

The door to the inn swung open, and two of the soldiers entered, squinting and swinging their gazes about the half-filled tavern. One soldier strode to the bar, leaning on it and addressing the innkeeper in a voice intentionally loud enough to be heard over the din of the room.

"We're here on behalf of Queen Danica of Midmere," he announced. Then he turned back to look at the rest of the tavern, given that he now had their attention. "For those of you who haven't heard the news, our king is dead, and a group of rogue magi have bewitched and kidnapped Princess Cassia. The queen will pay a handsome reward for any information as to the whereabouts of her daughter."

"Bewitched?" Everis whispered.

Wren's brow furrowed.

The soldier continued, "We believe the princess is in the company of magi Imaryllis Leif and magi Rue Brevil, although others may be with them whom we are unaware of at this time."

Everis and Wren exchanged anxious looks. Everis bit his tongue, trying not to speak up, to ask questions. The soldier rattled off brief descriptions of Imaryllis and Rue, informed the tavern patrons that they would be available all night should anyone wish to report anything, then took his leave back outside, likely to tend to his men and horses.

The moment he was gone, conversation within the pub picked up again, this time with a charged energy behind it, full of gossip and questions no one had answers for. Everis didn't dare try to discuss anything, not until Faulk gave a sign it was safe for them to step away from the table and their abandoned meals to slip upstairs.

With the door shut behind and away from prying ears, Wren whirled to face him, grasping his arms. "Cassia escaped the capitol."

"With Lady Imaryllis and Rue…"

"But no mention of Master Orin." A troubled crease returned to Wren's brow. He drew back, brimming with anxiety that had him pacing the small room. "Why would they leave him out?"

Everis tried to grasp for a comforting answer and came up with nothing good. "Maybe… Maybe they forgot? Maybe they were instructed not to say anything about him?"

"To what purpose? Unless they wanted to ensure it lured us back to Midmere rather than searching for Cassia's group." Wren paused, looking very much like he wanted to latch on to that theory but was having difficulty doing so. He turned back to Everis, their eyes meeting. "You don't think that's the case, though, do you?"

"No," he softly admitted. "I think if we were even on their minds, they'd have sent the news to Patish quickly, not had soldiers announcing it in random inns on the off-chance word might float back to us."

Oh, he hated the way Wren's expression fell. Neither of them wanted to think of the alternative, that Master Orin was trapped within the city limits. Or worse, that he was being held prisoner under Danica's watch.

Everis stepped closer, drawing Wren's face into his hands. "What is it he always tells us? Not to dwell on the unknown, but to anticipate it and plan accordingly."

Wren swallowed hard. "Yes. Yes, you're right. I shouldn't get all worked up. Lady Imaryllis is out there somewhere. She'll know what his plans are and what we should do."

"Any thoughts on how we do that? The whole finding her bit, that is."

"No. Faulk might, though."

Everis refrained from rolling his eyes. To say that his prickliness over Faulk's friendship with Wren was entirely gone would be inaccurate, but he'd settled a bit during their travels. Besides, this was too important to be soured over. If Faulk had the means of helping them reunite with their companions and, more crucially, their Master, Everis would get on his knees and grovel for Faulk's help if he had to. "Then we'll ask him."

Wren cracked a meager smile. "It's odd…"

"What is?"

"You, being the rational and comforting one."

It was meant as a compliment, but it stung Everis with a bit of shame and made him avert his gaze. Their situations were normally reversed, weren't they? With Wren being the logical, even-keeled one who didn't allow his emotions to get the best of him for long. Always roping Everis in when his temper flared. He'd seen Wren get angry before, but in moments when it *mattered*, he was the one that others looked to and counted on when Orin wasn't there. It wasn't fair to put that on him, especially not now when they both needed to be strong for one another. Wren being afraid was unfamiliar territory, but then again, it concerned Master Orin, so perhaps it wasn't so out of place.

"Is it an unwelcome change?" Everis asked, attempting to keep his tone light.

Wren touched his jaw, coaxing Ever to meet his gaze. "No. I thought it was quite sweet, actually. Thank you. You know that I wouldn't have been able to do this trip without you."

Everis's cheeks warmed, and he prayed it wasn't visible in the dim lighting. What did he say to that? *Thank you?* Or *You're welcome?*

He didn't end up needing to say anything as Wren leaned up to press a warm kiss to Ever's mouth. It didn't last nearly long enough before a brief knock sounded at their door. Just two sharp raps that, somehow, Ever knew belonged to Faulk because they were as curt and to the point as the man himself. He leaned to unlock the door and open it so that the assassin could step inside.

Faulk regarded them with a characteristically unreadable expression. "Guards are staying overnight. They've started questioning people directly. I suggest killing the lights and ignoring them if they come knocking."

"Won't that draw suspicion?" Wren asked.

"Perhaps, but it's safer than allowing them a proper look at your faces."

Everis hadn't recognized any of the soldiers, but that didn't mean anything. There were hundreds of them back home, coming in and out of training. The ones he knew by name all worked within the castle walls—people he saw and interacted with, at least occasionally. Yet he knew from experience that the guards often recognized the magi. They stood out more; there were fewer of them. Plenty of people knew of

Orin's two apprentices, and it would've been smart on Danica's part to have told them to keep an eye out if she suspected they were headed back from Patish.

"Do you think they were telling the truth about Cassia escaping the city?" Everis asked Faulk.

"Don't see what incentive they'd have to lie about it, really."

"Then do your people know where they are?"

"Oh, absolutely. We have an Owl positioned across every village and city on the continent who keeps track of the comings and goings of everyone."

Everis paused. "Really?"

Faulk deadpanned. "No."

"Oh."

"Look, the information we got today was news to us, too. Anything that's happened since we left Patish? It's as much a mystery to me as it is to you." He surveyed the crestfallen looks on their faces and sighed. "The twins have already set off on the main road. If the princess is smart, she'll head to her uncle. It's the only safe place for her right now. There are two ways they could have gone: by sea or through the mountains. If they wanted to go unrecognized, they wouldn't have risked a boat where a crew member might get a wild idea about ransoming her off to Danica."

Everis stared at Faulk, somewhere between impressed and annoyed. The precision and depth with which the assassin thought things through were worthy of admiration, but he also kind of wanted to hit him for it.

"If we wait here, we might run into them," Wren said softly.

"They'd be hard to miss, yes," Faulk agreed. "But those guards may have the same thought. Patrol the roads close to the pass, wait for them to inevitably make a run for it..."

Everis watched Wren from his periphery, the worried lines on his face twisting in frustration. He moved to the window to glance outside. Only barely could he spot two of the soldiers milling about near the corner of the building, scanning the horizon. "Do we know how many there are?"

Faulk folded his arms. "I've counted eight horses, but likely more if they have people out patrolling."

Everis inclined his chin. Images from the bandit attack flickered to the forefront of his memory. How many had there been? Twenty? Thirty? They'd beaten them back with a modest group of soldiers, even when surprised in the dead of night. Now, they had two magi and a crew of highly skilled and lethal assassins. They could pick off the soldiers one at a time after the sun went down.

You could handle them all on your own.

His pulse fluttered. His skin ached for the feel of his dark magic, the power coursing through his body.

You don't even need them.

You could handle the soldiers on your own.

"Ever?"

Wren's voice made him suck in a breath. He pushed his shoulders back and mentally tried to shake wherever it was his consciousness had tried to wander. "Sorry, I was just thinking. We could take them, couldn't we? If it came to that?"

Faulk frowned. "*If* it came to that, yes."

Everis looked back at him. "You're assassins. Isn't taking people out stealthily what you do?"

"It is... *when* the situation calls for it. And perhaps it may reach that. But right now, these are soldiers who think they're out here to rescue their princess." Faulk swung his gaze between Wren and Ever and back again. "Would you ask us to take the lives of people ultimately trying to defend the same person you are?"

Heat rushed to Everis's face, though he was mildly grateful for the look of shame that passed over Wren's as well, suggesting they'd been of like minds and felt equally chastised.

"No," Wren admitted. "But I doubt they're going to listen to us if we try to reason with them, either."

"Probably not, but that isn't for you to concern yourselves with right now." Faulk shrugged and headed for the door. "Your job is to get some rest—and keep the doors locked."

Everis turned from the window. "What are you going to do?"

Faulk barely glanced at him. "I'm going to do *my* job, magi."

FAULK

Faulk cracked open the window and breathed in. The fair weather had held throughout the mountains, but it was starting to smell like rain. If a storm came their way, it would make traveling slower—but it could also be used to their benefit. Easier to hide. Easier to mask sound. Easier to sneak around.

Stryder watched him from her place on the nearby bed. Elias and Jade had gotten themselves engrossed in a card game whose rules made no sense to Faulk, but it kept them occupied and from interrupting his thoughts while he tried to decide what to do next.

He took in one more deep breath and straightened. Perhaps it was that breath or the shift in his posture, but when he turned back to the room, all three of his companions were watching him.

"Well?" Jade asked.

"We'll give it two hours, time for the sun to fully set." Faulk leaned against the window frame. "Stryder, keep an eye on the magi. If you catch wind of anyone sniffing about their room, deal with it, discreetly. Get the two of them to their horses. Elias, you'll be keeping watch in the tavern. Plenty of people still down there drinking, soldiers included. Engage them if you can; see what loosened tongues might tell us.

240

"Jade, you're with me. We're going to cut their horses loose from the stable. It's not going to stop them, but it ought to slow them down. If anyone encounters any trouble, you know what to do."

Jade adjusted his glasses, giving a thoughtful *hmm* as his gaze dropped back to his hand of cards. "They likely have someone watching the horses, you realize."

"Then we'll handle them." He gave the man a pointed look. "Nonlethal means where possible. I hope I don't have to clarify that."

Stryder groaned. "That makes it a lot harder if they decide to be difficult, you know."

"Almost like it's part of your job to think on your feet and adapt to circumstances," Jade mused. "Although I'll admit, it *would* save us trouble down the line to simply get what information we can, then dispatch them. No risk of them coming after us later."

Faulk bit back a sigh. They weren't wrong. "Let's just spare who we can, shall we? I suspect there's going to be enough bloodshed when we reach Midmere."

An hour later, Elias departed for the tavern downstairs. An hour after that, Faulk and Jade slipped out the window, scaling the walls to drop silently to the damp grass. Faulk tipped his head back to look at Stryder, leaning out after them and keeping watch. He gave her a brief signal, and she ducked inside and closed the window. Together, he and Jade slinked through the drizzling darkness around the back of the inn, minding the windows they had to pass.

He stole a glance at Jade. Faulk had specifically asked him to come along on this mission. Jade was lethal and sharp, quick to act, and although he had a disturbing cold streak to him, he wasn't one who placed himself above the rules. And, on this job, the one who made the rules was Faulk. They'd known each other and worked together for as long as Faulk had been a member of the Dusk Court, and there was no one else he trusted to have his back in the same way.

The stables came into view. They pressed themselves to the outside wall, listening. Beyond the soft sounds of horses stirring and chewing, Faulk could make out voices. He could smell them, too: two people, beneath the scent of hay and manure and rain… No, three. A woman and two men.

He held up three fingers. Jade nodded and signaled to the window high overhead that led to what Faulk suspected was a hayloft. They parted ways. Faulk rounded the corner, crouched, and stole a cautious look around to the entrance. No one lingered outside. All three guards were inside the stables, taking shelter from the rain. Good.

He closed his eyes, straining to listen. Jade was so damn quiet that even Faulk's otherworldly senses couldn't tell where he was until he'd reached the window. Even then, it was the softest scuff of wood and the crunch of straw beneath boots. The guards' conversations didn't skip a beat. Jade had made it inside unnoticed. Faulk straightened, took one last surveying look around, and made for the door.

The soldiers were gathered around a small table, atop of which sat bowls, mugs, and a few candles. Faulk stepped inside and dragged the door shut before any of the soldiers took notice of him. Even then, the trio only stared, baffled by his presence.

"Need something?" the blond soldier asked, beginning to rise to his feet with a hand resting on the pommel of his sword.

Faulk advanced, taking in his surroundings. There were two ways in and out: the window in the hayloft that Jade had used—Faulk caught a glint of moonlight shining off the metal buckles of his clothes—and the main doors Faulk himself had entered. No simple escape. The stabled horses shifted nervously as they caught the scent of him.

"You're here from the capital, yeah?" he inquired. "Looking for the princess?"

The soldier visibly relaxed. His hand dropped from his sword. "That we are. You got some information to share with us?"

"Oh. No, not really. But I hoped you might answer some questions for me."

The three exchanged looks.

"What sort of questions?" the woman asked.

"Like, what exactly happened in the capital? Because I've been hearing quite a different story from what you were talking about inside."

The first soldier scowled. "Well, *our* information comes straight from the queen. What have you heard?"

Faulk absently lifted a hand to stroke the nose of his own horse, who craned her head out from her stall to nibble on his shoulder. She was used to the scent and unsettling feel of him. "That Danica conspired to have her husband murdered, and that's why Cassia fled, to keep herself safe."

The guards startled, all shouting their objections at once.

"That's absurd!"

"The queen would *never*!"

"Who would spread such rumors when the kingdom is in mourning?"

The blond man circled the table, stalking toward him. He stood about eye level with Faulk, though he was broader in build and looked accustomed to towering over people to make them feel small. "Who the fuck has been running their mouths?" Pause. "You been talking to the magi we're looking for? They been through here already?"

Faulk lifted his chin, unflinching. "Might have. Might be that they came through here days ago and you'll never catch up with them now. And it might be worth asking yourself, why would the princess head to Patish if she's under some sort of bewitchment?"

"The magi are working for Duke Ryland," he snapped. "They colluded together to murder the king, and once he's got the princess, he knows he can manipulate the queen to meet his demands."

So that's what she's playing at.

A sharp *crack* split the air outside, close enough that it had to be from the inn or somewhere nearby. A signal, either from Stryder or Elias. *Shit.*

"Interesting theory. Well thought out. Thank you, and sorry in advance."

"Sorry for wha—"

Faulk decked him. Hard. Hard enough that the larger man toppled back and was out cold before he hit the floor.

The remaining guards lurched to their feet. Jade slipped from the shadows and grabbed the woman. A well-placed pinch to the back of her neck made her eyes roll back before she, too, crumpled.

The last man drew his sword and scrambled away, looking between Faulk and Jade and back again, caught between them with no easy means of escape. "Who the fuck are you?"

"We're people who know more of the truth than you appear to," Faulk responded. "Stand down and maybe we can talk."

For half a second, the bloke looked like he might lower his blade and listen. At the last second, his lips pulled up into a fearful snarl, and he lunged for Faulk, taking a wide swing. Not intending to hurt, really, but to force Faulk aside so he could reach the door beyond him. Rather than side-step, Faulk caught the man's fist where it was wrapped around the hilt of his sword, stopping him in mid-swing.

"Stand down," Faulk repeated. "Notice we didn't kill your friends. We could help each other. I have information you lot could use."

"Fuck off," the guard snarled.

Faulk caught the glint of a dagger in the guard's other hand almost too late. Jade wasn't so careless. He cleared the small table, his own blade drawn, and slammed the pommel into the side of the man's skull. The soldier hit a support beam and slid down it, unconscious.

"Damn it." Faulk sighed, running a hand over his face. "Thank you."

Jade flashed him a pleasant smile, already moving to tie the guards up. "Your boyfriend would be awfully cross if you came home with a new set of scars on your face, my friend."

Faulk wrinkled his nose and didn't even try to argue that. He turned to look at the horses. If they weren't scared before, they certainly would be now. Only the horses they'd brought themselves were unbothered, either still sleeping, or else watching with mild curiosity.

The moment Faulk opened the stable doors and the stalls, it took little to send every one of the guards' mounts bolting off into the night.

WREN

Although their room held two beds, Wren and Ever still somehow agreed without having spoken a word that they were going to crowd together on a single. It was something Wren could get used to, having Everis at his back, spooned around him with an arm wrapped loosely about his middle. Wren could feel the rise and fall of his chest and the warm breath that tickled the back of his neck. On any ordinary night, it would've lulled him right to sleep.

Tonight, however, Wren couldn't sleep.

A cumulation of things plagued his thoughts, making it impossible to fully relax. Knowing Cassia was out there somewhere and they needed to find her. Listening to every creak and groan of the building, straining to hear any potential signs that someone was lurking outside their door. Knowing something very wrong was happening in Midmere... and that Master Orin was in the middle of it. The latter, more than anything, was enough to keep him wide awake.

Lady Imaryllis and Rue were supposedly with the princess. That was good. Rue was a young magi who didn't possess impressive combat capabilities, but she was a decent healer in her own right. Imaryllis was as deadly as she was kind, and there weren't many magi better suited to serving as a bodyguard.

But if those were the two who'd escaped, then what of the other magi? What had happened to Gilbert, Drake, Mace, Arabella, or the others? No matter Danica's power, she and her soldiers wouldn't have stood a chance against a group of magi. Unless she'd turned them on each other to retain the loyalty of some of them to even the playing field. He couldn't imagine who would've been foolish enough to believe their fellow magi would kidnap the princess, but then again, a lot had transpired lately that Wren would've once thought impossible.

Wren might not have been able to sleep, but his thoughts were racing so fast that soon he lost himself in them, envisioning too many horrible things and spiraling with the possibilities of what was to come. He'd delved deeply enough into the recesses of his mind that when a hand clamped over his mouth, he nearly shouted in surprise.

His eyes snapped open to Stryder leaning over them. She signaled him to be silent as she drew back, gesturing to Everis so that Wren could turn to him and shake him gently awake with a whispered, *"Quiet."*

Ever stirred blearily, confused, but sat up and surveyed him and Stryder without a sound.

Stryder inclined her chin toward the door. Wren stilled and listened, but couldn't hear anything out of the ordinary. Then he noticed the doorknob twitching, twisting slowly, as someone on the other side carefully tested to see if it was locked. His breath hitched. Ever's face twisted into a snarl, and he slid off the bed, prepared for a fight. Stryder caught him by the arm, shook her head, and instructed them both to head to the open window she'd entered through.

Swift and silent, they grabbed their things and fled into the night; the magi made the two-story drop with far less grace than Stryder did, but no ankles were broken, so Wren considered it a win. They scurried to the far end of the building. Wren wasn't sure where she was taking them, but she'd no doubt planned this out with Faulk in some discussion he and Ever hadn't been privy to.

As they neared the corner, a man's voice hollered behind them. Wren stole a glance over his shoulder, spotting one of the royal guards leaning out their window.

"Move it." Stryder's jog turned into a sprint. The magi followed suit.

Voices filled the previously silent night, guards calling to one another as they rushed from the inn. As they reached the back of the building, a soldier rounded the corner and nearly collided with them. He didn't draw his sword fast enough to fend off Stryder; she slammed him against the wall and had a dagger to his throat before he could fully register the precarious situation he'd found himself in.

Faulk's words stuck out loudly in Wren's mind, that these were people only doing their jobs, that they *thought* they were doing the right thing, trying to rescue the princess. He started to say something, to beg Stryder to spare his life, but she made no move to kill him.

"Why are you after us?" she growled, voice low.

The guard stared up at her, wide-eyed, voice quavering. He looked so young, barely out of training. "We... we spotted you in the tavern, and a few of us recognized the pair of them." His gaze flicked briefly to Wren and Everis. "They're apprentices to one of the traitors."

Everis stepped forward with a snarl. "Master Orin is no traitor!"

"Hush," Stryder hissed. They could all hear footsteps and rustling armor approaching from around the corner. A resounding *crack* near the front of the building momentarily deafened the sound, and Wren glimpsed an odd firecracker speckle of light in the sky. Whatever it was, it certainly had Stryder's attention. She looked down at the frightened boy. "You're going to tell them we went the other way."

He balked. "What?"

She pressed the blade into his throat. "You're going to tell your friends we went the other way. Aren't you?"

His face paled, voice coming out as a squeak. "Y-yes."

Stryder pulled back, grabbed him by the front of his chest plate, and shoved him to one side hard enough for him to land on his knees in the mud. Before he could get up again, she took off with Wren and Everis on her heels.

It had started to rain. The ground was already loamy and slick. Wren nearly lost his footing once, caught by Everis at his side. The last time they'd been like this, running for their lives in the dark, had been the night of the bandit attack in the pass... something Wren didn't want to think about.

They followed Stryder past two unconscious guards lying face down on the ground. As they approached the stables, the doors flew open, unleashing a stampede of horses from inside. The animals bolted, narrowly clearing the three people in their path. Wren pressed close to Ever's side, and Stryder remained steadfast at their backs, the three of them unable to do more than brace themselves and pray none of the herd decided they weren't worth moving *around* instead of *through*.

At the end of the horses came Faulk, astride his own horse and with the reins of another in hand. He galloped to them, shoving the reins into

Wren's grasp for him to scramble up into the saddle. There wasn't time to get all their horses saddled and ready to go. Everis climbed up behind him, an arm around his waist, and Stryder swung up behind Faulk. Jade brought up the rear atop his mare.

"Elias is toward the front," Stryder said, pointing.

Jade nodded, twisted his mount around, and took off in that direction. Faulk turned away from the inn down the main road.

Wren followed, falling in line beside him. "We aren't waiting?"

"No time. They'll catch up."

"How will they find us?"

"Leave my people to me, magi," Faulk called back, then put his heels to his horse.

They fled as fast as their horses could take them, south on the main road, from the inn and the mountains, until Faulk took an abrupt left off the beaten path and into the woods. Wren was accustomed to riding, but not like this. Nothing so hurried, chaotic, frantic. He and Everis mimicked Faulk and Stryder, ducking low to avoid the branches that whipped and clawed at their hair and clothes as their horses tore through the trees.

Somewhere in the distance, another firework crackled in the sky. Wren couldn't see it, nor could he really see where they were going. He could only trust that Faulk was a better rider than he was and that their horses weren't running as blind as Wren felt they were. One misstep, one misplaced stone or root to trip them up, would prove disastrous. He held his breath and the reins as tightly as Everis held him, face pressed into Wren's back.

They slowed after a few miles, letting their exhausted horses decrease their speed to a brisk trot. Wren wasn't sure how far they'd gone or how long they'd been riding, nor did he have any idea which direction they'd traveled. His body ached from the tension and rough ride, and his sides hurt from where Everis had latched on to him. He uncurled his tense fingers with a grimace. Faulk didn't appear to be lost. He meandered through the trees at a leisurely pace, though still alert and taking stock of the surrounding area. For the time being, Wren trusted he knew what he was doing and maintained his silence.

Everis's patience, as always, wore thin first. "Do we have any idea where we're going? What about the others? What if the guards follow us?"

"Difficult to do without their horses," Stryder mused.

"I imagine it won't take them long to snag a couple."

"And by then, they'll have lost their ability to give chase."

"But they—"

"Both of you shut up so I can hear," Faulk snapped.

Everis grumbled under his breath but did, in fact, shut up.

They kept their pace for another thirty minutes before Faulk drew to a stop at an outcropping of stone. It was too shallow to be considered a cave, but would keep out the wind and what rain the canopy of trees allowed through.

Faulk gave Stryder a nudge, and she slid down from the horse. "You three wait here. I'll be back shortly."

Wren didn't need to be told twice. Everis dismounted, offering an arm that Wren gladly accepted. Ever frowned in Faulk's direction. "Where are you going?"

"Do you ever stop asking questions?" Faulk sighed, already turning away.

"I'll stop asking when you start answering some of them."

"Learn some patience."

Everis opened his mouth to respond, but Faulk had already trotted off into the woods, swallowed by the towering trees.

"He spotted that second signal a ways back," Stryder explained, rolling her shoulders and toned arms into a stretch. "He's probably trying to track it down."

"So that was one of our people?" Wren asked. He'd suspected as much. Some sort of means of alerting one another. Hopefully, the guards hadn't taken too much notice of the direction it had come from—if they could see it from the inn.

Stryder laughed and clapped him on the back hard enough that it almost hurt. "*Our people*, he says. Are you thinking of becoming an Owl, little magi?"

He blushed. "No, of course not. I just meant... one of ours. A friend."

"Doubt it was Elias or Jade, if that's who you mean. Entirely wrong direction. No way they got that far ahead of us. It was probably the twins out on patrol. Spotted Elias's flare from the inn, maybe."

Wren glanced at Ever to see if those answers satisfied him. Not that it really answered much at all. They still weren't sure if Jade and Elias would catch up, if Faulk could locate the twins, if they were safe where they were, or what would happen next. The idea of their numbers being reduced from eight to four was worrisome, to say the least.

Although Everis had a frustrated crease to his brow, when he met Wren's gaze, he seemed to force his expression to soften and offered him a small, reassuring smile that made Wren's chest flutter. Once upon a time, years ago, Wren never would've imagined looking to Everis for safety and comfort. He'd only seen a little boy in need of protection and constant assurance. Somewhere, somehow, things had shifted to something more balanced, and he wasn't sure when that had happened... but he appreciated it.

Wren reached for Ever's hand, lacing their fingers together, and drew him down to the semi-dry floor of the cave. He had a feeling they'd be waiting awhile.

EVERIS

Faulk returned two hours later. Wren had started to doze, head on Everis's shoulder, and Everis was loath to wake him. He didn't think Wren had slept much, if at all, prior to being roused for their abrupt escape. But Faulk told them to get up and move, so he roused Wren reluctantly. He took the front of the saddle this time so that Wren could lean into him from behind and get some more rest, even if he couldn't outright sleep.

Surprising no one, Faulk didn't offer information as to where they were going, and Everis was too tired to prod him. It was late, cold, the fog had rolled in, and the dense forest meant little moonlight reached them. He wanted to get to wherever they were going and fall face-first into whatever sleeping surface was available.

An hour passed before a sharp whistle reached his ears. Faulk brought his fingers to his lips and let out one identical to it. Another weird Dusk Court Owl thing, Everis supposed. And when they neared what looked to be a small fire just outside a cave set deep into the mountainside, Everis saw not only the twins but several other figures, far more in number than their missing companions. Something akin to hope flickered inside him and made his chest tight.

"Is that—" he started.

"Might be."

"Why didn't you tell us?"

Faulk gave him a sidelong look, completely unreadable and yet still somehow obnoxiously amused. "You didn't ask."

Everis wanted to hug him and punch him. Instead, he urged his horse ahead, and the jostling stirred Wren from his rest. Together they laid eyes on Brant and Artesia, Magi Rue, and most importantly... Princess Cassia alongside Lady Imaryllis. Wren made a strangled sound, and they nearly tangled themselves up in one another in their hurry to get down from the horse. Wren might've lost his ability to speak, but Everis cried out. "Lady Imaryllis!"

Sheer joy lit Imaryllis's face. She rushed for them, gathering them up in a crushing embrace. Everis could recall gentle pats on the back over the years, the occasional playful hair ruffle, but never a hug like this. She held them as though she'd been convinced she'd never see them again. Perhaps she'd thought she wouldn't. Everis's eyes blurred, and he swallowed the lump of emotion in his throat.

"You're safe," Imaryllis gasped, her own voice choked. "*Sweet Mother*, you're safe."

Everis nearly laughed. "We could say the same about you."

She pulled back, a hand to each of their cheeks, looking them over. She brushed a thumb across the healing scar on Everis's face. Briefly, he could've sworn her eyes looked glassy. "You're both alright? In one piece? I've been worried sick."

Everis glanced askance. Wren's gaze was traversing the small camp, as though still holding on to the hope of spotting Orin. That despite everything they already knew, their master might've somehow played everyone and shown up when they so desperately needed him.

He swallowed hard and met Everis's eyes briefly before looking at Imaryllis with a forced smile. "Fairly certain we've been safer than the lot of you have."

Imaryllis studied his face. She was too observant for her own good. For a moment, Everis thought she might comment on it, but instead she pulled them in for another tight hug before drawing away completely.

"You two must be exhausted. Come on, let's get you warmed up and fed. We can catch up after that."

They turned to the group. Princess Cassia lingered near the fire with hands wrung together, wide-eyed and eager, as though struggling to maintain decorum and wait her turn to greet them. Despite their exhaustion, they both bowed, even if the gesture felt needless given how the princess promptly reached out to clasp their hands in her own.

It had only been weeks since they'd seen her last, and yet she looked... different. Older. Tired. Sad. It was easy to forget that Cassia was younger than him. She was royalty and acted like it. Oh, she had often played with them in the yards when they were much smaller, until her mother or governesses came to whisk her away with a scolding, and she'd always had a smile and kind word for them over the years... But she knew how to be poised and polite and seem older than her sixteen years.

Now, though, it occurred to Everis how much she'd been through in their absence. The loss of her father, the betrayal of her mother, being forced out of her home and without all the safety and comforts to which she was accustomed. Everis's heart hurt for her. He squeezed her hand.

"We're thrilled to see you safe, Your Grace," Wren said, and despite whatever sorrow he was feeling in that moment, Everis knew he meant it.

Cassia's smile widened. She drew them down next to the fire and made quick work of getting them each a flask of water and some cooked rabbit left over from their earlier supper.

Tired as he was, Everis gratefully dug into his meal, a bit charred for his liking but filling. He listened absently to Imaryllis speaking to Faulk and a woman he didn't recognize but quickly came to know as Gwyn, a Court member from Midmere. Gwyn and the other Owls in the capital had helped the princess escape. They'd encountered Sevin and Vesir earlier that morning, and it was the twins who'd struck the flare when they saw Elias's go off at the inn. Elias and Jade were still missing, but the Owls were convinced they would find one another soon enough.

It couldn't be helped that Everis's gaze at some point met Brant's across the fire. Was Ever surprised to see them there? That out of all the guards in the castle, they were the two who'd gone against the queen's orders and, as far as everyone else was concerned, turned traitor? He might've balked at such a thing, and yet they were often stationed close to Cassia. They knew her, were possibly even on friendly terms with her. The thought annoyed him, that they could be normal, *kind* people to everyone other than him. Brant gave him a thin, humorless smile and lifted his flask before taking a drink.

Eventually, everyone retired to their bedrolls within the cave, save for Gwyn, who remained near the fire to keep watch. Everis and Wren didn't have anything of their own—it'd all been left at the inn or in the stables—so Imaryllis brought a few spare blankets to where they sat huddled just inside the cave entrance and offered them.

"You boys should get some sleep. It'll be morning soon."

Everis reached for the blankets but found himself blurting, "Master Orin?"

Imaryllis's expression fell, and Ever's hopes fell with it. Surely, she'd known the question was coming. Everis was surprised Wren hadn't asked it sooner. She took a seat in front of them, rubbing the back of her neck. "Orin stayed behind to buy us time to escape."

Everis glanced at Wren. In the firelight, his face looked deathly pale and somber. "Captured, then...?"

There was a pause long enough that it made everything feel horribly wrong. "Perhaps. The last we saw of him before the gates closed, he was engaged with Drake."

"Drake?" Everis repeated, confused.

She looked between them. "You don't know?"

"Know *what*?" Wren pressed.

Imaryllis bit back a sigh. "I think we're going to be up for a while longer."

IMARYLLIS

They didn't go to bed until the early hours of the morning. Even then, Imaryllis lay near the dying embers of the fire and repeated the conversation again and again in her head, fixating on the new information, piecing it together with what she knew. Drake Reed and Danica, carrying on some sort of affair, conspiring to kill the king and princess... Before, Imaryllis hadn't been able to understand how a mother could do such a thing to her own child but knowing what she did now, that answer was a little clearer.

Still, Cassia had grown up as Danica's daughter. Cassia had run to her, clung to her, loved her as any little girl would love their mother, and despite their sometimes-strained relationship, Imaryllis found it difficult to accept Danica could be so cold-hearted as to *murder* her.

And now, the poor girl would be faced with learning this truth, and learning the fate of her birth mother, so soon after the death of her father. It was so much loss on top of the great expectations of a girl who now needed to fill the role of queen. Cassia was sixteen. Old enough, strong enough, to manage beneath the weight of it all, and yet... it wasn't fair. No one, let alone someone her age, ought to have to shoulder so much.

Orin would've known the best way to approach the topic. He would've found the right words to say, would've known the balance between being empathetic and firm, granting Cassia time to grieve while being able to guide her forward. He'd always been good at that. It was a quality he possessed Imaryllis had admired and tried to emulate, although she'd been told many a time that she was too strict and pushed too hard, that her expectations of herself and others were too high. How, then, did she navigate this? Not only with Cassia, but with Orin's two apprentices, as well.

She rolled over on her pallet, turning her gaze toward the cave where the boys had curled up with one another to sleep. The pair of them had always been close, yet something had changed. They were now wrapped up in one another in a way she would've thought appropriate for lovers. It made her smile. If Everis and Wren could find comfort with one another amid the chaos, she would be glad for it.

They were going to need each other more than ever.

She slept little that night but was up and moving not long after the sun had risen to peek through the thick canopy of trees. Brant had switched off with one of the Owls during the night. Imaryllis roused Artesia and Rue, leaving the work of waking the assassins to Gwyn. Despite hearing how they'd helped Wren and Everis get this far, she still couldn't help an inkling of wariness digging at the inside of her ribs.

Wren and Everis were slower to rise but were coaxed from their bedroll by the smell of venison cooking over an open fire. Imaryllis ventured further into the cave to look for Cassia, expecting to have to wake her, but she found the princess already upright with a blanket about her shoulders and a neatly folded piece of parchment in her hands.

Imaryllis paused a few feet away. "Your Grace?"

Cassia turned the parchment slowly in her fingers, sparing a glance up. "Good morning, Lady Imaryllis."

"Good morning." She paused a moment, then sank down beside Cassia, their backs to the smooth cave wall. "Are you alright?"

"Yes. I mean… I think so. I wanted to ask last night, but I felt there were more important conversations to be had… What are we going to do now?"

Her brow furrowed. It was a good question. Until this point, their goal had been to get Cassia to Patish. Now that they'd been joined by others who intended to return to the capital… "Wren and Everis are going back to Midmere to confront Drake," she finally settled on. "The assassins will go with them."

Cassia worried at her lower lip. "Do you think they stand a chance? If Master Orin couldn't beat Drake…"

"Separately? No. Together…" Imaryllis trailed off. The boys were intelligent and skilled. They'd been trained by Orin, Imaryllis, even Drake Reed himself. But she'd never had reason to see them at their full potential, not in a training yard or a battlefield. To say that they could face down a man of Drake's ability, on top of the city guards and whatever magi followers of Drake's remained alive…

"You have to go with them, don't you?" Cassia asked.

Imaryllis tipped her head back to rest against the wall. "My duty right now is to protect you."

"Then I will go back with you."

"No." The answer came short and clipped, unyielding. "We sacrificed much to escape the city and get this far. I will not rest until I've seen you safely to your uncle's home. I'm more confident now than ever that he'll protect you with every bit of strength he possesses."

Cassia looked down at her hands. "I don't want anyone else to get hurt because of me."

"All the more reason to continue onward to Patish."

"But people are going to Midmere to fight… in my name."

Imaryllis looked over at her, sympathetic. "Yes. That's correct. But not just for you, Cassia. For your father and his memory, for the people of Midmere. They will fight because it's the right thing. They wouldn't remain faithful to you if they thought you unworthy."

The poor girl's eyes were glassy with unshed tears that she valiantly attempted to hold back. "You might be the greatest warrior we have in this group. I'm not convinced they can do it without you."

What would Orin say or do? "At the end of the day, you are the one we're here to follow, Princess. We can advise you, we can guide you, but the choice is yours. Tell me what you want, and it will be done."

Cassia remained silent for several long moments, lost in thought, before turning to meet her eyes intently. "I want you to tell me truthfully. Do they stand a better chance with you there?"

Imaryllis could answer that with ease. "Yes."

It had nothing to do with pride; it was a simple fact. She knew the city better than anyone except Gwyn. She had the most combat experience. She'd witnessed Drake fighting and knew at least some of what he was capable of.

Cassia nodded. "Then you will return to Midmere with them. I'll continue to Patish with whomever you think is most capable of accompanying me."

If she could've had her way, she would've sent Wren and Everis along with her, just to keep all of them safe. It would never happen. The boys were bound and determined to return home, and she couldn't blame them.

"Then so shall it be, Your Grace. I think it's a wise decision." She watched Cassia's nervous fingers twirl about the folded paper again. "What is that?"

Cassia looked somewhere between ashamed and sad. "Master Orin slipped it to me just before we left. He asked me to deliver it to Wren and Everis when I saw them."

"Have you read it?"

"No, but I wanted to." She held out the paper for Imaryllis to take. "I figured it must be something personal, though. I didn't want to intrude."

Imaryllis turned the letter around in her hands. Everis and Wren's names were written in Orin's neat scrawl across one side. It would've been easy to unfold it and read it, wrap it back up and pretend she hadn't. Such a thing felt like sacrilege, though, especially now. "Do you intend to give it to them?"

"Do you think you could?" Cassia hugged herself. "It doesn't really feel appropriate right now, does it?"

No, Imaryllis thought. She studied the paper a moment longer, then tucked it safely away into her pocket. "I'll give it to them when the time is right, then."

Cassia gave her the ghost of a smile. "Thank you… for all that you've done."

Imaryllis needed to tell her about her mother—both of them. Yet the words caught in her throat, and she couldn't figure out how to make them less barbed, less painful. She didn't want the last conversation she possibly ever had with the princess to be laced with hurt. But would it be fair to send her off to Duke Ryland's and allow her to get the story from him? Someone she'd seen maybe once as a baby?

Cassia must've seen the conflict in her eyes, or perhaps it was the way her mouth opened and closed while she struggled to speak. "Something's bothering you."

"A great many things are bothering me, Princess."

"I know you're worried about me. But whatever it is, I can handle it."

"I know you can, but it doesn't mean you should have to." Imaryllis looked down at her, pained. "Nothing of what I have to say is pleasant. All of it will hurt."

Briefly, Cassia seemed to flinch—so briefly it was hard to say if Imaryllis had imagined it. She squared her shoulders and straightened, shifting from a small, tired, frightened girl to a regal young woman in the blink of an eye. The youth and the sadness weren't banished completely, but the change was remarkable all the same.

"We're all hurting, Lady Imaryllis. What's one more hurt on top of it?"

WREN

Breakfast was a somber event. They ate alongside Rue, who tried to be polite and conversational, but Wren couldn't find it in himself to maintain small talk for long. Artesia and Brant moved in relative silence about the small camp with the Owls, packing, preparing the horses.

Throughout all of it, Wren kept replaying pieces of last night's conversation in his head. Of all the magi within Midmere, one of the last he'd ever have considered capable of betrayal was Drake Reed. Not even betraying the crown, but betraying *Orin*. The two had been so close for as long as Wren could remember. Orin had plenty of people he was friendly with, but if Wren had to pick a single person other than King Faramond to consider a confidant or partner, it would've been Drake. He recalled dinners with the pair sitting beside one another and how Drake would lean into Orin, murmuring something that made Orin laugh. Wren been almost jealous of it sometimes.

The betrayal burned deep. He could feel the anger seeping out of Everis now and again, that prickle of darkness that made the hair along the nape of Wren's neck stand on end... Yet every time, Ever reined himself back in quickly enough that neither of the other magi present seemed to notice. Perhaps his training with Ivy, no matter how brief, had done some good.

Imaryllis and Princess Cassia emerged from the cave well after the rest of them had finished eating, their expressions bleak. Cassia appeared to have been crying, though her eyes were presently dry.

She approached the fire with an air of authority. "Excuse me, everyone, if I could have your ears for a moment."

They all slowed or stopped what they were doing to give her their attention.

Princess Cassia exchanged looks with Imaryllis, who gave an encouraging nod. "Foremost, I don't feel I've properly expressed my gratitude to all of you for everything you've done. Lady Imaryllis, Rue, Brant, Artesia, Gwyn... You put your lives in danger to protect and help me escape the city, all while mourning those we had to leave behind. Gwyn, you weren't even oath-bound to do so, and still you sought us out to lend your aid.

"The same for the Owls from Patish. Not only have you risked yourselves, but you've outed your organization to more people than I imagine you ever wanted to."

She turned to Everis and Wren. "Ever, you already saved my life once. You two could've stayed in Patish, where it was safe, and no one would've blamed you for it. I dare say that Master Orin and Imaryllis would've preferred it. Yet without hesitation, you came back."

Wren's face warmed a bit, and Everis ducked his head and rubbed the back of his neck. They didn't try to respond, not wanting to interrupt the flow of Cassia's speech.

"Drake Reed has revealed himself as a powerful blood magi. For those who aren't familiar with the term, it's a forbidden form of magic that draws from the very life around them. You can imagine how on a battlefield, where blood flows like water, this makes a blood magi a formidable opponent. What's worse, he has several other magi on his side, along with the city guard working under my mother's orders.

"At this point, I fear we're running out of time to change our minds about the paths we've chosen. Those who choose to go on to Midmere will step into the viper's pit, and I'm sick with worry that I won't see some of you again. And so, I want to make it clear that anyone who doesn't wish to do this has my permission and my blessing to leave now. Travel wherever you wish, start a life anew. I will not hold it against you and will be grateful to know that you're safe."

She paused then, scanning the group, waiting for anyone who might look as though they were considering the offer. Wren wasn't surprised to see that no one moved an inch. The Owls did nothing without thorough forethought and precision. As for him and Ever, well, they had their own reasons for returning home—and only a few of those had to do with Cassia.

"We're with you, Your Grace," Rue spoke up. Her timid voice wavered, but there was determination behind it. It made Wren smile, and he placed a reassuring hand on her arm.

Princess Cassia swallowed hard, briefly overcome with emotion. "I would ask Gwyn, Artesia, and Rue to accompany me the rest of the way to Patish. Anyone else who feels ill-equipped to fight back at the capital is also welcome."

"Lady Imaryllis is returning with us?" Wren asked, meeting Imaryllis's eyes.

"The princess has requested it," Imaryllis agreed.

He couldn't help it; some of the tension he'd been carting around eased from his chest and shoulders. Wren hadn't realized just how afraid he'd been to return to Midmere, to walk into the unexpected, without someone more experienced there to guide him.

"I hope she won't be the only one." Wren looked over at Faulk, who rolled his shoulders into a shrug.

"We see things through, magi. As it stands, we also have siblings in Midmere who no doubt could use our assistance. Sevin and Vesir can return to Patish with the princess. They'll be able to deal with things if the bandits in the pass get any ideas."

Wren smiled. It was spoken so casually, and yet he'd come to understand the concern beneath Faulk's chilly exterior. "Thank you, Faulk."

Imaryllis clapped her hands together. "Then it sounds like we know where each of us belongs. Come on. We need to be on our way before we waste any more time. We have important places to be."

CASSIA

They departed within the hour. It felt rushed. Too soon. Lady Imaryllis had taken her by the shoulders, leaning down to meet her gaze. "No matter what happens, you will persevere," she'd said. Then she drew Cassia into a hug—an embrace that ought to have been inappropriate between a royal and a servant of the crown—but Cassia latched onto her for dear life. It was the first time anyone had hugged her since her father. She would use that moment of comfort to help brace herself for what was to come.

Wren and Everis saw her off with smiles and well-wishes, reassurances that they'd see her again soon. As Cassia watched them mount their horses and head off in the opposite direction, leaving her, Gwyn, Artesia, and Rue, and the twins alone, she couldn't help but wonder if she would see any of them ever again.

The question hung heavy around her heart and made her eyes well with tears. She fought them back. She'd spent far too much time crying over the last two days, and she wouldn't allow herself to dwell. This was the way of things, and she had her own demons to face from here on out—something she would have to do without Master Orin or Lady Imaryllis at her side.

She turned in her saddle to look at Rue and Gwyn, who were waiting with the utmost patience. Rue offered a kind smile. "I'm certain they'll be alright, Your Grace."

Cassia managed a weak smile in response, giving the reins a tug and nudging her horse into a trot. "For the sake of the kingdom, I hope so."

EVERIS

Lady Imaryllis kept them to the main road as much as possible, though now and again Faulk instructed them to deviate, to disappear into the woods and lie low. How in the world that man could sense when someone was coming long before the rest of them could, Everis didn't know, and any attempt to ask was answered with a shrug and a roll of Faulk's eyes.

The trip gave them sufficient time to plan. The city gates would be heavily guarded, but Faulk insisted there was another way in through the city's underground waterways.

"Have you been to Midmere before?" Everis asked.

"It's been a while, but Gwyn refreshed my memory."

"You're full of surprises."

Faulk gave a short laugh. "You have no idea, magi."

When they stopped at night, Everis retreated with his supper and sat away from the group. He didn't mind Wren's company, of course, but he needed the time to clear his head and think.

They would be sneaking into Midmere like common criminals. From there, their aim was to—hopefully—infiltrate the castle while avoiding an enormous battle. The less bloodshed, the weaker Drake would be.

And the weaker you will be, too.

He shivered, shaking off the rumblings in the back of his mind.

Wren came to join him with his own food and drink, taking a seat at his side so they were hip to hip, overlooking the valley speckled with trees stretched out before them. "Are you alright?"

"No better or worse than you." He leaned into Wren, taking comfort in his presence and the warmth and calm he radiated. "Just thinking."

"Any luck?" Wren picked at his food with a sigh. "Because I find my head just spinning itself into circles when I try to think too much about any of this."

Everis squinted. He thought, just maybe, he could see the outline of Midmere far in the distance, but it could've been a trick of the vanishing daylight. "I was thinking we might not be strong enough to beat Drake as we are."

"As we are?"

"I mean, what if we have to fight fire with fire? A blood magi against a blood magi." He looked down at his untouched food.

Wren no longer tensed when the subject of blood magic came up. It seemed the more openly they spoke of it, the easier it became for them both. After so many years of pretending it didn't exist, it was a relief.

"I've been thinking of that," Wren reluctantly admitted. "But, you know, the more we've found out about your powers, the less I think that what you're doing is blood magic."

Everis frowned. "How do you figure?"

"Ivy said it, didn't she? Blood magic requires the spilling of blood itself. Ichor is the most powerful generator of magical energy. But you don't have to do that. You *can*, but you don't *have* to."

"No, I just sap the life out of things without even meaning to," he muttered.

"But it's still different. If you're capable of doing that, of stealing something's lifeforce without resorting to bloodshed, could you potentially do that to Drake himself?"

Everis opened his mouth, closed it again, his frown deepening in thought. "I... I don't know. I've never tried. It's always been unintentional and uncontrolled."

"We have a few days for you to practice, then." Wren smiled faintly. "This isn't me telling you to lose yourself to your magic, Ever. Don't slip down dark paths where I can't follow you. I'm just saying, if it means the lives and well-being of an entire kingdom..."

"And if it means putting a stop to Drake," Everis finished quietly.

Wren let out a slow breath. He set his bowl aside and reached for

Everis's hand, sliding their fingers together, intertwining them. "I love you, Ever. Whatever happens when we reach Midmere, you and I will face it together. If you slip, I'll be there to bring you back. Always."

He swallowed the lump in his throat and looked at Wren. He'd meant it when he'd said he would burn down the entire kingdom if it meant keeping Wren safe. Whatever battles awaited them in Midmere would test their skills more than anything they'd faced so far. The thought of Wren getting hurt, of Drake so much as laying a single spell on him... It made the dark parts of his magic churn beneath his skin like fire, burning and insatiable and furious. He squeezed Wren's hand, staring into his deep blue eyes, using the familiarity there to draw him back to where he belonged.

He didn't know if the others were paying them any attention, but it didn't matter what they thought, anyway. Everis leaned in, pressing his mouth warmly to Wren's, savoring the way Wren melted into him without an ounce of hesitation. Wren kissed him desperately, sealing a fierce promise of the words he'd spoken, said as though he could burn it into their lips.

They would take care of each other. Always.

THE CARVERS
THE BASICS OF MAGIC, VOLUME I

A unique form of magic less commonly spoken of is carving magic. Not to be confused with the scribes who quite literally carve their spells into inanimate objects, carvers instead carve their spells directly into their own skin.

By doing so, it's said that spells can be summoned swiftly and in rapid succession with no verbal cues, a unique and useful ability for magi on the battlefield. By no surprise, this form of magic is frowned upon due to its unstable nature. Once a spell has been carved into human skin, it remains there indefinitely, and attempts to heal the wounds are often met with mixed results. As such, a magi with a spell written into their body that is constantly active may suffer side-effects including, but not limited to, uncontrolled magical outbursts and debilitating pain.

Although carving is not strictly prohibited by the Citadel at this time, it is strongly discouraged.

WREN

Three days of careful travel later, they stood amongst the trees atop a hill overlooking Midmere's valley. In the past, Wren had always loved these views; the sight of his home up ahead had promised familiar faces, a warm bed, and a good meal. Now, everything about the city, from the castle walls to the outlying farmland, appeared dangerous and unwelcoming. It was late enough that they ought to have camped out, but Faulk insisted they keep going. They had a contact amongst those farmhouses, he said, and they could rest awhile and decide what time would be best to sneak into the city proper.

They crept down into the valley beneath a setting sun, picking their way as discreetly as possible. Normally, even at this time of evening, Wren would've expected to see a fair number of people still out and about. Everything was eerily quiet. Even the cows and horses they passed seemed subdued and kept their heads down.

Faulk led them to a small farmhouse on the outskirts, unassuming, simple, with lights burning warmly from its windows. Wren must've ridden past it many times over the years in his comings and goings without ever having given it a second glance.

The moment they drew up, a couple opened the door to greet them.

If he had to guess, they were close to Master Orin in age. When Faulk dismounted and approached, tugging up his sleeve to show them the owl tattoo on his forearm, the pair gave him a nod and extended their own arms, which bore matching, albeit faded, marks of the Dusk Court. Not a word was exchanged as they stepped inside, not until the door had been closed and latched behind them. And then—

"Thought you lot would never make it," Elias announced from the kitchen table, sporting a wide smile. Jade sat across from him.

Wren let out a quiet laugh of relief. How they'd missed the pair of them along the way, he didn't know, but Faulk and Stryder looked unsurprised.

"We'd hoped we'd lost the two of you," Faulk said dryly, taking a seat beside Jade.

"As if you could be so lucky. And look—you've brought along some new friends." He eyed Imaryllis and Brant with some scrutiny.

"Another magi to help even our odds," Stryder said with a gesture and a smile in Imaryllis's direction. "And, ah... a defected guard? Is that right?"

Brant frowned and opened his mouth like he wanted to protest. "I— uh. Yes. I guess that's about right."

"Lovely. Well, you're in the home of Marcel and Paul. Semi-retired Owls who keep their home open to those of us passing through."

"And serving as a means to get in and out of the city undetected," the woman named Marcel said pleasantly. "The main gates have all been closed up tight. No one in or out. Even the farmers here on the outskirts haven't the foggiest what's going on inside, and our people have been coming only as often as needed to deliver updates."

Imaryllis frowned. "If there's a secret passage out of the city, why didn't we bring Cassia through that way?"

"Gwyn asked us about that," Marcel said. "But the exit was on the opposite side of the city from where the princess was hiding, and before we could think of a way to secure safe travel through the streets, they found you lot. Besides, horses can't get through that passageway, and I doubt you'd have gotten far without them."

Wren shifted his weight from one foot to the other. "If we have our entrance, shouldn't we be going?"

"They won't grant you passage this time of evening," Paul said. "Too risky, where it's located. Best to go in the early hours of morning—then someone will be waiting to let you through."

Wren cast a cursory look out the windows. The rain was coming down heavier now, an overcast sky making it difficult to tell how late in the day it was. It was dark enough as far as he was concerned. The sooner they got beyond those walls, the sooner they could find Master Orin.

Marcel moved away from the counter. "You look exhausted. Let me fetch you all some stew, then we'll show you where you can clean yourselves up and get some rest, hm?"

Without needing further prompting, everyone else in the room moved to take a seat wherever they could—given that space was limited—but Wren lingered near the door, too restless to sit. The longer they waited, the worse things could become inside the city. Home was within reach, and they were all content to wait as though time wasn't of the essence.

Everis drifted to his side with a bowl of stew, and when Wren didn't immediately take it, he pushed it gently into his hands.

"Eat," he instructed.

"I don't know if my nerves will let me."

"Try. For me. Please? We're going to want our strength."

Wren bit back a sigh, but reluctantly took a few small bites. It wasn't bad. A bit bland, but the meat was tender and the potatoes fresh. Ever, too, only picked at his meal as though every spoonful required a great deal of mental fortitude to swallow. Wren set his bowl aside after a moment, fingers seeking the front of Ever's tunic and curling into the fabric and leather, searching for some sort of comfort without drawing attention from a roomful of people. Everis took the hint, drifting forward, positioning himself between Wren and the rest of the room, granting Wren the ability to drop his head against Ever's chest and close his eyes and just *breathe* through the grief and worry and frustration of having to wait, wait, *wait*.

Everis placed his own bowl aside on the windowsill, brushing some of Wren's blond hair back. He used to wear it so meticulously, always tidy. These days, there was no point. It looked as frazzled as Wren felt.

After everyone had eaten their fill, Faulk and Lady Imaryllis worked with Paul and Marcel to orchestrate their next steps. They would nap while they could. In the early hours of the morning, they would make their way through the flood tunnels into Midmere, where another Owl would grant them access on the other side. Faulk would head straight away to meet up with some of Midmere's faction of the Court for any further information. Lady Imaryllis, Brant, Everis, and himself could move through the city so long as they were careful and kept a low profile. Although Faulk instructed Jade, Stryder, and Elias to gather information, there was something in the way he looked at them that suggested he wanted them to keep an eye on the three magi and make sure they didn't get themselves into further trouble.

Wren didn't argue against this plan. Whatever happened beyond that would be decided after scoping the place out and, he hoped, involved sneaking into the castle. They didn't have time to wait for Ryland's men to arrive. They could handle Drake on their own if they were quick and careful and smart about it.

As the others settled into their small bedrolls in the cellar for the night, Wren watched Everis beside him through the dim flicker of nearby candlelight. Since his early teenage years, he'd had such a lean face and sharp features. Now, though, they looked too gaunt, too tired. He ran his fingertips along Ever's jaw, traced the forming scar along his cheek from the bandit attack. His abdomen ached with the memory of his own injury.

"Do you feel it?" Ever whispered.

"Your face? I do. It's quite nice."

"Mm, no. The darkness. From inside the city."

Wren closed his eyes and took a slow breath. Something did feel off. Whether it was the uncomfortable tension roiling across the outer limits of the city or the fear and anxiety he was carting around in his chest, he didn't know. "Tell me what *you* feel."

Everis wet his lips, and his gaze grew unfocused, a faint sliver of red visible in his eyes. "It feels... familiar. Black. Cloying. Drake isn't trying to hide what he's doing anymore. What if regular magi aren't enough to deal with him?" He paused, but didn't give Wren a chance to respond. "I know what you said before, but if I have to use blood magic to stand up against him—"

Wren caught him by the chin, forcing Everis's gaze to refocus on him as he firmly spoke. "You are not a blood magi, Ever."

"I'm capable of hurting people with my magic."

"Yes, but that isn't your intention. You aren't murdering for the sake of power."

Everis stared at him, A single name hung in the air between them. *Maliel.* Wren refused to dwell on it and shook his head.

"I don't know what it will be like to face a magi far more powerful than us, but we aren't alone. We have Imaryllis, we have the Owls, and Gods willing, we'll have Master Orin. Together, we can do it."

Ever lowered his long lashes, half obscuring his dark eyes. When he spoke again, his voice was achingly soft and small and young. "If it comes down to it, to protect everyone, to protect you... I will use whatever magic I must."

"Ever—"

"I mean it. Whatever it takes." He forced his gaze up. "I will protect you, and I will raze the entire fucking city to the ground to keep you safe."

"This isn't about me and you," Wren tried to say, but then Ever's mouth pressed very insistently against his, desperate and offering reassurance as much as seeking it. Wren submitted without a fight because, in the end, what Everis had said was true for them both. They wanted to avenge their king, to protect Cassia, to rescue Orin, to see justice served... But far and above all else, they needed each other to come out of this in one piece.

The rest of the kingdom be damned.

EVERIS

Paul woke them in the early morning. Everyone roused with barely a word, accepting the offered coffee and bread laid out by Marcel. With little fanfare, they dressed. The assassins were back in their dark, nondescript clothing, and all of them donned cloaks and hoods. Faulk presented the magi and Brant with sets of similar clothing, something that would help them blend in. Then they filed into the narrow passageway hidden at the far end of the cellar behind a heavy stack of barrels.

It was a long walk in tight, damp, and dark quarters. The taller members of the group—Everis included—had to hunch to fit, and it wasn't long before an ache formed in his back and neck.

Faulk led the way. Somehow, despite the darkness and the various twists and turns and tunnels branching off, he seemed to know where he was going, like some sort of hound following a scent. After nearly an hour of meandering in what *had* to be a big circle, they came out of the passageway and into the flood tunnels beneath Midmere. The scent had been discernible for a while, but now, right alongside it, it was overpowering and made Ever's stomach turn. The water flowing through these sewers was the Waste Water, and even the assassins, ever so ready to get their hands dirty, didn't look inclined to get quite *that* dirty.

They inched along the narrow ledge following the water. Everis tried to envision the city overhead and their place in relation to it. Everyone remained deathly silent, and he didn't dare break that hush. It wasn't until they branched off yet again into another narrow tunnel system and reached a dead end that Faulk came to a stop. He offered the lantern to Stryder and reached up into the darkness where there was, apparently, a trapdoor that he knocked on three times. After a long moment of silence, someone knocked back twice, and Faulk responded with one last single knock. The hatch unlocked and opened, spilling light into the tunnel.

They clambered out of the darkness and into a brightly lit cellar full of perishable goods and supplies that might've belonged to some sort of general store. Everis gulped in several lungfuls of air, grateful for the fresh scent of mixed herbs. An ordinary-looking man in shopkeeper's garb looked them over, exchanged a few quiet words with Faulk, then disappeared back upstairs. Faulk turned to survey them, scrutinizing Wren, Lady Imaryllis, Brant, and himself.

"I would have the lot of you stay behind, honestly, if I thought you'd listen. So instead, I'm telling you this: we're going to check in with some of our contacts to figure out what's been happening and see if we have a secure way into the castle. If you're going to wander the city, I suggest you don't do so as a group and keep your heads down." Faulk's gaze zeroed in on Everis. "Heads down, and mouths shut. Do not draw attention to yourselves. Do you understand?"

Everis flushed, chastised. "Yes."

"Good. We'll leave separately. Wait about ten minutes between each departure."

One at a time or in pairs, they climbed up into the main shop and then out of the store and into the city. Lady Imaryllis intended to go last, and she gave Wren and Everis a reassuring but wary smile as they left.

The sun had risen while they were underground. The morning merchants had long since set up in the streets, which were bustling with shoppers and sellers alike. It made it easy to slip out into the crowd with Wren at his side, to keep their hoods up and blend in amongst a sea of unfamiliar faces.

He'd walked this city a thousand times since he was a child, and never had it felt like this. A heavy gloom hung over everything. Guards were stationed on various corners, keeping a watchful eye—for what? For them? Wren remained stone-faced beside him, yet only a brief glance showed Everis the turmoil in his eyes.

There was no sign of Faulk or the others, and yet Everis couldn't help but feel like they were being watched. He wouldn't be surprised if an Owl or two had been saddled with keeping an eye on them.

"The queen's gone mad," someone said as they rounded a corner. "This isn't wartime."

It might be soon, he thought dismally.

"Stringing men up like that for all to see…"

Stringing men up? Executions happened now and again in the city, the punishment for rapists and murderers. Usually, the execution took place, and the body was removed, sometimes sent to the magi for research if no next of kin laid claim to it. There were only a few instances in Everis's memory where a criminal had been left for viewing afterward. Typically, it had been a particularly notorious crime, where the people demanded the corpse be left for the birds.

Ever's stomach turned with nerves, but his feet carried him to the large square, the space just before the castle where royal announcements were made from the parapets and, naturally, where executions were held.

A crowd had formed there, denser than any Everis could remember seeing. He weeded his way through, nearly losing Wren in the process. Every step made his heart race a little faster. Something was wrong.

We shouldn't be here.

Before they could push their way to the front, he caught sight of the gallows and came to an abrupt halt. It was all he could do to grab for Wren's hand and hold on for dear life.

No, no, no, please—

Don't let him see…

WREN

Everis dragged him to a stop, and Wren couldn't fully process why.

Even when his gaze fell on the bodies strung from the gallows.

Even when he recognized the first one by his ginger hair as Gilbert, and next to him—

A cry caught in Wren's throat. The sounds of the crowd hollowed out in his ears, became dim and distant. He stared into Master Orin's face, seeing but not believing. Those clouded, glassy eyes that had always been so full of love and kindness, that long hair always meticulously pulled back from his face, now tangled and matted with blood.

They had stripped Orin down to nearly nothing, showing off every gash and wound and bruise to serve as a warning. He'd been dead for days. Had he been hanging there as long? A spectacle to show off outside the castle walls? Orin had served the realm faithfully for decades. He'd held the king and queen's confidences, helped win their battles, tended to their sick and dying.

He'd given everything of himself… and they'd murdered him.

Wren willed his legs to move. He needed to do something. Anything.

He needed to find Drake Reed and string him up with his own innards.

Everis squeezed his hand, trying to draw him back to the present. Wren's head spun when he turned to look at him, the faces in the crowd blurring, his legs threatening to buckle. Ever said something Wren couldn't make out. Tugged on his hand. *We should go.*

No. No.

We can't leave Master Orin here.

I can't breathe. Why can't I breathe?

Because if they left, they would let Orin down yet again. How long would Drake and Danica leave him out there? Naked and rotting in the rain and sun, like a gallery exhibit put on show for the entire city. And these people who Orin had served for decades—had not one of them seen fit to do something? Did none of them care?

Wren pulled free of Ever's grasp and stumbled through the assembly for the gallows. He planted his hands against the platform and hauled himself up, drawing the assassin's dagger from his belt. Everis was on his heels, no longer trying to talk him down, prepared to walk into this trap right alongside him. And it *was* a trap. Wren knew it somewhere in his gut. A trap laid out by Drake, and Wren was falling for it like a fool.

"Oi! Get down from there!" someone barked.

Wren stopped and turned toward the guard ascending the steps.

The man's steps faltered when he laid eyes on the pair of them, and he drew his sword. "It's them. It's the magi traitors!"

Wren whirled on the man with a snarl. "Traitors? *Traitors?* The people you've left to rot here did nothing wrong! They were no traitors to the crown, and neither are we. The only traitors are in *there.*" He thrust a finger toward the castle. Fury and grief made it difficult to control his voice. Twisted his normally calm and even speech into a roar. "Many of you knew these magi. You knew them as your healers and protectors. These soldiers were your sisters and brothers. How much convincing did it take for you to strike them down?!"

The ascending soldiers paused beneath the weight of his words, exchanging looks. Yes. They felt guilty. Yet they'd valued their own lives and likely the lives of their families and so had gone along with their orders, regardless of how they felt. Yet if all of them had risen together, perhaps...

Perhaps his master would still be alive.

Their hesitation was short-lived, however. *Fucking cowards.* They advanced on Wren and Everis, swords drawn. Everis drew his own sword, turning to meet one of the incoming blades. He spared only the briefest of glances at Wren.

"If you're going to cut them down, hurry it up!"

Then he parried the guard's attack, turned, and struck. The steel slid through the skin and muscle of the guard's throat. The splatter of blood that rained across his boots snapped Wren into action. He stood up on tiptoe and sawed at the rope.

It's all right. I'll get you down. Everything is going to be fine...

Townspeople began to shout and stir, shocked by the bloodshed, uncertain what to think of it. More guards rushed for the stairs, and Everis turned to face the crowd with a snarl.

Wren shivered, stopping, watching Ever.

What have I done?

A ripple tore through the square, a tremor Wren felt all the way to his bones and in the air's displacement around him he could only barely see. The guards on the platform were thrown back, clear from the gallows, tossed into the fray of fleeing townspeople like sacks of grain. His own feet slid precariously on the worn wood, yet his hold on Everis's arm seemed to render him otherwise immune to being cast back.

"Magi Everis, Magi Wren!" one guard bellowed, a man whose face was familiar to Wren. "You're under arrest. Please, come peacefully."

Wren grimaced. This wouldn't go well.

Everis turned his burning stare in their direction, stilled a moment, then tore from Wren's grasp so swiftly it caught him by surprise. His blade shimmered, crackling with magic and glinting in the light while Everis's eyes smoldered. He met the city guards, all five of them, armed with nothing more than a simple sword... and the frightening magic that poured from him like an overflowing fountain. Stunning to watch.

Ethereal.

And *terrifying.*

The earlier hum of the crowd transformed into a thunderous roar as townspeople stampeded to safety. Wren's mind reeled. He turned back to Orin, lifted his eyes to his master's face. It looked nothing like him, and yet there was no one else it could be. He felt as cold to the touch as the blood in Wren's veins. He willed his arms into movement, to resume sawing at the rope.

A pair of thick arms grabbed him from behind and wrenched him away, plate mail pressing against his back as a guard attempted to wrestle Wren to the platform with his arms twisted behind him. With a hiss, Wren thrashed and shoved his weight back. The guard grunted, took one step further than he should have, and they both went toppling off the platform to the cobblestone below. Winded, Wren rolled to his back, dizzy as he gazed up at the sky. From one of the castle walls, he spotted movement: the familiar soft blue of a magi's cloak and then the shimmer of a spell being cast.

They were aiming right for him.

The fire raged down onto the square, bolstered by blood magic. It should have incinerated him, the guards, and every corpse upon the gallows.

There came a brilliant flash of light as Lady Imaryllis appeared and raised her arm, and the spells engraved with such care and skill upon her bracer glowed white. The air shivered and rippled, a shimmering wall going up before them. They braced themselves regardless. The fire crashed against the magical shield, furiously licking across the surface, searching for an entry point. Imaryllis leaned into it with all her weight, jaw clenched, and held firm until the fire dissipated and it was safe to drop the spell.

Then she whirled that fury onto them.

"Have you two lost your fool minds?" she hissed. "The idea was to do this undetected!"

Wren could only stare at her. His voice wouldn't cooperate. She wouldn't understand. No one could.

Imaryllis leaped down from the gallows and gave him a shove, pointing toward the edge of the square. "Go with Faulk. Get yourself to safety, and I'll go after your idiot boyfriend."

Wren staggered a half step, bumping into Faulk, who'd slipped up behind him. His gaze darted back. Seeing Master Orin on the gallows made his body seize up with anguish all over again. "The bodies..."

"Go!" she snapped.

Wren briefly squeezed his eyes shut, turned, and ran. Chaos flooded the square as guards marching in collided with townspeople rushing out. Somewhere in that fray was Ever, and Wren could feel the rippling of powerful magic washing over him even from a distance. Faulk snagged him by the front of his tunic and dragged him through the commotion. They weaved through the smoke and dust and bodies until Wren did not know which direction they'd gone. Faulk hauled him into a small, unassuming building.

The door heaved shut, muffling the noise outside. For the first time in a while, Wren could make out the ragged sound of his own breathing and the pulse beating in his ears. His hands shook. His stomach turned.

Faulk took a few steps away from him, winded, shoving his hands through his silver hair. When he turned back around, his scarred face had screwed up into a snarl and his eyes were wild and terrifying. "What the fuck was that? Now the entire bloody city knows you're here!"

The image of Orin and Gilbert hanging from the gallows snuffed whatever guilt Wren felt. The image burned into the back of his eyelids. "Those people up there, they were our colleagues, our fellow magi. That was my *master*. I couldn't just leave him hanging there!"

The assassin groaned as though this answer were somehow predictable but no less infuriating. "Well, they're *dead,* so I don't think they much care!"

Wren jerked back, stricken, and his vision blurred. Yes.

Master Orin was dead.

Never again would Wren see his reassuring smile or feel a calming hand upon his shoulder. He'd never hear that low voice giving him patient instruction as he fumbled through a new spell. There would be no more trips. No more late-night conversations. No more name-day celebrations or holidays.

In the blink of an eye, it was all just... gone.

Everis's words rang in his head: *have you ever lost someone?* The answer at the time had been no. Wren had struggled to grasp the depth of what it meant to truly lose anyone. Everis had known. He'd faced it as a small boy, and again when Wren had been injured. No wonder he'd been pushed to darkness trying to save him. In that moment, trying to cut Master Orin's body free, Wren had wished so fervently for the capability of bringing him back—even if it meant sacrificing someone else.

He sank to the ground, fingers latched together behind his neck, head bowed toward his knees as he fought back a wave of nausea. He couldn't stop shaking.

Faulk sighed, did a few more circles about the empty storefront, and faced him again. "Look, we need to get you back out of the city. The others will try to help Everis and keep him from getting his fool-self detained. Are you up to another jaunt?"

"I can't leave Ever behind," he managed. "If they catch him..."

"Then they're capable of catching you both. They know what you look like. My people will help him better than you can." Faulk's voice was laced with strained patience, trying to be understanding, but clearly it wasn't his strong suit.

"You're a bunch of average people going up against blood magi," Wren snapped.

Faulk's jaw tightened. "And you're a fucking apprentice, *boy*. My people have gone up against magi, werewolves, vampires, and everything in between. Yes, it's going to mean a lot of casualties for us. People I consider friends and family will probably die. We're putting our lives on the line for your cause."

"I didn't mean——" Wren started.

His voice raised. "So, I suggest you get your head out of your arse and recognize that you aren't the only one who's lost something important. And you won't be the only one who *continues* to suffer loss until we deal with these magi, and that involves you not wallowing in your grief. There is time for that later."

Their eyes locked as Faulk spoke, no matter how badly Wren wanted to look away. His sorrow was a deep, overflowing well, and he'd presumed that no one could possibly understand what that was like. It was an unfair assumption.

He thought of Cassia, so positive and strong, although she had just lost her father, her mother, and so many people she'd thought she could trust. He thought of Imaryllis, who would face down the very guards and soldiers she had trained for years.

Faulk was right. He'd been careless and selfish. It didn't matter that the bodies of people he loved were out there. They were dead, and he was not. He'd blown their element of surprise out of sorrow, and Drake had known he would. His priority *needed* to be protecting Cassia, reclaiming the throne for her. It was what Orin would've told him—no doubt while setting off to rescue Everis himself.

Could Ever take care of himself, though, without Wren at his side? The concept of them being separated left him feeling nauseated all over again. Ever had worked as much as he could during the trip home, practicing using his abilities without stumbling.

Wren hoped it was enough.

He forced himself to his feet, drawing the hood back up around his face. "I'm ready."

EVERIS

In his mind's eye, Everis saw the city burning around him. It would've been effective, some dark part of him thought. Every guard, every knight and servant and townsperson who'd stood by while Master Orin was murdered would pay for it.

Focus.

Everis had no plan in mind other than to lead the soldiers away from Wren. It had been foolish to expose themselves like that, and yet he could hardly blame him. But now—he needed to keep his wits about him, needed to remember why he was here, what he wanted to protect. He had to remember what Master Orin would've wanted from him.

He tore through the city streets, which had begun to blur together. Every street brought with it new soldiers hunting him down, shouting voices—some of which he recognized—calling his name, begging him to turn himself in. Fools. All of them.

With practiced ease, he launched himself up and over a fence, onto a low storefront, and to the rooftops, hopping and climbing from one to the next. An arrow sang dangerously close to his face, and he stopped, dropped, and flattened himself against the rooftop with a hiss.

"Magi!"

A glance across the street revealed Stryder on the opposite rooftop, waving him over. Out of breath and lungs burning, he crossed over, only barely managing the leap from the top of an inn to an apothecary. He trusted Stryder to lead the way, and before long they'd evaded the guards below, leaving them huddling in the shade of a building while they caught their breaths.

"Did Faulk have you watching us?" he finally rasped.

Stryder laughed. "After a fashion. He instructed us to stick nearby in case of trouble. Good thing we did."

Ever licked his dry lips anxiously. "I have to go back and find Wren."

"It's being taken care of, I promise. Faulk was heading to fetch him."

"Even so—"

"Look, you two have already blown our cover, which is somehow surprising and yet not."

He started to relent, prepared to fall in line and go… wherever it was Stryder intended to lead him like a dog to a kennel. But a prickle of magic worked its way up his spine, distracting him from those intentions and drawing his attention back in the direction of the square.

Regardless of whether Wren and Ivy believed him to be a blood magi, Everis knew blood magic when he felt it. And this blood magic… it wasn't the same that had come at them from the apprentice on the castle walls. It was heavier and stronger than any magic he'd ever felt.

Drake.

He tipped his head back, studying the outline of the castle's tallest spires. The royal wing, now occupied by a false queen. The magi tower, the place he'd called home for most of his life. The pulse of magic was too blatant to be an accident. Drake had spent years hiding his dark magic from even Master Orin.

No. He was intentionally projecting it now. He was calling to them. *Taunting* them.

It was an invitation.

"Everis."

He heard her, but the sound didn't register quite right in his head. His gaze was tilted toward the castle.

She clasped his shoulder, startling him. "Magi, we need to go."

Everis's head snapped toward her. He licked his lips. "Can you get me to the south side of the castle?"

Stryder paused. "What?"

"There's an entrance through the southern gates. Small, poorly guarded. Used mostly for merchants making deliveries to the kitchens.

Can you get me there and help dispatch the guards so I can get inside?"

"Are you bloody mad? You can't go in there alone!"

"You're welcome to come with me, if it pleases you."

"What—no!"

"Then I suppose I'm going alone."

She tightened her grip on his arm. Everis snarled and yanked it free.

"You saw what they did. They took everything important to Wren and me and destroyed it. Now I'm going to destroy them—I'm the only one strong enough to do it. Go back to the others. Look after Wren."

Stryder looked as though she were fighting back a laugh. Everis knew what she had to be thinking. If a trained group of assassins and a magi master hadn't been able to reach Drake Reed, what hope did an apprentice have?

Yet she stared into his eyes and slowly, the annoyed smile faded from her mouth. She turned away, shoving her hands through her short hair with a groan. Either she helped him or she let him go alone and put him in greater danger. It didn't matter to Everis which she chose.

"Fine. Fine, I'll help you."

WREN

The city flew past them in a blur. Faulk took down the few groups of guards they encountered with a blood-curdling ferocity that would've stunned Wren any other day. They retreated to the general store they'd emerged from, then back into the tunnels beneath the city. This time, Faulk brought him down a different route without as much as a lantern to guide their way. Wren stumbled. Faulk growled, the sound animal and feral, and instructed him to hold on to his cloak.

Wren did as he was told, squeezing his eyes shut so he'd stop straining to see in the dark. "How are you doing this?" he finally asked, breaking the maddening silence.

"I have a good nose, and I see well in the dark." Faulk's voice was clipped but not unkind.

"Peculiar."

"Is it? Magi aren't the only creatures in this world capable of inhuman feats."

"Are you saying you're not human?"

Faulk chuckled and said nothing more than, "Sometimes I wonder."

Finally, they emerged into a set of man-made caverns lit by a series of sconces lining the walls. They weren't alone. Owls scurried about, some huddled together and speaking in hushed tones. When they stepped into the large room, several people stopped to regard them. A few gave Faulk acknowledging nods. Then everyone went back to what they were doing.

Faulk brought him to the next room, filled with cots and crates and barrels. He stepped aside, gestured. "I want you to wait here while we locate the other magi."

Wren couldn't bring himself to argue. He was left alone to take a seat on one of the cots in the corner, listening absently to the hum of conversations in the adjoining cavern, although nothing was truly loud enough for him to make out. It was simply noise. Something to fill his head, something to focus on rather than sitting and reflecting on his own feelings and worries. Was Ever alright? Lady Imaryllis? Had the other Owls been able to find them and bring them to safety?

The sound of approaching footsteps drew his attention as several Owls came into the room, carrying bodies wrapped in shrouds. Wren's stomach turned, roiling with nerves that pushed him to the edge of his seat. One by one, the wrapped bodies were laid out on empty cots. A few glanced his way, and Wren thought he saw sympathy and pity in their eyes. One of them gave him a brief nod, not only acknowledging him but granting him privacy as they exited as quietly as they arrived.

Wren wrung his hands, not daring to move for several long moments. When he finally drew the blanket from the body in the cot beside his own, Gilbert's eyes were half-open, gazing up into nothing. His body, too, was littered with stab wounds. Wren moved to the next body. A vaguely familiar guard. Seemingly uninjured but dead all the same, with the aroma of dark magic clinging to her like a second shroud. Onto the next. An unfamiliar soldier, and another—though this one looked so young. A trainee, perhaps. Brave enough to stand against the traitors, only to be struck down.

The next—

He'd known Master Orin had to be amongst the retrieved bodies, and yet when Wren uncovered him, he flinched back as though burned. Slowly, he sat on the edge of the cot, watching Orin, studying his face, refusing to let his gaze wander to the injuries he'd suffered. Wren placed a hand on his master's chest, as though he might feel the flicker of a heartbeat somewhere within the depths of his body.

Only a short time ago, death had seemed like such a faraway thing, a sorrow that couldn't touch him, but from the moment of the attempt on Cassia's life, that illusion had been shattered. So much loss, so much death, and grief… All because Drake and Danica were hungry for power.

So many had died for it. Orin had died for it.

"You were his pride and joy, you know. He was so proud of you."

Wren didn't look up at Lady Imaryllis. "I've let him down."

"How? We were all fooled, Wren." Soft footfalls as she crossed the room, circling around, pulling up a chair to take a seat at Orin's other side. "Drake hid himself beneath our noses for years. If anyone's to blame, it's those of us who should've been able to see some sort of sign."

Wren, silent, took one of Orin's hands in his. He traced his fingers over his knuckles, over old scars and new. Perhaps she was right, but it didn't matter. He never should've left. He should've been there when Orin needed him. Part of him understood there was nothing he could've done even if he'd been there and that he likely would've died right alongside him—but the bigger part felt he'd failed his master by not having known somehow, by not having been able to protect him.

Imaryllis sighed softly. She reached into a pocket and drew out a rumpled piece of parchment, which she offered to him. "Orin gave this to Cassia before we parted ways. It's for you." When he didn't immediately take it, she placed it beside him. Whatever that letter said would surely break what little was left of his composure. She stood, but before she could walk away, Wren spoke.

"I don't remember much about my family," he offered softly. "I don't even remember missing them, really. I remember being angry, hurt, but that's all."

Imaryllis stopped. Turned. Watched him, listening.

"Everis does, though. He wears the memories of his mother like armor and scars, always in his line of sight. I never understood it before." Wren took a slow, deep breath. The room had begun to stink of death. "I saw plenty of death, of course, and yet never truly grasped that I or anyone I loved was within its reach."

"It's a terrifying thing," Imaryllis murmured. "You almost lost your own life during the trip to Patish. That didn't frighten you?"

"Not really, no. Not like this."

"Like what? Are you afraid of Drake?"

He bit back a sharp, dry laugh. "No. I'm afraid... of losing Everis. More than anything else, I'm afraid something will happen or that he'll go somewhere I can't follow."

She frowned, not grasping his meaning. He hadn't expected her to.

He shook his head. "Nothing. I'm sorry, I'm tired and not making much sense. I'll be better after some sleep and a meal. Have we heard from Ever yet?"

"Stryder was with him, last I heard. They may have holed up elsewhere until the streets clear a bit."

With a sigh and a nod, Wren's shoulders slumped. That wasn't comforting, not until he knew for certain Everis was safe.

Lady Imaryllis left. Wren glanced at the letter. It was rumpled and worn. It had come on quite a journey from Master Orin's hand to his own. After a long moment of debate, he finally sat back and unfolded it. Already, his heart was clambering into his throat.

My dearest Wren and Everis,

I write this to you in hopes we'll be reunited soon, but knowing it may not be a possibility. And so, I find myself faced with a lifetime of regrets and what-ifs, self-doubts, reflecting on whether I've done right by you both.

Wren, when I brought you under my care, you were an angry little boy, hurting from the abandonment of your family. There were times I was certain you hated me, resented me. And yet somehow, you blossomed into the type of young man I wish I had been: intelligent, steadfast, loyal, and above all else—just.

Everis, despite your magical leanings, you have one of the biggest hearts I've ever seen in a person. You see the value in all life where I didn't at your age. You are compassionate and strong, a combination that will lead you to greatness one day.

I've done many things in my life I'm not proud of. I haven't the time or parchment to write it all down here. But should you regain access to my rooms back home, you'll find my journals there, and they will grant you insight into 'before.' Before I came to Midmere. Before I found a family I would've done anything for.

My regrets don't just stem from my past, but from my time with you two, as well. Did I do enough to protect you, to prepare you? It was easy during periods of peace to think we had all the time in the world, and yet now, I fear I did not.

More than anything, having seen the fearsome might of Drake's powers, I fear that in stifling Everis's powers, in not teaching him what they meant and how to better harness them rather than simply suppress them, I might've made things harder on him. I was so focused on ensuring no one else ever found out... Did I hurt him in the process? And I have saddled you both with handling the aftermath of my choices. Whatever happens next, you will be forced to face it without me.

You won't be alone, however. I've come to realize that if there was anyone I could've trusted with Everis's secret, it was Imaryllis and Gilbert. Confide in them. I think they will understand and hopefully succeed in helping him where I failed.

With this letter, you will find one more, addressed to the Citadel. Wren, consider this my encouragement to you.

I'm so proud of you and so undeniably fortunate to have had you for my apprentices.

I love you.

Orin

Wren's eyes had long since blurred, but he turned to the second page. A letter addressed to the Citadel, a master's recommendation for his apprentice to take the exams required to become a fully fledged magi. Grief washed over him anew. He wasn't ready for this.

He wasn't ready to live in a world without the man who'd raised him.

IMARYLLIS

She couldn't recall the last time she'd used a preservation charm. Normally, she placed them on bodies the magi would be studying or investigating. Now, she did it to keep the bodies of Orin and the others in as good shape as possible until they could be properly interred. The charm wasn't indefinite, and if the bodies were exposed to the elements, they wouldn't hold up no matter what she did. Still, it was what she could offer. It was all she could do with a situation that otherwise made her feel utterly helpless.

Wren had vanished for a bit. Hopefully, he was getting himself cleaned up and fed. She'd done as much already, even though eating at a time like this was no easy feat. Now she sat, surveying the assembled Owls, marveling at them. There were at least twenty of them, coming and going, looking over maps and speaking in hushed tones. Even unable to hear what they were saying, Imaryllis could determine several things, like who present was the most important. People who held some sort of ranking within the organization. They were the ones at the center of every conversation, who would step away only to be accosted by another group seeking approval or advice.

Faulk was one of those. Despite this not being his home, the Owls rallied around him and sought him out. Imaryllis hadn't been able to get a word in to him yet about what would happen next.

She curled her fingers tightly around the mug of lukewarm coffee she'd been nursing for the last thirty minutes. What she truly wanted was sleep, but she had no interest in trying, not until she knew Everis was safe.

Stryder's entrance turned a few heads, hers included. She sprang to her feet as the assassin met her eyes and strode across the cavernous room to meet her. The grim approach made Imaryllis's heart plummet.

"Where is he?"

Stryder glanced askance at Faulk, catching his eye and waving him over while she led Imaryllis into a spare storage room. Once Faulk stepped in behind them, Stryder grimaced as she rubbed the back of her neck.

"So... the magi changed the plans."

Faulk's eyebrows shot up. "Pardon?"

"He went into the castle."

Imaryllis didn't even try to bite back the immediate groan that escaped her as she dropped her face into her hands. That was so very much like Everis, wasn't it? Thinking he could take on the world by himself, rushing headfirst into danger, thinking that by doing so, he could protect everyone else. "No..."

"He insisted he could handle it," Stryder lamented, not cowering beneath Faulk's intense, disapproving stare but still looking sheepish.

"He's barely considered an adult by *anyone's* standards, and you just let him go... because he said he could 'handle it'?"

"Ah, well, when you put it like that, it sounds like an awful idea. But you know, for some reason... I believed him."

"His confidence isn't necessarily misplaced," Wren said from the doorway.

Imaryllis turned to look at him, frowning. "You were worried sick earlier."

"I still am, because that's what I do." Wren meandered over, and true to form, the crease between his brows suggested he was warring between emotions. "But if I'm honest, I worry more about him facing soldiers than facing Drake one on one."

Faulk snorted. "Reed is the one we're all tiptoeing around trying to figure out how to handle. What makes you say that?"

Wren looked down. The folded letter Imaryllis had given him was in his hand. Silently, he offered it to her, as though it possessed the answers they needed.

Imaryllis read it, but all it left her with were more questions. "I don't understand. What's he saying?"

"Everis has... a unique set of magical abilities," Wren said slowly. "For years, we thought it was a leaning toward blood magic, but I'm not so certain that's what it is. He doesn't require blood to be spilled, and he doesn't need incantations or text to cast. I've watched him work spells with his eyes closed and without saying a word."

Imaryllis tried to wrap her head around this. She knew Everis as a self-conscious, overly sensitive boy who often grew frustrated that Wren's spellcasting was so much more advanced than his own. To think he had that kind of power... It was difficult to imagine.

"What Everis is capable of, it's terrifying and incredible," Wren continued, lowering his lashes and looking far away, "and it frightens me because I know it also pulls him to a dark place. I worry for him. I think he has the power to beat Drake, but..."

"But would he lose himself in the process?" Faulk finished. Something akin to sympathy flickered across his face.

Wren closed his eyes. "That's what frightens me, yes."

Whether what Everis was capable of was blood magic or not, would the Citadel care? Clearly, Orin had been worried he'd be persecuted if anyone were to find out.

Imaryllis looked at the letter again.

...if there was anyone I could've trusted with Everis's secret, it was Imaryllis and Gilbert. Confide in them.

Hells, he was putting her in a spot, even in death. Although was it truly anything other than Orin knowing she couldn't have turned either of the boys over without clear proof they were some sort of threat? She loved them. She couldn't envision Everis intentionally harming anyone, either. But if using this magic of his risked him and everything he was, then...

"Well," Imaryllis huffed, "if he's in danger, I suppose we ought to get to him as quickly as we can."

Wren lifted his head and gave her a small, grateful smile.

EVERIS

The southernmost entrance had only a single guard posted, easy enough to dispatch and toss into the bushes. It would give Everis a few hours of sneaking around, hopefully undetected, and if he could locate Drake and kill him… perhaps it would spare them an all-out bloodbath.

This feels like a trap, Stryder had said, and she was probably right. But if he was right about Drake summoning him, he still had the upper hand. Drake had no knowledge of the extent of Ever's abilities. If he could catch him off guard…

Everis snuck through the familiar hallways he'd played in as a boy, stealthy and cautious, avoiding a few servants who nearly crossed his path. He knew which turns to steer clear off and which halls to take slowly, which ones were the best for hiding. He didn't want to kill people if he didn't have to, least of all servants completely unskilled in combat.

All he needed to do was find Drake and kill him, then locate Danica and place her under arrest. Revenge was the only thing on his mind.

He reached the west wing and crossed the courtyard, same as he had the night of Cassia's attempted assassination. As he crept along the walls, not wanting to be spotted from the windows overhead, he damned near tripped over someone napping in the grass. The guard startled awake and scrambled to his feet as Everis drew his sword, and for a moment, they just stared at one another, taken aback.

"If you don't tell anyone I'm here, I won't tell them you were sleeping on the job," he offered.

The guard scowled, unsheathed his sword, and lunged. Everis dodged and slit the man's throat with a grimace. The spilling of blood made his mind cloudy, fuzzy. Made him pause and breathe deeply. There'd been so much of it today—so much life lost, and it was becoming more and more difficult to think around the hunger for revenge. He leaned into the wall, focusing on the cold stone, the sound of the nearby fountain, his pulse in his ears, the flapping of wings…

Wings?

His eyes snapped open, spotting a fluttering of white feathers and red eyes shimmering from a nearby bush.

For a moment, his vision blurred with tears. "Nova, you're still here."

He stepped toward her. She cocked her head, fluffed her feathers, and turned to flutter away to a tree. Then she looked back, bidding him to follow. With a frown, Everis headed after her.

Nova moved from tree to bush to tree, leading him across the courtyard. When they reached a door, she perched on his shoulder until he opened it and slipped inside. From there, the white raven glided down the halls and stairwells, through familiar paths that now felt heavy with darkness and grief. She hopped and flew from sconces to windowsills to tables, periodically looking back to ensure Ever was keeping up. He was. The halls were eerily silent and devoid of security.

Perhaps most of the soldiers are out in the city. They don't expect any threat coming into the castle.

Before he knew it, Nova had led him right to Master Orin's bedroom door at the top of the tower. He stilled, heart in his throat, struggling to bring himself to try the door. How many days had he spent in this very room? Namedays, holidays, regular days when the weather was miserable and Master Orin had him and Wren bundle up and settle in. Instead of lessons, they read and drew and played games while the storms outside raged. They were some of Everis's most precious memories. Now, they were so far out of his reach that it made it hard to breathe.

On his shoulder, Nova tugged at his hair. With a grimace, Everis opened the door and stepped inside.

Orin's room lay suspended in time. A cup of cold tea sat at his bedside, along with an open book, facedown, that he would never get to finish reading. Ever slowly moved to the wardrobe and opened it, removing one of the robes from inside. He wrapped it around himself, pressing his face into the fabric and breathing in. Sandalwood, rain, home.

Nova perched on the footboard of the bed, surveying the room. She looked lost.

"Do you know that he's gone, Nova?" Everis asked softly. "Do you understand what that means?"

She looked at him. Something in her eyes had always felt so human. Now, the understanding Everis saw there made him think she knew perfectly well that Orin was dead and felt the loss just as he did.

"Why did you bring me here?"

Not that he expected an answer. And yet, perhaps coming here had been the right idea. For the first time since they'd stepped foot into the city, Ever's head felt clearer. The darkness of this place was affecting him more than he cared to admit. He took a seat, pressing his face to the sleeve of Orin's robe again. He needed to stay grounded. Needed to remember the real reason he was here: to kill Drake. Protect Wren. Restore Cassia to her rightful place on the throne.

After a few moments, Nova fluttered to the window, then took flight, leaving Everis alone. He lingered, not wanting to leave this space where he felt safe. Where, at any moment, he could envision Wren or Orin walking through the door. He stood and moved about the room, not wanting to go through his things, but... searching. For something, anything, he might use. He located a few potions, a few runes. Nothing he would have much use for. Finally, he went to the door, giving the room one last long look.

I'm trying, Master. I want to make you proud.

He drew up the hood of Orin's robe, took a deep breath, and left.

Drake could be anywhere, but the magi study seemed as good a place to look as any. If he could find and dispose of the other magi while he was at it, all the better.

As he headed back down the tower, a door swung open and a familiar woman stepped out. Ever moved on instinct, grabbing the startled magi and backing her into the room with a dagger to her throat. He pressed her to the wall with a snarl while she stared up at him, eyes wide and horrified.

"Everis!"

"Hello, Pava. Scream, and I'll slit your throat so fast you'll bleed out before anyone hears you." He hadn't forgotten that this woman had sold out Lady Imaryllis.

"I won't scream," she whispered. "I swear on my life. Please."

Ever didn't budge. "Are you working with him? With Drake?"

"I... No. I... It's complicated."

"I suggest you uncomplicate it quickly." The steel bit into her flesh, drawing a thin line of blood.

She sucked in a breath. "I'm not doing blood magic if that's what you're asking."

"Are you going to try to tell me it wasn't you that betrayed Lady Imaryllis's trust?"

Pava opened her mouth, closed it, fumbled for words. "I... I was afraid. Imaryllis was talking about betraying the queen, and if they'd found out, *when* they—"

Ever narrowed his eyes. "So, you sold everyone out to save your own skin."

She whimpered in response but said nothing to try to argue that fact. What was he supposed to do? He'd been fully prepared to kill anyone he encountered for being a traitor, but so many of these people had just been afraid, going along in order to stay alive. Maybe it wasn't a forgivable offense, but he had a hard time bringing himself to kill her when she wasn't even fighting back. He couldn't just let her go, either.

He drew away, and she exhaled in relief. Pava was a researcher, not a fighter. She no doubt knew offensive spells, but that wasn't her area of expertise, and if she wasn't a complete idiot, she'd know she was no match for him and her best bet was to play along for the time being.

He sighed. "You're coming with me."

"What?"

"I'm not repeating myself. But I will give you a warning: if I think for even a second that you're planning on fucking me over, I *will* kill you, and I will not feel bad about it."

She bit her lower lip but nodded in eager understanding.

Pava didn't ask him any questions as they crept out of the magi tower and headed down into the dungeons, still not encountering a single guard. Ever paused, momentarily caught by the faint smell of decay, and saw the body lying within one of the cells.

Cassia's would-be assassin. Still down here from before they'd even left. The chill of being underground kept the stench to a minimum, but it was still enough to make his lungs itch and his eyes burn as he approached and stepped inside. No one had reason to come down here, so it likely hadn't occurred to Drake to get rid of the body.

"Where can I find Danica?" he asked.

Pava lingered at his side, soft face paling at the sight of a rotting corpse. "Queen Danica spends much of her time in her chambers, surrounded by guards."

Everis watched her. Before she could ask what they were doing, he stepped out of the cell and swung the door shut, letting the lock click into place. Pava startled, rushing to the bars and trying to grab his sleeve through them. He stepped out of reach.

"No, no! Please don't leave me here!"

"You're lucky this is all I'm doing," Ever snapped. "Your betrayal caused a chain reaction of events. Master Orin's dead because of you."

She froze, her eyes turning glassy. "That's not true."

"You told Drake where to find them. Orin gave his life to protect Cassia, *your queen*. If you care at all, if you have any remorse, you'll spend your time down here regretting what you did."

He didn't wait for a response. He turned and marched up the stairs before the roiling darkness within him made him change his mind.

WREN

"There are two primary entrances to the castle," Faulk said. "They're marked on the map." Wren knows them intimately. The main gate to the north and the merchant's entrance at the back. "Our best bet is to get in there now and apprehend Danica, if at all possible. Once she's in our custody, the rest of the city guard will fall in line. At that point, we might be wise to await Ryland's men to go after Reed."

Faulk had already talked this all over with his own people, and now he was delivering the plan to Wren and Lady Imaryllis. Wren lifted his head to look at her.

She studied the map with a critical eye. "I don't think we should wait for anyone."

"No?"

"Not if an opportunity presents itself, no. The longer we wait, the more time we're giving those apprentices of Drake's to grow stronger. They're fledglings right now. We can take them."

She'd spent an hour teaching the assembled Owls how to best fight a blood magi, something that even Wren had never received lessons on. Not that there was much advice to give beyond the obvious: *Don't bleed. Don't give them an opening. Work fast, and don't strike to injure because they can*

299

utilize their own blood just as well as anyone else's. That was easier said than done, but it was why the element of surprise was so important. If they could find Drake's apprentices and catch them off guard, overwhelm them, it could be done.

Drake, Wren knew, wouldn't be so easily taken.

Faulk folded his arms across his chest. "You two will put on some of our clothes, something to make you indistinguishable from us. I don't want you easily picked out in a crowd. Imaryllis, you and Jade will lead the charge at the front of the castle. Sevin and Vesir will take others in through the back. It's unlikely they'll gain access to the castle, but that's fine. They'll serve as a diversion. Wren and I will be slipping in through the final entrance."

Wren frowned. "Those are the only two ways in and out of the castle."

Faulk smiled thinly. "No, there's one more. What can you tell me about Drake's three apprentices?"

"Arabella Clearwater, Beatty Stone, and Quinton Fray." Imaryllis said their names with distaste and barely repressed anger.

Wren felt it, too. Beatty and Arabella were older than him by a few years, but Quinton was closer in age to Imaryllis and had been one of his teachers on occasion. The betrayal stung.

Imaryllis continued, "Quinton's specialty is hexes and illusions, a dangerous one. Beatty and Arabella are younger, without specialties... which might be good for us in the sense that they're inexperienced, but bad because I couldn't tell you what subjects they might've been studying and improving in ever since teaming up with Drake."

"If possible, write down descriptions of each of them so we know who we're dealing with. Sounds like this Quinton will be the one to watch for."

Imaryllis frowned. "I can do that, but I'm not certain I like the idea of the pair of you going off on your own."

"The goal is to sneak in undetected while the occupants of the castle are distracted by the attack on both entrances. I'll select one or two others to accompany us."

"And you'll storm in there with a single magi and a bunch of humans and hope you can handle several blood magi?" she asked.

"You aren't giving the Owls enough credit." Faulk inclined his chin. "I'm asking you to trust my judgment on this one. We're limited on time, people, and... well, magi, frankly. The biggest battle will be at the main gates, and that's why you need to be there."

For a moment, Wren was certain Lady Imaryllis would argue. She

even looked at him as though expecting Wren to side with her, but...
he felt lost in this situation. It all felt so large and beyond the scope of
anything and everything he'd ever had to deal with. Planning a siege? His
mind blanked when he tried to formulate any semblance of a plan.

Imaryllis seemed to understand, though, because she gave a curt,
resigned nod. "Very well, but I'm placing Wren under your care and so
help me, if he gets hurt..."

"We're all at risk of injury here." Faulk smiled faintly. "But I will put
my own life on the line to keep the kid safe. You have my word."

"*Kid*," Wren muttered.

Within the hour, everyone had assembled. They would leave through
different entrances into the city, with Imaryllis's group exiting closest to
the main gates. Imaryllis gave Wren a tight hug and a promise that they
would see each other soon. Jade would travel deeper into the tunnels to
exit somewhere near the southern borders of the city, then backtrack to
the merchant's door. Before they parted ways, Jade sidled up to Faulk,
slapping him on the back before pulling him into a tight, albeit brief, hug.
His words were soft, but Wren was lingering close enough to make them
out. "Don't lose your head, pup. I don't want to have to be the one to tell
your lover why you aren't coming home."

Faulk only scoffed, but he returned the hug with a single arm,
awkwardly, and shoved the taller man away. The way he grumbled, "Get
lost," sounded somehow affectionate.

Their own group consisted of Faulk, Brant, Elias, and himself. Why
Brant was included, Wren didn't know, but the soldier had more than
proven his willingness to go into battle. Perhaps it was personal. He'd
watched a lot of his contemporaries and friends both die for and betray
the throne.

They departed two hours after the other groups, and Wren spent
that time seated with Master Orin, eyes closed, meditating. Centering
himself within the comfort of his magic and trying to seek out Everis's
in any way he could. Normally, he could view it in the distance as a sort
of comforting, warm glow.

Now, though, he only saw red. Red and mist so thick he could swirl
it about his fingers. Threads tangled together into a mess of gold and
crimson.

Everis was lost in there somewhere.

Wren would unravel those threads or die trying.

EVERIS

Pava had been telling the truth about one thing, at least: there were guards stationed around the royal wing. Ever positioned himself around a corner and waited, exercising every bit of strained patience he possessed to not simply rush into things. Eventually, it paid off, and he was able to dispatch two of the guards as they changed shifts and were distracted, allowing him to slip into the tower stairwell and slink upstairs.

The last time he'd been here was the night he'd followed Cassia's assassin. Now, he was the one being as silent as he could, prepared to slaughter anyone in his way—Queen Danica included.

Yes, that's right.

Perhaps he'd been looking at this wrong. Perhaps Drake wasn't who they needed to deal with first. If they took Danica down, the rest of the kingdom might fall in line behind Cassia. They would have more help *against* Drake.

Security within the tower was tight. He met another guard coming down the stairs as he went up. Everis slammed him into the wall with a hand over his face, fire crackling from his fingertips over the man's skin and down into his throat and lungs, burning and suffocating him

302

before he had a chance to scream. There were four more guards posted outside Danica's chambers. With no easy way to sneak up on them, Everis focused, summoning smoke into the hall, thick and black and blinding and, most of all, distracting. The guards promptly began to search for the source of the apparent fire, which gave Everis ample time to slide in and drive his dagger into the base of their skulls and backs and throats.

His head had gone fuzzy again. *You are not a blood magi,* Wren had insisted, but he wondered if that was entirely right because the blood around him, on his hands, on his blade, his clothes… it certainly made him feel stronger. Powerful. *Unstoppable.* When he closed his eyes, the threads he saw were *all* glittering red.

He choked on a sound, struggling to regain his composure.

Orin. Cassia. Imaryllis.

Wren.

He needed to keep his head. They were counting on him.

Everis sheathed his dagger and drew his sword, anticipating more guards within the room itself. He'd refrain from using any more magic if he could help it. Spells weren't needed against humans where his blade would do the trick.

He threw open the door.

There were no guards in the room. No Danica, either. Instead, Everis stared at Drake Reed, seated comfortably in a chair beside the open balcony windows, a gentle breeze sweeping in and upsetting his long, blond hair. Drake smiled, the same warm smile Everis had known all his life, a kind, familiar face—save for the fact that he now wore a patch over his right eye.

"Welcome home, Ever."

Everis swallowed his burning temper. "Where's Danica?"

"The queen is elsewhere. Safe, of course." Drake delicately marked his place in the book he'd been reading and set it aside. "When I realized you were here, I felt it prudent for her to be relocated."

"When you realized…" Everis's face warmed. The smirk on Drake's mouth was so smug he wanted to hit him. "And when was that, exactly?"

"The moment you came in through the merchant's entrance, of course. Nothing happens within these walls without me knowing. Although I'll admit, I'm surprised you showed up alone." He tipped his head. "Where's your shadow?"

Everis didn't respond.

"Nothing to say? You've never been one to hold your tongue. Orin always said you were too impulsive for your own good." Drake spat out

303

Orin's name like venom, and Ever's vision flashed red.

He raised his hand, snarling out a spell that sparked fire around his hand and the dagger he held. He launched the blade in Drake's direction. All done in a fraction of a second.

Drake's reflexes were faster. He flipped the table before him, launching it into the air where the dagger embedded itself and the flames scorched and licked across the wood. Barely taking a breath, Everis prepared to launch another attack, but the second the table hit the ground, Drake fired off a spell, spoken in a tongue that sounded dark and unearthly, made his voice drip like poison. Before Ever could figure out what he'd done, ghostly fingers clutched his throat. They shoved him across the room, lifting his feet off the floor. He grasped at nothing, choking on air, his thrashing futile against the unseen.

"Sore at me over your master, are you?" Drake *tsk*ed. "No one is more disappointed in that outcome than I am, dear boy. I respected Orin. I loved him. I hoped he'd have the common sense to work with me instead of against me... a mistake you and Wren could rectify."

He unclenched his hand. The ghost fingers released Ever. He landed amongst a pile of books and papers stacked on the floor, wincing. Drake had given him an opening to play along. He ought to take it. And yet he could think of nothing worse than any sort of feigned kindness toward Drake.

"He was a good man," Everis rasped, rubbing at his bruised throat. "A better one than you could ever hope to be. You think I would want anything to do with you except to see your head removed from your fucking shoulders?"

"Hurtful." Drake sighed. He didn't move to attack again. Instead, he made a sweeping gesture to the mess of books strewn about Everis's landing spot. Everis glanced down, then did a double take. He would've recognized Master Orin's handwriting anywhere.

Sucking in a breath, he slowly picked up one of the open books. No, not books... Journals. Orin's journals. The ones he and Wren had watched their master write in every day without fail. They belonged in Orin's room, though, not here. Not in the possession of the man who'd murdered him.

"What..."

"You should give them a read. The entries regarding you are quite interesting. Perhaps it might give you some insight into all the ways your master let you down."

Despite himself, Everis paused. Just briefly.

No doubt, Drake saw the split second of hesitation, the chink in his armor. His wolfish smile widened a notch. "Go on. Have a look. I'd never attack a man while his back was turned."

The image of Master Orin's body hanging from the gallows blinked through his mind. Wren's trembling fingers clutching his arm, the utter devastation and pain wringing out his voice and clouding his eyes... Everis wanted to tear this man apart for that, for the sight of Wren in such pain. Could he, though? If he attacked now, if he put his all behind it, if he utilized the magic he'd been trying to suppress, could he win? He'd come to the castle because he'd been so sure of it. Now, faced directly with the challenge, his confidence wavered.

Patience, Orin would've said. *Don't let your impulsiveness shove you into a battle you aren't prepared for.*

He closed his eyes and took a calculated breath. Opened them again. Slowly, he flipped through the pages. Notes. Spells. Scribbles of plants and Nova. A sketch of Wren and Everis hunched over their work in the magi tower, lost in concentration.

There are decades of memories documented in these.

He would've loved nothing more than to sit with Wren and pore over them, searching for a way to feel closer to Orin, for some way to reclaim him while the loss was so raw and tender.

Yet he soon realized that there were pages within the journal that Drake had dog-eared. He flipped to one, chest tight. It was dated years prior. In fact, the same year Everis had come to live at the castle. His heart lurched in his chest. Whatever this was, did he truly want to read it? Did he need to know? Some things were better left buried.

And yet...

...Wren questions whether it was a wise choice to have brought Everis here, and the answer is: I do not know. His mother was ill, yes, but she bore no symptoms of the strange wasting sickness that took the rest of the town.

The only conclusion I can come to is that Everis drew on the lifeforce of those around him in his bid to save her.

Imagine it. A single boy his age, so mired in grief that he felled an entire city to try to bring someone back to life. All without knowing a thing about what he was doing. The power that required... I cannot begin to fathom the dangers it could present. The Citadel would surely see him as a threat and put him to death, or imprison him at the least, and that is not something I can allow. He is only a child, and a child can learn. We can curb this darkness within him. I'm certain of that. He will have a home here, a family, and I will see that he knows only the good he's capable of doing.

He re-read.

…Everis drew on the lifeforce of those around him in his bid to save her. Perhaps he could have, if he'd known what he was doing.

The weight of an entire city of deaths weighed down on him. No, that wasn't right. Other people had gotten sick first, and then his mother… right? Wasn't that how it had gone? Mother couldn't have been the first. He couldn't be the one responsible for thousands of deaths. He bowed his head, eyes closed, trying to remember how to breathe around a broken heart. "Why are you showing me this?"

Drake's voice dripped with saccharine sympathy. "Because you deserve to know exactly how much he let you down. All these years, he placed a lid on a boiling pot when he should've tempered the water. He's made it all worse for you, Everis. Had he told anyone else, we could've helped. *I* could've helped and seen that you were trained. Not stifled and shut away like a dirty secret."

Would such a thing have been possible? Ivy seemed to think he could control it. Had he received proper training as a boy, how much of this pain and fear could've been avoided?

This time, the voice in his head was Imaryllis's, scoffing. *He's baiting you.*

Drake had risen to his feet. He approached now, slow, relaxed. "Orin hid the truth from you because he felt it was your fault and didn't want you to carry the burden. *I'm* telling you the truth because the truth is that it *wasn't* your fault. You were only a boy."

Everis's shoulders sagged beneath the weight of those words. "And you think you could teach me now? How to control it?"

"Yes." Excitement slid beneath the edges of his words. "More than that, I think we can learn from each other. I know the technical aspects, but you—*you* have the raw talent, Everis. You just need a skilled magi to help draw it out."

The words in the journal blurred. Everis blinked back tears. What would it have been like to grow up not feeling as though he were a freak of nature? If Master Orin had even just *talked* to him about it, had tried to help him learn about it rather than shut it all away and hope that was enough?

He looked at Drake.

"…You are not a magi like me."

He reached for the red threads. Grasped. *Pulled.* Allowed the magic to wash over him in a brilliant rush. Electricity crackled across his hands as he brought them up to grab Drake, prepared to filter enough lightning through the other magi's body to kill a small army.

His hands passed through Drake with no resistance, nothing more than smoke and ash that shuddered as the illusion dissipated. Everis floundered, left with nowhere to channel that magic, unable to regain his bearings long enough to react as the real Drake appeared behind him.

A solid hand clamped over his mouth, the leather of Drake's gloves muffling the snarl he tried to let loose. Drake held on to him tightly, and it took him a second too long to register the scent. Clove. No, cypher. Sedatives—strong ones. Everis's eyes rolled back. He strained to keep hold of his rage, his magic, clutching at threads in hopes they could save him…

He was unconscious before Drake allowed his body to hit the floor.

WREN

TEN YEARS AGO

They could smell the rotting corpses before they arrived in Balerno. The stench was something that would surely etch itself into Wren's head and lungs for years to come. And the heat... Oh, the heat. The sun had set nearly an hour ago, yet Wren's tunic and cloak were heavy and itchy with sweat. He couldn't imagine how the knights felt beneath their heavy armor.

Master Orin appeared unduly calm and unbothered by the weather. Then again, his master came from a region where the summers were brutal, and rain fell heavily year round, so perhaps he was used to the sweltering humidity. Although the heat might not have bothered him, his master looked troubled when they finally saw the bodies.

Even at fifteen years old, this wasn't Wren's first foray into dealing with the dead. Some of his lessons involved studying human anatomy to learn the right magic to cure the things that ailed it. Master Orin could mend a broken bone, a fractured arm, wounds from arrows and knives and dog bites, all things Wren had witnessed during the years he'd been Orin's apprentice.

Not even a magi as skilled as his master could do much about a plague.

Large red Xs were splashed across doors, behind some of which Wren could hear the occasional sobs and cries. Bodies had been six and seven high on the dark streets. No one had bothered to come through and light the nighttime torches, and so they operated by torchlight from their own entourage and the nearly full moon overhead.

Wren drew his horse closer to Orin's. "Shouldn't they be burning the corpses, Master?"

"They should," Orin agreed. "But look around. Much of the town is dead or soon will be. They've no way of keeping up with the bodies."

An entire city felled by illness in the span of a month. Wren had a difficult time wrapping his mind around such a travesty.

A woman with a bundled infant in her arms hobbled down the road ahead. When she saw the magi with the royal guards, she staggered up to Wren's horse, forcing him to draw the mare to a swift halt, and latched on to his thigh. He lifted his lantern, spilling light across her narrow face and cheekbones hollowed by the wasting sickness. The Silent Plague. Aside from her hollowed-out features and paper thin skin, she looked fine. No boils, no rash.

"Are you here to help my baby?" the woman rasped, lifting the bundle at him. Had she not been so weak, she'd have no doubt shoved the infant into his arms.

His horse stamped her hooves and reared her head away. Wren gave the reins a tug to keep her in place, his voice catching in his throat. "I…"

Two of the guards dismounted and now closed in, taking the woman and leading her gently away. Briefly, he felt Master Orin's hand upon his shoulder, reassuring, although it did little to settle Wren's nerves. "Is there really nothing we can do for her?"

Orin shook his head. "Nothing I could offer her would help. The knights can give her something if she's in pain."

"What about the child?"

The look on his master's face clouded over with pity. "Already dead." He put his heels to his horse and continued down the street.

The knights busied themselves searching for survivors. They would bring any they found to a quarantine camp several miles away, tended to by magi who would watch them for the next few weeks to ensure they showed no signs of disease. After that, they could travel to the capital of Midmere.

There was no saving the city of Balerno. Once a plague took hold of a town… there was no coming back from it.

Master Orin seemed to have a destination in mind, and soon it was just the pair of them, alone in the oppressive darkness. He knew better than to ask questions. When Master Orin wanted him to know something, he would tell him. Until then, it was best to remain quiet and watch, listen, and learn.

They passed through the town square where more bodies lay, covered by blankets that did nothing to mask the stink. Wren couldn't help but stare down at them. If their troops had arrived sooner, more of these people could've been saved. He and Master Orin could've cast a few protective charms, the same ones they and the knights had donned before stepping foot through the city gates. It wasn't foolproof, but it was the best form of protection anyone could have against this type of disease.

As they neared the opposite end of the square, Wren's mare whickered nervously and drew to a halt, prancing back a few steps. Master Orin's horse resisted as well.

"Master, look." Wren pointed. "What is that?"

A fine mist had crept into the square, not unusual save for its deep crimson color. Master Orin swung down from his saddle and tied the reins to a nearby produce stall. He studied the tendrils of red snaking across the ground like fog rolling in from the sea, his expression dark and distant and unlike anything Wren had seen him wear before.

Then he straightened and said, "You may wait here, Wren."

It was less an order and more a granting of permission. If Wren was afraid, he didn't need to go along. But the only thing that worried Wren more than going into that fog was sitting there idly while Master Orin went in alone. He dismounted, fastened his mare next to Master Orin's, and went after the older magi without a word of protest.

Where the red mist had only been barely noticeable in the square, it became thick and roiling down the road. It had no scent, really, at least none strong enough to overtake the cloying stench of death. Yet the further they walked and the thicker the mist grew, the harder it became to breathe and the queasier Wren felt. Master Orin tracked it with dogged determination.

Wren stumbled once over a body lying prone in the street. Orin caught him by the arm to help right him, then pointed straight ahead. The mist was heavily concentrated around one small, dilapidated house, tucked between others much like it. And like most of the other homes they'd passed, this one had a large red X painted across its door, signifying that those inside were diseased or deceased.

Master Orin stopped shy of the house and looked down at him as though undecided. Wren caught hold of the sleeve of his master's robe, not wanting to be left behind.

"Stay close," Orin murmured.

He tried the door. It had no lock and was held shut by a flimsy table, easily pushed aside. Mist rolled out in large, velvety plumes, blinding Wren and making his eyes water. He sucked in a breath and held it. Inside the hovel, it was pitch black. They stepped in slowly and carefully, and Master Orin reached along the wall until he found a window to open the shutters and allow in some moonlight. It cast the room in an eerie glow, providing enough illumination that Wren could see the body on the floor. He gasped, took a quick step back, and nearly stumbled over a chair. Master Orin steadied him again with a hand to his back, then stepped over to kneel beside the woman.

She lay upon a pallet of threadbare woolen blankets, her hands clasped loosely over her stomach. There were no signs of decay to be seen.

"She *is* dead, isn't she?" Wren whispered.

"Quite." Orin withdrew. A troubled look crossed his usually serene face. "Someone has been using magic to keep her preserved... and judging by this mist, I would presume it's not the kind of magic we want to be involved in."

Wren's skin prickled. He'd learned of the magics forbidden by the Magi Citadel, dark arts that required death and sacrifice in exchange for power. Some magi were born with a leaning toward it, others steered in its direction due to troubled pasts or difficulty managing their emotions. Magi did not make magic, after all; they only served as a conductor for it. The better one's connection to the earth and every living thing on it, the better a conduit one could be. And there was no stronger, clearer conduit for magic than life—than blood.

A faint scuffle from the back of the room caught their attention. Orin followed it to an old, tilted armoire. When he flung open the door, Wren half-expected a rat to come skittering out. Instead, there sat a small boy curled in on himself, peering out at them with eyes wide as saucers.

Is this our blood magi? No, not possible. The boy was younger than him. Surely a child wasn't capable of... whatever all this was.

Yet Master Orin spoke to the boy so softly, and soon they were leaving with this child called Everis in tow and Wren with a knot of unease in his stomach. Orin would say nothing as long as the boy was with them. He would have to wait.

The mist had already begun to evaporate by the time they returned to their horses.

They reconvened with the knights, who'd rounded up close to thirty survivors. Not a large number, considering the population of the city. Master Orin explained to Everis that he would need to remain in quarantine until they had cleared everyone of any illness. Everis's eyes grew wide with uncertainty, but he put on a brave face and nodded, allowing himself to be left in the care of a married couple.

Orin returned to Wren, placing a hand against his back and leading him to their horses. The survivors would be loaded into wagons and transported some ten miles south to the quarantine camp. Wren and Orin would ride ahead to ensure the other magi had everything prepared for treatment. The magi would see that every person who arrived received a ward of healing in the event they were exposed to any illness in the camp and to prevent anyone who might be sick from spreading it further. Their wards could do little for an already infected person, but they could help to prevent the disease from spreading.

Wren didn't speak a word as they mounted their horses and set off. When questioning Master Orin, he needed to tread carefully. Orin did nothing without thinking it through thoroughly, and many times Wren had tried to argue with him, only to find himself frustrated because Master Orin had a rebuttal for *everything*. They rode in silence for the better part of an hour before Orin spoke without Wren needing to ask a thing.

"You're wondering what I'm doing, offering to bring him home with us."

Wren bit back a sigh. "The thought had crossed my mind, Master. I'm sure you have your reasons."

"I do," he agreed, glancing at him. "You know what they would do to Everis if they thought he was a blood magi?"

"They would kill him."

"Or send him to the Citadel to be imprisoned, which might be worse."

"So, you're trying to save a child, is that it? Regardless of the potential danger?" Plenty of times during their years together, Wren had argued with Orin for the sake of arguing. He'd been a willful child with a lot of opinions on a great many things. This wasn't one of those times. He only wanted to understand.

Orin looked straight ahead. "Do you remember when you first came to me and we had an argument about botanical growth spells? You lost your temper and unintentionally shattered every tube and colander in the laboratory."

Heat flooded Wren's face. It hadn't been one of his finer moments as an apprentice. More of that willfulness; when he was younger, he'd struggled mightily to learn to pick his battles. "I remember."

"All children have difficulty controlling their emotions, Wren," Master Orin said gently. "Everis is no different. He has the raw potential to do great things with his magic, if someone were to show him how to use it properly."

Wren remained silent for a long moment. "Did he do all of this, Master? Not just preserving his mother's corpse, but the rest of it?"

Orin's expression didn't change. He didn't answer, either. That, in and of itself, was answer enough. Wren's stomach turned.

In the end, it didn't matter what he thought. The boy seemed so small and innocent, not at all what he'd have expected of a blood magi. But if Master Orin was right, and this had all been an accident, wouldn't it be cruel to hand Everis over? Or were they putting everyone in danger by subjecting them to someone who could potentially hurt them without even meaning to? The boy had unwittingly brought death to the doorstep of an entire village. His chest hurt. He could see the difficulty of the decision Master Orin was making and couldn't decide whether he agreed with it.

Or maybe he simply couldn't get the image of Everis out of his head, huddled in a closet, surrounded by death and disease yet untouched himself. Long after they'd reached camp and settled for the night, he could still see Everis's face behind his closed eyelids.

In his dreams, the boy's eyes met his, and in their depths lay a blood-red glow.

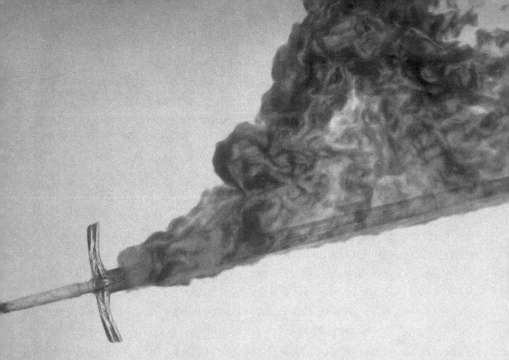

IMARYLLIS

Imaryllis had taken part in her fair share of battles, but this would be unlike any before it. Laying siege to her own home? Against people she'd known for decades? It hardly seemed fair. Or real.

She allowed Jade to lead the charge. He knew the roads to take, the alleys to sneak down, even with their limited numbers, so that they went unnoticed until the last possible moment before arriving at the castle gates. They'd anticipated there would be soldiers and city guards armed and waiting for them, yet the castle gates stood open.

As they filed cautiously into the central courtyard, Imaryllis scanned the parapets, expecting a trap.

All she could see, however, were bodies.

Several piles of them stacked haphazardly about the courtyard.

"What a tacky storage method," Jade muttered.

"Some kind of warning, perhaps," Imaryllis said.

When the gates slammed shut behind them, the bodies stirred.

Jade's cautious expression deadpanned. "Mm, I don't think so."

Imaryllis watched in abject confusion and then horror as the piles writhed and the corpses rose, clumsy and uncoordinated, and shambled toward them. She drew her swords, summoned her magic to wrap around them, and braced herself.

If Drake and his apprentices were capable of making the dead rise, she wasn't sure this was a fight they could win.

WREN

Trying to follow the two assassins in the dark made Wren feel unwieldy. Elias and Faulk moved in total silence while he and Brant lumbered after them, cringing at every noisy footfall. At least Brant had been required to change out of his armor in favor of the same leathers the Owls wore. Faulk insisted the armor would be a hindrance where they needed to go.

"I don't know what other entrance he's talking about," Brant muttered to Wren as they navigated the city streets. "I've lived in that castle all my life. If there were hidden passages, I'd know about it. I've looked."

"I'm inclined to say the same, but he clearly knows something we don't."

Was this the first time they'd ever spoken about anything not having to do with Everis? He'd never personally had much of an issue with the guard. Certainly, Brant had been crass and rude and a bully when they were children, but Everis hadn't been the easiest to get along with, either. The pair of them needled each other and threw insults—and punches— quickly and without reserve. Perhaps he'd disliked Brant on Ever's behalf for a while, but they'd grown up. Brant had become a bit of an annoyance, but not a terrible person. If nothing else, Wren had seen his dedication to his work. To Cassia, to Faramond. That was commendable when so many had betrayed their call to duty.

Brant asked, "Do you think Everis is alright?"

The question caught him off guard. He blinked once, surprised. "He's... Well, for the time being, he's alright. I think. I can sense him, and I don't believe he's injured, so..."

"Huh." Brant scratched his jaw, scruffy with a few days' worth of growth. "You guys can do that? Like... feel each other?"

"After a fashion. It's more that every magi's magic has its own unique feel to it. Like how apples and pears smell different? Maybe that's a poor analogy because it isn't a scent, exactly..." His brow furrowed in thought. Their magic was deeper than normal senses. It wasn't a sight, a smell, a touch, a sound. It was *everything* compounded into one. A sixth sense. "Sometimes the differences are so subtle I can't make them out. But there are two people I've always been able to sense easily and without fail, like an extension of myself."

"Everis and...?"

Wren looked straight ahead. His chest ached with the emptiness. "Master Orin."

Idly, he wondered if the fighting at the front of the castle had started. Lady Imaryllis was there. He ought to be, too. She was one lone magi, and no matter how skilled she was, if she had to face Drake or his apprentices, she'd be outnumbered.

He heard Master Orin's voice in his head. *Concentrate on the present and what you're setting out to do.*

His mission right now was here, with Faulk and Elias and Brant, to get into the castle and find Danica. If he worried too much about everyone and everything else, he wouldn't be able to put his all into the task at hand... and that task might very well include going up against one of Drake's apprentices himself.

Under the cover of night, Faulk led them to the towering castle walls. In the marshy grass and sloping hills, the footing was precarious, and a few times Brant and Wren had to grab each other not to slip. Just when Wren was about to ask where in the world they were headed, they reached a narrow pathway leading from the castle walls down to the streets below and at the head of it, a small archway within the wall itself. It took Wren a second to recognize it, but the moment they stepped inside and the smell of waste and death washed over him strong enough to make him gag, he realized—

"The death chute?"

The chute began in the dungeons and, unlike some of the trash chutes elsewhere, was wide enough that a body could be deposited and dropped below for easy retrieval. It wasn't used often these days—at least, not like it had been in centuries past when plague and war meant plenty of bodies to dispose of from within the castle.

Elias adjusted the sword on his back and looked at them, eyebrows raised. "It leads into the castle, doesn't it?"

"Yes, but…" Brant bit his tongue at a stern look from Faulk. He'd promised to listen if they brought him along.

Elias went first. Faulk hoisted him up high enough that he could grab a narrow lip of stone at the base of the chute, where he could pull himself up. Then it was a matter of bracing his shoulders against one side and his legs against the other and slowly crawling up like some sort of awkward spider.

Wren went next. Elias had done it with such ease that it surely couldn't be that hard. However, the moment he positioned himself with his shoulders against one grimy, cold stone wall and his boots against the other… How did he even move without falling? He studied Elias above him. *One arm at a time. Shift your shoulders. One leg, the other leg.* Grimacing, Wren pushed with his legs to slide his shoulders along, then walked his feet along the wall to catch up. Slow but steady.

It sounded like Brant was having as hard a time beneath him. He heard a string of curses at one point and bit back a laugh. "Bet you're glad you didn't wear all that armor after all."

"Shove it," Brant panted.

Even though the dungeons were set at the base of the castle, the raised structure meant they were still high above the ground. Elias had long since reached the top and disappeared, and Wren silently wished the man would toss down a rope or something, because surely that had to be easier than this. Finally, Wren reached the top, snagging the ledge and hauling himself over with a grunt.

"Thanks for the hel—" Wren stopped. Elias stood a few feet away in front of a closed cell, and within that cell was a familiar face. "Pava?"

"Wren?" Pava had her fingers wrapped tight around the bars and appeared to have been in the process of begging Elias to let her out.

Elias glanced back, his eyebrows raised. "You know her?"

"She's a fellow magi." Wren dusted himself off and approached, though he kept a careful distance. She'd betrayed Lady Imaryllis. He hadn't forgotten that. "What happened? Why are you locked up?"

"Everis found me and put me in here."

That had his attention. "Ever? Was he alright?"

"Last I saw him, yes." She chewed at her bottom lip, looking from Elias to Wren and back again as though unsure who to try to appeal to the most. "Please, let me out. I can help with whatever you need."

Elias moved away, peering into the cell at the assassin's corpse.

Wren held up a hand to silence Pava and drifted to the man's side. "Do you recognize her?"

Elias folded his arms over his chest. "Her name was Mateen."

"A friend?"

"Hm, no, I wouldn't say that. We worked a few missions together, but not necessarily well." He shook his head. "She liked to do what she wanted to do, orders be damned. Not a big surprise she ended up going behind the Court's back to take on an unsanctioned job. A damn waste of talent."

Brant joined them, groaning as he stretched out his back. "That's a tight fit—what the hell is she doing here? Er, in there?"

"Ever locked her up," Wren said, giving Pava a pointed look. "And she's going to stay there."

The woman's face fell. "But—"

"But nothing. I don't trust you. You betrayed Imaryllis to save your own skin. How do I know you won't do the same to us?" Wren gave her a thin smile. "Be grateful Ever didn't kill you instead of locking you up."

Pava drew back slowly, sinking to the floor at the far end of the cell as though no longer trusting being near them. She didn't argue, though.

Faulk made it up the chute with surprising ease and swiftness. He hauled himself out of the cramped space and to his feet without having broken a sweat and took a moment to assess what was going on. He joined Elias, looking in at Mateen's rotting body within the cell. If he was sad about it, it didn't show on his face.

He *tsk*ed softly, turned, and stared at Pava. "Who is still within the castle?"

"W-what?"

"People. There are people in the castle, yes?"

"Um, yes."

"But probably not the same people as usual, correct?"

"Oh—no, many of them were ordered to leave."

"Fewer people in the castle means less concern about mutiny," Faulk explained in response to Wren's and Brant's confused looks. "Then back to my question: who is still within the castle?"

Pava wrung her hands. "A couple of the guards, though most of them were sent to the barracks and aren't allowed to enter the castle itself.

A skeleton crew of servants. Ten, maybe… maybe fifteen? I'm not sure."

"And the magi," Wren amended.

Pava lowered her gaze. "Yes. And the magi."

With a little more prodding, Pava informed them that Danica spent much of her time in her quarters with Drake in her company more often than not. Which wasn't the greatest news, given that they'd hoped to encounter Danica on her own and spare themselves a face-off with Drake just yet.

They left Pava behind, ascending the stairs out of the dungeon. Out in the hallway, Wren fell into step alongside Faulk, voice low. "With any luck, the fighting out front will distract Drake."

"We can hope, but it means he likely left someone watching over Danica, too." Faulk kept his gaze straight ahead. There was something so fascinating about watching him work, the intensity with which his eyes took in everything and how his head tilted ever so slightly, like he could somehow hear someone coming from a mile away.

Yet despite Faulk's keen senses, after a few moments, it was Brant who came to a halt and scowled, turning in a circle. "Is it just me, or did we just come down this hall?"

The other three stopped, looking at each other. Faulk had a similar frown on his face. "We're going in the right direction. At least, we should be." He sighed. "But things in here are… a bit muddled, for lack of a better word."

"*Your* senses are muddled?" Elias groaned. "Then we're fucked."

"They're muddled, but they aren't useless. Give me a second to orient myself." Faulk closed his eyes, trying to concentrate. On what, Wren hadn't a clue. When Faulk began to walk again, still without watching where he was going, Wren kept close. They paused outside an archway with a door, tried it—unlocked, thankfully—and stepped through.

The door slammed shut behind them. Wren whirled, grabbing the handle to drag it back open, half expecting it to be locked. It wasn't and opened easily, yet the hallway on the other side wasn't the same one they'd exited from. What was more, Elias and Brant were nowhere in sight.

Faulk swore.

"Quinton's specialty is illusions," Wren said. "This must be his doing."

"Lovely. And he's the strongest of the three, isn't he?"

"Barring any unforeseen circumstances? Yes."

Faulk grunted, shoving a hand through his silver hair. "Then a fight may be likely after all. And if that's the case, there's something I need you to promise me."

Wren frowned. "What is it?"

"I need your primary focus to be on defeating the blood magi we encounter, no matter what. That means you cannot be worrying about anyone else. Do you understand?"

"I don't understand. You're my friend. We would protect each other in battle, wouldn't we?"

"I don't need your protection, magi," Faulk said, his tone stern. "No matter what, you'll just have to trust that I can look after myself."

Wren faltered. This wasn't like any other battle where he knew he needed to have the backs of those he fought with—and that they would have his. Faulk was a lone wolf, but surely against a type of enemy he'd never faced before, they would both need all the help they could get.

"I…"

"If you consider us allies or friends or whatever sentimental nonsense, then promise me." Faulk turned to face him fully, standing close enough that it made Wren's cheeks warm a little.

Wren didn't flinch away from his intense stare. "I promise. I won't put myself at risk to help you if it comes down to it."

"Good lad." Faulk gave his shoulder a squeeze, released it, then turned to head down the hall.

Wren hurried after him. "So, since we're friends, I overheard something Jade said…"

"I already don't like where this is going."

"You have someone? A lover, back in Patish?"

Faulk's expression remained a blank slate, of course. There might've been the briefest flash of something indiscernible in his eyes, but it was gone just as quickly as it had appeared. "I suppose you could say that."

"What are they like?"

"We should really focus, magi."

"I'm stressed. This helps me focus."

He snorted. Hesitated. Sighed. "He's… intelligent. Witty. A complete headache."

"Is he part of the Dusk Court too?"

"He's not an Owl, no, though he's aware of us. He's too gentle and compassionate to do the things we do. I've only ever seen him kill a man once, and it still haunts him."

Wren couldn't help but smile. Faulk's voice softened as he spoke, a gentle fondness creeping in. It was strange to think that someone as gruff and no-nonsense as him had a lover who was gentle and nonviolent. He and Everis were different, but they shared some commonalities. Their tempers—even though Wren had learned to deal with his much better than Everis had—and their compassion and care for life. Their love of magic and everything it entailed.

His chest ached. He and Ever had rarely been apart for any length of time, come to think of it. When they traveled, they traveled together. They ate their meals together, studied together, trained and fought and bickered and played together. When was it, Wren wondered, that Everis had gone from being a thorn in his side to the person he loved most in the world?

He lapsed into silence, mulling this over as they moved through the castle. None of the hallways made sense. He knew this building by heart, yet they were taking turns that shouldn't have existed and doorways that ought to have led in completely opposite directions. Now and again, Faulk would stop, close his eyes, reorient himself, and try again, but Wren could sense the frustration building in him.

Wren surveyed the tapestries and paintings on the wall as they passed. Yes, they'd gone through this hallway at least eight times. Sometimes twice in a row if they turned left at the corner up ahead…

"Make a right," he instructed.

Faulk glanced back with an arched brow, but did as instructed. At the end of that hall, Wren instructed him to take another right, followed by another. They continued making rights. It ought to have taken them in a giant circle, and yet, finally, the surroundings began to change and they found themselves staring out over the empty training yard and the drooping willow he and Everis had spent so many years climbing. He laughed.

A disembodied voice greeted them with cheer. "Congratulations! Is this what you were trying to reach? Seems an odd destination."

Faulk bristled, lips pulling back into a snarl. He took a step forward, eyes locked upon the willow.

Wren placed a hand on the hilt of his sword, taking a deep breath. "Hello, Arabella."

IMARYLLIS

The dead didn't stop.

They struck one down only for another to rise, and it seemed the only way to get rid of them was to burn them. The Owls tried to keep them off her while she cast repeated variations of fire spells; despite that, the dead didn't slow. The acrid smell of burning flesh hung heavy in the air. The smoke made her eyes water. Yet every time she turned around, more of them had appeared out of nowhere.

Something wasn't right.

One of the dead shambled up to her, and she stared into its face, noting every tiny detail. It reached for her, and she let it. Let it sink its teeth into her shoulder.

Nothing. No pain.

Imaryllis laughed, short and bitter. She shoved the illusion away and turned her gaze toward the parapets as she cast another fire spell. The heat swirled between her hands as it formed, and she gathered it, molded it, then cast it up toward the walls. The spell landed in the center of the walkway atop the wall and exploded. Imaryllis turned, cast again, and sent it to another area. This time, it must've hit home because there came a series of unholy screams and the illusion engulfing the yard shimmered and melted away in a dizzying blur. The dead vanished. She and the Owls were standing in an empty yard.

Imaryllis swore under her breath. Illusions were cheap, nasty things with no place on a battlefield as far as she was concerned. "Tricks!"

On the ramparts, she finally spotted Quinton, half his face blistered and burning, his mouth pulled into a sneer. He began to cast. He could cook the lot of them there in the yard like some oversized frying pan, but Imaryllis was prepared for that—and had prepared the Owls, too.

"*Shield!*" she yelled.

As Quinton finished his spell, Imaryllis raised her arm and activated the engraving on her bracer. The barrier it cast was large enough to cover herself and anyone within a thirty-foot radius.

Quinton's attack rained down on them in a devastating deluge, fireballs cracking the earth where they struck, rattling Imaryllis's barrier and forcing her down to one knee as she braced herself against the impact. The magic crackled and strained beneath the onslaught. She closed her eyes, focused everything behind it. She could feel Stryder and Jade moving to her sides, pressing their hands to her back to physically support her.

These people, these assassins, who had no real reason to help them, were *her* soldiers right now.

She would protect them with everything she had.

WREN

Arabella stepped into view from behind the old willow tree. She was as lovely as ever, full-figured, with dark curls that cascaded down to her lower back. Her hazel eyes glinted with a familiar red shimmer that made Wren's stomach turn. It was all he could do to be grateful they were running into her and not Quinton.

"That was a deceptively easy puzzle to solve," Wren noted.

Arabella shrugged. "Quin's busy elsewhere, so he did what he could on short notice. Still, you wasted some time, hm? Oh, goodness, where are your two friends? Don't tell me you got split up." Bella had always been a playful sort, but not always in a way that others found amusing.

Wren knew better than to take the bait. He stepped forward, signaling Faulk to give him a chance to handle this. "This isn't right, and you know it. Cassia is alive and well. What Drake has you doing... It's going to get you all killed or locked in the Citadel dungeons for the rest of your life."

She smiled, all teeth. "The Citadel has an entire team dedicated to hunting down blood magi. Did you know that? An entire team for one person. Do you really think they're prepared to handle an entire kingdom run by us? We're just the beginning, Wren. Others will join, and those idiots at the Citadel will either fall in line or simply fall."

His heart sank. But if he couldn't reason with her, he'd use another tactic. "One blood magi who's been suppressing his powers for years and a few half-baked apprentices who wouldn't know their arse from their nose? I think we can handle it before the Citadel needs to bother sending a team."

Arabella's smirk faded from her pretty face, twisting into a snarl before she sank her teeth into the meat of her arm, spilling blood. It was their only warning before she attacked.

The force of a wind spell came at him like a hurricane, scarcely giving Wren a chance to construct a barrier. The burst shoved him and Faulk back, their boots sliding along the stone. This wasn't right. This wasn't strength he would've ever expected from Bella—certainly never anything he'd felt from her during their training sessions.

The second the spell faded, Wren dropped the barrier and raised his hands, reaching through the fog in his mind until he found the magic he needed to send a blast of fire spiraling across the courtyard. In the blink of an eye, Bella was gone, but the fire enveloped the willow and sent it up in flames. Bella reappeared a few feet away in a crouch, blood smeared across her lips and dripping down her arm.

Faulk lunged from behind Wren, faster than humanly possible, fast enough that it caught Arabella off guard. He took a swipe with his dagger that looked somehow clumsy for him, and Bella twisted to avoid it. Faulk's free hand came up, raking across Bella's face. She reared back with a distressed scream, blood leaking from several sizable gashes across her eyes.

How did he do that?

Bella brought a hand to her face, gaping. One of her eyes squinched shut, but she only needed one to be dangerous.

"Down!" Wren shouted to Faulk.

The assassin listened without a moment's hesitation, dropping to the ground. Instead of launching another attack at Bella, a flurry of snow and mist came from Wren's outstretched hands and submerged the area, reducing visibility to zero. He couldn't see Bella, but he couldn't see Faulk, either.

Wren drew his sword and darted through the haze, spotting Bella's silhouette, and lunged with every intention of driving the blade right through her. He was met with a bloody smile and raised hand, accompanied by a blinding flash of light that sent him staggering and grasping his face, his vision completely whited out and burning in his skull.

He couldn't see to put up another barrier. Couldn't see to cast anything.

All he could do was lift his sword, useless, in a miserable attempt to ward off any attacks. He could vaguely hear Bella mumbling in a language he'd come to recognize as blood magic. It crackled in the air like fragments of glass.

Wren squeezed his eyes shut and prayed.

He braced for pain that never came. Instead, a woman's howling scream ripped through the air, followed by retreating footsteps. Wren gasped, still trying to clear his vision. Shapes and shadows came into fuzzy focus, enough that he could see Arabella fleeing across the training yard for the magi tower, and Faulk trying to run after her. The assassin took a few steps, however, then staggered and dropped to his knees. Wren rushed to his side, helping him lie back. The front of Faulk's body was riddled with open wounds, glittering shards of ice jutting out of his abdomen and chest.

Faulk took a few raspy breaths and tried to sit up, groaned, and swore. "Fuck."

"Easy, easy, let me just… I can—Gods…" Wren swallowed hard. He didn't have the equipment for this. Faulk's blood was everywhere. His vision was still hazy, white around the edges, like an impending migraine. "What happened to not getting in each other's way, you stupid—"

"Stop, stop," he growled, grabbing Wren's arm. "She's injured. Hurry and go after her."

Wren looked in the direction Bella had fled, then back down. Faulk had lost so much blood. His vision blurred, this time from tears. He thought of Jade, and Stryder, and Elias, and Faulk's other friends, all the Owls who looked up to him. He thought of Faulk's lover, waiting for him back in Patish.

"Go," Faulk snapped again, giving him a weak shove. "Before… she gets away… I'll catch up…"

"Liar." Wren choked back a sound somewhere between a laugh and a sob. Carefully, he laid Faulk down and got to his feet. Blood on his clothes. Hands. Everywhere. He trembled. But he couldn't allow Arabella to get away, not after this. He'd give her no chance to hide or heal herself.

He gave his friend one last look before turning to give chase.

EVERIS

Everis woke to darkness.

Not a dark room. Not a dark cell. But *darkness*—all-encompassing nothingness. The cold swaddled him gently but made his skin burn. Despite the endless stretch of emptiness, he didn't feel as though he was alone. There were eyes on him from every direction. Faces in the shadows he could only ever catch in his periphery; they vanished like ghosts when he turned to look.

Then there were the voices. Master Orin. Lady Imaryllis. Ivy.

This sort of power needs to be hidden. Ever.

It's dangerous.

Blood magi ought to be locked up for life.

if you ask me. No second chances for that sort of thing.

I used to hunt blood magi for the Citadel when

I was younger. I could've hunted you if I'd wanted to.

The words slithered down his spine like droplets of ice water. He shuddered, curled in on himself, put his hands to his ears.

Stop.

Don't get me wrong—

if I have any inkling that you're a threat

I will come after you myself.

Please stop. I don't want to hurt anyone.

I don't understand: Maliel was doing so much better.

Then I left him alone with that boy...

I had to protect Wren. It was only to protect Wren...

Wren questions whether it was a wise choice

to have brought Everis here... I do not know.

The Citadel would surely see him as a threat

and put him to death.

Everis curled in tighter. Bit back a sob. He couldn't run, couldn't escape. All he could do was to drag his magic around him like a shell, wrap himself in threads of gold and crimson, bury his face in his arms, and pray for it to stop... or for Drake to end it so the voices would go silent.

WREN

Wren scarcely recognized the interior of the magi tower. He stopped short, sucking in a breath. His vision had mostly cleared, enough that he could take in the surrounding sight. Books and papers and shelves lay strewn about. A battle had taken place here, and no one had bothered to clean up after it. Heartbreaking.

Arabella had left a trail of blood in her wake, winding across the ground floor. Wren followed it, trembling. She'd been his peer once, a member of his family here at the castle, even if not a close one.

But Faulk...

Even though the assassin had been closed off, in just a few weeks, he'd become closer to Faulk than he ever had been to Arabella in all the years they'd lived together within the castle walls.

Abruptly, the blood trail ended behind a bookshelf. Wren frowned, turning full circle. She couldn't have simply vanished.

He heard her casting behind him just in time to leap to one side. A gust of wind sent the bookshelf skidding across the floor and crashing into its neighbor before toppling them both. Wren rolled to all fours, scrambling for a spell to use. Fire in here would send centuries' worth of important texts up in flames. A lifetime of being taught to respect the

330

history within this room left him paralyzed, unsure of what to do.

Wren could see now where Faulk had left deep gashes across Bella's abdomen, like some sort of wild animal rather than any human-made weaponry. Arabella redirected toward him, hands raised, a more involved chant falling from her lips. Wren lurched to his feet to run.

A massive, ghostly hand slammed into the ground where he'd been. Its fingers curled, monstrous claws leaving gouges in the stone. It moved as Bella moved, following Wren across the room, blocking him from effectively reaching Bella to break her concentration—or having a moment to cast anything himself. Instead, he wove in and out of the bookshelves, trying to make Bella lose sight of him. She cursed his name loudly. He ducked low around a corner as the ghost hand swept past him, and he dove beneath a research desk, huddled and hiding, catching his breath.

"You can't win this," Bella sneered. "Come out now, and I'll take you to Master Reed. Maybe he'll spare you if you ask *very* nicely."

Wren gritted his teeth. This was one of the weaker apprentices. If he couldn't beat Bella, how in the world was he supposed to go up against any of the others? How was he supposed to go against *Drake*?

I can't do this without Ever.

No, he couldn't rely on Everis. That he'd all but vanished suggested he was in trouble. Not dead—Wren would've sensed the absence of him—but locked up or injured or both. Wren needed to be stronger than this. He had to be capable of fighting on his own.

He scrubbed his palms against his trousers and closed his eyes, breathing deep. Centering. Concentrating. He blocked out the chaos of Bella's spells, wreaking havoc across the room as she searched for him, and willed his heart rate to slow. Like Master Orin had taught him. Focus. Calm.

When one of her spells knocked the desk across the room, exposing Wren, he was already halfway through his spell. Something more in-depth than he was accustomed to, but he could do it. He knew he could.

"Got you," Arabella jeered.

Wren's fingers formed an O. He opened his eyes, looking at her through the center as he spoke the last word. Shackles of shimmering energy clamped around Arabella's body, pinning her arms to her sides, fastening her ankles together. It forced her spells to drop. The ghost hand dissipated a mere inch in front of Wren's face. She threw her head back and shrieked in fury, thrashing against the magical restraints.

Wren slowly got to his feet, careful not to break his concentration.

As he approached, she shook with rage, eyes burning a brilliant red. He stopped in front of her. "Got you."

Arabella laughed. "You won't kill me, though, will you? You're thinking of all the ways you could keep me alive."

She had him there. Wren should kill her. He had the means to do so, and he was likely going to have to, but he didn't want to. He'd rather lock her up, send her to the Citadel. A lifetime sealed away seemed a far more fitting punishment for murdering Faulk than a painless death.

"Pathetic little apprentice. And *stupid*," Bella continued. "The moment your guard is down, I'm going to rip your throat—"

Through the open doors lunged a shadow so swift that Wren couldn't immediately register its presence. The giant wolf sank its teeth into the junction of Bella's neck and shoulder, puncturing her throat. Her eyes flew wide, mouth opening in a scream. The binding spell dropped, and Wren stood, paralyzed by horror and fear as the great beast shook Arabella like a rag doll. The sound of her neck snapping broke Wren out of his terror, and he shrank back, readying himself for another fight.

But the wolf dropped Arabella and turned to him, blood-stained mouth pulled back into a snarl as it licked its chops. Its body was humanoid, bipedal, with arms and large, clawed hands. Stooped over on all fours, it was nearly eye level with Wren. Were it to stand up properly, it would tower over him.

Wren stared, a tremor working across his body from adrenaline and fear. Yet the beast stared at him calmly, and in its gold eyes, he saw something he recognized.

"Faulk?" he whispered.

It all made sense.

The uncanny ability to navigate in the woods, in the dark, in the tunnels. The wounds he'd inflicted upon Bella outside. There'd been signs every step of the way, and he'd missed them. Faulk had even said, *I'll catch up with you.*

Damn him and his secrets.

At the sound of his name, Faulk stepped closer with his head bowed. Not a threat. Wren swallowed hard, reaching a shaking hand to touch the wolf's head. His fingers slid into the coarse fur. Then, unable to help himself, he wrapped his arms around the wolf's neck and hugged him tightly.

"I thought you were dead."

Faulk snorted. He allowed himself to be hugged for a moment before shaking Wren off, and Wren watched in morbid fascination as the beast convulsed and shifted. His bones cracked, and Faulk whined, low and pained, as his body morphed back down into its human shape. When he sank to the floor on all fours, catching his breath, the open wounds on his body that he'd gotten while defending Wren were no more than fresh pink marks, healed over.

Wren kneeled at his side, a gentle hand upon his shoulder. He knew little about werewolves except that his master had met one once that he'd deemed *not a threat, and so he had let him live,* but the process he'd just witnessed looked excruciating. "Are you alright…?"

"Clothes," Faulk muttered, voice hoarse. "Outside."

Wren's face warmed, but he nodded and ran out of the tower, stealing a look around to ensure no other surprises awaited them. He fetched the discarded clothing and brought it back.

As Faulk dressed, Wren circled up the spiral staircase of the magi tower to one of the uppermost floors, surveying the damage. It would be impossible to locate any of the texts he'd been hoping for, but he had his own small writing desk where he'd kept a few books and notes that were, thankfully, undisturbed. He took a seat and flipped through them, searching the potion recipes, spells, and charms scattered throughout for something that would be of use.

He couldn't transform like Faulk. He couldn't scribe like Lady Imaryllis. His spells weren't as strong as Master Orin's. He couldn't cast without speaking and signing like Everis…

Or could he?

Wren stared down at the few spells he'd plucked from the books and notes. He shoved one of his sleeves up and slid the assassin's dagger from his belt, hesitated, then brought the tip of the blade to his skin.

If they were going to survive this…

Drastic measures were needed.

BRANT

"These fucking halls." Elias delivered a swift kick to the door they'd just passed through. "I swear, if we pass that tapestry one more time…"

"Well, we can't just stand here and do nothing." Brant sighed, shoving a hand through his hair. He wasn't certain how much time had passed since they were separated from Wren and Faulk, but it felt like too long, and that they hadn't encountered a single person was concerning. They were caught in a loop of the same three hallways, and every time they seemed to select the path that broke the trend, they found themselves wrapped up in it once again with another wrong turn.

Brant was about to suggest they stop for a bit to rest when the air around them seemed to shudder and shimmer, a dizzying blur of texture and color that made his head hurt. Then the illusion faded, leaving in its wake an entirely different hall than the one he'd thought they were in. Rather than the north end of the castle near the ballroom, they were somewhere east, a few turns away from the library. "What's happened?"

Elias stood at attention, alert, confused. "Maybe whatever magi was casting the illusions got his arse handed to him?"

"We can hope. Come on." With renewed excitement, Brant pressed onward, now with a sense of direction. They would head to the tower where the royals slept in search of Danica.

At the end of the hall, Elias grabbed his arm and yanked him to a halt, signaling him to keep quiet. In tandem, they peeked around the corner, spotting nearly a dozen guards positioned outside a set of double doors.

"Where do those lead?" Elias whispered.

"The library."

"Anything worth guarding in a library?"

"Um…" Brant blinked. "Books?"

"Doubt they care much about protecting books at a time like this." Elias rolled his eyes. "Willing to wager they're looking after some*one*."

Brant raised his eyebrows. "If that someone is a magi, are we really the two who ought to be stopping to say hello?"

"Maybe not, but do you fancy hanging out here to wait for backup?"

He bit back another sigh, shoulders slumping. "Yeah, alright. Got a plan?"

Elias pulled a set of knives from his belt, grinned, and swung around the corner. "Ahoy, gents!" he crowed, strolling down the hall toward the guards. "Got a second? I can't seem to find where I left my bloody horse." The moment the soldiers drew their swords, Elias flicked the knives with expert grace and aim, piercing two of the men's throats.

Brant stared, open-mouthed, until one guard took a swing at the assassin. Swearing under his breath, Brant drew his own sword and raced after him, catching the guard's blade and knocking it away.

"Brant?" one of the guards called.

"Sylvia." He pointed his sword at the lot of them where they'd paused. They didn't all recognize each other, but he saw a few faces he knew, and knew well. "What are you doing? You've lost your damned minds, working alongside blood magi!"

Sylvia hesitated. Not only her, but many of the others. They were frightened, cowed by Drake Reed and Danica into following orders. "We can't defy the queen," Sylvia said.

"Danica is no longer queen," Brant hissed. "Stand down. Help us reclaim the castle for Cassia. She's the one you should be loyal to!"

A few glances were exchanged, but no one moved. Was he going mad? Had *he* chosen the wrong side? How were they so willing to skew their view of duty?

"We've seen what happens to those who try to lie down their arms," Sylvia whispered. "We're just following orders. I'm sorry, Brant."

Brant raised his sword, jaw clenched. "So am I."

They met with a clash of blades. Elias slithered amongst the group with the grace of someone used to close combat, his reflexes fine-tuned.

Brant tried not to think. Tried not to pay attention to whom he cut down, to the familiarity of their faces, the pain in their eyes. If he acknowledged that, if he allowed the hurt to seep in, he would surely fall to pieces.

At least Artesia wasn't there. She was safe in Patish with Cassia, and she'd be waiting for him when this was over. If he faltered here, if he died, she would no doubt blame herself for not having come along. Brant couldn't allow that.

Thinking of his best friend renewed his resolve. He allowed his mind to blank, to think only of the sword in his hand, to see the people before him as nothing more than enemies to contend with. And at the end of it all, he stood amongst the bodies, breathless and trembling, nursing a gash in his side and another on his thigh. He looked at Elias, who wiped his daggers clean on a fallen soldier's cloak and tucked them back into his belt before straightening up. His hair was mussed, but otherwise, he appeared unharmed.

The assassin flashed him a grin. "Nicely done."

Brant surveyed the fallen with a knot in his stomach. He swallowed hard and nodded. *I did what I had to do.* He couldn't force his voice to work, so he straightened as much as his wounds would allow and reached for the door instead.

He pulled the library doors open. A blinding light flashed before his eyes. Elias grabbed the back of his shirt and yanked him aside just as a stream of crackling lightning zipped past where he'd been standing. Its proximity made the hair on his body stand on end.

"What the fuck—"

"Magi," Elias hissed.

They braced themselves. This wasn't a fight they were likely to win.

"We just want to talk," Brant called.

No answer.

"You know perfectly well we aren't capable of beating you, magi. So, grant us a few minutes of your time."

Still, silence. No more spells, nothing. Brant and Elias looked at each other, frowning.

"You may enter," came a voice.

Slowly, the pair stepped through the doorway, on guard, prepared for some kind of trick. Instead, they saw Danica with a knife in hand, standing over magi Beatty's throat-slit corpse. She stared at them, something unreadable in her gaze, then dropped the knife and turned to move away.

Baffled, Brant lowered his sword. He closed and locked the doors behind them and inched into the room. Danica had taken a seat at a table and stared off at nothing.

"Your Grace?" The respect came automatically and without thought, after too many years of viewing this woman as his queen. She said nothing, hands against her belly. "You killed the blood magi. Why? I thought you were working with them."

"I was," she murmured. "But that was before."

"Before?"

"Before I realized what a fool I was."

Brant and Elias exchanged looks once more. Brant pulled up a chair and sat. "I don't follow."

"It's not an excited story."

"Yeah, well, we've got nothing but time right now, so start talking," Elias said.

Danica took a slow breath. "...I fell in love with Drake years ago. He was handsome, charming, and what's more... he paid attention to me. Loved me. I had not shared myself with Faramond in years and he never so much as asked. He had his daughter. That was all he cared about. His wife didn't matter.

"Cassia isn't truly my child. When I admitted as much to Drake, he filled my head with worries. What would happen after Faramond was gone? Would the people who knew the truth use it to discount my place here? I lost sleep over it."

"So, you started to poison the king?"

"Drake's doing, and I didn't realize it was him for a long while. When he told me, I was horrified... but the fact of the matter was, my life *had* been better without my husband in the picture. He could have stayed sick, for all I cared. I had my freedom. I had Drake..."

Brant's gaze dropped briefly, then lifted to her face again. "And then you got pregnant."

Danica placed her fingers against her stomach. The swell was barely noticeable, but it was there. She gave a grim smile. "I refused to share Faramond's bed for years and he never pushed. And then everything spiraled out of control. Drake has gone mad. I tried to reason with him, but after he killed Orin, something in him... seemed to snap. Whatever Cassia wishes to do with me, I deserve. I only ask mercy for the child I carry." Finally, she looked at Brant. "Please, stop him."

Despite it all, Brant's heart hurt a little for her. The unspoken pain in her eyes told of a story deeper than Brant could comprehend with her condensed explanation.

"Others more qualified are working on that, Your Grace," he said softly. "We'll stay here with you. In the meantime, why don't you start at the beginning?"

WREN

The castle was far too sturdy a structure to be brought down by the outside fighting, and yet the sounds of the battle raging out there echoed throughout the building and, likely, the entire city. That they were still going meant that they hadn't yet lost—but they hadn't won, either. Wren asked Faulk only once if he'd go back to join them because they were going to need his strength. Faulk leveled a long look at him, and Wren got the point.

The illusions in the hallways had vanished. Finally, Wren could navigate them to where they needed to go. Danica's chambers were empty, although a few dead guards just outside them suggested that Ever had been here.

Then where is he now?

Wren turned a full circle, struggling not to cry out in frustration. He flexed his left hand and used the sting of pain radiating up his arm to keep himself from spiraling into desperation. He'd followed the pull of Everis's magic—faint as it was—here, and here led them nowhere.

"Can you pick up on Reed's magic the way you did Everis's?" Faulk asked, wandering the room. Now that Wren knew his secret, it was easier to recognize what he was doing. Analyzing, listening, smelling, hunting for clues.

"I keep trying, but there's so much going on, so much magic, and Quinton's still lingers all over the castle from his illusions..." Wren sighed, shoving his hands through his hair. "If he *wanted* me to find him, I could, but so far, nothing."

"Think he's fled?"

"Running away isn't really Drake Reed's style, but then again, I never thought him capable of any of this." Wren came upon the pile of journals in the corner and frowned, stooping to pick one up.

"These were..."

He opened it. The sight of the familiar writing was a punch to the gut.

"...Master Orin's."

Faulk drifted to his side. "All of them?"

"Oh, yes." Wren smiled faintly. "He wrote or drew in them almost every night, either in his study or by the fire in his room, always with a cup of tea and—Nova!"

"What?"

Wren's smile grew wide, filled with sincere happiness. He pointed to the balcony doors, rushing over to pull them open. The raven hopped inside, fluttered her wings, and perched on Wren's outstretched hand with a throaty caw. "Faulk, this is Nova. She belonged to Master Orin."

Faulk stared at the bird. Wren half-expected the usual questions about her peculiar appearance. She didn't look like an ordinary raven, after all, and even her eyes were... different. Aside from being red, when one stared into them, there was a level of understanding there that even the most intelligent of bird species lacked.

Faulk bypassed such questions and asked instead, "Can she help us find Everis or Reed?"

"Maybe." Wren looked at the corvid. Yes, she was smart, but *how* smart? "Nova, we're looking for Everis and Drake. Do you know how to find them?"

She fluffed her feathers and regarded him with a quizzical tip of her head. For a moment, Wren felt utterly ridiculous for having asked such a thing when she was likely waiting to see what treats he had in his pockets for her, but then she spread her wings and took off, gliding back out the door and into the halls. Faulk and Wren hurried after.

They followed Nova out of the tower and back into the winding castle hallways. She stopped long enough to ensure they were following, and soon, they entered a hall where a large group of guards were positioned near the door leading to the belly of the castle. The only two important things beyond that point were the throne room and the banquet hall. Wren and Faulk skidded to a stop and stared while at least two dozen startled guards stared back at them. They had a matter of seconds to formulate a plan.

"Think he's beyond that door?" Faulk murmured.

"I'd bet on it."

"Then get in there and go after him. I'll deal with this." He took a step forward. The soldiers were recovering from their surprise, drawing their swords.

Wren's heart leaped into his throat. "You can't. You're still recov—"

Faulk was already shifting, the bones in his shoulders and spine cracking and popping as his body broke free of its mold, the seams of his tunic beginning to pull and tear. His voice came out deep and reverberating, more a growl and barely discernible.

"*Go.*"

He advanced on the guards with his teeth bared. His transformation had their full attention.

Jaw clenched, Wren waited for the right moment. When Faulk launched into the group of armed men and women, still half-morphed but full of fangs and claws and fury, every man and woman focused on him. Wren shot forward. He drew his sword, parrying the blade of a single soldier in his path and knocking her to the ground.

By some miracle, the doors were unlocked. Wren dragged them open enough to slip through, heaved them shut, and after a second of intense debate, he slid his sword into the door handles to keep the guards from following. It wouldn't stop them if they were determined, but at the very least, it bought him some time.

As he jogged down the hall, the sounds of the fight steadily growing dimmer, it dawned on Wren how very alone he was now. Nova hadn't abandoned her perch on his shoulder, but when it came to fighting, he was worried about her safety. He stopped as he neared the throne room doors, coaxing her up onto his hand and then onto a wall sconce.

"Thank you, sweet girl. But I need to go on alone now. I don't want you to get hurt." He scratched the top of her head gently. "You're all we have left of Master Orin, so I want you to stay safe. Do you understand?"

She pecked at his sleeve when he withdrew, but remained put as he backed off.

This might be the last time I see you.

He turned away and marched for the throne room doors looming at the end of the massive, red, mist-filled hall. It made his vision blur; briefly, he could've sworn he was fifteen years old and in Balerno again. He could feel the faintest flicker of familiar magic, like a soft heartbeat next to his own.

Ever.

He reached the doors, breathless, arm throbbing, and shoved them open.

Hold on, I'm coming.

EVERIS

Worthless.

You need to get up.

You can end this.

Stop.

He's responsible for the destruction of Balerno.

We couldn't trust you enough.

Too dangerous.

Please stop.

The voices had melded into one malformed, hideous entity, ringing within the blackness, striking from every direction.

He was so cold.

They wanted to keep you from reaching

your true potential, Everis.

Drake. The only voice that stood out from the others.

Yes, Drake had him here in the darkness. Everis could see, feel, hear nothing beyond it, and that was fine with him.

He wanted to curl up and hide.

He wanted to be left alone.

Perhaps he deserved this, though. Perhaps this—the assault of voices, the cold, the pain—was his punishment. It was no wonder Master Orin hadn't told him the truth. He hadn't wanted Everis to think himself a monster, even though he was. He'd been responsible for so many deaths since leaving the capital. He'd killed an innocent man, one of their own soldiers. He'd been brutal and merciless in battle, all at the mercy of his own magic.

And even still, he wanted more. The magic sang and swelled around him, called forth by the darkness within the castle, the blood spilled nearby. Every time someone died, Everis felt it like a needle beneath his ribs, prodding, coaxing, tempting.

You aren't meant to fight it. Everis.

You can learn to control it. I can teach you.

Was that true? Drake seemed to have control over his magic. Could Everis learn to do the same? Could he use this power to protect the people he loved? He'd already failed Master Orin. He couldn't fail those who were left. He couldn't fail Wren.

Wren. Wren, Wren, Wren.

Everis couldn't hear his voice, no matter how hard he strained. Couldn't sense him, either. Couldn't sense anything or anyone beyond Drake Reed, whose presence swaddled him like an infant as though he could protect Everis from the rest of the world.

Could he?

Was he fighting against all the wrong things?

He didn't want to fail again.

WREN

Red mist coated the floor of the throne room so thickly that Wren could scarcely see his own boots. But he could see Drake Reed perfectly, lounging upon the throne like some big, lazy cat, flashing him a wide smile.

"I was wondering if you'd make it."

Wren clenched his hand. Magic thrummed beneath his skin, itching, aching. "Where's Everis?"

"Where's Cassia? We could trade."

"Cassia's far from here and safe, but don't pretend you didn't know that already."

Drake shrugged. He rose smoothly from the chair, pushing his long braid back over his shoulder. "I suspected, but, goodness, I'm not *omnipotent*, Wren. How kind of you to think I am. Did you kill my apprentices?"

"You don't even know that much?" Wren scoffed.

"More that it doesn't ultimately matter. They were here to serve a purpose, and they've done so. I'm aiming my sights higher for a better apprentice." He smiled again, and when he descended the dais and stepped around the body huddled in the mist at the base, Wren recognized who it was.

His heart about stopped. On his knees, hands behind his back, and blindfolded, Everis lay motionless but… alive, yes. That was the most important part.

Wren didn't think twice. He made a dash for Everis, desperate to make sure he was alright. Drake began to cast beneath his breath. Only a few feet away from Ever, Wren blinked and found himself right back at the door where he'd started. He staggered and skidded to a stop.

"He can't hear you, I'm afraid." Drake advanced across the room at a leisurely stroll, his sugary tone echoing off the walls. "I've put him somewhere for a bit to… think some things over."

Wren's jaw clenched, fury radiating down his body. "You have no right."

"I have every right." Drake laughed. "Answer me something, Wren. What makes a king a king?"

"I… What?"

"What makes a king more worthy to rule over a kingdom than any other person?" Drake tipped his head. "Because he was *born* into it? Regardless of skill or strength or intelligence or compassion, monarchs are only in charge because of the blood they carry. They think themselves worthy, as though it's their divine *right* to rule over those they see as lesser."

Wren hesitated. Yes, of course he'd wondered such things before, but it was simply the way of the world. "King Faramond was a good man. He cared about his people. You'd have not found a more compassionate king."

"Faramond had empathy; that's true." Drake stepped closer until they stood nearly toe to toe. His eyes shone with the same brilliant crimson Wren had seen in Everis's eyes, but his was constant, sinister, darker somehow. "…But he wasn't strong. If he had been, he'd never have taken up with a woman who wasn't his wife. He wouldn't have humiliated Danica in such a way. What did Danica get out of their marriage? He overrode her every decision because she wasn't a Starling, then vowed to put a child on the throne that wasn't *theirs*. Only his. Faramond may've been well loved by the people, but do not claim he was a good husband by any stretch of the imagination."

"And he deserved to die for that?" Wren asked. "Him aside, what about everyone else? Every innocent townsperson, Cassia, Master Orin… You can stand there and claim this was all right and proper because Faramond hurt people with his choices, but at the end of the day, *you* are the one who's stolen innocent lives because of it."

Drake smiled his slow, wolfish smile, all teeth. "Sweet, naïve boy. That's because I have what Faramond lacked. I have the strength. That alone makes me the only one qualified to rule."

There was no way he could cast before Drake could stop him, not at such close range. But the proximity was the opportunity Wren had been hoping for.

He lifted a hand, exposing the palm he'd meticulously carved his spell into, and finally relinquished his hold on the magic that had been crawling through his body like a feral animal waiting to get out.

The flash spell ignited, a extraordinary white light, mere inches from Drake's good eye. Drake reared back with a gasp, one arm across his face, the other reaching for the sword at his belt. Swinging blindly was all he could do. That trick was unlikely to work twice.

Pain radiated hotly up Wren's hand and arm and made the room spin. He dashed for Ever, dropping to his knees before him and yanking the blindfold from his head. Everis's eyes burned crimson, but he stared off at nothing, unresponsive even as Wren took his face in his hands. He didn't have much time.

"Ever, Ever, can you hear me? I need you to snap out of it. *Ever!*"

"Insolent little welp," Drake roared. He squinted in Wren's direction, vision likely still blurry but returning. He raised his hand and chanted.

Wren lurched to his feet and leaped back, not wanting Everis to get caught in the crossfire of their battle. His arm still throbbed, but he had more than one trick up his sleeve—literally. He looked at his arm and focused on the other spell he'd carved into his flesh; one he'd memorized from years of studying Lady Imaryllis's scribe work. He envisioned a sword in his hand, not forged from steel, but from magic and energy and light, an extension of himself and his power. The carvings *burned*, a pain so brilliant and raw that Wren's entire body went rigid with it. But it worked. The blade grew itself, a glow that seeped from the wounds themselves and snaked down to his wrist and hand, extending outward to form a blade. Wren reeled from the hurt, but the entire process had taken a mere second, and Drake hadn't had time to finish casting.

Wren charged for him and swung. His magical sword met Drake's silver blade with a clash of magical sparks.

"*Ever!*" he cried again. "Ever, you need to wake up!"

Drake parried the blow and again tried to cast, but Wren didn't give him the chance. He pressed the attack. Drake still had his control over Everis to maintain. He couldn't do that, sword-fight, and try to cast something new all at once. One of the three would have to falter, and Wren was counting on that. Every time their blades met, pain sang anew up Wren's arm, jostling him, making him see white. It crept into his shoulder and threatened to seep into his chest.

How long could he do this?

For as long as you must, he could hear Orin say.

Wren pressed forward, letting out the agony with an anguished scream, putting every ounce of his magic—his very energy, his life—into his swings to keep going. Just a little longer.

For as long as he must.

EVERIS

The voices went quiet.

For the first time in an eternity, Everis could hear his own thoughts. His chest could unclench. Finally, the silence he'd been longing for. Even Drake's voice had vanished, leaving him in a dull haze where the only sound he could hear was his own heartbeat.

Yes. This was where he belonged. In this nothingness where he couldn't hurt anyone. Where he wasn't considering how Drake Reed could help him while simultaneously replaying in his head over and over and over how Drake had murdered Master Orin.

The thought made his chest hurt all over again, and he bit back a sob, wanting to curl in on himself, wanting to hide, to vanish into nothing.

Nothing.

Nothing.

Nothing.

"Don't go somewhere I can't follow!"

He took in the first breath he could recall breathing in some time. Wren's voice was distant but clear, so beautifully clear. Ever tried to look around, tried to see him through the tangled mess of threads that bound him.

"EVER!"

Wren.

He yanked at the threads, gold and red alike. Clawed at them, at himself, to get free. Tried to open his mouth to yell back, but the sound wouldn't come. His body ached. His arms hurt. He ripped at the threads until his hands bled, then crawled, dragged himself through the razor-sharp formations of magic, not knowing where he was going other than *away.*

Wren was calling for him.

Wren needed him.

Wren didn't care about his powers, about what he'd done, only that they were safe and together. No matter what, Everis had to protect him.

Without Wren—

No, there was no without Wren. There was only with Wren… and Nothingness.

He'd wanted that moments ago, hadn't he? To fade into oblivion. Now, all he could think of was reaching Wren. He would burn down the entire castle to get to him.

Be still, Drake's voice hissed.

The confines of the spell pressed back against him. Everis growled, shoved back, extending his own magic. Drake was strong, but Ever could be stronger. He looked to the side and spotted a red thread.

Grabbed it.

Pulled.

Everis's eyes snapped open, and he threw back his head with a choked gasp. His shoulders and back throbbed because, in the real world, beyond the dark place that Drake had put him, his hands were shackled behind his back and the throne room was hazy and so very, very bright. They were fighting, Drake and Wren. Everis couldn't make heads or tails of it at first, but he could feel the flow of magic from them both. The fury, the rage, the defiance.

Ever strained against the shackles. Envisioned them, frozen and brittle. The iron grew cold until it burned his wrists as he strained against them. Finally, they gave way and shattered, frozen pieces disappearing into the red fog as Ever slowly pushed to his feet.

Knowing his spell had been broken, Drake looked his way. His expression twisted into something wild and crazed. How could he have thought, even for a moment, that this man could train him? That he had control over his magic?

Drake had no control over anything.

The world felt crooked. Off-kilter. Drake's voice, hollow and far away. The only thing he could focus on was the magic pulsing through his body, sharpening his senses, almost overwhelmingly so.

And Wren, Wren, *Wren.*

Wren needed him.

For that, he would claw his way out of the darkness.

WREN

Drake growled.

Wren stopped mid-swing, looking back, and his eyes grew wide. Ever had risen to his feet, shoulders squared, glowing gaze zeroed in on them.

Drake took the opportunity presented within the blink of an eye. He grabbed Wren from behind, twisted his carved arm sharply behind his back. The jostling made Wren's vision distort, and he gasped. The resulting sting of the blade now against his throat forced him to swallow the hurt and be still.

"How are you feeling, Ever?" Drake called. "Do you see what your friend is doing? Carving spells into himself. No different from self-inflicted blood magic, if you ask me. Perhaps Wren can become a magi like us, after all."

Wren clenched his teeth. He flexed his fingers. From this angle, unable to see Drake, he couldn't cast any spells at him. Even with the power no doubt coursing through him from all the bloodshed that had happened there today, Everis couldn't possibly be fast enough. He would be stronger, but so was Drake.

Ever tipped his head as though listening. Rather than answer, he lifted a hand.

Snapped his fingers.

Out of nowhere, Nova tore from the red haze, beak and claws rending the side of Drake's face as though she'd returned for his other eye. Drake released Wren with a horrible scream. "*Fucking nuisance!*" He caught her by a wing and flung her roughly aside.

Wren staggered. Ever darted forward and caught him, drew him close, took stock of the carvings upon his arm and hand. "What did you do...?"

"What needed to be done," Wren murmured. He righted himself, unsteady on his feet. The spells written into his skin had served him well, but it sapped his energy to use them. The fatigue made his limbs leaden and his vision swim and twirl. "I'm not sure how much longer I can continue."

"Then leave this to me." Everis tightened his arm around him, protective, then released Wren and turned to face Drake.

He didn't hurry. Instead, Everis moved for Drake, slow and calculating, a predator stalking its prey. Drake sneered, raised his hands, and spoke in that ugly language that made Wren shudder.

The windows of the throne room vibrated, then shattered. Rather than fall, the shards angled themselves at Ever and fired off like arrows in a vicious onslaught. Wren's voice caught in his throat. Ever made no move to dodge or shield himself. When the glass came at him from all angles, he gave a wave of his hand, and the shards all halted. Turned. Took aim at Drake.

Drake's eyes grew wide. His quick reflexes brought up a barrier spell, though not before the first few shards had pierced his leg and arm and torso. The rest collided with the shield and slid to the floor in a horrendous cacophony.

"How—" Drake started to ask.

He didn't know, Wren realized. *He didn't know Ever could cast without speaking.*

Ever moved faster than Wren could track him. He closed the distance between Drake and himself, brought a hand up, fingers splayed. Drake reared back, crossing his arms protectively in front of himself, but the burst that came from Everis's outstretched hand sent him off his feet and slamming into a towering pillar.

Drake gasped, winded, and dropped to one knee. He slammed his hands to the floor and ground out a spell; the marbled tile cracked and caved and shattered, zipping a line straight for Everis. Ever leaped to one side, narrowly avoiding the path of destruction. But the rubble trembled and raised into the air, hovered a moment, and launched at Everis so fast he couldn't deflect it. Rather than strike him, it surrounded him, forming a prison of stone and marble that engulfed him completely.

For a few heart-pounding seconds, the room went silent. Then the stone prison exploded, and even Wren had to duck and cover as the debris rained down. When he dared to look again, Everis and Drake had lunged for one another.

Their spells came fast, yet even with Everis casting wordlessly, Drake kept up with his incantations and signs. The throne room pillars split from base to top. The ceiling cracked, raining down large chunks of stone. Everything trembled beneath Wren's feet, a silent threat that even this room couldn't bear witness to this battle indefinitely.

A falling piece of ceiling half Wren's size landed nearby, and in the swirling mist that briefly cleared, Wren spotted Nova's prone form. He scooped up her still body, cradling her gently to his chest before retreating to the dais. She was so still, one of her wings twisted at a wrong angle. Carefully, he laid her beneath the queen's throne, where he hoped she'd be safe from any further falling debris.

His arm pulsed.

He flexed his fingers. A little more. He could give a little more. Could bear the pain a bit longer.

Wren turned to the fight and let the magic flow over him to reform the blade from his arm, magic spilling from the raw wounds once more.

He ran into the fray, coming at Drake from the side. The older magi narrowly spotted him in his periphery, catching Wren's blade with his own, a barrier on his other side blocking Everis's attack. Drake panted, eyes wide and filled with a fervor and fury Wren had never seen in a human being.

This time, he and Everis attacked in unison, coming at Drake from all sides, wearing him down with one relentless assault after another. Fire coursed through Wren's body, making it hard to think, and he pressed onward still.

Master Orin.

He let the warmth of memories push him.

Everis and Orin. Cold winter nights around a fire.

Stories. Studying.

Treats Orin snuck from the kitchens, which he brought to them with a smile and a wink.

Nova. Perched on the back of Orin's chair, preening herself. Occasionally trying to preen his long hair with limited success.

His life. His family.

Drake had taken that from him.

There it was—an opening. A misstep, a moment too slow, wherein Drake raised his sword high over his head to bring it down on Ever. Wren wouldn't allow him to take any more.

EVERIS

The thrum of magic fueled every movement he made. Every step, every spell. He didn't fight it. But he didn't allow it to overwhelm him, either.

Ever let it fill him, let it meld with him, and then he used it. Natural. Easy. Symbiotic.

Drake cloaked himself in it as though it would shield him, let it control him, not understanding his mistake. This magic didn't care about them. It wasn't there to protect them, only to bring ruin and death.

It *consumed*.

Drake raised his sword.

Foolish.

Wren came in behind him. The magical blade passed through Drake's body with little resistance, piercing straight through to the other side. Drake seized, arched, pupils blown wide. There was no way Wren hadn't struck something vital. A lung, an artery. Ever wanted nothing more than for Wren to twist the blade, drag it down, make sure it hurt as much as possible.

That was the magic talking. *Hungry.*

"The Citadel will want him," he said instead, voice calm and collected and in control.

He met Wren's eyes. They could bind Drake, take his other eye, render him useless as a magi, and turn him over to the Citadel. Wren's expression wavered. Sweet, gentle Wren, who never wanted Ever to resort to violence unless he had to…

Wren nodded once.

Drake breathed slowly, carefully. His gaze dropped to Everis. There was clarity there again, even if only a little. "How can you cast without…" he tried to say. Coughed. Blood trickled from the corner of his mouth.

Everis pressed a palm flat to Drake's chest, above his racing heart. "I tried to tell you," he said. "You and I are not the same."

The force that slid through his hand and into Drake's body was subtle, at least from the outside. Inwardly, Everis envisioned it.

Crush.

Heart, lungs, ribs.

Everything.

Ruin it.

Wren withdrew his blade. Drake's body collapsed in a heap, his one good eye staring off into the darkness, no longer glowing red.

WREN

He stared at Drake's body until the sight blurred and his legs gave out. Everis caught him, cradled him against his chest, murmured something too distant for Wren to make out at first. The swoon didn't last long, but even when his senses returned, his entire body trembled with pain and exhaustion.

"It's done," Everis said softly.

Wren swallowed hard. "It is done. But Nova…"

Everis helped him back to the dais, where they retrieved Nova and sank onto the steps. Wren stroked her head. She opened her beak, but no sound came out. She was alive, but barely. He didn't need any special magic to know she was in pain.

"We should…" Wren started, stopped, steadied his voice—and his resolve. "We shouldn't let her suffer."

Ever nodded. He reached for Nova, and Wren let him take her. He wasn't certain he could kill her, even if it meant putting her out of her misery, even if it was kind. Was he truly so selfish? The one last living link to Orin, and he'd failed to protect her, too.

Everis cradled the white raven in his lap, resting a gentle hand atop her, and closed his eyes.

The flow of magic was subtle at first, and yet somehow familiar. An inkling of a night that seemed forever ago when Wren had been mortally wounded… A soft glow emanated from Ever's hands, and the magic washed outward, propelled away the red mist, and encased Nova's body—then Ever's, and then Wren's.

The pain in Wren's arm ebbed. Feeling returned to his fingers. He watched as the spells he'd carved into his skin healed one by one, leaving only fresh pink scars behind.

Still, Ever's magic crept outwards, wider and wider, stronger and stronger, thrusting away the crimson mist and banishing it to the far reaches of the room where it dissipated completely. Wren watched Ever's face, noted the concentration, the strength he was putting behind this one last spell. Everything he had was going into this.

Wren reached out, placing his hands over Ever's, lending whatever strength he had left.

If they could save anyone, anywhere, he wanted to help.

FAULK

Blood.

Everything smelled of blood.

He hadn't moved from the floor, where he lay in a fetal position, human again. His wounds were struggling to heal. The guards hadn't fought with silver, but even a werewolf could only take so much.

Maybe this is it.

He'd done what he set out to do, and he could only hope it meant something. That his death wasn't in vain. If Wren and Everis could take down Drake, if the kingdom could be saved... that was what mattered.

I protected your apprentices as best as I could, Orin. I hope we're even now.

He closed his eyes.

So much blood.

He drifted off. Something washed over his naked form like a soft, warm blanket. It cooled his burning wounds, soothed his bruised and battered limbs. Cradled him with promises of gentle dreams and no more pain. Was this what death felt like? Comforting. Welcoming.

Asher, I'm sorry.

IMARYLLIS

Stryder was dying.

She'd fought back-to-back with Imaryllis, protecting her while the magi fired off spells. Imaryllis hadn't seen exactly what happened, but at some point, they had been surrounded and when she looked back, Stryder had hit the ground on her knees.

Imaryllis had patched her up as best she could. Healed the outermost wounds to the best of her ability, but healing wasn't her specialty. All she could do was make her comfortable. She retrieved what little she could from the magi tower—herbs and poultices and tonics for the pain—but there wasn't enough to go around. Not for all the wounded.

She moved through the ranks and the red haze that had settled over the yard in a dazed silence, stopping where needed. But there was nothing left to give. They'd won this battle, but at the cost of so many lives—on both sides. Of course, she'd treated their fallen enemies. They'd been her soldiers once, too. She made them comfortable. Offered them kind words and held their hands as they died. She forgave them in their last moments because after so much loss, so much grief, she couldn't bring herself to be the cause of anyone dying with regret. For now, at least, she would swallow her anger and resentment to bring peace.

It was what Cassia would want.

It was what Orin would've done.

The fighting inside had finished. She'd been prepared to head into the castle, to find the boys, find Drake, but somehow—the moment the battle was over, she sensed it like a loosening in her chest. All she could do was tend to the people who needed her right now and pray that those inside made it out alive.

"Look," someone nearby gasped. A few other sounds of surprise arose, and Imaryllis turned.

Steadily, the red mist was being pushed out of the court as though by an unseen breeze coming from the castle. When it reached her, a soft warmth washed across her skin and she could feel the magic, the familiarity of it soothing her aches and pains.

Ever. Wren.

Please, sweet Mother of us all, let them be okay. If no one else, let them be okay.

Imaryllis looked down. A gash just above her elbow had healed. So had the one on her leg. All her injuries had mended, and looking across the yard, other injured were stirring, some of them sitting up, looking themselves over in a mixture of confusion and awe.

Whatever Wren and Ever had done, it was helping. She laughed, turning to rush through the crowd to the place where she'd left Stryder under Jade's care.

"Look, look what they've done!" she cried, dropping to the woman's side. Stryder was still asleep, hadn't stirred.

No, that's not...

Imaryllis touched her shoulder, looking at the mortal wound in her abdomen. It hadn't healed. She looked at Jade, and he shook his head, mouth downturned. Her chest cinched tight once more, eyes brimming with tears. Jade looked away as though granting her privacy, but he murmured in a voice that suggested years of similar grief and loss.

"We can never save everyone."

FAULK

He woke to something jabbing his cheek. When he opened his eyes, Orin's white bird was peering at him, her beady red eyes blinking curiously. Wren came into view a moment later, kneeling before him amongst the blood and bodies. The look of relief that washed over his face when he saw Faulk awake was almost touching.

"You're alright," the magi said.

"I'm not dead," Faulk hoarsely agreed. As the two magi draped him in a cloak and helped him to his feet, he found he was tired, shaky, but his injuries had healed. He remembered the scent he'd caught just before slipping into unconsciousness, and he got that same scent off Everis as the pair helped him out of the castle. Curious.

"So, a werewolf," Ever said, somewhere between amused and annoyed. "And you decided not to tell us."

"You didn't ask."

They left the castle and joined the others set up in the main yard just inside the gates. They handed Faulk off to Jade, who laughed at his state of undress and led him away to get cleaned up.

Only once they were alone did Faulk dare to ask, "How many did we lose?"

Jade offered him a flask. He'd hoped for something stronger than water and was disappointed when he took a drink.

"About half. Stryder among them."

Faulk flinched. Stryder… He'd worked with her for years, found her sharp and pleasant and optimistic—something he needed sometimes, even if he didn't want to admit it. How many people had he lost during his years as a member of the Dusk Court? They all knew what they signed up for, but that didn't make the pain any less. It still hurt.

He leaned back, watching across the yard as Lady Imaryllis reunited with Everis and Wren, gathering them up for a tearful hug. "We'll compile a list of names to bring back with us."

When Jade had no quip or smart-assed remark to offer, Faulk looked at him. It was strange, seeing him so solemn and downtrodden. Asher wouldn't have liked it, and so he fumbled for something comforting to say. "… I'm glad you aren't dead."

Jade gave him a quizzical stare, raised an eyebrow, and laughed. "I would've hated to have to tell my brother something had happened to his big, dumb dog."

"Gee, thanks."

"We've lost a lot of good people today, but we're still here. Somehow. We'll have to deliver a lot of bad news back home." Jade gave him a smile that mirrored his brother's nicely and made Faulk homesick. "But I suppose, dear pup, I'm glad you aren't dead, too."

WREN

The entire city felt purified. Everywhere in the castle, they were met with broad smiles and congratulations and *thank-you*'s. So many thank-you's.

And yet Wren couldn't help the heaviness and dread weighing on his heart.

Everis had scarcely left their rooms. He'd exhausted himself, yes, but it was more than that. Wren could see the haunted glimmer in his eyes when Everis thought he wasn't looking. The magic he'd used, regardless of how he'd used it, had taken a toll on him. A heavy one.

Wren gazed down at his lover asleep beside him. He brushed a mismatched strand of Everis's hair back from his face. No longer black like the rest of his hair but shot through with silver. Wren had noticed it the morning after their battle, but Everis had only frowned in the mirror, unsettled.

It was well past lunch, but he'd been reluctant to wake Ever to eat. If sleep was what he needed, then Wren wanted that for him. The only reason Wren had even come up here was to let Everis know they had company.

Everis sighed, stirred, frowned, and finally lifted his lashes the slightest bit. "Hm?"

Wren smiled. "Good morning."

"Not morning…"

"Not in the slightest." He shifted to accommodate Everis as the taller man curled around him, shoving his face into Wren's neck with a grumble. "Captain Annaliese and the others have arrived. I thought we might go down to greet them together."

Ever made a low noise.

"Ivy's with them."

Another noise, though this one was slightly more interested. "What? Why?"

"I haven't spoken with her, so maybe you should ask her yourself."

With a soft groan, Everis untangled from Wren and dragged himself out of bed to wash and dress. Wren watched with quiet amusement and a little relief. It was the first time Everis had gotten up and done much of anything in days. To see him brushing his unkempt hair, pulling on fresh clothes, and tidying himself made some of that dread lift from his chest.

Together, they ventured down from their room—Wren's room, really, that they'd been sharing—and into the bustling belly of the castle. There was still cleanup to be done there and across the city, but the townspeople had certainly stepped up and handled a fair bit of it. Cassia would no doubt ensure all of them were well compensated when she arrived. She had remained with Artesia, Rue, and her uncle while Annaliese and the army sailed back. Now that the fighting was over, they had sent a raven to Patish.

In the meantime, there was debris and rubble and bodies to tend to. Burials and cremations to be arranged. The dungeons were full to bursting with prisoners. Pava included. Wren had made sure of that. Many of them would no doubt receive pardons from Queen Cassia, but some would not. Those who'd led the charge, those who'd gone out of their way to bend to Drake's will despite chances to do the right thing… Many of the soldiers had been reluctantly following orders out of fear. Many had not.

Wren spotted several familiar faces as they moved through the castle. Everis kept close to his side, seeming uncomfortable with the presence of so many. Soldiers, infantrymen from Patish, servants, hired help scuttling about doing repairs and cleanup…

Someone told them that Magi Ivy had been spotted near the magi tower, so that was where Wren headed. As they crossed the training yard where Wren had fought Bella only a few days prior, Everis faltered and tensed beside him. He glanced sideways, following the other magi's gaze, and spotted a group of soldiers near a pile of training dummies. Among them were Brant and Sanda.

Rather than Brant being the one causing Everis's mood to sour, however, it was Sanda, whose gaze was locked on them. No... On Ever.

Ever averted his eyes, shifting closer to Wren's side, even as Wren whispered, "Look at her, Ever. She deserves that much."

Everis grimaced, stopped, and turned toward the soldiers. He met Sanda's gaze, as though he might somehow convey his pain and regret and an apology to her. As though it would really mean anything. It wouldn't, Wren knew, but Everis still owed it to her.

Everis held her gaze and then bowed deeply, humbling himself before her. Sanda's expression didn't fully change, but she turned her head away. It wasn't forgiveness, not exactly, but it was as much acknowledgment as they were likely to get.

Before they could resume walking, Brant spotted them and lifted a hand in a wave with a wide grin. And Everis, confused, uncertain, and reluctant, slowly lifted a hand and gave a curt nod in Brant's direction.

Wren smiled.

Progress, no matter how small, was still progress.

They continued to the magi tower. With so few magi left in the city, it had yet to receive much attention. Wren found Ivy at Master Orin's desk, trying to make sense of piles of papers, determining which ones had been ripped from book bindings and which were free floating and belonged with others. She had her work cut out for her.

"We didn't expect to see you here," Everis greeted.

Ivy wrinkled her nose at the interruption, but she placed her papers aside and swiveled in her seat to look at them with a brow raised. "Hello, boys."

"What happened to sticking by Ryland's side where you belonged?" Wren asked.

"Had a guilty conscience, I suppose." She sighed. "I'm sorry. I should've gone with you from the outset."

Ever shook his head. "You don't owe us an apology. You stayed where your duty dictated. There's nothing wrong with that."

"Yes, well. I'm here now, and I suspect you have much to catch me up on."

Wren and Everis exchanged looks. Yes. Yes, they did.

They left nothing out—the exception being Faulk's werewolf status—including Everis collecting the remaining dark magic that had been spilled in the castle and turning it into... something new. Something different. Something that had enabled him to heal rather than hurt.

Ivy listened in quiet fascination, her gaze never once leaving them. When they finished, she dropped her head back against the chair, looking ceilingward.

"Fascinating."

"Fascinating? That's it? Not... blood-magic-y?" Everis asked.

"I don't know how to answer that, truthfully. Yes... and no. I told you, I fully believe you're something apart from what the Citadel views as a blood magi. For one, you're still sane. I think."

"As much as he ever was," Wren mused.

She rolled her eyes. "Word's been sent to Patish, I take it."

"Yes. Princess—Queen Cassia will arrive with Duke Ryland himself and an entourage. I suspect he'll stay a bit, just to help Cassia settle things here. After all, the city's happy she's alive, but organizing the mess Drake Reed and Danica left behind won't be easy."

"Where is Danica, anyway?"

"Being kept in her chambers under constant surveillance," Ever said.

"What do you suppose your new queen will do about her?"

"Even if Cassia were persuaded to have her executed, Danica is with child. I don't think she could do it. Besides that, I don't believe her capable of depriving a child of its mother." Wren shook his head. "More than likely, she'll be given a sum of money and banished, sent to another city somewhere to live out her life."

Ivy wrinkled her nose. "Kinder than she deserves."

"I don't know. Maybe." Wren stole a glance at Everis, thinking of the family they needed to visit and inform of Maliel's death. "People can do awful things for love."

EVERIS

They buried Master Orin atop a hill overlooking the city, beneath the shade of the towering sentinel trees where a soft breeze carried fog down into the valley every morning and swept it away by noon. They'd had a picnic here once, the three of them, one of Ever's earliest memories of his time under Orin's care.

Nova foraged nearby. She'd watched when Orin had been laid to rest, and she'd stayed there after the others left, holding a silent vigil over the grave.

That had been several days ago. Now, Everis stood there, alone for the first time, just as much at a loss for what to say as he had been during the small funeral held for his master. He had so many questions. About his magic, about life, about Orin's life, now knowing that Orin had spent so many years locked away for the use of blood magic.

"We have your journals," he finally said, wincing at how loud his voice felt, how vulnerable, out in the open. It was hard to envision that he was truly alone. "I hope you don't mind. They're precious to us. And perhaps we can learn something from them—about you, if nothing else. You might have told us about the blood magic someday, perhaps when you viewed us as equals and not your students. That's what I'd like to

369

think, anyway."

He took a breath.

"I forgive you, by the way. For not telling me the truth. I understand why you did it, and I can't say for certain whether or not it was the right call. Maybe it was. Maybe it wasn't. But what matters is that you did it to protect me, because you were a good man, and even if I had to choose, you and Wren are the family I would ask for, over and over again. We will look after each other, I promise."

Nova lifted her head and croaked, alerting him to the steady hoofbeats coming up the trail. He inclined his chin, greeting Wren with the faintest of smiles.

"Am I interrupting?"

"Not at all. We were just finishing up, I think."

Wren dismounted, still favoring his inscribed arm and hand. There wasn't a mark left on it, but a time or two, Everis and Wren had spotted the brief glimmer of magic crawling across his skin where the spells had been carved. No healing spell of Ever's could fully rid Wren of what he'd done to himself, it seemed... But how that would affect him in the long run, Everis couldn't say.

"How's the arm?"

"Oh, fine, fine." Wren waved him off, leaving the horse to graze nearby while he moved up alongside Everis to gaze down at Orin's headstone. "Hello again, Master."

They lapsed into silence, both quietly searching for some sign of Orin there with them. Sometimes, Ever thought, when he closed his eyes and reached into the recesses of his own magic, he could swear he sensed Master Orin there somewhere. A warm, calming sensation, like a hand against his back.

Ever opened his eyes and took a deep breath. "So... First to Armos for you to visit the Citadel."

"I suppose. I still don't like the idea of splitting up, even if only for a bit."

"I won't be far outside the city, Wren. But I don't think it's safe for me to go waltzing into the Citadel right now. You'll take your exams, and I'll be waiting when you're done."

Wren made a face, but they'd taken this argument in circles already. Wren had his letter of recommendation from their Master. It would benefit them both if he received his proper title in an official manner.

But the Citadel no doubt knew what had taken place here and were taking steps to send a team if one wasn't already en route. They would question everyone, and although Ever trusted his fellow magi, there were certain people—Sanda, for instance—who would be happy to tell them the things they'd witnessed. It could be enough to make Everis a person of interest, and he wasn't convinced he should be around anyone who was accustomed to sensing dark magic on a person.

"Well," Wren relented, "while I'm at the Citadel, I may as well do some reading. See if I can learn something about Magi Astra or any other magi who might be like you."

"Like me?"

"Of course. You're very special, Ever, but I doubt you're one of a kind."

They exchanged playful grins before Wren's expression sobered.

"What about after, though, do you think? If we don't return here, where will we go? What will we do?"

"I don't know," Ever admitted. He watched Nova hop from side to side before taking flight to land on Wren's shoulder. "I don't suppose I care much, though."

"You don't care?"

"Not particularly." He slid his hand into Wren's, squeezing. He cast a glance out over the valley, the city he'd called home for the last decade, before turning back to his lover with a tilt of his head. "As long as we're together, that's really all that matters, isn't it?"

Wren's expression softened. He smiled. "Quite."

The End

ACKNOWLEDGMENTS

Okay. Wow. This book was a long time in the making.

I started writing *Into the Glittering Dark* shortly before COVID hit. I was racing through this story like I never have with anything before, and it felt great.

Enter the pandemic, and my creativity crash-landed along with my mental health and physical health. Writing felt impossible. All I could do was struggle to keep up with work while dealing with the effects of being even more isolated than usual. Add on my grandmother's death (thankfully not COVID-related), financial struggles, moving, and more… We had a rough time. (Didn't we all?)

Finally, in 2023, I realized this story was so close to done. I had a gorgeous cover I had commissioned for the story, and I needed to get off my ass and finish writing it. So, slowly, painfully, I did. It turned into the longest book I've penned to date, and I'm glad for that because I felt satisfied with the world-building I was able to include. When I first started writing so many years ago, I desperately wanted to write fantasy. I tried and have several half-baked attempts, but I wasn't a strong enough writer to figure out how to make it all work, how to create a world, magic system, and characters that flowed together. I ended up starting with YA contemporary, and then tiptoed into historical/horror/paranormal. *Into the Glittering Dark* is my first terrifying foray into fantasy. I invested so much time, money, love, tears, and blood into this book. If it makes even a few people happy, I'll consider it worth it.

Early reviews pointed out that the romance element of the story isn't very prominent. During edits, I adjusted some scenes and included a few more, but really, this book was never meant to be a romance. It's a dark fantasy following morally gray characters, and some of those characters just happen to be in love. I'm sorry if this disappoints anyone, but not everything needs to be romance-centric. *Into the Glittering Dark* ended up being so much about addiction, friendships, and family... and yet, it's worth noting that almost every choice Everis and Wren make in this book is made for love of each other and Orin. It's not hot and steamy, not in-your-face, but it's there in every single page and decision.

So, I hope everyone reads and gets enjoyment out of those elements. I owe a massive thank you to my wife, who pushed me on this when I felt it was never going to happen. Also to my editors, Karen and Danielle, and my beta readers—of which there were many!—who caught typos and inconsistencies, and sometimes asked, "Does this character realize how awful the choice they've made is?" (HA! That's what makes it fun.)

Although *Into the Glittering Dark* was written as a standalone, keep your eyes open, because I'm not done with them just yet...

-Kelley

Printed in the USA
CPSIA information can be obtained
at www.ICGtesting.com
LVHW040216061023
760346LV00008B/14/J